ADVANCE PRAISE *for*

Below the Moon

PRAISE *for* BOOK 1 *in the* SERIES

Above the Star

"Will hold you spellbound until the last page."

—*Reader's Favorite*

"Think of Star Wars, The Lord of the Rings and Homer's *Odyssey* all wrapped up together."

— Raymond Gariepy, editor of *WestWord* magazine

"Shows readers that there is a power within all of us to change the world."

—Jessica Kluthe, author of *Rosina, The Midwife*

Below the Moon

The 8th Island Trilogy

BOOK 2

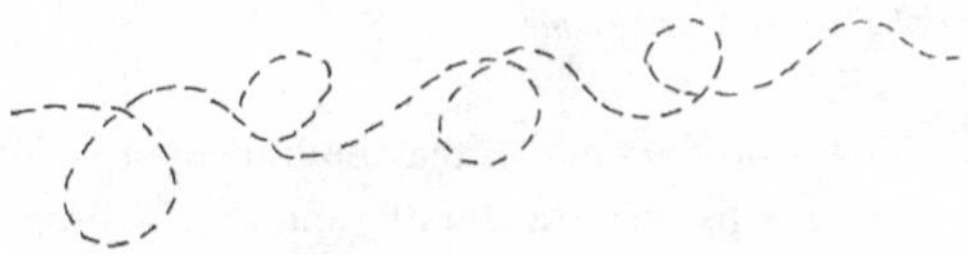

BY

Alexis Marie Chute

Published by SparkPress, a BookSparks imprint,
A division of SparkPoint Studio, LLC
Phoenix, Arizona, USA, 85007
www.gosparkpress.com

Published 2019
Printed in the United States of America
ISBN: 978-1-68463-004-2 (pbk)
ISBN: 978-1-68463-005-9 (ebk)

Library of Congress Control Number: [LOCCN]

Book design by Stacey Aaronson
Interior artwork by Alexis Marie Chute

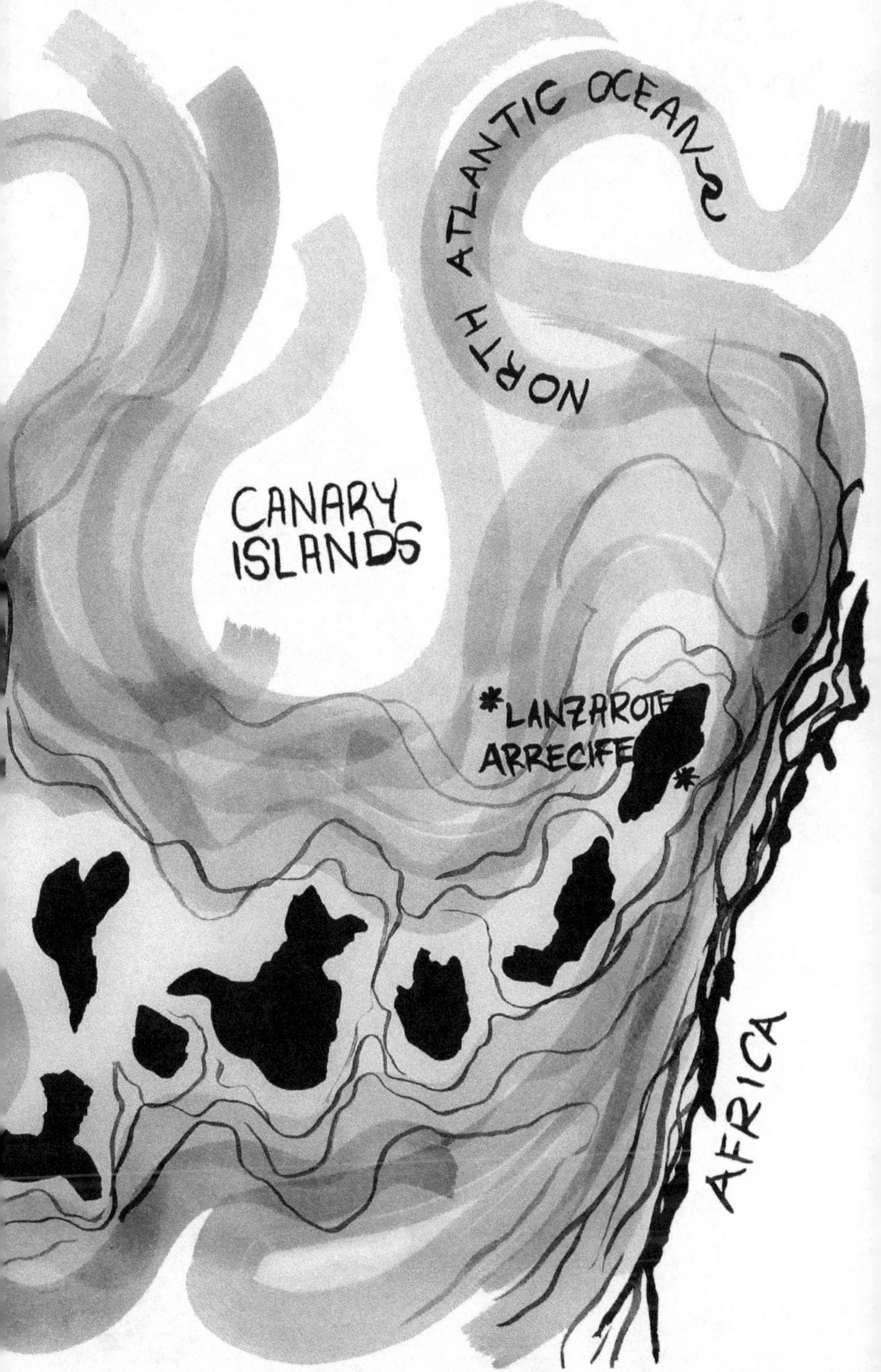

NORTH ATLANTIC OCEAN

CANARY
ISLANDS

*LANZAROTE
ARRECIFE*

AFRICA

JARR-
WYA
N
W E
S
SEA OF
SELFDOM
FAI
VINE-
GLASS
CITY
BL
FORE

BANGOL
FORTRESS
EASTERN
BEACH
ROLACE
WEB
BALUURWA
THE DOOMFUL
FORSAKE
FORTRES
CREEK OF
SECRETS
WHITE
FOREST
MILLIA
VILLAGE

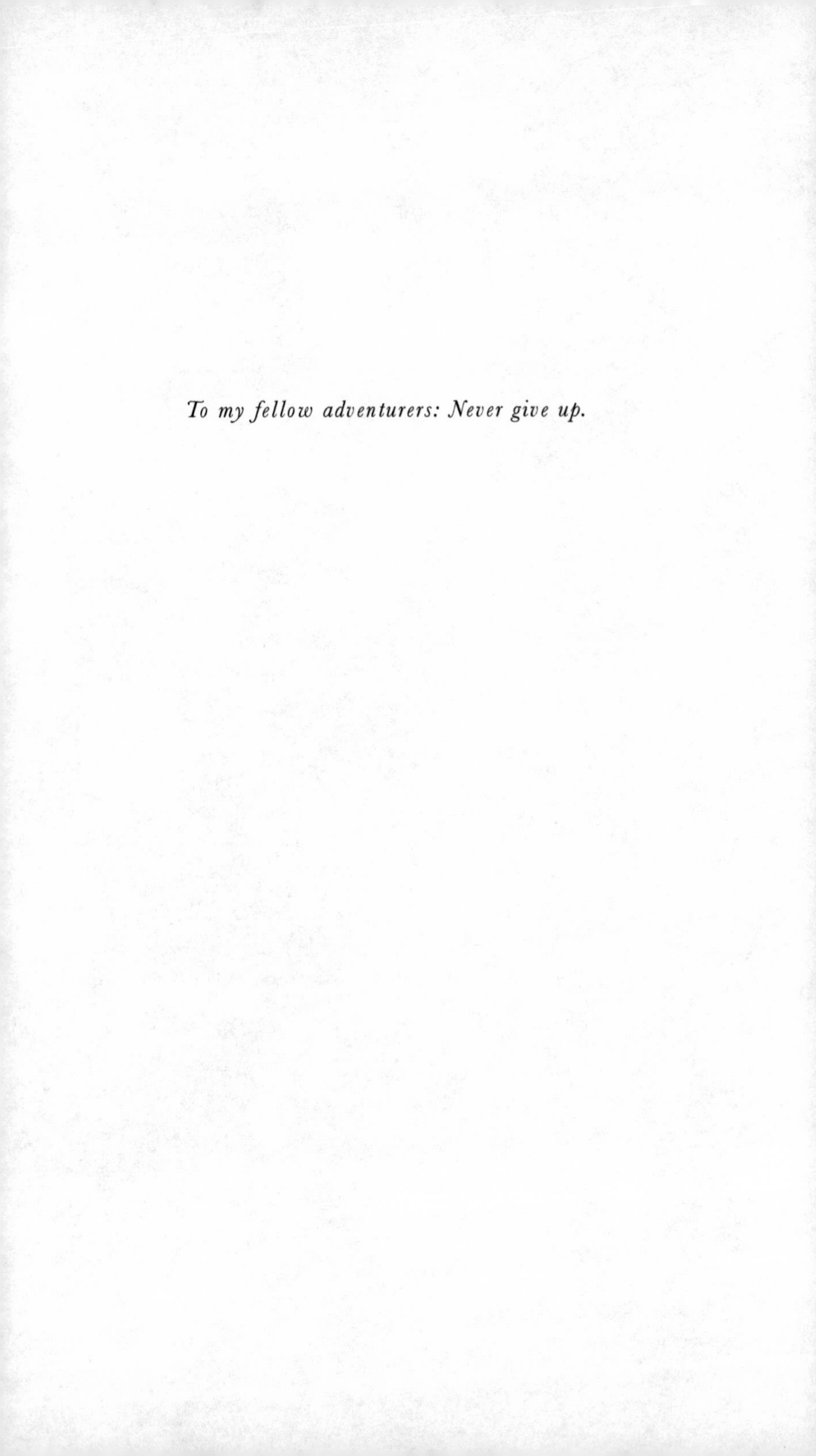

To my fellow adventurers: Never give up.

chapter 1

Ella

Lightning illuminates the sparse room where Luggie and I stand in silence, and causes a lapse in opacity across the enchanted glass walls of his chamber. For a moment, I can see beyond to all buildings and inhabitants of the city. Olearons prepare the wryst drink and vulai bread in the great kitchen for our imminent journey to the Star. Inside a molded-glass nursery, a red-skinned mother rocks her frightened baby. The Lord of Olearon struts around in his fanciest garb, overseeing everything but doing nothing. In contrast, Grandpa Archie and Dad dash here and there helping everyone. Olearons and humans sit at long glass tables, eating the tiny harvest, while others struggle to sleep. Then I see Mom and Captain Nate. Ugh. Their flirting is disgusting. I can't stomach the sight of them, so I look up.

The dark sky is lit with splashes of purple, yellow, and blue as the pronged fork of electricity lacerates the atmosphere, cracking it to pieces like shattered pottery. Through the grassy pathways between the geometric buildings, past the warrior-training paddocks, and beyond to the western pasture, I can make out more tall slim red bodies going about their normal lives—though nothing is normal. Not for me in this new world called Jarr, not for the Olearons, or any race on the island of Jarr-Wya.

Luggie's yellow eyes squint at me, distrusting. He shoves a tunic into a sack. Both were given to him by the Olearons, and he accepted them begrudgingly. The tunic is for protection from the erratic weather on Jarr-Wya. He needs it. We all do. The sun is pale like an unripe peach. It looks ill in the sky and gives little warmth. It's easy for me to relate to its feeble quality. I wonder if I'm fading away like the sun and exactly how much fight I have left in me to resist.

The sack was given to Luggie to carry his belongings on our journey to Baluurwa the Doomful, the mountain where our new company hopes to find a tunnel to the hiding place of the Star. Not all of us will set out on this mission. Not the dead ones: Olen; the Maiden of Olearon; Eek; or Valarie, the cruise director, twice-killed. Luggie's sister Nanjee wasn't the only casualty.

Luggie is painfully stubborn, like me—though I'd never admit that to Mom. He is almost six thousand sunsets old, which, if my math is right, makes him sixteen in human years. He's still learning to wield the Bangols' control over the earth, rock, and clay. His head-stones have grown in, but they're not like the ones that also break through the skin of the adult Bangols above their cheekbones. He's immature, which is obvious from his stubbornness alone.

Luggie is mad at me. He hasn't spoken a word since we were rescued by the Olearon Kameelo out of the eastern sea and flown to the glass city. True, I had to punch Luggie in the face to knock him out. If I hadn't, he'd have continued to resist Kameelo and might have drowned all three of us.

I smile weakly in Luggie's direction—a white flag of peace—but this only further sours his mood.

Rain begins to patter against the glass. *Great.* Yes, I'm being sarcastic. The only thing my cancer hates more than physical exertion is physical exertion through mud. The one solace I have is that right about now I'm missing my grade nine social studies exam on technology through the ages. I intended to study on Constellations Cruise Line, aboard the *Atlantic Odyssey*, but then Grandpa Archie used the portal jumper, a Tillastrion, and accidentally transported our whole ship to Jarr.

Besides causing the exhaustion, my cancer has stolen my ability to speak. It's been months. The no-talking thing hasn't truly bothered me until now, when I have something important to say.

"What do I have? What here is my own?" Luggie says, fuming, finally speaking to me as he stares at the sack that hangs in his hands like a deflated balloon. The tunic the Olearons gave him is a brilliant blue like their warriors' jumpsuits. "How can I wear it, Ella? The color alone makes me want to wretch. I have loathed the Olearons right from when I was birthed from stone. And it is justified, I might add. Stop shaking your head at me, Ella—I have learned what humans mean when they turn their necks like that."

I can't yell at him to tell him to grow up, to stop whining. Maybe it's a good thing I'm unable to communicate except through my drawings with ink. I care about Luggie, but there are many things I want to say in the heat of this moment that I might regret. I, too, stubbornly believe I'm right.

"One day I will shred this garment, or bury it, or enact one of ten other ways to dispose of something so putrid."

I can't help but roll my eyes at him. Luggie continues to mumble under his breath, now in the Bangols' sharp dialect, as he concocts more ideas of how to destroy the tunic at his first opportunity. Tentatively, I take the three steps across Luggie's small room in the Olearons' glass city. I touch his arm, but he wrenches it away.

"I have packed it not because I forgive them, or you, but just in case," he says, relenting. He nudges his shoulder against the glass wall that is cut so precisely that its molded magic curves are barely discernible. The wave of cloudy glass shimmers and turns transparent at his touch. He's learned how his place of refuge among the Olearons functions, and he now watches the red creatures through the translucent shimmer as they hustle to and fro in the rain, donning the overgrown leaves of the blue forest like storm slickers.

"How can I trust you after your blow to my face and Kameelo's hot hands on me, stealing me from the eastern shore? You two stopped me from mourning my fallen Bangol soldiers, friends, and family. From mourning Nanjee." Luggie nearly chokes. I can tell he feels a pang of sadness at his sister's name. He shuts his eyes, dulling their lemon light to a faint glow that radiates through his eyelids.

Nanjee is my only regret. I've never had a sibling. It's hard for me to understand how Luggie feels, though I have lost someone I love—Grandma Suzie. I know that grief is like being cut in two. My annoyance toward Luggie wanes. Yes, I saved his life by punching him, but in doing so I delivered him into the care of his enemy. I'd be mad, too—and heartbroken. I think back to when Grandma Suzie died; that was my first experience with death, and I don't think I've become much better at dealing with it since.

One moment, Grandma Suzie occupied space in the world. There was an energy around her that caused anyone nearby to light up, to smile. I remember running from room to room in our Seattle bungalow, searching for that feeling, for Grandma after she died. All I discovered was weak traces of her on her clothing and books, in her stained teapot decorated with painted strawberries and their curling vines, and on the breeze when I ran along her daily walking path. For a while, the ruts from her walker inscribed that path like handwriting, but the ruts grew shallower, fainter, like my memory. In the spring, they remained, frozen in time. Even now I imagine her smile and creased cheeks when I close my eyes.

I suspect no one ever becomes better at grief. It's not like practice makes it easier. Humans—I can't speak for the Bangols or Olearons—must learn to hide its pang stealthily. I did my best to comfort Grandpa Archie, but I was too young. All I understood about grief was the confusion of absence without explanation. I brought Grandpa my favorite toys and rolled myself into a ball on his lap, his heart beating against my cheek so it wasn't terribly lonely in his chest. Grandpa Archie had me and Mom—and Dad, too, until he disappeared—to lean on. Luggie must feel all alone.

"My first desire is to weep," Luggie admits, as if reading my face and wandering thoughts.

I'm startled briefly, pulled away from missing Grandma to be present in Luggie's glass room with its grass carpet—back to this Bangol who peers over his shoulder to where I stand awkwardly.

He goes on. "But my second desire is to avenge. If Kameelo had not robbed me of my right to mourn, I would have climbed from the sea and up the stone pillar that supported the cells above it. I would have collected what was left of Nanjee's body and given her the ritual burial that is the Bangols' way, not the scorching ceremony of the Olearons. We Bangols are of the earth. Our bones are made of clay. Our blood flows with the waters of the deep. Our eyes are shards of sunshine, scattered in tiny quantities, sunbeams planted in the dirt. Can you even understand this, Ella? I am speaking your language, but can you understand?"

My head bobbles quickly in a nod that is both an effort and apology. I lift my hand to touch his smooth grey skin, but he shuffles beyond my reach. Luggie smashes the sack onto the grass. He exposes his teeth. I don't mean to, but I stumble back, afraid.

Luggie says, raging, "The sunlight grows into our beaming eyes, giving vision to our young, touching us with light. The Bangols come from the foundation of Jarr, from the very island of Jarr-Wya. It is only right that Nanjee, the princess of the Bangols, be returned to the place from where she was birthed. Those Olearons, they knew. Taking me away from the east . . . I will get back there. Maybe all that will remain is bones, but I know Nanjee's head-stones. I will find her. I will honor her life: my beautiful, brilliant sister."

Luggie lifts a hand to the glass wall and scratches five straight lines with his sharp nails. He steps away so the distortion returns, shielding him and me from the activities of the city. The opaque reflectiveness is a dull mirror, though it vibrates at the cut lines.

Luggie's muscles are tight, rippling through him to his clenched fists. I'm sure his nails puncture his palms. He grinds his dagger-fine teeth and growls. "And Ella"—Luggie whispers now—"Ella, why them? Why did you choose them over me?"

He kicks the sack. It bounces against the glass door, which shimmers, and for a moment the mirror returns to glossy translucency, allowing Luggie and me to catch a glimpse of Duggie-Sky running by. The boy pauses, then steps back as he notices us. The four-year-old rushes to the door and presses his nose into a pancake against it. I can't help but laugh, which comes out horribly. Cancer has corrupted even my laugh, trapping me in a silent world, though it's loud in my head, the place where I collect all the things I wish to say.

Duggie-Sky has a square of the Olearons' vulai bread in one hand and a drying mud ball in the other. His face still presses against the glass as he raps on the door with his elbow. Luggie swings it open.

"Hi!" says Duggie-Sky cheerfully. His dark brown skin glows with raindrops, and his boyish round cheeks are flushed from evading the young Olearon tasked with minding him until our company departs. Since the transformation gifted to him by Rolace the man-spider in his web, not only is Duggie-Sky as fast as a blink, but he's also grown smarter. Perceptive.

"You sad, Luggie?" Duggie-Sky asks. "Wanna play catch?" The boy moves with the agility of a basketball player. His eyes tell me he understands what's going on around here—probably better than I do—though his voice hasn't lost the childlike slur.

Hi, I say in my head and wave at the boy who stands two feet shorter than me. Duggie-Sky beams and takes a bite of vulai bread. His tight black curls bounce as he chews. Luggie doesn't turn, so I smile and raise my hands. Duggie-Sky tosses me the ball, a perfect sphere of mud just like the ones the conniving Bangol, Zeno, taught him to make.

"Snack?" Duggie-Sky asks, holding the bread toward me first, then Luggie. I shake my head and toss the ball back with terrible aim. Without pausing mid-chew, Duggie-Sky zips to successfully catch the mud in his free hand. He laughs and vulai breadcrumbs fall from his lips.

"Ugh, I cannot stomach more vulai." Luggie grimaces.

Duggie-Sky darts around Luggie and peeks at me for a second before disappearing behind the narrow glass wardrobe. The gift of teleportation, imbued with the magic life force of Naiu, is well used, and daily. Duggie-Sky even exercises it in pestering Grandpa Archie, who is always a good sport and even does much of the initiating on his own.

I jump behind Luggie. As I peek around his stocky body, Duggie-Sky leans out of his hiding place, then vanishes again. Suddenly, I feel a *tap, tap, tap* on my back. I jump and turn at the same moment and thrust my hands forward to tickle the boy's belly. He giggles, scrunching his neck, and tumbles down onto the grass floor of the chamber, pulling me down by the wrists. I can't help but laugh. "Aweeak!" I sound horrible and am suddenly self-conscious. Luggie catches my gaze.

"Be careful, child," he says. "She is not well."

My weakness, the nausea and frailty from the tumor, are my business, and I would say as much if I could even whisper the words. The way Duggie-Sky looks at me now, less like a playmate than a fragile decoration on a mantel, to be appreciated from afar and certainly not touched . . . ugh, I hate that look. I remember that expression on the faces of my classmates at school. It's true—physically I couldn't keep up with them, but I was still me.

Luggie turns away from Duggie-Sky and me, and the unbalanced feeling fills the modest space. To tip the energy toward peace, I sweep my hands outward, one to the left and one to the right, as if brushing away crumbs after a meal. The gesture is American Sign Language, meaning *finished*. Duggie-Sky gets the idea and leaps to his feet.

"They're almost ready out there," he says happily, and on his way out adds, "Okay, bye!" Duggie-Sky disappears with a swoosh through the entryway.

"Why does he bother with doors?" Luggie mumbles.

Before the door clicks shut behind the gleeful child, I catch the edge of it and take a step out. It's clear that I'm wasting my time here; I'm sure I can help with packing in the octagon paddock, if they'll let me. My eyes find Luggie's and I shrug, wave goodbye, and step out into the drizzling, windswept pathway.

"Wait," he says.

I want to scream. Instead, I close my eyes at the whipping of the breeze. It animates my long blond hair, dancing it around my face like a puppet's strings. The wind has been erratic: strong like a bull, wild like a snake. It's one effect of the Star's poisoning of the island, making the Bangols—their king Tuggeron, whom I call Tuggs—crazy-hungry to expand their territory. The Star is also to blame for creating the Millia sands, which leeched the blood from half the Constellations Cruise Line passengers—people I sat beside at the ship's mammoth tables in the dining hall and swam with in the bean-shaped pool on the deck. I can't help but shudder.

The Star must be stopped.

"Your laugh . . ." Luggie begins. "It is jarring, a pained screech. I do not understand how the illness at your neck saddens you, how it makes you weak, but still your sounds are beautiful to me. Even in my anger, Ella Wellsley, I need to protect your laugh."

My hand is on the triangular glass handle. I'm unable to walk away, to leave Luggie alone with his sack and the despised blue tunic. I'm also stubbornly unwilling to return to his chamber. Again, I find my blue eyes locked with Luggie's vibrant yellows. He is the first to look away. I can't hold back the tears.

I give in.

Ella

chapter 2

Luggie

Luggie softens as Ella brushes past him. He swallows hard to mask the breath-stealing effect she has on him. She sits on the carelessly strewn sheets of Luggie's bed, smoothing them, then patting the spot beside her, beckoning him to join her. *If only she could speak*, he wishes, then laments: *Even if she were to write the words of an apology, I cannot read her language.*

Ella's gaze once made Luggie's head-stones ache with affection, though now her eyes send an unnerving shiver down his spine. When he blinks, he still senses the place where Ella struck him. That one act, he realizes, was the unraveling of them, of their trust. Luggie was rendered unable to protect Nanjee's body from being picked apart by the hungry black flyers with their curled talons and scavenging, pecking beaks—black flyers that have morphed since the arrival of the Star and now bear two heads and overgrown wingspans. Their great shadows arrive with a chill before them.

Luggie and Ella had formed a plan to escape that didn't involve flying Kameelo or the Olearons. He planned to sneak the keys to her cell from his father, and in the night they would paddle the makeshift raft Luggie constructed to the next arching stone bridge to save Nanjee. The three would head north by sea to the Bangols' fortress at the head of Jarr-Wya. The other part of the plan, which Luggie had not articulated, a fantasy of impossibility, stretched many sunsets into the future.

He had imagined hiding Ella within the stone fortress until he could convince his father—King Tuggeron—that she played no part in thwarting the ruler's plan to capture and wield the power of the Star. Then a lifetime with Ella . . .

Luggie sobers at the thought of Tuggeron, which pains him more than his healing wound. Everyone knows the king is mad and selfish, desiring immortality and, most of all, the Star. The Olearons believe Tuggeron must die. They have spoken of their desire plainly in Luggie's presence.

He agrees that his father must be stopped, but a sliver of love still lives in his heart for the Bangol who raised him—for the father who taught him to manipulate earth and stone, and to fly the awakin butterfly balloons. He feels love, even for the king who beats him.

Luggie frets over the look of betrayal that will greet him on the faces of all Bangols when he arrives on Baluurwa the Doomful with a company of Olearons. They will surely see; the Bangols have eyes on the mountain at all times, as Tuggeron's paranoia never sleeps. They keep watch for a lone Steffanus, a winged creature they might capture to use in the operation of a Tillastrion. The Bangols have never ventured to the derivative world—the human Earth—themselves, to Luggie's knowledge, except for the twin heirs of the previous king whom Tuggeron successfully banished.

Luggie strains to remember back many sunsets to his childhood, to recall whether his father ever touched him kindly. *Was he good before the mysterious Star crashed into the sea beneath Jarr-Wya?*

He sighs deeply and his shoulders fall. *No.* Tuggeron never loved him. He loved Luggie's sister, Nanjee. *My father will be furious with me.* Luggie clenches his teeth. *If I return without Nanjee, without even her head-stones, that will be it. He will kill me and seek immortal dominion more fervently. Who was I fooling? Tuggeron was never grooming me to rule—only to serve him without objection, without a mind of my own.*

Dejected, Luggie plunks himself down beside Ella. The bed, enchanted to gift the sleeper pleasant dreams, rests on a glass frame and is firm with little give. Ella shifts to face him. Her hands graze his cheeks. Tenderly, she turns his head to check on the stitches where his ear had been blown off by the Maiden of Olearon's blast. The Maiden sacrificed herself to destroy the manifestation of the cruise director, Valarie, in her massive carakwa horde, though not to save the Bangols. Luggie's kin had been consumed by the lizard-beetle horde hungry for blood and vengeance.

Luggie pulls sharply away from Ella's embrace. Her eyes fall, and her hands, too. She takes a deep breath. Her lips make silent shapes, mouthing his name. He shakes his head, as Ella had done moments before. "Ewwwwwaaaaa," she says aloud as she tries to speak. The tears that had clung to her fair eyelashes, and glistened on the bright whites of her eyes, now surrender and plummet. He watches her sadness rise and fall in her chest.

"Don't, Ella," Luggie says weakly. "You broke me. You betrayed me. Your touch was the only kindness in my life, other than Nanjee, but now . . ."

Ella pulls a parchment book from her sack, which she wears with the handles slung over her shoulders like her school backpack, long lost in the fire on the eastern shore. She produces a paintbrush and vial of black ink. Luggie cannot help but compare the artist tools of the Olearons to those of the Bangols. The ornately constructed and decorated book he and Nanjee had given Ella was by far more precious than the simple, modestly stitched pages of the Olearons. Even the blue-bark brush and long silver vial of ink look primitive and minimally adorned. *Just like the thin red bodies*. Luggie grimaces.

Luggie hates the sight of the art tools in Ella's hands. He looks away while she draws. The paintbrush makes a gentle scraping sound against the paper, and, with it, his mind becomes entangled in thought once more. When he looks back, he sees Ella's drawings. He studies the pages, which she has torn free and laid across the bed so their dampness will evaporate. A black drip slips off one page and stains the immaculate white bedding.

Ella points at one drawing, then at another, and another. Luggie begins to recognize the invisible journey that connects each image. *Ella has a plan!* Luggie fills with understanding—and with hope.

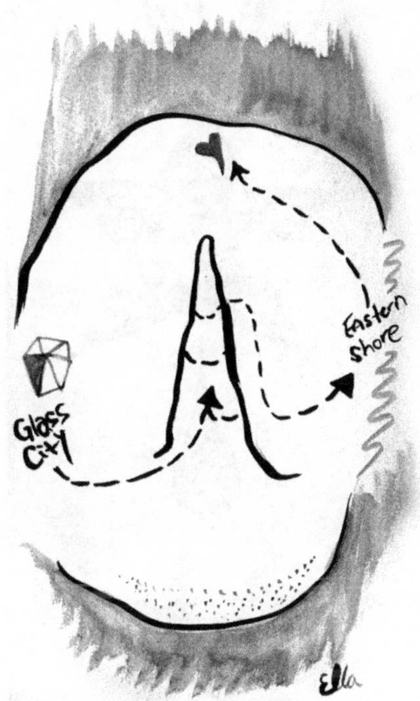

Ella

NANJEE
Ella

"Are we too late for this?" Luggie asks, resigning himself to sadness, hope being too dangerous. *Look where hope left me not many sunsets past!* The flicker of possibility dulls in him.

"I loved you, Ella. Then you delivered me into the fire. I loved you . . . The word *love* is more beautiful in my language."

Luggie takes the book of paper and roughly tears free a new page. Ella slips the blue handle of the paintbrush into Luggie's callused hand. He draws the letters. One at a time, slowly, thoughtfully. He blows the bubbles of ink dry, then turns the paper to show Ella. Her eyes trace the lines.

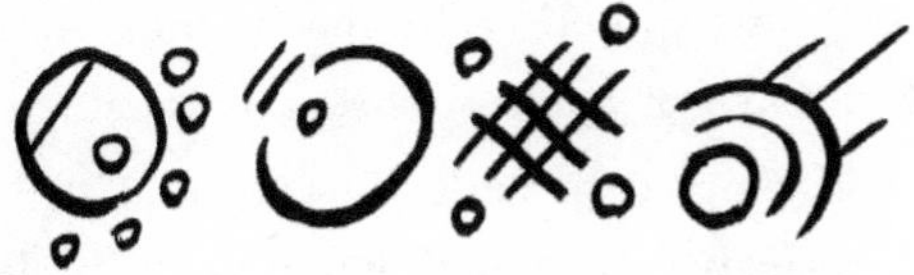

She reaches, and Luggie thinks she means to take the paper—but her hands find his. He lets the drawn *Love* fall to rest on the bed between them. Ella scoots closer, rising to her knees, filling the distance between them. The paper crumples beneath her. Her pink lips brush against Luggie's. Once more he feels Ella's weakening effect over him. She pulls back a shallow breath's distance and pauses. Her taste is sweet on his nearly black lips. He inhales her. She waits. For what feels like a thousand breaths, Luggie's heart hammers away his dwindling resolve until he can no longer sit unflinching like a stone. Then he, too, leans forward.

Their kiss is full and long. It is laced with the desperation of too much time spent waiting and the pain of the vast distance between their two worlds. Neither knows how to encapsulate their bizarre love, which only makes sense removed from race and land and magic and language and hate and the Star.

Luggie touches Ella's shoulders, her neck, and her ears. His pointed nails delicately part her hair, now messy and tangled, until he feels the crest of the scar at the back of her neck.

"Oh," he says without thinking, the word spoken inside Ella's mouth. "I'm sorry." Luggie winces. He shakes his head and is about to speak again, fretting that he may have hurt her.

Ella smiles, broad and encompassing. Her teeth are dull edged like a spoon, the white of Jarr's moon. She laughs—the cackle of illness, and all Luggie has ever known of her mirth. His worry turns to vapor and is gone.

As if they both know what the other needs in that moment, they fold their arms around each other in a desperate embrace. The cherished touch of two lost ones, separated from their predictable courses, forced to endure each night in the abyss of unknown, and lacking the sun to guide them by day. They remain entangled until their breathing harmonizes, heart to beating heart. Luggie is sure Ella feels it: the racing in his chest.

He briefly forgets that they sit in his enemy's city, that Ella's father has transitioned—in body and mind—to an Olearon within Rolace's web, and that the Bangols were abandoned and deceived by the company led by Ella's mother, Tessa, and grandfather, Archibald Wellsley. Luggie forgets that he and Ella have somewhere to be, that the new company is venturing out at any moment to begin a new quest to defeat the Star and find Ella's cure, which is impossibly intertwined with the fate of all worlds.

Without warning, someone raps on the door to Luggie's chamber as loudly as the lightning beyond its reflective walls. The door clicks open. There, standing erect and unflinching in the rain, is the 30th Lord of Olearon. His scowl is menacing, though subtle enough that one might miss it on his polished face. Pinned to one shoulder, the Lord wears the distinctive patch once worn by his deceased Maiden. The patch is animal hide, dyed red and stitched with gold amidst a pattern of rainbow bands. The ten-foot-tall doorway is shy of the ruler's towering height, so the Lord rounds his angular shoulders to enter, then tips his chin in solemn greeting.

Luggie stands to face the Lord. Behind him Ella ruffles papers as she collects the drawings and shoves them hastily inside her sack, slinging it over her back in one swift motion. Understanding settles over Luggie: *Ella does not want the Lord to see her plan.* He relishes the thought. *Maybe she is on my side of this war after all.*

Luggie does his best to block the Lord's view—pulling his shoulders back and resting his thick hands on his hips—though the Olearon is a towering presence, seeing everything. The youthful Bangol forces down a nervous gulp. When the Lord finally opens his mouth after studying the scene, all he says to Ella is, "It is time. The company awaits, and you two are the last to assemble. Go now, human."

Beneath the Lord's squinting black eyes, Ella retreats through the narrow doorway. She looks back, but the Lord seals the door. Once she is gone, leaving behind the floral smell of her hair and the bitter odor of ink on the sheets, Luggie is alone with the looming being, who radiates heat.

Suddenly, the Lord's shoulders tremble violently. Luggie startles at the motion, so alien for the composed, even-tempered Lord. A shiver of what Luggie can only guess is disgust creeps over the Olearon like a robe. The Lord's posture grows even more plank-rigid. His ruddy lips pull back in a snarl.

"Tell me, Bangol," begins the Olearon. "Why should I trust you to join the company on this journey? You stone-heads are devious scavengers and oath-breakers. I would rather roast you here and report to the others that I was provoked, that you rose from the earth to swallow me whole. My actions would be seen as self-defense."

Luggie's courage—bolstered by Ella's plan—burns hungrily in his chest. "Now who is the devious one?" Luggie says with scorn. "You may be the Lord of Olearon, but you are not my king."

The Lord pauses, considering. He grits his ash-white teeth. "It would give me pleasure to turn your flesh to dust, but for now, I have a higher purpose in keeping you alive."

Luggie puffs out his chest. "I am going to Baluurwa to protect Ella, then get myself back to where I belong—"

"Or so you think," the Lord says with a twisted chuckle. "While you may not believe this—because of the falsehoods your foolish forefathers hammered into your thick rock skull—the Olearons desire peace. We use war to achieve this when there are no other options, and I regret that this is one such occasion."

The Lord continues as he studies Luggie, circling him. "I do perceive that you are not as foolhardy and selfish as your father, or as the many who follow Tuggeron without a mind of their own. The Maiden in me has shown me these things—both the cruelty of Tuggeron and your bravery, Luggie. You are capable of restraint, which I have witnessed since you arrived in my city. And you are prone to love, though of this strangeness I need say no more. What this tells me is that you should be king—King of the Bangols."

Luggie waits. The Lord's words strike him mute, silent like Ella, at the ludicrous proposition. Some—like Winzun and Zeno, the sons of the last Bangol king—would fight each other till their grey skin returned to earth and insect grub for the title the Lord so curiously just dangles before Luggie. Yet Luggie refuses to be blinded by power like his father. Bangol skepticism rises in his throat, a resolute distrust of the Lord that solidifies into an even deeper loathing. *It must be a joke*, Luggie finally concludes. But before he can reply, the Lord continues.

"If the Bangols were to live peacefully amongst all on Jarr-Wya, if they were to submit to wisdom"—the word *wisdom* clearly meaning Olearon rule—"I foresee the flourishing of your race, within reason. Things would change, of course. No wild pursuits of a foreign star. No thievery of the Olearon harvest or of the crop from the Fairy Vineyard. No warmongering."

"Obedience."

"Yes. Obedience." The Lord bends. He touches the damp bedsheet where the ink drip is slowly drying. "I will need one to lead this new way of life for the Bangols—one I may counsel and guide. Will you be that one, Luggie?" The Lord burns a perfect circle into the white sheet so no remnant of ink remains. A wisp of smoke rises in a thin, tangled line.

"What choice do I have?"

"The choice is a clear one between life and death. Between death and love."

Every cell in Luggie's body aches to call forth the earth, slap it down in a wave of dirt and roots and shattered glass, to make true the lie of the Lord. To destroy the bloodthirsty, hypocritical Lord of Olearon would earn the respect of the Bangols and perhaps forgiveness from his father. The act must be done before the Lord speaks lies and poisons minds against him; otherwise, Luggie will never succeed in returning home. *What sweet retribution*, Luggie thinks, *for Nanjee and the true-hearted Bangol warriors.* Luggie's friends—the dutiful who reluctantly followed Tuggeron's orders to drown the humans to bait the Star and coax it out from its hiding place in the sea beneath the island.

The Lord's closeness makes it impossible to shift the grassy earth beneath their feet quickly enough for Luggie to beat the Lord's blaze of fire to scorch everything in the room in half the time. The Lord knows this as well. His red neck and face emit a heat that trickles down Luggie's brow in silver drops of fear.

The Lord is too close. He whispers, "After the Star and its power are mine, and our company descend Baluurwa for the Bangols' northern fortress, I will call upon you. Obedience. You will stand straight, proud, fierce. Your stones will be clean and your head clear. Tuggeron will burn. But not you. And not those who cross the line of fire to stand at your side. You will lead them in serving me, and in striving for true peace for all Jarrwians.

"And about the human girl," adds the Lord, sneering. "She uses you for a purpose, as do I, though hers saves only herself, while mine spares thousands. If you truly possess affection for her, remember how closely I control those she holds dear: her mother and her grandfather, Tessa and Archibald Wellsley. And of course her father, faithful Ardenal. Do not give her cause to blame you.

"Like you, I once knew complicated love." The Lord's voice is tight. "It was ripped from me. Love is worth the fight to protect it—in the name of peace, of course, Luggie. You would be wise to remember this."

Luggie is startled. *Who is the Lord speaking of?* To his knowledge, the Lord ruled with his Maiden before her death, as had all Olearon rulers before them. *How was their love complicated? How was it ripped from him?*

Since the Maiden's blaze consumed both herself and the monster incarnation of cruise director Valarie, the Maiden came to inhabit the body of her Lord. They must be joined in spirit now—in the closest, most intimate way. Luggie cannot make sense of the Lord's confession. Luggie grinds his teeth, ignoring whatever vulnerability the Lord reveals. *Likely for a purpose*, he reasons. He growls, "And if I do not obey . . ."

"Consider it, yes, but know disobedience ends in death. The rule of the Bangols will fail, your race will be annihilated in my unforgiving fire, and you will watch them burn. I will bestow one final mercy on you: to live a long life. We Olearons will write about you, the last stone-head, in our histories, as the rest of your kin fade from memory."

"And Ella?"

"In every thread weaving the present into what will become the history of Jarr, I see her inevitable end. Her death. She cannot live. If she were to bear your child, that life would be the unity of us all, which I will not have. It must never come to pass."

A haunting shudder throws back the Lord's head. His eyes search the sloping glass ceiling, as if he orients himself in the city. The shiver works through him from head to booted foot. Finally, he takes a rounder, softer stance. Luggie watches dumbly, baffled, unsure if he should help or escape in these fleeting breaths.

Luggie timidly asks, "Do you need the healer?" He takes a step away as he speaks, worried that the Lord will scald him if his movements are not predictable.

"What foolishness is this? Why have you not followed the human girl? Out with you, or I will leave you behind."

"You held me back," Luggie says, fuming.

The Lord scowls at Luggie and turns, leaving him alone with his questions in the glass chamber.

Coolness rushes in at the Lord's departure, and Luggie wipes sweat from his flushed brow. He blinks in confusion, flashing his glowing yellow eyes. It is as if the Lord forgot their conversation entirely, as if the convulsions induced immediate amnesia.

What did the Lord mean that a child birthed of Luggie and Ella would unite all? That babe would be new, that was true—one part Bangol, the other human—but Ella had no Olearon blood in her veins. Her father, Ardenal, had transitioned into an Olearon after he arrived on Jarr-Wya, after his encounter with the magical man-spider's web.

The Lord is confused, Luggie reasons. *Poisoned with lust for the Star, just like my father.*

The memory of Ella's drawings, done just minutes before, fill his vision. Would a child be their future?

Luggie's attention shifts to his bed, beneath which the secret history of the Olearons lies tucked between mattress and frame. He does not know if the Lord has yet interrogated Archibald about the mysterious record. Archie stole the secret history from the Olearon throne before the original company ventured to the Bangols' eastern arching bridges in search of Ella. The Maiden confiscated the glass object from him before she died. All believe that in her sacrifice to wipe out carakwa-Valarie, the history was lost to the sea. None know that Luggie found and concealed it. Not even Ella.

For now, Luggie is content to keep quiet about the survival of the history. The wisdom burned into its glass calls to him, even when preparing for the new mission. *Perhaps*, Luggie thinks, *I can barter the object in exchange for something—or someone—more precious.*

"Obedience is earned." Luggie's voice is scratchy. He tenderly slips the envelope containing the secret history into his sack. "The Lord, like my father, soon will see: I am not as easy to control as they believe."

chapter 3

Archie

The journey to Baluurwa the Doomful points the company toward Jarr-Wya's interior, where the blue forest butts up against the black rock on the west, between the Olearon field and mountain. Baluurwa rises sharply out of the island's center, its angle dangerous, though smaller fragments of ground—grass, dirt, and rock—float on all sides. These levitating pieces of earth connect to the mountain by twisting vines and step-sized stones that magnetize the whole offshoot, binding it together. From many of these mini airborne islands spill flowers and sloping trees, their roots dangling out through the dirt to drink from low, sweeping clouds.

To Archie, Baluurwa appears like a looming squid, its tall pointed head directing everyone's eyes up toward the storm. The sky remains dark, the color of bruised plums. *It's been this way all day, as we trekked toward the mount, every waking hour*, Archie reflects nervously. No sunlight fights its way through the wounded atmosphere. The dusky sky is impenetrable. *Is there even a sun up there?* he worries. The massive squid-like mountain reaches into the space around it with tentacles of vines and stone. There, chunks of land sway lazily in the churning storm, dropping pebbles and leaves that forget from where they fell by the time they setting on the ground far below. Archie looks at his watch.

It is a nervous habit, but a futile one. His watch of a long-defunct brand, with a chipped face and tired leather band, no longer ticks. Its face looks back at him blankly, showing the time it stopped.

Eleven-thirty.

Archie wonders if that was the nighttime hour when the *Atlantic Odyssey* was overtaken by Olearon warriors after the ship jumped to the waters of Jarr-Wya. Or late morning, when the vessel crashed on the Millia's shore. Archie taps the face mindlessly, as if he can startle the watch from its hibernation to tell him how long they have been on the magical island. Days bleed into nights, and the dark overshadows everything. There once was the richness of color and life here and the touch of Jarr's sun imbued Naiu, but the Star has stolen the light. The weather is not the only element driven into madness.

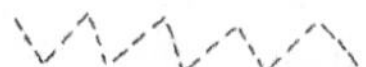

THE company that ventures to Baluurwa includes humans and Olearons, plus Luggie. Archie points his finger as he counts. There is the Lord of Olearon and his two henchmen; Yuleeo and Islo. Junin trails them. She is mother to a young red-skinned daughter who was fast friends with Duggie-Sky. Archie commended Duggie-Sky for his brave tear-filled goodbye to the girl. Junin, accustomed to goodbyes, is a warrior from the contingent that rescued half the passengers who survived the *Atlantic Odyssey* crash and the evil Millia sands' demand for blood. Archie trusts Junin, though he has less confidence in the one she serves.

Azkar and Nameris, and their youngest sibling Kameelo, who was gifted the power of flight inside Rolace's web, also stand guard over the Lord. They still grieve the deaths of their other brothers, Olen and Eek. Kameelo keeps watch of the new company from above, where he flies in the dim sky. Since they proved their strength and loyalty on the trek east, the Lord keeps the three brothers closer than all but Yuleeo and Islo, his most intimate advisors and guards.

Ardenal is the eighth Olearon, though he treks apart from the others, beside Archie and Duggie-Sky, whose four-year-old legs have not yet tired. Archie peers past the boy to his son. Arden—Ardenal on Jarr-Wya—wears the blue of an Olearon warrior, but that is not all he shares with them. His skin is warm red, his eyes the endless black of midnight. His hair is unlike it was when he was human; now, it is matted and forming a Mohawk across his skull.

Ardenal, too, like born Olearons, can control fire, calling it forth from the nape of his neck, weaving blades of grass into weapons of flame and igniting his whole body. Even with this unexpected transformation, Archie relishes the closeness of Arden, who had been lost to Earth for two confusing years. It didn't take long for Archie to recognize the ruddy, gangly creature as his son, though Tessa—Archie's daughter-in-law, Ella's mom, and Arden's wife—was slower to recognize what Arden had become.

Tessa and the captain of the *Atlantic Odyssey*, Nathanial Billows, talk in quiet voices on the periphery of the company. Archie scowls in Nate's direction. He resents the closeness between Tessa and Nate, though a small part of him understands. He, too, longs for companionship—for his late wife Suzie—and accepts that Arden has changed. Archie's mission of reuniting his family was complete when they found each other at the glass city, yet the fractured feeling between Tessa and Arden continues to divide them.

Archie next counts his granddaughter, Ella, and the Bangol,

Luggie, who walk close together, watching the tall branches of the blue forest for the compound eyes of the carakwas or the concealed bodies of the black flyers. Regretting his granddaughter's fear, which he would remove if he could, Archie is thankful for Luggie—for Luggie's hand on Ella's back as he guides her, watching out for her.

Archie knows the friendship of a Bangol himself, despite Zeno's abrupt departure in the east. Zeno did not say goodbye, not to Archie or to any of them, and yet Archie's forgiveness reaches his friend, no matter where he may be. Zeno rebutted his kindnesses and his trust, yet there was evidence that the selfish Bangol cared for the human who sought him out in the Haria marketplace on the island of Lanzarote on Earth, the human who helped him return to the island of Jarr-Wya and his fellow Bangols. Zeno leaped in front of Archie when the Maiden's anger, and her fire, flared at discovering the secret glass in Archie's hands.

At the tail end of the company is the Spanish opera singer, Lady Sophia. The skin on her pudgy arms and neck grow patchy white and red with exertion. She still dons her ball gown, which she wore when the *Atlantic Odyssey* crashed on the Millia's southern beach and dirtied on the rescue mission east. At the time, she scoffed at the idea of changing into more sensible trekking attire.

"It's the only way I can judge how much weight I've sweated from my hips," she bellowed in protest in the glass city. The outspoken woman pestered Junin for a needle and thread so she could stitch two folds into the gown, allowing her thick ankles and calves to march unobstructed. Lady Sophia relented enough to slice the heels off her shoes with a glass blade. Her other demand was to join the new company.

"I hated how the Maiden used me—being thrown off a

bridge into the ocean as a ruse," she said. "Still, the exhilaration of it inspired me to write songs of my own. Oh, I can only imagine what new arias will bubble up out of me on this new adventure."

The Lord scolded Lady Sophia, emphasizing the seriousness of their mission to defeat the Star—and with that, reverse all it altered: the poisoning of Jarr-Wya, the erratic weather, morphed creatures, corrupted minds, and the presence of the Millia sands.

Lady Sophia shooed the Lord away, as only she seemed capable of doing, her cheerful mood unsullied by his ferocity. She merrily went on packing loaf after loaf of vulai bread, enough for five warriors, and told the Lord, "Now who'd sing you all to sleep? Couldn't have that on my conscience!" She chuckled.

Finally, Archie counts himself. Fifteen in all.

There are fifteen in their quiet company, all leery of what may come when they reach Baluurwa. No one ventured to the mountain since the last Olearon Lord: Telmakus, the 29th. Archie read about him in the secret history of the Olearons, which he discovered in the armrest of the glass throne in the citadel. When the Maiden discovered him reading the glass history, she confiscated it, threatening to scorch Archie. At Ardenal's insistence, she showed mercy instead.

Archie's fingers ache for the magical square of glass. At his touch, it revealed to him, in his own language, many things deemed private by the Lord. As he longs for the secret history, Archie laments its demise along with the Maiden, who had it with her when she faced the Bangols in the east and revolted against Valarie. *How could the glass survive a blast of fire so hot it killed millions of carakwas? It can't have survived, Archibald, you old fool!*

Archie stretches his hands, his arms, his back. How youthfulness crept into him from the first moment he touched the Tillastrion made by Zeno, he has no idea. This, too, like the glowing white words he read on the glass, he tells no one. Day by day, Archie feels himself straighten out, his crooked back no longer a wilted flower. His skin grows thick and conceals the web of veins that once rose as blue tributaries on the tops of his hands. He runs his fingers through his hair, savoring its thickness where he was once bald and speckled with age spots.

"Grandpa Archie, carry me?" Duggie-Sky says in a whining tone, and though Ardenal reaches his toned red arms for the boy, Archie shoos him away. Archie scoops up the child without effort and swings him onto his shoulders. As the boy perches there, the muscles in Archie's chest tighten and bulge in the pleasing way he remembers from the decades he spent as a roofer in Seattle. He was lean and strong then. Archie is certain he is changing, bizarrely, back into that shape.

The pace of the company's hike, compared with the urgency with which they had rushed east to rescue Ella and challenge the Bangols, is indeed slower and more calculated. The Lord is a looming presence amongst them, and all are more careful with each step. At the company's center, the Lord discusses with Yuleeo and Islo in hushed voices their strategy for climbing the mountain and navigating its tunnels.

"Losing the Maiden was the greatest tragedy," the Lord said to the company as the glass city disappeared behind them, hidden by thick blue trunks as they entered the forest. "This time, none will be that careless."

No one in the company had the courage to speak up for the successes of that mission. Ella was saved. The contingent of Bangols were annihilated, except for King Tuggeron. Most in their company returned to the glass city with only minor injuries. Yet, what they brought with them were haunted memories. They do not disagree with the Lord.

All remember Valarie's haunting voice as she emerged into

consciousness on the eastern beach in the monstrous amalgamation of linked carakwas. The original company that remained after the expansive blast mourned the Maiden but are grateful. The spiteful words of the Lord only add pain to their misery. The Maiden's mercy, how she spared them—if not all Jarr-Wya—from Valarie's vengeance is an enduring debt.

Back in Seattle, while Archie snored on the couch, Ella ascended into their attic and poured over her lost father's notebooks. Those journals were filled with his research and sketches—drawings that became etched in Ella's mind, which she later realized were clues to locating the remedy for her cancer—a remedy entangled with the fate of the worlds. She recreated these drawings to lead the company to the Star and, hopefully, her cure.

Azkar grips Ella's drawings in his hand as he treks, while Archie immediately memorized the images. His mind now traces their inky contours. *What must we crack open?* he wonders. *Who must burn in a blazing fire? And how must a brain, heart, and flame unite, leading from one to the other?* For Archie, the ink drawings elicit more questions than answers.

Azkar studies one drawing with dotted lines that trace the exterior of Baluurwa, then point inward, through the center of the mountain. "This drawing is too simple, Lord. The Steffanus race burrowed many, if not hundreds, of tunnels through the rock . . ." His face is pinched in consternation. The black scar that runs from beneath his eye, down his left cheek, and to his collarbone puckers and pulls at his red skin.

Nameris snatches the drawing. "Azkar is right. We could be lost for countless sunsets within Baluurwa."

Nameris is by far the most studious of the warriors. Due to his time spent studying—instead of training—he is rail thin, though fast on his feet. He reminds Archie of a friend of Arden's from university. The young history student was a tall skeleton, as if his back had no bend, so he looked down on everyone—quite literally, but also as one who believes he knows much more than the rest.

Yuleeo speaks up thoughtlessly, "If only a Steffanus remained, so that she might lead us to the right path—"

The Lord cuts off Yuleeo. "Never wish for such a thing. The last of the Steffanus race died when the 29th Lord—my uncle, Telmakus—burned through the mountain before his end. This is a debt we owe to him, never to be forgotten. The last Steffanus nearly drove him mad with her ill-intended oracles, her wicked lava eyes, and her cunning voice. We all must take care"—the Lord raises his voice—"to mind the lies still carried on the wind. Report immediately to Islo anything heard on a whisper."

Islo nods solemnly. His black eyes meet those of each of the company. His gaze is controlled, mechanical, as he analyzes each member. Archie feels x-rayed, and for the first time since stealing the secret history of the Olearons, he is glad it is not tucked inside his bag.

Islo, like Azkar, is broad shouldered for an Olearon, his arms and back bulging with toned muscle. His hands are firm as boulders, and through his thick neck glow orange veins that throb indiscreetly. Islo's eyes finally rest on Azkar. The two Olearons were childhood playmates, though more like adversaries, Azkar told Archie back in the glass city. With held breath, Archie watches them scowl at each other. Azkar breaks the gaze and turns forward, his march now a storm that sweeps the company through the blue forest.

"No members of the Steffanus race remain on Baluurwa," says Junin, comforting the humans. "They have been gone many sunsets. No oracles have been scratched onto our glass city. No fires light up the western face of Baluurwa like stars in the black. While we seek to appease the Millia to the south and the

Bangols to the north, the heart of the island is calm. We should have no trouble upon our arrival."

"No trouble except finding the safest way in, and through," grumbles Nameris.

Archie peers at the Lord of Olearon. The towering red leader insisted on accompanying the newly formed company, certain, like Junin, that nothing lurked in the shadow of Baluurwa. Archie does not worry about the Steffanus sisters. It is the thought of Bangols that tears through his nerves like the colorful sparks of lightning cutting through the plum sky. In the glass city, Ella drew for Archie all she had experienced as a prisoner in the Bangols' journey east—from her time in their clay baskets, protected by the young sibling Bangols she befriended, to the stone-heads' camps as blue forest turned to white, then to sand and sea air. Archie could sense her fear as she painted images of her days locked in a stone cell at the end of a bridge over the eastern sea, where King Tuggeron bound humans to stones and let them sink to the Star at the bottom of the sea.

What if the Bangols lay in wait for them in the tunnels of Baluurwa? Archie feels too cowardly to present this concern to the Lord. The ruler is only concerned with the Star. All he speaks of is finding and destroying the dark sphere beneath Jarr-Wya, while Tessa's only desire is to unravel the cure for Ella, to disentangle it from the mystery of the Star. *These two desires—health for the island and health for my granddaughter—while often appearing to conflict*, Archie thinks, *are finally aligned.*

Archie can hear Duggie-Sky's stomach grumble from where the boy sits on his shoulders. "Hungry, little fella?"

"Uh-huh. Dinner soon?" the boy says.

"We must put more ground behind us," Islo barks.

Azkar nods slowly, annoyed to support Islo. "It is almost night—"

"How can you tell?" says Tessa, who shuts her mouth quickly with a click of her teeth.

Azkar glares at her, squinting so tightly that his eyes appear like black smudges of soot. "—and since our speed is slow, we will camp at the base, then scale the mountain by day."

Nate, still walking close beside Tessa, asks, "How much longer?"

"Depends on our pace," Nameris answers, looking back at Lady Sophia.

"Oh, my darling, thank you for noticing! I really am doing well, aren't I?" The singer laughs. She claps her hands and flashes Nameris a smile. The Olearon looks forward and continues to march without speaking.

"I'm guessing about three hours," Nate says, answering himself. "From my time captaining ships, I've grown skilled at eyeing distances. I'd guess about ten miles if we keep on like this."

Lady Sophia's laugh is a trill amongst the gloom, and not just Archie finds himself grinning. "Is that all?" she says. "Well, we'll certainly earn our supper!" She looks up at Duggie-Sky. "At least, most of us." She scrunches her nose playfully at the boy, who disappears from Archie's shoulders and reappears at Lady Sophia's side, where he slips his hand into hers. "Now that's better." She giggles.

"Too much delay and frivolity," the Lord grumbles to himself. He grits his teeth and hastens his stride.

If the Lord is so concerned about speed, why bring any of the humans along? Archie wonders. This is not the only thing that perturbs him about the Lord of Olearon; Archie also finds his attire a curious choice.

When the Lord overtook the *Atlantic Odyssey,* capturing its passengers and the Constellations Cruise Line staff, he wore the royal-blue battle jumpsuit, the same as his warriors beside him, though not rolled up at the sleeves and legs. Archie made out the Lord's ruddy flesh of his chest, ankles, forearms. Now, however, he is clothed in royal attire. He wears fitted silver-gold breeches that sheathe him past his shins and a matching doublet decorated with clear and silver gems surrounding a glass breastplate. Over all this, he wears a robe with folds of golden fabric that begin at sharp points rising from his shoulders and draping down to his feet like Naiu-rich waterfalls. The robe is dirty at the hem. It features a firm swirl of fabric beneath his chin that swoops down to his wrists, concealing his red-hot skin in an iridescence like ice.

The Lord's hands are sheathed in tight gloves decorated in colored gemstones that conceal his skin, as do his warrior boots. The only red flesh visible is that of the Lord's face, with its sharp, angular cheekbones reminiscent of the glass city, dark eyes like dying embers, and blood-hued lips. The black eyes are unreadable to Archie and ever searching. The Lord's broad forehead leads up to the steep rise of his Mohawk of thick dreadlocks, decorated with vivid-colored glass beads. *Like those that hopscotch along the perimeter of the secret history,* Archie remembers.

"I have been desiring to speak with you, Archibald Wellsley," the Lord begins. He startles Archie out of his wandering thoughts. The others in the company notice but keep their eyes on the blue bark trunks beneath the tree's large carrot-colored leaves. Archie was staring so intently at the Lord that he didn't realize he was being studied with equal scrutiny. He slips one hand inside one of his trouser pockets and grazes its contents.

Archie's fingertips tingle where they graze with a leaf folded around one of his reeking socks. What the makeshift packaging contains offers him the slightest bit of comfort, especially with the Lord glaring at him. No one but Duggie-Sky knows what he carries; the boy watched earlier as Archie collected the magical plant. Archie dreaded this particular conversation with the Lord and hoped the Olearon's preoccupation with the Star would prove a permanent distraction. "Are you sure it's even necessary, Lord?" Archie begins. "I barely looked at the glass, and I'm terribly sorry, truly—"

The Lord's words cut off Archie with an abruptness that causes Ardenal, Tessa, Nate, and Lady Sophia—though not Duggie-Sky, who is oblivious—to shuffle away nervously. The opera singer tugs the boy gently. The red of the Lord's face burns at Archie, as if all his heat was relocated to his cheeks to sizzle in place of the absent sun. "In your world," the Lord continues, "what is the penalty for stealing from a king?"

"Well, I can't say I rightly know one way or anoth—"

"Because in the world of Jarr, on the island of Jarr-Wya, we Olearons punish, by scorching, those who rob the ruler—though, this is not enacted kindly as in the ceremony for our warriors, for the Maiden." The Lord rests a hand on his chest as he speaks her title with affection.

Archie learned from these red beings that their connection to their lovers transcends even death—that they are connected from one life to the next, one world to another, on one lavish journey together through time and all manner of creation that Naiu had conceived. The bond between Lord and Maiden, the rulers of the Olearons, becomes therefore exponentially more intimate over time. When one dies, that one's spirit comes to reside in the body of the living member of the pair. In one manner of thinking, the Maiden, upon her death, arrived first at the glass city to be with her Lord before the rest of the bedraggled company ventured back on foot.

The Maiden, now inhabiting the body of her Lord, is silent

to all but him, and she shares her wisdom with him. The one piece of information Archie wishes the Lord would be blind to is that he is guilty of removing the secret history from the throne within the glass-domed citadel.

"I stumbled in by accident, Lord, really." Archie blunders over his words. His lies are insects on his tongue, and he spits them out bitterly, repulsed at his pathetic attempt to save himself. The Lord sees his words for what they are. Archie resigns himself to the truth.

"This place, this island . . . it's doing something strange to me, inside of me," he says. "I'm bolder, braver than I've ever been, and more foolish, too, obviously." His hand remains on the bundle in his pocket. Contained inside the leaf and sock is a small bouquet of Banji flowers. The first company delivered the flora to the man-spider Rolace, who needed the Naiu they possess to spin his power-giving web. The flowers are also a hallucinogenic and can disorient and disarm an enemy quickly. Archie collected his stash of Banji—*As an insurance policy*, he thought—when the others weren't looking, swearing Duggie-Sky to secrecy, and proceeded to forgot about it. Until now.

"Certainly more foolish, Archibald Wellsley." The Lord points with his chin. "Pause here," he says to Islo and Yuleeo, who grunt out orders to the company. "A moment alone, Archibald." He gestures to a patch of darkness in the shade of the azure forest.

Ardenal steps past Yuleeo's guiding arm, approaching his father. "Lord, I beseech you—"

"You will have your goodbye, warrior, though that time has not come," the Lord snarls at Ardenal. "Stand down."

Archie is led between the blue trunks, which shine dully without the sun. "I understand there are things you must do," whispers Archie. "But, please, not until we save Ella. The reason

I sought out Zeno and his Tillastrion and portal jumped to Jarr-Wya was to reunite my family, together and well. Even if I must die . . . please, Lord, not until I've done my part to save my granddaughter." His hushed voice grows impassioned. "Please, I know I can be of use on this one last mission. Then you may dole out your judgment on me and burn my breath away till I'm nothing. Please—"

"Archie!" The Lord's pitch is higher, and his voice suffused with feminine softness. "Archibald, cease your blubbering."

Archie looks to the Lord, confusion rippling his forehead like troubled waters. He scratches the thick new growth of black-flecked stubble on his chin. "Lord, are you all right? Your voice, it—"

"Shhh! Do none in your world possess a sliver of tact? Go, now, farther that way." The Lord points, still speaking strangely.

Azkar and Islo, their shoulders butting up against each other, elbow through the wood behind them. "Is something amiss, my Lord?" Islo asks first.

"No, fools! Guard the child. If she is indeed needed to destroy the Star, she must not fall into the Bangols' hands. Go!"

When the two warriors are long strides away and Archie is alone with the Lord, the red face bends low and the leader asks, "Can you not sense who I am?"

"You are," Archie begins tentatively, "the Lord of Olearon." He pronounces each word slowly, as if his declaration might ensnare him more tightly. He observes the softened expression on the Lord's face. The lips that now curl upward, but not with anger or disgust. The wide, waiting eyes. The angled way the Lord stands. And the voice. Higher and kinder.

Archie brightens. "How can it be? How can you speak through him?" He releases the package of Banji flowers and removes his hand from his pocket.

The Lord smiles, and the expression is at odds with the fabric of the silvery-gold suit. "Do you remember what I told you and our original company when we stood on the precipice of facing the Bangols on the eastern shore? I have worked tirelessly to bind up my soul into one singular entity, to lie to the one I love, to my soul's other half."

"Yes, Maiden. I do." The memory resurfaces in Archie's mind and hovers on the cusp of his understanding. "And so you can do this, be with the Lord and speak through him . . ."

"Without his knowing."

"Amazing, Maiden."

"I cannot sever the connection between us for long, so listen closely." The Maiden, in the Lord's body, stoops, dropping to a breathy whisper Archie strains to hear. "There is much I must weigh. What to reveal and to whom. Everything will burn in its appointed time. Dying when I did . . . my moment of passing was a choice, you must understand, Archibald. Yes, to save our company in the east, but also so the rest of you might go on to save all the worlds."

"Maiden—I don't understand."

"My love and I are united in this form, but we are not alone. Do you not recall anything I told you, foolish human? That the Lord is not himself?" The Maiden scowls, which is more befitting the Lord's demeanor. Slowly the memory of her confession slips back through Archie's ears and he hears it anew. His jaw falls open. The Maiden's frown dissolves. "It is true. There is another who dwells—harshly and wickedly—inside this shell. I have built up my reserves for many hundreds, if not thousands, of sunsets, to withhold my wisdom from both Lords, to save us all once more."

"The Lords?" Archie mumbles the words as if the insect wings and legs have returned to his mouth. It does not make sense. His tongue forms the beginning of many uncomfortable questions, forbidden questions he should never ask, as they would reveal the knowledge he gained from the secret history. Archie is mute, the words trapped behind his teeth. Just when he has settled on the *one* question he must have an answer to—*Which Lords?*—something in the Maiden's expression changes.

Archie sees a flicker of grey light glimmer ever so subtly across the charcoal eyes. A shiver rises from the Lord's feet to knock his knees together and ascend through his spine, stitching tight his posture so it is erect once more. When the Maiden speaks again, the voice is gravelly and bottomless. The words cause the hot sweat on Archie's forehead to freeze in place. He tumbles back onto the moss bed of the forest floor.

"Archibald Wellsley! Where have you taken me?" roars the Lord of Olearon.

chapter 9

Tessa

Tessa's head snaps toward the trees, where the Lord called out. While the Olearons talk in a huddle of blue jumpsuits and red skin, she slips away from the company. Ella sees her, but Tessa raises her pointer finger to her lips, even though Ella cannot speak. Nate does not notice Tessa as he plays catch with Duggie-Sky using a violet-colored fruit. Nor does Lady Sophia, who plunked herself on a root, her back cradled there as she fans her face with several orange leaves. Her eyes are closed.

Tessa tiptoes through the blue forest. It is easy to spot where the Lord has taken Archie. The Olearon's face illuminates the blanket of diffused light that hangs over the trees. She ducks behind a stump, not wanting to startle the Lord and cause his fire to burst from his neck to burn a hole through her heart.

Archie is looking frantically from side to side. He slinks backward through the moss and the skeletons of dead leaves. Patches of mud coat his hands.

The one word her ears catch perturbs Tessa, and it rattles around in her head. Archie called the Lord *Maiden*. "Maiden?" she breathes.

The Lord sends from his face a band of hot breath that quivers in the damp forest air and distorts Tessa's view like the summer heat on a southern highway.

"Why do you address me as such, Archibald Wellsley?" The Lord spits. "To wound me? Impossible." His laughter knots Tessa's stomach into a twisted ball, and her mouth turns to sand. "With every passing sunset, my power grows. Family is a weakness. The others will be more loyal without you. We all will have less to lose."

The Lord pounces. He is on his hands and knees, looming over Archie. Tessa creeps forward. She bites her lip. *I should turn back for the others. Ardenal will help*, she thinks. *Or perhaps I could dart out and startle the Lord? Maybe he'll be startled long enough for Archie and me to get away . . .*

"It was glorious to crush Dillmus between my arms, to squelch his reign over his flame, to let it run wild through his veins and consume him. I watched as his fire burned through his eyes, melting them, and glowed upon me like the firm touch of the midday sun in days now past. It was beautiful. It helped me to see that nothing can remain in the wake of flame and desire. Except for me, that is."

"Dillmus?" Archie stutters, seeming to Tessa that he remembers the name vaguely. *How can he know that?* Tessa wonders. She sees Archie slip one hand inside his pants pocket.

"To see the skin of Dillmus curl, his fingernails transform from black to wisps of ash. I breathed him in. Every Olearon cowered in fear, but not I. Oh no, Archibald Wellsley. Too much had been taken from me. It was my honor to steal the life of another. And it was just the beginning. And why not you, too, human?"

"Please, Lord—"

The Lord narrows his eyes. He pinches the finger of one black glove and slides it off, then the other. Archie gasps. Tessa covers her mouth. The red skin of the Olearon is no longer even in tone. Patches of the Lord's hands are pinky-orange and tender, inflamed and creased in distinct scars that join it to the blazing red as if adhered with an unskilled touch.

"What happened to you?" Archie says, wheezing.

"*Who* happened to me." The Lord chuckles, his mouth falling open and his teeth glaring as he looms over Archie, casting a dark shadow across the old man. His ruddy lips are on fire, his tongue one great flame. The Lord's jaw cracks open to a gaping hole and the flame creeps out in a band of sweltering light. It curls through the space between him and Archie, who retreats until his back is flush to a blue tree. The old man's eyes reflect the snake of fire.

Archie fumbles with something in his pocket. *Maybe he's struggling to retrieve the glass dagger from the Olearons*, Tessa hopes. *But why would he keep it in there, where it might stab him in the leg? No, he's got something else in that pocket. Whatever it is, he's not pulling it out quick enough to save himself.*

Tessa has no time to gather the others or even call out for help. She finds a palm-sized rock at her feet and hurls it. It smashes against the Lord's head, just above his left ear, with a painful crack. All at once he is on the ground, and Tessa on her feet. She rushes to Archie. Together they watch the Lord's body convulse. His silver robes are sullied with smears of green moss and damp earth.

"Should we do something?" Tessa chokes on the words.

"If we touch him, he'll burn us," Archie says with a wheeze, his eyes wide and his face as pale as the bark of the white woodland. Even in his quivering state, the Lord spreads his hands along the ground, feeling for the gloves, which he finds and puts on with difficulty.

Tessa and Archie turn toward the trees, suddenly ablaze with light. Ardenal appears, the flame at his neck engulfing his hair and shoulders, and he rushes to his father and wife. By this time, the Lord is still, the quivering abated, and he pulls himself to sit upright. Azkar and Islo arrive, their bodies also aflame, and Kameelo swoops down to land on a branch overhead.

Islo bares his teeth. "What has happened here?" He stoops to collect the Lord. The ruler accepts the help and straightens to his feet, leaning heavily on his warrior.

"I do not know," the Lord says tentatively.

"You wished to speak with the human," Azkar reminds him.

"We spoke." Archie's voice breaks, and he clears his throat. "Don't you remember, Lord? I offered you the debt of my service, till my final days, as payment for my crime."

The Lord touches his head where a tiny trickle of blood oozes and simmers lightly against his skin. "Then how am I wounded?" he asks, on the cusp of rage.

"The rock," Tessa answers. "I saw it fall." She points to one tiny floating island above them. Beneath the chunk of levitating earth, dirt hangs in the air where roots blow in the wind. Hovering stones and curling vines connect the enchanted island to Baluurwa. "I saw the rock dislodge and drop, so I ran and tracked it here. It struck you to the ground, Lord."

The Lord presses his fingers to the gash to cauterize the wound. He appears to consider Tessa's words carefully. While she desires to swallow the lump choking her throat, she holds back, unwilling to break her composure. In the periphery, the remainder of the company arrive in the clearing.

The Lord's countenance is muddied in confusion before he says, "Service until your death, Archibald. Yes, I accept this for your thievery, though we all may die prematurely if we do not carry on and find cover at the base of Baluurwa."

"You are right, Lord." Nameris nods. "The sky is slipping into black. It will be harder to evade the debris of the mountain by nightfall."

Kameelo leaps down from the tree. "I flew ahead. There is a cave not far away. It may be the start of a tunnel."

chapter 5

Tessa

Tell me what really happened, Mom.

I don't think I can, Ella.

What good is your gift of telepathy if you won't talk candidly? Spill the beans, please! The vibe feels weird now.

I didn't see it all, and what I did doesn't make sense. I wish I could get into the head of the Lord . . . Something's happening to him. Don't ask me what because I don't know. The skin on his hands . . . it's . . . it's . . . unnatural . . .

Unnatural how?

It's like a . . . like a poorly stitched quilt. Some parts are red, but mostly he is a sickly orange. Splotchy. Freckled with tiny dots of black. His skin puckers.

Like my scar.

Yeah, like your scar. But in all the wrong places. It might cover all of him, but I only saw his hands, and only for a moment . . .

Hmm.

We're trusting him for now, Ella, but not forever. Something's going on here. If only I could whisper to Archie without all the others hearing.

Is what Grandpa said true? Did the Lord really let him off for stealing the glass?

I don't know that part. All I know is that when I arrived, Archie was on the ground. The look on his face was not that of someone who'd been shown mercy, who'd made a deal that saved his life. He was terrified—

Of the Lord?

Yes. The Lord was on all fours, like an animal. And his fire looked like a serpent, slithering out of him to kill Archie. The Lord said family is weakness and talked about some Olearon named Dillmus.

Do you know who that is, Mom?

No. Not a clue. But whoever it is, he's dead now. The Lord killed him.

What do we do, Mom? I'm freaking out!

Don't let anyone see on your face that something's wrong.

Tessa looks over at Ella on the other side of the company hiking through the dark, lit by the Olearon's flames. She says out loud, "Hey, Ell, want to walk with me for a bit? Luggie, do you mind?" The Bangol shakes his head of protruding stones. Ella winds her way through the group. Tessa laces her fingers through her daughter's. "Love you, Ell." Ella nods and smiles weakly. The warmth of Ella's hand is weak. Tessa continues to comfort her daughter, though her lips do not move.

We're going to be okay, Ella.

How do you know?

I don't.

Well, that's inspiring!

Ella, you're squeezing my hand too tightly.

Sorry, Mom.

We'll figure this out. We always do, right? When you were diagnosed with cancer at ten. When your dad left two years ago. When six months ago, you woke up unable to talk. We always figure things out, and this is another one of those times. Once everyone is asleep, I'll speak with your grandpa Archie. If the Lord is dangerous, we'll sneak away in the night, leave the Olearons in the cave.

With Luggie, too?

Yes, of course. He knows this place. Maybe he can hide us somewhere the Olearons and Bangols can't find us. We'll make our own way into the mountain. Locate the Star, whatever it is, and your cure. The Bangols know how to make Tillastrions to transport people between Jarr and Earth. Luggie will help us. We'll get you healthy and then get home.

And what about Dad?

Tessa bites her lip and doesn't answer. Ella tugs on her arm and squeezes her hand harder than before. Finally, Tessa turns to her daughter and shrugs.

Tessa peers through the crowd at an Olearon half a foot shorter than the rest. He speaks in the musical tongue of the fire beings, which could be a foreign language of one of Lady Sophia's arias. It is smooth and ringing, like silk and bells. Ardenal's skin is fiery embers, his eyes coal. His hair is matted into a tall Mohawk—a style the Arden that Tessa remembers could never have pulled off—beneath which a flame roars in the settling dusk, giving light and heat.

Ardenal wears the royal-blue warrior jumpsuit and heavy black boots. When the sun was hot, many sunsets ago, Tessa watched as Ardenal removed the top of his jumpsuit and tied the arms around his waist. His back and chest shone like a dew-kissed rose at first light. Tight skin, even in tone, and rippling like the turbulent ocean when the *Atlantic Odyssey* first embarked from Barcelona. Their voyage feels like it was lifetimes ago, and Tessa strains to think back years. In her mind, his red skin pales to peach, his lyrical language becomes awkward, and the blazing hotness shifts to a comfortable seventy-two degrees Fahrenheit.

When they married, Arden's hair was a deep chestnut that fell in his eyes. His blue eyes, like Ella's, the color of a pale sea, sparkled with a boyish whimsy that caused Tessa's chest to burn. His eyes touched her heart through his chunky black glasses, which had the habit of slipping down the gentle slope of his nose. Like Archie fumbling with his watch, so, too, was Arden with his glasses—endearing habits. Arden would push up the frames with one exacting finger to touch the space between his eyebrows, and then he would smile, seeing the world sharply once more.

Tessa and Arden wed in Archie and Suzie's yard. It was early summer and the goatsbeard plants in the garden were already five feet tall, their blossoms tipping their stems with plentiful white plumes. The flowers bowed to the alpine strawberries and the hot-pink fireweed that favored the Pacific Northwest. Tessa's dress had a modest amount of lace and was ankle length and flowing, like her hair, which spilled down her back in loose blond curls mimicking the sway of a woman's hips. Arden was barefoot and laughed at himself. "Khaki pants and plaid!" he had joked with a gasp. His fellow PhD candidates wore pale suit jackets and bow ties.

Their vows had been simple and personalized: "My friend, my lover, my equal, I choose you today, and in every tomorrow. I vow to stand beside you in sadness and in joy, in argument and in laughter, in body and in spirit. You are the light of my life, and my enduring treasure. Whatever our tomorrows may bring, I give you my heart. Keep it safe, as I will yours."

Tessa had memorized the vow, not wanting to read it but to look directly into Arden's eyes, meaning every word. Still, she tripped up, saying, "My friend, my lover, my sequel," to which their friends and family sniggered. Tessa did, too. When it was Arden's turn, he matched her fumble with his own. "You are the light of my life, and my enduring pleasure." The blush of his cheeks turned Olearon-red. "Treasure! I mean, treasure!" Their first kiss was long and warm, and smelled of mingling flowers and sweet summer sun, and forever.

Tessa smiles to herself now. How could she have known there would be another part to their relationship, a sequel in its own right? Arden walked out of their home and lives two years ago, without a goodbye, only a note that Tessa alone read before crumpling it. She hadn't told Archie or Ella. All it said was, "Love you, Tess. Be back soon." It didn't mean anything to her that morning. Not even that night. Arden often stayed late at the university, researching Egyptian dynasties, or so she thought. She now knew the truth. Arden's search for Ella's cure led them here, to the stony faces of the Bangols, to the simmering heat rippling the air above the Olearon's necks, and to the doom of the mountain before them as they approach its base.

When Arden didn't returned to their cozy Seattle home after a day, after a week, Tessa panicked. She phoned the police, the university, and all of his friends and colleagues. She stalked every one of his favorite spots: the friendly university pub, the looming graduate library on the second floor, the quad between buildings where freshmen sprawled over textbooks and each other, but there was only Arden's ghost—evidence of him, but not him: the patch of dirt in the quad where the considerate oak tree cast the perfect shade for reading; his favorite beer on the pub menu, Pike Brewing Company's Scottish ale; and, his books.

There were stacks and stacks of books in his shared office at Seattle University, where the wall shelves were filled in with hardcover volumes, and at home, too. Books filled the nooks of his bedside table and under his side of the bed. Books lined the useless space between their kitchen cabinets and the ceiling, though never gathered dust. Arden would move through their bungalow like a Roomba, avoiding collisions though never really seeing. His nose and glasses were locked in a peculiar intimacy between the hard covers of textbooks or historical records. From room to room he would navigate, connecting one sentence in one ancient book to a paragraph in another.

What sequel can Tessa and Arden have now?

Tessa received no word from Arden in seven hundred days. She counted: seven hundred nightmares of chasing his ghost; seven hundred calendar pages carrying the weight of everything—Ella's cancer, the bills, full- and part-time jobs, Archie (oh, helpless Archie) and her own shadow of loneliness. She was alone. That was a fact. Arden was the one she confided in and also the one who understood not to ask the questions about her family that would send pangs of self-pity through her like waves in a storm, beating her down. It always reminded her.

Tessa was alone.

Arden's absence echoed her early-life solitude, which broke her as a child. It was a wild pain then, but not since. She vowed never to let it be again. After the first hundred days of Arden's disappearance, she built up the walls around her heart so high that they passed the sun and moon to dwell amongst the stars. *I'll never let anyone in again*, she vowed.

Even Ella's illness, her ever-present turmoil, makes Tessa dizzy. It is sure to be another loss too great to bear. Higher go Tessa's walls—more fortified, more enduring. She squeezes Ella's hand as they walk through the blue forest. Her daughter's warm, petite hand fits so perfectly within her own, like a baby bird nestling beneath its mother's wing.

Suddenly, Kameelo appears from above in the inky sky. He lands with a thud at the front of their company. "The cave is a hundred breaths ahead. Its mouth is twelve feet tall, and much, much deeper though, unfortunately not a tunnel. It is empty, however, with space for us all."

"Thank you, Kameelo," the Lord replies. "We will rest the remainder of the night there. Eat, sleep, and then by dawn's light—as little of it as we are offered—ascend Baluurwa. Islo will divide our company into five groups of three who will search out the tunnels by quadrants, in even increments of time.

When the time is spent, we will return to the center of the first quadrant, report, and redraw our searching boundaries."

"There will be at least one Olearon per group . . ." Islo begins.

Under her breath, Tessa whispers sarcastically, "Of course."

". . . I will inform you of your group before dawn," Islo finishes.

"To the cave!" orders the Lord.

chapter 6

Luggie

Ella surrenders to fatigue and is limp in Luggie's arms as the company crosses the uneven threshold into the mouth of the cave at the foot of Baluurwa the Doomful. Luggie cradles the girl's head, and her hair—blond like her mother's—slips through his fingers and bounces in playful waves in the moonlight. Ella's pale pink lips are parted and her breathing is shallow. It is only in sleep that her body betrays her illness; her awake self presents a confident facade.

Tessa, Archie, and Ardenal flock to ensure Ella is laid snugly on the cave floor before they scatter to plot strategy for the next day's unknowns.

Luggie sits on the far side of Ella, her body buffering him from the rest of the company. No eyes flit in his direction. The hunger for the secret history of the Olearons burns in his chest. He calculates the risk of retrieving the enchanted glass square from his sack without arousing suspicion. The burning desire for knowledge outweighs the fear that pricks his mind with warnings.

The glass feels like power in Luggie's hands, the sensation heightened by the possibility of discovery. The perimeter of the square is lined with gemstones that sparkle in every color. At his touch, a silent thunderstorm appears on the surface, where a swirling black void consumes angry clouds until white lettering—in Bangol—rises, spilling its secrets like candlelight in the dark cave. Luggie, shielding the light with his shoulders, devours the history that blossoms and disappears before his eyes.

It was in our season of harvest in the lands beyond the glass city when I—the 30th Lord of Olearon, Dunakkus—first noticed the peculiar way I felt upon the glass throne.

One day I returned to the citadel, weary from the long hours spent before sunset, cutting, culling, and reaping the twelve-foot-tall stalks. Naiu, the life force that feeds everything, was strong then in the many sunsets at the beginning of my reign; I was crowned when only a child and grew to maturity within my post. The magic flowed from the sun through crystal columns—the crystaliths—in our western field, intensifying and radiating from their bases into the soil. The Naiu was great and our harvest was rich and abundant. I, as all other Olearon Lords before me, did not sit idly by as my warriors worked until the light was spent and their children asleep. I bore the effort alongside my subjects.

On this particular day, I returned to the citadel and ascended the steps to my crystal throne.

My Maiden, my soul partner, knew my state. She left me to fetch vulai bread and the silver wryst to drink, knowing I needed restoration. I was left alone but for the green birds and the awakin butterflies that fluttered above me high at the apex of the citadel, though they, too, were weary. The birds were eager for rest, and the awakins unfurled their second set of wings, their nighttime pair, never risking to land.

The glass throne was cold despite the warmth of my exertion, but that was not the only sensation it elicited. A deep rumbling seemed to rise from beneath me, as if the earth were contracting in labor. Swift pricks of energy, like sparks, nipped at my thighs. I leaped down from the seat and ran my hands over the glass. It was frigid, though hummed with a vibration that caused my fire to quiver.

Suddenly, one rectangular section of glass from the fire-molded throne clicked open a finger's length. Out of the crack blasted light so intensely white and piercing that I shielded my eyes. The birds overhead fluttered in confusion, and I, too, could not comprehend. The rectangle pulled free from the throne, and then I realized it was a seamless drawer, not meant to be discovered.

The throne had been polished countless times each sunrise and sunset, so I presumed that access to this drawer was the ruler's alone. This caused me trepidation. The Lord before me, my uncle Telmakus, was a conflicted and suspicious figure. If he had hidden an object in the throne, I could only surmise that it would cause me, and my loved ones, much turmoil.

When my eyes adjusted, I could see that there, in the glass drawer, was an outfit so beautiful that I immediately wished to cloak myself in it. There were gloves, a neckpiece, and a crimson undergarment and leggings to be worn beneath my gold and silver robes.

I slid my hand into a glove and noticed how strange it felt against my skin—flush and tight like lizard scales. The seams appeared nearly invisible, as if I had been adorned by my own flesh. The red was a different shade, however; rusty, orangey, and sickly, I had to acknowledge. I likened it to the elder Olearons—those nearing death, ill, or inept.

The glove did not feel old or unwell. Instead it felt powerful.

I flexed my fingers and brought them together into a tight fist.

The hum of energy was now inside me, tingling at my fingertips. I brought forth fire and stretched it by fanning my hand. Tiny lightning bolts jumped from my thumb to my fingertips, then back again. The sound crackled and snapped, growled and hummed. Around my wrist I could see where the glove pinched my skin.

In the distance, the Maiden's footsteps began to click softly at first, and I did not wish to frighten her. I withdrew the glove and replaced it into the drawer, slipping the rectangular compartment back into the side of the throne.

The next day, I again visited the hidden drawer.

I found a piece of the orangey-speckled garment that vibrated within my palm. It jerked away from me, rose of its own will into the air warmed by my breath, then hovered and placed itself on an exposed section of skin on my forearm. There the rough-edged fragment fused itself, as if it had melted to me. It brought with it a surge of energy, hot and radiating, and much stronger than I had felt the day before.

I knew an attendant or warrior would pass through shortly, so I struggled to remove the garment. To my bewilderment, there was no edge to peel back. My crimson-hued skin was level with the tingling surface. I clawed and even gnawed with my teeth, but the scrap of cloth had melded to my arm.

As expected, an attendant knocked at the citadel's tall glass doors before opening and bowing, then striding quickly to the foot of the throne. Anticipating this, I turned my back to the drawer, which shut as I leaned against it. I swung forward my thick, black mane, with the distinguished beading of the Lords, and folded my arms beneath it, concealing the adhered patch.

The attendant delivered news that my nervous mind refused to hear, and I never once dropped my eyes to my forearm. At his departure, I hurried through the glass tunnels and elevated passageways from the citadel to the ruler's quarters. I found a blue warrior jumpsuit without cropped sleeves and changed into it before returning to the field.

That was the start of it: my daily appointments with the secret drawer. Yes, as time passed, more sections of the spotted orange garment wafted before me, securing themselves to the places they knew they belonged. Soon, my legs were a patchwork of my own skin and the enchanted flesh.

With each piece that was placed on me, I grew in power. At midday, I would dismiss my attendants and the Maiden to be alone in the citadel, alone with my new wardrobe. The fire I conjured between my fingers throbbed with light that sparkled. It was loud now, bringing with it a wind that only fed the flame. I raised my hands and a fiery bolt shot out, piercing a green bird through the heart. Its body was caught mid-fall by its friends and the awakins, who carried it to the bird's perch, hoping to sing it back to life, but to no avail.

The green birds that had once landed on the sharp points of the throne began to remain high at the apex of the glass-domed citadel, perching on the branches of the blue-bark trees the structure was built to encircle.

I learned many things from the energy that emanated from the secret glass compartment. It became clear to me that the Olearons were the first children of Jarr-Wya, from the initial spark of creation.

The Bangols' pitiful presence and lust for the land was an infestation. I grew to loathe their grey skin and polished head-

stones. I saw them for what they truly were: a disease upon our island, a digging, dirty presence that altered Jarr-Wya, uprooting its clay and shifting its stones. It was clear that this could not be allowed to continue. I realized that at my first opportunity, I must exterminate them from the island, and not by banishment, but by blood. Blood and death and restoration.

I have always loved peace, but something was changing in me.

In my dreams, I laughed as fire overtook Jarr-Wya. I imagined even the Steffanus race incapable of flying high enough to escape the curl of my flame. I saw myself, my Maiden, and our warriors. We walked through the fire, which fed our strength, unsinged, unified, and reborn as the stewards of Naiu in all of Jarr.

These nighttime dreams soon led to rumination by day. I called to my most intimate chambers the advisors and elders I trusted most. They spoke of a secret record written by my uncle, Telmakus, that must be passed into my hands. They said that within it, many of my questions would be answered, and the impetus behind my desires explained. They showed me where to hide the record, in a thin slit on the right armrest of the glass throne. Its existence was a guarded secret.

It is within this record that I now add my experience, with the hopes of—

ARCHIE bustles around, assembling the company, some members more willing than others. His voice is jovial and singsong. Ella stirs beside Luggie, who swiftly resheathes the glass inside the envelope and within his sack—just in time.

"Today is a special day," Archie says, bubbling with enthusiasm. "Wake up, Ella! Join us, Luggie!"

As if the words Luggie read are imprinted on his eyes and may project on the rough cave walls, he shuts his eyes quickly and rubs his eyelids. He cannot look at the Lord, nor even Archie, for that matter. Luggie helps a groggy Ella to her feet, where her grandfather takes her arm. The old man taps his watch, yammering about the date. It is hard for Luggie to focus. He struggles with one nagging desire that dims the happenings around him:

I must kill the Lord of Olearon.

chapter 7

Ella

The calendar date slips my mind—that is, until Grandpa Archie wakes me from my nap in the cave, towing me to where Dad waits. His fingers are lit in fragile flames at the tips. Grandpa says, "Blow out your candles!" Then I remember. My birthday!

I turned fifteen sometime in the last day or so, though it's hard to mark time here. Without the strength of Jarr-Wya's sun, the azure bark of the forest is dark like the sky on a night with a crescent moon, not electric sapphire as it was when we first arrived. Their carrot-colored leaves are a dull brown. Our shadows have disappeared on their own errands. It's like traveling through a dream, and I'm one to know what that's like. I glance at Mom but don't say anything through my mind.

Grandpa smiles so sheepishly when I hug the air out of him and kiss his cheek. He is old-fashioned in all the best ways and beautifully forward-thinking in others. He gives me space to do what I want and be who I am. Before my cancer, when Mom tried to enroll me in ballet, Grandpa slid her the slow-pitch registration instead. When I hated slow-pitch, he and I would go for ice cream during the games while Mom was at work—until she found out, that is. Then Grandpa was in the doghouse.

When my cancer threatened to change who I was, without my permission, Grandpa helped me to hold onto myself. Words have never been his way. He gave me love by spending hours with me at our scratched-up kitchen table, painting with dollar-store acrylics, laughing full throated at our creations. Until the cancer stole my laugh, too.

Now Mom brings over a mound of Lady Sophia's store of vulai loaves, which are square, bland, and yellowish like corn bread. For the vulai, Dad retrieves a syrupy liquid—"ellag currants," he tells me—which flows purple and tastes like honey. Junin and Grandpa bring over travel vials of the silvery wryst drink. Since recovering in the glass city, I've learned that the magical liquid not only renews my strength, but also makes me tipsy, which I don't mind tonight.

It's my birthday! I'm fifteen!

The storm of the morning continues in the night—popcorn lightning with its offshoots of crackling reds and blues and yellows. Its trumpeting song that follows serenades us, as does a hollow voice that whistles through the trees. I've overheard the Olearons grumbling that the voice of the wind is different since the Star crashed beneath the island. They say they don't know the language that now whispers through the forest, but whatever it is, it sounds harmonic to me, like an echoing chorus of children singing a cappella in a cathedral.

My family and new friends sing to me: "Happy birthday to you . . ." Lady Sophia is the loudest and draws out the final notes so passionately that I cover my ears and can't help but let out my scratched-record laugh.

I press my fingers to my lips and blow kisses as silent thank-yous to those who have gathered: To Mom and Dad, and Captain Nate, who's annoyingly always at Mom's side. To Grandpa Archie and Duggie-Sky, who perches on Grandpa's shoulders because he's too short to see our hilarity—so normal, but in such a strange setting. To the salty-skinned and beaming Lady

Sophia. To goofy Kameelo and kind Junin, who stood there dumbly as the humans sang. I'm glad the other Olearons—the Lord, Islo, Yuleeo, Azkar, and Nameris—are in the corner scheming. They would have dampened the vibe, which is all smiles, congratulations, and exclamations of "Happy birthday!" Mom is near tears, but I ignore her. She doesn't dare say, "This may be your last birthday," but I know she's thinking it.

My stomach is full of grainy vulai bread and my head buzzes from the syrupy wryst. If I'm not going to make it to my sweet sixteenth, I might as well make fifteen one to remember.

Since I can't thank anyone beyond the kisses and repeated sign language gesture or even engage in the normal birthday party banter, I excuse myself and Luggie, too. His actions since I drew my plan for our future—if I have a future—tell me he's forgiven me. He was close by my side as we trekked here. I love how protective he is of me.

True, I'm ill, and thus slow and clumsy, but Luggie matched my pace. He growled at the others to ease up our speed, which embarrassed me but also made me crack up. Lady Sophia burst into a grin she had hoped to hide and supported him, saying, "Let's pace ourselves, for Ella." Her words make me smile again now as my brain is loopy and my head heavy. Not long after she said that, she asked Kameelo for a ride on his back. A cramped calf muscle, she claimed. He tried to fly with her pudgy arms wrapped too tightly around his dangerous ruby neck. Her glistening white thighs were thick around his narrow waist.

Boy, her scream was loud. If anyone actually lived on the mountain, they would have heard her whoops and hollers half a day before we arrived. Lady Sophia, first screaming but eventually laughing, suddenly lost her grip and slipped off, nearly pulling Kameelo's jumpsuit off with her. Kameelo only managed to get to the Lord's height—about ten or so feet—off the ground, so when Lady Sophia landed on her rear, she bounced twice on the mossy path before settling like a flipped pancake. She seemed fine enough.

Now I'm the one leading Luggie behind me, away from the party, and through the cave. Grandpa Archie gives me a closed-mouth grin. Mom's forehead is scrunched with worry and her lips curl with disapproval, but who is she to judge? She still hasn't told me how her and Nate's flirting is a part of our plan to find my cure, but I haven't made a fuss about it. She looks happy for the first time since before my diagnosis. I hate Nate for the way he gazes at her—yuck, seriously?—but I do want Mom to have a life, even if it has nothing to do with me. The two emotions that bubble up in my gut—anger for Dad and happiness for Mom—don't sit well with the dense Olearon fare. But tonight, right now, it's not about any of them.

Luggie and I trace our way along the wall of the cave. Its rock is jagged and angry, black as the night between the broken bursts of vibrant stormy pyrotechnics and strangely warm to the touch, even when we've moved far enough away from the Olearon's heat. Eventually, the warmth of their flames fades, too, so Luggie and I hug the insides of the cave, drawing comfort from Baluurwa and from each other.

We take tentative steps into a narrow offshoot of the roughly carved space. The rock is only an inch above my head, about two inches above Luggie's, with less than an arm's width of space on each side. It's dark now, the Olearons' light nothing more than a flickering glow behind us—dark but for Luggie's eyes. They create a small pocket of shadowy light where we can make out each other's faces when we are nose to nose. I can taste the wryst on Luggie's breath, which only makes my head spin more quickly.

We are chest to chest. Beneath my shirt, I feel against my

ribs the long chain of my necklace, from which hangs two objects I hold dear. One is the locket I wore on Constellations Cruise Line, aboard the *Atlantic Odyssey*. Thankfully it's suffered only slight tarnishing in the soggy island air. It was Grandma Suzie's locket and holds two photographs: one of Grandpa Archie and the other of Dad as a baby, cut from old photos that once hung in their living room. Grandpa gave it to me when Grandma Suzie died.

The other object dangling there is an ornate metal key. I dug it out from a hidden pocket of the blank book Luggie and Nanjee gave me to draw in to communicate. I found the pocket and the key while I was a Bangol captive, trapped in a sack as Luggie and Nanjee flew our balloon to higher elevations on the wings of the awakin butterflies. The trees of the blue forest faded into the white woodland beneath us. The key vibrated in my hand. I knew I was not meant to find it. I wondered, *Had Luggie's dad, Tuggs, king of the Bangols, hidden the key inside this book?* The clean, creamy pages were intended to be filled with Tuggs's slanted history of the Bangols—before Luggie and Nanjee stole it, that is. I didn't tell Luggie about the key, for which I now feel a pang of guilt. It belongs to his kind. Still, something about it makes me want to be sneaky and keep it to myself.

It's too dark in the cave to draw anything new. I pull out from my sack what drawings I made during our rest stops earlier today. Luggie smiles at them faintly, but his attention is halfhearted. When we stood close, Luggie felt what I conceal. He puts his hand on my chest, where the locket and key sit nuzzled against my ribs. I've been too careless, but it's too late now. His brow creases ever so slightly, and his gaze follows his touch, which emboldens me. I must keep my secret safe and also have a happy birthday. Releasing the black ink drawings to be gobbled by the darkness at our feet, I cup Luggie's face in my hands.

Kissing is just the distraction we both need. His eyes close, and our lips find each other in the dim, buttery glow of his eyes, even when closed, that only ever fades completely when a Bangol is dead.

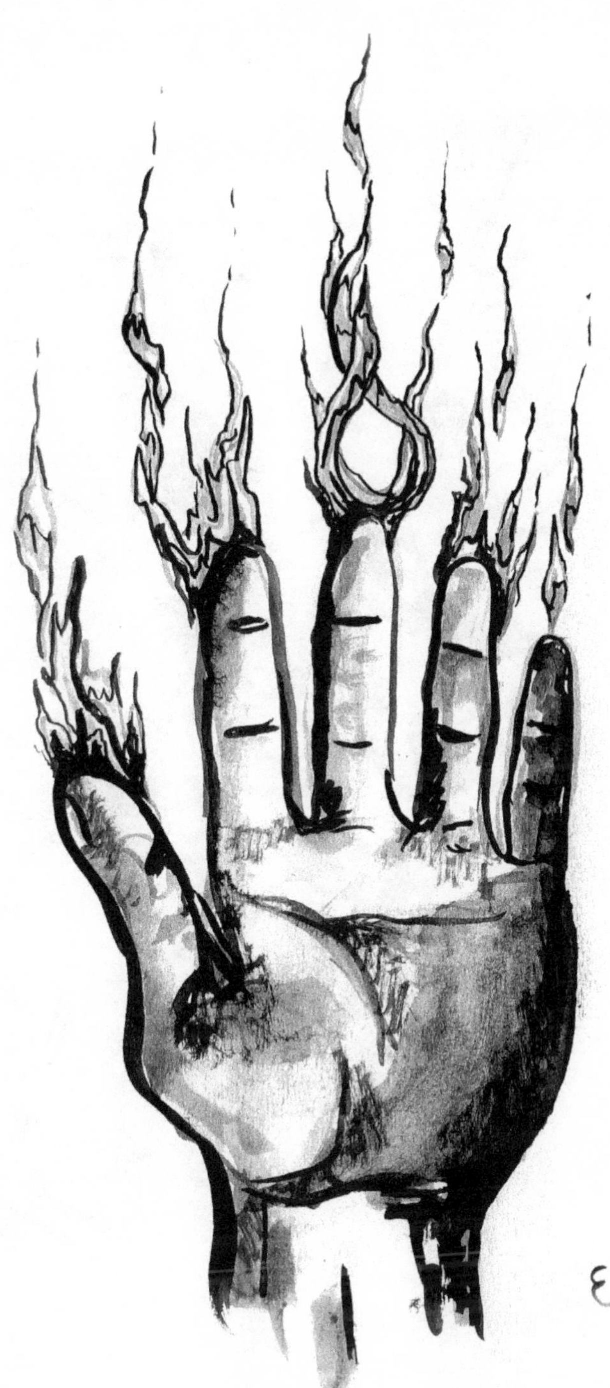
Ella

FOR Ella's EYES ONLY!!!!

Ella

chapter 8

Tessa

Tessa leans against the opening to the cave, staring into the distance. A feeling of foolishness thuds in her chest as she realizes that, until now, she did not notice the life that throbs at the heart of the island. The subtle, which life does not value confrontation or even acknowledgment but merely exists to live and to die, in perfect succession. Breath and no breath. Hunting and hunted. Motion and stillness.

Tessa not that long ago believed that Jarr-Wya was home only to the Millia, Bangols, Olearons, and, in a generation past, the Steffanus race. She laughs at her small-mindedness. In the dark sky, the great black flyers are silhouettes outlined in moonbeam silver. The awakin butterflies, each airborne by night with a purple pair of wings, flutter sleepily. They choose never to land, afraid to risk contact with the hallucinogenic Banji flowers—Tessa knows this all too well from her time carrying the flora to the man-spider, Rolace. The awakins also fear the sky hunters, those silver silhouettes that stalk them like the shadows of clouds. The awakins hover between branches, above and below the palm-sized leaves of the blue forest and the nests of the sleeping green birds. The awakins' tireless energy prompts Tessa to yawn.

Just beyond the trees, the moon also illuminates the slick fur and innocent faces of what first appears to be a pack of fluffy rabbits. Their coats are brown, like the dusty earth where they huddle. Junin approaches silently and startles Tessa.

"My apology, Tessa Wellsley. I only meant to escape the endless plotting. May I join you?"

Tessa nods, and Junin stands beside her on the threshold of the cave. The Olearon inhales deeply as her almond-shaped eyes adjust to the darkness without the illumination of fire.

"What you so keenly observes," Junin begins, "are the huppers."

"Those there? Huddled together?" Tessa points. "They look like rabbits."

"Do your rabbits have glowing whiskers that attract the lightning bugs?"

"No."

"The insects believe their host hupper to be a friend, and they are, in one manner of thinking. Until the hupper grows hungry."

Tessa watches the pack of huppers shuffle through the dirt. They scurry into a patch of moonlight, which reveals their lengthy corkscrew tails and massive ears, easily two feet tall, which stand erect despite untamed tufts of shaggy hair. Suddenly, a twig snaps in two—a predator is nearing—and all thirty pairs of bushy ears turn back.

Tessa shifts on her feet. "What's coming?"

"It is only the sasars. They hunt the huppers. Calm yourself; they have never ventured near an Olearon habitation. They fear our fire."

Tessa's mouth hangs agape as the group of huppers disperse, leaping from the ground through the air and landing on the vertical planes of the nearest trees. Midair, their brown fur loses its copper highlights and fades to ashy black, matching the night sky. The moment the huppers' small feet connect with the bark, they transform to pale starlight-blue, then become fully azure from the tips of their ears to the ends of their tails.

"Do your huppers hide from hunters in this way?"

"N-no," stutters Tessa.

The huppers remain fixed in place, as if held motionless to the blue trunks by some magnetic force, and just in time. Three sasars stroll into the moonlight. The white fur-covered bodies are as big as bears, Tessa notes, and she blinks rapidly in disbelief. Her mouth feels dry.

"You're sure they won't come this way?"

Junin shakes her head. The sasars weave around the trees like cats at a scratching post. They stand on their broad hind legs and claw at the bark. When they open their mouths, black fangs stand out against their ghostly fur. Their howl is a nightmare made audible, bloodthirsty and savage, and it rattles at the end like the clatter of empty spray paint cans.

"Since the Star arrived many sunsets ago, it has broken not only the island, but all that live upon it. Like the sasars—no longer can they smell their prey. They must listen hard or starve."

Nate appears at Tessa's back and wraps his arms around her. "You all right?" he asks before connecting the terrifying sound to the massive white beasts. He curses and pulls her inside the cave.

"It's okay." Tessa smiles weakly.

She takes his hand, and they return to Junin's side. The Olearon watches the scene with indifference, her muscles relaxed.

Just as the sasars are about to move on, one nervous hupper twitches its whiskers and leaps from its trunk. Not fast enough. A sasar lunges after it and bats it out of the air. The small creature smashes against the earth, changing swiftly to brown. Its small skull cracked upon impact. Its color flashes between jade and lemon, pumpkin and scarlet, slate and sky; this sequence is repeated until it becomes white to match the three sasars that feast on its sinews.

Tessa nearly shrieks when Nameris steps up close behind her.

"A word, human?"

Tessa turns to look back at the Olearon, and she shrugs and nods at the same time. Nate scowls. He looks at her with apprehension, but she releases his hand.

"Excuse us, Captain Nathanial Billows, Junin," says Nameris.

The female Olearon nods. She and Nate return to the shelter of the cave and a pocket of orange light.

"Archibald, a moment," Nameris calls.

Archie leaves Duggie-Sky with Ardenal and joins Tessa and Nameris at the cave's entrance.

When Nameris sees they are alone, he speaks. "As you both know, my power, gained within Rolace's web, is to sense the truthfulness of the spoken word."

There is a silence as his words hang in the air like the metallic smell of the hupper's blood. Tessa is afraid to breathe. She remembers the feel of the rock in her hand, its solidity, and then the strain of her muscles as she lofted it toward her target: the Lord.

Her mind is flooded with memories of Rolace. The man-spider's body was massive, boasting twelve hairy legs and a spinneret that stretched through his human mouth. His eyes, when not split into four reflective orbs, were the eyes of a man much older than Archie. *Kind eyes*, Tessa thinks. He first spoke to her through the Creek of Secrets. His need of the Banji flowers was great. One effect of the Star's poison flowing into the island is the lifeless stretches of desert, which choke out the nurturing power of Naiu. Rolace was desperate for the enchanted flowers needed to spin his magical cocoons and web through the white woodland.

The Banji flowers are powerful, Tessa reflects sadly. *And they're disappearing.*

The scene that flashes across Tessa's mind is grim, laced with regret. She sees the unsettled black sea beat against the eastern beach and the Bangols' arching bridges. She smells the sickening odor of death carried on the lizard-legs of the millions of carakwas that scurried past the place where she hid in the tall grasses on the edge of the beach between slender white trees. The sound of the clicking, screeching carakwa horde was deafening, and Valarie's taunting voice through the creatures' mouths was nearly enough to fatally arrest her heart. Valarie murdered Rolace. Her evil outlived him, and his web would crumble to dust, returning its spell of Naiu to the island.

Tessa can feel her heart squeeze painfully as these recollections haunt her. Silently, she thanks the Maiden for sacrificing herself in the blast of flame. The Maiden saved Ella. She saved them all that night. Thankfully, Valarie is no longer a worry. Tessa exhales all the stale air she had been holding in her chest.

"Have you nothing to say?" Nameris says, interrupting Tessa's tangle of regret and gratitude. "I know your lies," he continues, looking between Archie and Tessa, who are both tongue-tied like guilty children. "The Lord did not pardon you, Archibald. He would never release anyone from a crime unscathed. And you"—he stares down at Tessa—"what really happened with that stone?"

Tessa and Archie begin to babble at the same time, making excuses, fumbling between half truths and part lies. Nameris clenches his white teeth, revealing them between his thin ruddy lips. "Cease this idiocy at once!" He pauses to lower his voice. "I am on your side." He places his broad red hands on the humans' shoulders. "I have sensed a sinister energy in the Lord since we returned from the east. He is crueler. Quicker to anger. More inclined to bloodshed. That is not the Lord to whom I pledged myself. He is a mystery to me, a terrifying contraction, and I suspect you two can help me to understand."

"The Maiden—" Archie begins, so quietly that Tessa and Nameris lean in close enough to feel his breath. "The Maiden spoke to me. Through the Lord. It nearly scared the pants off me. But I trust the Maiden. It was her voice. She was struggling for control. She said there was another in that shell of a body, not only her and the 30th Lord."

"The Maiden," Tessa repeats, her relief peppered with bewilderment. "She's alive!"

"As alive as she can be in her second state," whispers Nameris. "However, I have never heard of a Maiden speaking through her partner's body after her death, though she does cohabitate with him. Our Maiden, she was extraordinary—in life as in death." Nameris rubs his brow in contemplation. "She said that the Lord is not as he seems. She confessed this to our first company. Remember, Archibald? She said she practiced lying to the Lord, which was against the truthfulness of her nature. This, she said, might one day save both her and her love."

"I remember." Archie scratches the blackening stubble on his chin.

"I surmise that if she learned to strengthen her will and harden her half of their shared heart, she could think and even communicate without the Lord knowing. It would be dangerous for her. The bonds of love are strong but fragile. It is the most delicate of balances. If she strains too much toward separation, it could fracture them forever. A life of loneliness, and not only now, but in every life to follow."

"But why would she go through all this pain and sacrifice?

Why risk it?" Tessa asks, as if Nameris understands the confusing web in which they find themselves hopelessly entangled. "What could she have to tell us that's worth eternal loneliness?" The thought of that potential existence sends shivers down Tessa's spine.

"To save us," Archie replies. "To save Jarr. And all the worlds."

"All the worlds," Tessa and Nameris repeat in unison.

"All the worlds."

Tessa finally speaks, remembering a name. "I heard the Lord, whoever he is, say the name Dillmus. That he killed Dillmus. Does that mean anything to you, Nameris?"

"There is no logic in that. Dillmus was slain by his brother, Telmakus, the 29th Lord of Olearon. Our Lord must have been confused. Were these words spoken after the rock fell from the sky?"

"Before. And I threw the rock," Tessa confesses. "The Lord had Archie cornered against a tree. He was on all fours, beastly, and his fire was . . . was like a serpent slithering out of him, hungry—"

"He meant to kill me." Archie's voice quivers.

Tessa's stomach churns and she wipes her sweating palms on her dress. "His hands. The Lord's hands . . . there was something wrong with them, as if they'd been mangled by an animal, grown infected, and been stitched together poorly."

"I cannot make sense of this alone." Nameris's neck erupts in flame, like a spark catching in gas. "We must speak with the Maiden."

chapter 9

Ella

I'm sure you're as sick of the wretched vulai bread as I am, but it will calm the waters sloshing in your head," says Luggie, smirking. "I snuck it from Lady Sophia." He hands me a square of vulai.

I take a tentative bite—I'm not hungry but am humoring him. Immediately, I'm struck with the disappointment that the vulai is bare of the sweet ellag currants from my party. The bread creeps its way down my throat like a sled on a disappearing skiff of Seattle snow, and down farther it settles into a hard lump in the corner of my stomach.

I smile at Luggie. He's always taking care of me. I hope to one day return the favor.

The wryst drink has strengthened my body as if I'm ten years old again. Usually people get stronger as they mature, but with cancer as my companion, I'm the opposite. I'm invigorated, yet also intoxicated. My body surges with energy, but not my head, where a drumming beat refuses to let up. Luggie has it right. My ears feel plugged with water that slips from one side of my brain to the other, tipping my balance.

"You're so small," Luggie says. "Bones and skin holding up that beautiful face. I truly do love you, Ella."

My eyes fill with tears at my Bangol's words, and briefly I

wonder if the water in my head is leaking, but no—just tears. I feel the same way about Luggie. My heartbeats speak to him the same words he bestowed upon me—words like a gift, words that heal and bring hope.

I point to my mouth, which I lock shut, and shake my head. The sounds I produce embarrass me, though I can taste my "I love you, too" on my tongue. Back home, friends I thought would be lifelong eventually shied away from me when I opened my throat and let myself spill out. They said I sounded like a car crash or like our school principal's voice during morning announcements: screeching with microphone feedback. They told me this with a laugh, as if I were a humorous addition to a Google list of the Top Ten Most Terrible Sounds on Earth. I learned to be quiet. Though they said they didn't mind my sounds, I could tell they were relieved. Still, they faded from my life like flowers at first frost.

Luggie takes my hand from my lips and holds it between his grey palms, careful not to scratch me with his pointed nails. He brings our tangle of fingers to his chest, against the place where his rough skin and bones made of earth separate me from his heart.

"Speak," he says. "I am not afraid."

I can't contain the geyser of humility and gratitude and love that erupts from me, as if the pressure has been building for years.

"Ewwwk uuugphygolfla gllleeeeckkkkkzceogidifi . . ." I can't stop now. The sounds flow and cascade, smash against each other, and make a terrible racket. Olearons turn; I can feel their light shine in our direction, into our pocket of privacy at the back of the cave. Grandpa Archie and Dad rush over, Mom, too, but I wave them away. The tears stream into my smile, so long overdue that I'm sure I emit a light all my own, and they see. Everyone sees: on every freckle of my nose; in every fleck of icy blue in my eyes; in my posture, thanks in part to the wryst; in my awkward squawks that terrify Mom but also tell her I'm okay.

They leave Luggie and me alone. I talk and tell him my every thought and impression of Jarr-Wya and theories about the Star. We slip to the floor of the cave and sit with our legs wrapped around each other like pretzels. He holds my hands. He leans into me as if I'm telling him the greatest story he has ever heard. He listens without wincing, without even a flash of boredom across his great yellow eyes. He can't possibly understand, but in my hopelessly illness-defined life, I feel heard for the first time in months, if not years.

Luggie brushes a tear from his cheek, where I can see small stones waiting to push up through his skin like molars through fleshy pink gums. Adult Bangols, in addition to the rocks growing out of their grey heads from infancy, have stones that slice out from each cheekbone. It's a mark of maturity, a coming of age. While Luggie is young and painfully stubborn, he's also wise beyond his sunsets. Kind. Thoughtful. Tender, too. I'm sure these stones will rise soon; I only hope I'll be around to see it happen.

I regret every hour I spent wishing some boy at school would look at me and care, that he'd offer even the smallest fraction of Luggie's affection. I pull him close to me, as if our breath in each other's mouths isn't close enough. He may not have understood my speech, but he understands my kiss. It's my sign language to him—my translation of everything I had to say.

As we pull apart, hot against the black stone of Baluurwa, one of Luggie's sharp incisors grazes my bottom lip. It draws a red line that soon buds with crimson.

"Oh no, Ella! I'm terribly sorry!"

I feel the burn of a paper cut and shrug it off, but the worry etched in wrinkles across Luggie's folded brow tells me this isn't trivial. First, I feel an itch as my blood trickles down my chin; then, I sense it drip. As if time holds its breath along with us, we watch the scarlet drop plummet in a graceful spiral through the dank cave air, until it strikes the black rock with a tiny patter that quivers before coming to rest.

That is the exact moment Baluurwa awakes.

It starts as a groan from within the jagged rocks, which unsettles them with its baritone. Cracks appear in our nook, then shift like dislodging puzzle pieces, spewing dust and pebbles on our heads. Luggie's wide eyes illuminate the shifting mountain. We grab our sacks and dash into the orange light of the Olearons, tugging at the nearest arms. I hold tight to Duggie-Sky. Luggie realizes he's grabbed the Lord, and lets go. There is something strange in Luggie's expression, but it's only a flash. Then, he's pulling Grandpa Archie and Lady Sophia.

"Out! Out!" Luggie hollers. His voice is panicked yet commanding. "Baluurwa's coming down!"

Our company races out of the cave's crumbling opening. Boulders skid past on either side of us in the weak light, their smoothly cut black faces reflecting the moon into our eyes. We tumble over each other into the trees. The groan of Baluurwa turns to a growl, and the cracks and crashes are louder than the lightning that claps excitedly overhead. The night is clouded with dust, which glows like millions of stars, brightening the terrible scene. We watch Baluurwa over our shoulders. It shudders.

I can't help but plug my ears with my fingers, worrying they may bleed at the sound like my cut lip, which I suck nervously, tasting my own life slip down my throat. Was it a coincidence that the avalanche began the second my blood hit the cave floor? Nah, it must be something else.

Luggie hoists me up unexpectedly and carries me in his arms like I'm a child. The company darts through the trees. On one side of me, Grandpa Archie trips over a bloody skeleton of a small recently ravaged animal. He picks himself up easily and flings Lady Sophia onto his back. I blink and shake my head. *Did that just happen?* It makes sense that an Olearon could carry the full-bodied opera singer, but Grandpa Archie?

On my other side, I see Duggie-Sky disappear as a boulder rumbles through the air to dent the forest floor, splintering two blue trees. The boy reappears ahead, unharmed. Again he vanishes, only to reemerge farther along in the forest. It's obvious to all that Duggie-Sky loves his gift. He told me that Rolace's prerequisite for someone receiving a "superpower," as Duggie-Sky calls it, is that the person's "will is strong and heart is brave."

I sigh. The one shortcoming of the boy's gift is obvious: he perceives himself as indestructible. So far, his teleportation ability has been his saving grace, but I can't help but worry that it will one day be his undoing.

All in the company cough and choke on dust and debris. A piece of rock crashes behind Luggie and me, and I lean back in Luggie's embrace, just in time to see Dad's bicep slice open and blood stream out of the wound. I call to him but the screech is in vain. No one can hear.

Nate runs hand in hand with Mom, but they're not as fast as the Olearons. Even with his injury, Dad shoves Nate away and slips Mom onto his back, despite her scowl and impassioned protests.

Dad races by us. "Faster, Luggie," he orders.

"I can run on my own!" Mom yells, but it is a whisper among the crashes, and those who do hear ignore her.

The noise—if it's even possible—grows louder, like discordant trumpets. The ground beneath our feet shifts and cracks into deep fissures. Luggie leaps over a gorge of broken earth and we both tumble onto the other side. He manipulates broken ground to push me away, so I don't land on his stones or am cut by his nails. Just as quickly, he commands to alertness the grasses and mosses and stones around us. They quake with Naiu and snap together like magnets, forming a barrier above us. Boulders from the mountain crash upon our shelter and push our bodies into the forest floor, but we're safe.

As abruptly as the earthquake began, it stops.

The dust remains, giving form to the wind. All rocks shuffle to rest. Luggie lifts his hand, and an invisible force cracks our barrier in two and we slip out to stand within its opening. Baluurwa has quieted, but my body continues to shake. I shove my hands beneath my armpits to still them. Slowly, one by one, our company join Luggie and me in the earthquake-formed clearing. Between us and Baluurwa, the blue forest is flattened. A large white animal, stained with red, breathes its last among the rubble. Chunks of Baluurwa puncture the ground and form a sinister slope up the western side of the mountain.

My ears are ringing. I search Baluurwa for our cave, the place where I celebrated my fifteenth birthday, but what's left of it is buried beneath hundreds, if not thousands, of pounds of unforgiving rock.

"Our supplies are gone." Junin says in a voice I can barely decipher.

"Argh!" Dad screams in pain—though it sounds like a whimper to my aching ears—as his friend and fellow warriors, Azkar and Kameelo, pin him to the ground to clean and cauterize his bloody arm. Junin, too, seals my cut lip with the slightest graze of one red finger. I don't know what hurt more, the cut or the burn, but at least it's no longer bleeding. Mom wipes Dad's blood from her pale pink dress and paces around him nervously.

She's such a nurse. Or is it something else that causes her to stay close?

"You're okay," Luggie tells me, and I believe him. But I'm not worried about me. The avalanche of rock has made our hike up the mountain that much more perilous. Tears leak from my eyes and turn muddy on my filthy cheeks. I can tell, because when I wipe them away, not wanting anyone to see my despair, brown smears my arm. Baluurwa was our hope of finding my cure, but, more importantly, of saving the island I've come to love.

Luggie leaves me in the crack of our barrier to check on the others. Along with Nate and Grandpa Archie, they search for Duggie-Sky. They spot the boy high in a tree, the next in line to be flattened by the wild boulders. Duggie-Sky doesn't flinch or teleport down from the nook where he sits shivering.

"I peed my pants," he cries to Grandpa Archie.

"That's all right, little fella! I think I did, too!" Grandpa replies before climbing the thick trunk to pull Duggie-Sky into his arms. Grandpa leaps down and leads the boy to clean up in the shelter of the unharmed trees to the west.

While the Olearons and humans, along with Luggie, pace and talk at the base of the avalanche, I stay put. The Star has caused too much pain on Jarr-Wya. I curse it. I damn it for how it might separate my family, even after my cancer has claimed me. I blame it for ruining my future with Luggie—for ruining everything.

I know I'm having a teenage temper tantrum. I can't help myself. Plunking down within the divided barricade, I press my eyes closed. I wish the Star away. I pray for a happy ending for those I love, even if that means a happiness I will never know.

I feel my cancer symptoms flare up. The headache threatens to split my skull as if it were this barricade cracking at Luggie's will. I curse cancer. How evil it is that even now, when I have bigger things to worry about, it must show its nasty face and reduce my body to a helpless collection of organs and bone. My illness humbles me when what I need is to be strong.

I wobble to my feet. After scooping two rocks into my hands, I throw the first. The distance it travels is pathetic. The second makes it a hair farther. My frustration needs an outlet. Too much hangs on the fragile divide between oblivion and life. I pick up another black stone, toying with it in my hands, bracing my muscles to let it fly.

I don't know where the strength will come from, but I refuse to sit idly by and let others fight and die for me.

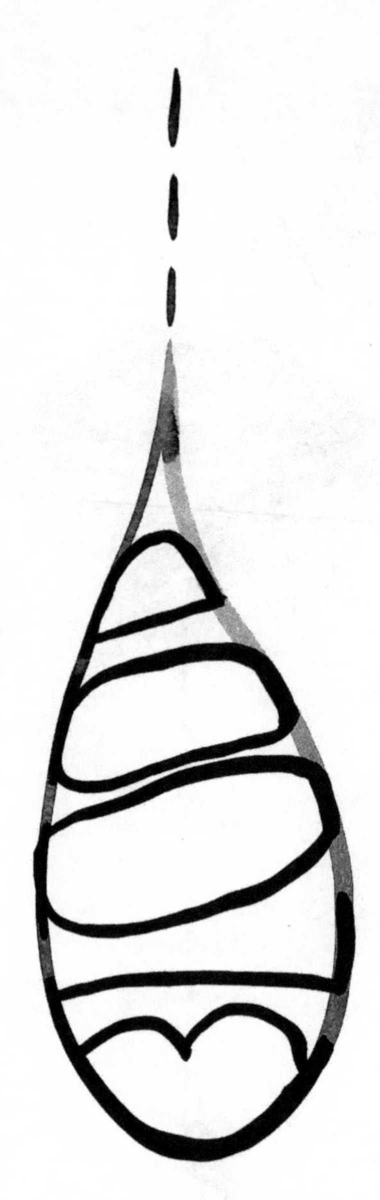

chapter 10

Archie

The Olearons take stock of the surviving supplies. The only satchel of food belongs to Lady Sophia, who escaped the cave clinging to what she values most: a stockpile of vulai greater than anyone anticipated, however small it is now after Ella's party. Archie watches the woman outstretch her arm with a hand to halt Nameris, insisting she carry the remaining bread and wryst drink for the company. The frustration on Nameris's face is thick, and the two squabble within his pocket of fiery light.

Azkar shakes his head at what is left. "Five squares of vulai, half a flask of ellag currants, and three vials of wryst, barely enough of the healing drink to strengthen a third of our company," he bemoans.

The only serious injury—most are plum-colored bruises and shallow cuts—is to Ardenal's arm. The place where Azkar cauterized the wound with his flame now blackens, burned to a flaky crisp. The wound stretches from mid-forearm to just above his elbow. The charcoal flesh has little give, and Ardenal winces as he stretches.

"Is that safe?" Archie whispers to Tessa. "What the Olearons did? Was there any skin left to burn, or was it just muscle they torched?"

Tessa shrugs helplessly. "I didn't get a good look at the wound," she says. The guilt of fighting Ardenal while he carried her out of the avalanche shows itself as the woman gnaws on one filthy fingernail. "My nursing skills seem like child's play out here," she continues in a murmur. "I wish there was more I could do."

Archie puts a comforting arm around Tessa. "It looks like he's in pain. And that's saying something. He's usually the first to put on a brave face."

"That's Arden's way. Never ask for help. Never confide in anyone. Just like all those months before he left. He wrestled with Ella's illness all alone, though he didn't have to. It was *our* pain to bear, to share and spread the weight between us." Tessa spits out a fingernail.

Archie and Tessa watch Ardenal join the Olearons who scavenge the debris for salvageable supplies. The tall lean bodies flex as they lift and toss warm boulders, newly settled at the broad slope of the wreckage. Each one ignites their fire, emblazing them from their boots to three feet above their Mohawks. Their eyes, remaining black, appear like haunting, scathing embers as they search.

"He needs rest, Archie. He's going to strain the wound. Can you make him stop and sit down?"

"I think that message would come better from the nurse. From his wife."

Tessa bristles at Archie's words and she does not reply. She marches toward the eight Olearons that light up the foot of Baluurwa like a ring of bonfires at midnight, leaving Archie alone with his thoughts. "Thank goodness the mountain's deserted. We certainly fail at ambush," he says to himself.

Duggie-Sky startles Archie as the boy appears at his side. Archie curses, then bites his tongue. "You scared me, little fella.

Why not spook Nameris instead, or Lady Sophia—she's always up for a good laugh—or save it for the bad guys?" He regrets his words immediately.

"Bad guys?"

"Yeah, you know . . . well, uh, you never know who we'll meet out here." Archie grimaces.

Duggie-Sky ponders Archie's words, his round brown face flashing with conflicting emotions before he settles on courage. "You're right, Grandpa." His voice reveals a trace of his childish drawl. "I chose this name for a reason. Duggie-Sky. After the Douglas Skywarrior." He looks down to his T-shirt, where a grey airplane carries a cartoon superhero barely visible through the grime and stains from their treks across Jarr-Wya. "I want to be a hero—"

"Oh, my boy—"

"And this gift chose me."

"Yes, but—"

"So I'm going to use it for good! Not evil. Not even scaring Lady Sophia!"

"That's a good choice, little fella." Archie regrets every idea he has inadvertently planted in the child's mind. He worries what mistakes will tumble out of his mouth if he keeps blathering on. "Time to rest, my boy. Come up here." Duggie-Sky disappears as if erased, then reappears in Archie's arms. The old man gently rocks the boy, who has grown quickly since the *Atlantic Odyssey* crashed onto the island.

Archie's eyes search for Ella. He spots her. She is sitting on the forest floor, in a shadow of rock. She does not meet his eyes, which Archie has learned means she wishes to be left alone.

Archie sighs. While the boy in his arms grows and flourishes, his granddaughter wanes. Ella was always stubborn, in all the best ways, she once told him, but Archie wonders if her strength of determination is enough to get her to the Star, to find her cure, before . . . he refuses to think of that end. He resolves never to share this fear with Ella. *If she believes she'll make it and she sees that I feel the same, together we'll succeed. Together we'll do whatever is needed to save her and Jarr-Wya. It's the only way.*

THE Lord declares to the company that they will mobilize at dawn.

For some, sleep is unescapable. Olearon warriors take shifts, watching the tree line and mountain. Others in the company are wide awake though off duty, like Nameris, whose gaze never strays from the Lord. The ruler of the Olearons appears to be frozen in the quiet place between slumber and consciousness, his eyes partially cracked while his breathing is deep.

Those who do rest sleep through the uneven crack and pop of lightning and thunder, sounds that have become background static for Archie. He barely hears it. Suddenly, however, a noise scratches through his wandering, worrying mind. It is Ella.

"Eeeeweeahhh!" she screeches, so loudly that her broken voice carries up the slope of Baluurwa and echoes back to them. Ella stands, her face a pale sheen that matches the wide whites of her eyes. One trembling hand points up through the tentacles of the floating earth islands above, into the black expanse where the color of the lightning dissolves into stars.

Archie leaps to his feet, startling Duggie-Sky from sleep, and the boy's first word is "Woooow."

A planet melts into view through the dark sky. It is perfectly round with three bands of blue encircling its emerald-and-purple speckled surface. It nears Jarr, slowly growing and becoming clearer. Archie can now see that the blue rings are spinning around the planet in a seamless whirl; his only clue to this motion is the variance in their hues.

As if rising out of black water, a smaller planet begins as an outline of silver, then takes on form. This planet is of ombré hues, tangerine fading to sunflower yellow.

The two planets are connected, Archie realizes when he squints. It is as if a rubber band has encircled both and been pulled taut between them. The light contained within the connecting band throbs vibrantly, pulsing as it rotates through violet, dusty blue, and pine green. In this shifting channel between planets, black flecks like dead stars pass from one sphere to the other, traveling in both directions.

Archie notices Tessa and Ardenal stand to flank Ella on both sides. Luggie is behind her, bracing her waist. Their mouths hang open. All in the company gaze at the weight of the atmosphere above, which has taken on such density and gravity of meaning that no one speaks for quite some time, lulled in an awestruck trance.

Nameris is the first to give voice to his awe, "The old rumors are true. What we believed as myth is now painted with a magnificent brush before us. A Naiu-rich world connected to its derivative."

"This is how it began with the Star. A great sight in the sky, dazzling us, came to mark the sunsets till our doom," rumbles Azkar. "We mustn't be fooled by this beauty. It is an omen of our impending destruction."

"Why are the planets pulled toward Jarr?" Lady Sophia asks.

Azkar spits. "It's the Star. Is it not obvious, human?"

"We must flee home! Back to the glass city," Kameelo whispers timidly to his eldest brother. "To say goodbye to our mother, to come together and burn as one before our end."

Azkar's expression does not betray sympathy for his sibling. Instead, his jaw clenches and his muscles flex.

"No one here will return to the glass city." The Lord's voice is flat. "We would never make it. And being fearful is not our mission, warrior." The Lord scowls at Kameelo, who drops his head. "We came here to wipe out what threatens our lives, our families, our home. Now is the time for bravery. Now is the time to die for our seas, our shores, and all that we love. For peace. I do not, however, believe death is our fate. No. The Star is not my Lord. We will see the light of the sun once more, when all of this is finished."

The Lord falls silent. The ferocity on his features melts to dread. The company sees what happens before they hear it. The connected band between the two nearing planets breaks apart like a fractured bone; there is a ground-shaking snap a breath later. Now all cover their ears. The dead and blackened stars scatter from the river of color like spilled sand. The blue rings of the larger planet wobble and collide. They bash into each other and into the landmass, dislodging chunks of green and violet. These pieces ricochet off one another until they are clear of the debris. The broken planet cascades through the dead stars and fragments of itself until it slices its smaller orange derivative into two uneven halves.

The sound of the collision a moment later is the crinkle and stretch of resistant metal, and the smell, which arrives immediately after, is first rich with benzene, like mothballs and gasoline, then stronger still with a gust of rotting fruit and burning rubber. Finally, everyone's nostrils fill with the odor of morning, earth, and dew. It is the only peace that lingers after the carnage in the sky. What was once two brilliant, connected planets look like table crumbs swept into a corner of the galaxy. Finally, the sky overhead is still.

chapter 11

Archie

Run to Baluurwa. Ascend now!" the Lord orders. "Our mission is at our doorstep. We must act before we are watched so casually in someone else's sky."

The company grab what meager supplies they dug out of the rubble, and climb. Ella waves away her parents, leaving Tessa bookended by Ardenal and Captain Nate. Kameelo forfeits flight to take Lady Sophia's hand and carry her satchel of vulai bread.

"Want me to carry you, little fella?" asks Archie, but Duggie-Sky only grins.

"No thanks, Grandpa." The boy vanishes from Archie's side and materializes twenty steps ahead.

Ella leans heavily on Luggie. They both wear their travel sacks, though in truth they rarely take them off. Archie sprints to them and is struck by Ella's state—weary and even more pale than before. He begins to slip off her sack, wishing to give her bony shoulders a rest, but she screeches, "Awwek!" which Archie can tell is a firm *no*, and he takes her arm instead.

The debris in the air—Baluurwa's dust and the slowly settling, finely ground planet powder from above—amalgamates into clouds in what should have been a morning sky. The moon still glows, subtly illuminating the blackness with pockets of silver. The Olearons lead by their light. The stratus clouds fan out in long wisps. The storm, which the company had ignored as they watched the catastrophe in the sky, now whips their hair and stirs the clouds like blown silk scarves. The cloud cover tangles around Baluurwa the Doomful, ensnaring it in an ominous haze of white.

The company climb frantically and slice their fingers on the warm black rock. Scaling the avalanche rubble is precarious, as many boulders balance on shifting edges. There are several narrow misses. Luggie does his best to wield his power over the stones, but he is inexperienced and lacks the strength of an adult Bangol. *Luggie's youth*, Archie reflects, *wasn't spent guided by a nurturing hand but beneath the thumb of a cruel father*. Archie encourages the young Bangol as best he can and takes Ella on his back, as he had Lady Sophia when they fled the landslide. He barely feels Ella's weight, which mirrors that of Duggie-Sky, nearly a decade younger than the girl, though the boy has grown in stature and maturity significantly beyond any normal human four-year-old.

Ella's weight had trailed that of her peers since the cancer grew bold and hungry. The bones of her face still hold their pretty shape—she has round cheekbones like Tessa's, a freckled nose, and a bewitching smile. Yet now her cheeks are hollow and the skin beneath her eyes is the pale blue of a winter shadow.

Archie clings to Ella's meatless legs, mere skin and bone, and she tightly clutches his neck. With a steady foot, he lunges from one boulder to the next, dodging slipping silt and shifting pebbles as the clouds swell to a damp fog.

"When you come across a tunnel, holler!" Nate calls to the company through the mist.

"We have passed the cusp of the avalanche," replies Nameris. "We should come across the lowest rung of tunnels any moment now."

Azkar growls as his boot slips. He spits. His deep black scar twists the skin from his left eye down to his collarbone. "We welcome trouble by scaling Baluurwa by this wicked light."

"The sun may never come," Junin answers in a motherly tone, though she appears only as an orange glow in the fog. "The moon is not terrible. It grants us what it can."

"But it cannot bestow warmth to our young in the city, those who have not yet mastered their flames," retorts Nameris, ever the pessimist. The thin Olearon shudders. "Or gift us with the Naiu our crops need to flourish."

"True," Junin says calmly. "Though I am thankful for the moon nonetheless. And as for the children, we will be their warmth."

"If we survive this," grumbles Nameris, climbing on.

The Lord speaks next. "There is no time for caution. You are all right, but none of our woes will be eased unless we proceed with ruthless determination. We must find the Star and roast it."

Archie cannot tell which Lord is speaking. He regrets that he did not have more time in the cave to initiate conversation with the Maiden.

Suddenly, an unfamiliar voice cuts through the Olearons' debate. The voice is high and ringing, reverberating like a bell, but is also low and gravelly. Female. Angry. At its sound, the company halt and stand motionless in various poses of ascent. Their breath is caught in their throats as their ears prick into heightened awareness. The white cloak around Baluurwa, moments ago an annoyance as they climbed, is now a crippling vulnerability.

"You will not harm the Star!" The voice slices through the fog, bouncing off the icy rain that begins to fall. "You will not harm the Star!" The voice enunciates each word, carefully, deliberately.

Through the wind and rain and mist emerges, ever so slowly, a face. It is silver, though Archie cannot tell if it is just a trick of the moon. The eyes are blue cut by fiery red lightning and edged in black. The woman scowls. Her long eyelashes grow into feathers that reach above her ears. Her hair is brown and blond, braided and long, and hangs past her navel. Her lips are glossy, pale, and twisted into a grimace.

The wind twirls the mist around her. Great reaching antlers sprout from her temples. They are polished bone and woven with coils of gold at their tips, extending their magnificence. Across her right breast and shoulder she wears a carved-gold shield, perfectly fitted to her feminine form. Ever so slowly, she reaches behind her and, from sheaths strapped to her back, retrieves twin daggers.

"The Star is our only hope," she says, and again her voice reflects a duality of hate and love: hate for the haggard company before her, love for the Star. "I will protect it with my life."

The storm beats back the cloud, and the woman can be seen plainly. *She's taller than me*, Archie realizes. She wears no shoes. Her gown is formed of strips of fabric. They are ruby-hued and braided over one shoulder. The gown is carried by the erratic wind, revealing pieces of silver and black fabric and patches of chameleon hupper fur, which changes with the color of the flickering lightning overhead.

The Lord steps forward. "What is your name, Steffanus?" he asks evenly.

"Wouldn't you like to know!" she replies sharply. Her daggers are at her sides, but Archie notices how her thumbs stroke the gold hilts, decorated with tiny leaves, as if she channels all her loathing into her hands, ready to strike.

"Her name is Tanius." A small girl steps out from behind the Steffanus.

Tanius turns and bares her teeth at her. "Get back, now!" she orders the child, but the girl ignores her and marches forward, smiling.

Archie's muscles twitch. He looks at the child's menacing teeth, gleaming through her girlish grin. His mind is at odds with itself. *Should I run down the mountain, or shake her hand?*

"I am Xlea. I am ten in human years. I know because I have been to your world." The young Steffanus looks at Archie, who still carries Ella, and at Tessa, Lady Sophia, and Nate. "I have recorded all my adventures on Earth in this book." Xlea holds up a worn paper journal bursting with drawings and writing, scraps and mementos, and dried flowers—so full that its pages fan. She rattles on. "I'm the only Steffanus birthed of the current blossoms. My sisters weren't ready, not like me. I was eager to fly and explore."

"Impatient," adds Tanius through gritted teeth.

Duggie-Sky appears out of the vapor only a few steps away from Xlea.

"Oh! Hullo!" she says, startled. "And who might you be?"

"We do not have time for this, Xlea!" Tanius growls.

"I'm Duggie-Sky," the boy says proudly.

"Oh, wonderful!" sings Xlea and she claps her silver hands. "But there is something not quite right about you. Hmm." She puts a finger to the end of her nose as she studies Duggie-Sky. He stares at her sheepishly and scratches his head of curly black hair. "I know!" Xlea claps again. "May I?" she asks as she approaches and reaches for the boy. He willingly gives her his hands.

"I would not—" warns Yuleeo. The Lord's warrior is grim.

Archie notices the throbbing orange heat coursing through the Olearon's veins, and the balling of heat and light on his palms as he readies to attack.

While Archie's throat is pinched in indecision, he manages to say, "Duggie-Sky, be careful . . ."

Xlea pulls Duggie-Sky close to her. She is dressed in a vivid yellow gown, cut and braided with shreds of fabric similar to those Tanius wears, though hers is not the color of death but of sunflowers and sunshine and cheer. The girl looks like the kiss of Naiu amidst the angry sky and jolting gale. Xlea bends down and rests her silver forehead against Duggie-Sky's deep brown one, scabbed where the boy had been attacked by a carakwa in the blue forest not long after the *Atlantic Odyssey* crashed on the Millia's southern shore. She closes her eyes. Duggie-Sky mirrors her.

Xlea's antlers are small, mere coils of ivory and gold. They graze Duggie-Sky's curls. The minute feels like an hour for Archie, who holds his breath. Finally, the girl pulls back.

"There!" she says and bites her lower lip. "Any moment, I am sure of it, just wait . . ." She nearly dances atop the black rock in her bare feet.

Duggie-Sky begins to shiver. His fingers twitch as if he plays music on an invisible instrument. His shoulders hop and bulge. Every movable joint flexes, contracts, and clicks loudly. Even his neck snaps to the side.

With this movement, Ella pushes from Archie's back and lunges forward. She races to Duggie-Sky and struggles to calm his convulsing body. She turns to the others and cries out, "Ewwhoo cankkkeeah!"

The Steffanus woman and girl cover their ears at the screech, and Tanius yanks Xlea away from Ella and Duggie-Sky. Tanius thrusts forward one of her hands, where semi-translucent bands of power surge beyond her fingertips like electricity. Ella's hair rises and stretches toward the Steffanus. Tanius's pursed lips curve into a smile as she blinks quickly, mischievously.

Scrunching her brows in determination, Ella whips around

to meet the ice-blue and lava-red eyes of the two beings. She points back to Duggie-Sky, who continues to contort. Ella's glare is fierce and protective. This time, when she opens her mouth, instead of an earsplitting shriek, something else emerges.

"Ell!" Tessa screams.

"Ella, what is it?" Ardenal races to his daughter's side.

Ella turns away from Tanius and Xlea toward the company, and parts her lips widely. First, a beak emerges, then a small round head covered in green feathers with human eyes that bat thick lashes.

"A green bird?" the Lord whispers.

Archie knows the birds well, as does the Lord. Archie first met the happy fowl in the forest to the south as he escaped the Millia sands, then again in the glass citadel. The citadel, home to the piercing glass throne at the heart of the Olearons' city, is a finely cut and fused-mirror structure with a dome that rises around and above crystal columns and blue-bark trees. At their topmost branches, green birds nest and frolic. When Archie had snuck into the citadel, finding the secret history of the Olearons, the green birds serenaded him with merry chirps. They spun emerald ribbons of light behind them as they played.

Ella gags. The green bird shrugs, shifting itself out of Ella's mouth until it is free. It briefly perches its velvety padded feet on her lower lip before flying off into the blackness.

Nate barges forward as Ella stands motionless, dumbfounded and embarrassed. "What have you done to her?" he yells at the looming Steffanus.

"I could not stand that abhorrent sound a moment longer." Tanius sighs, looking relieved. "I have heard it throughout this night, within Baluurwa, and even above the rumble of destruction you have brought to our home. I thought you kept a beast, but no matter. We will only hear pretty chirps from now on."

Ella opens her mouth and screams. There is no sound, not even the cackle of cancer, only a flock of green birds that pours from between her lips and creates an emerald cloud in the sky. Her lips quiver. Two fat tears plummet from her blue eyes. She shrinks away from the Steffanus beings and slinks over to where Duggie-Sky still writhes. She wraps her arms around him, as if his transformation will surely be as mortifying as hers.

"Don't worry, Ella and Grandpa." Duggie-Sky chokes out the words to comfort them, though Ella is apparently beyond a shred of hope. "It feels strange, but good." Every part of him quivers with energy.

Xlea approaches them. "Your body needs to catch up with your mind, Duggie-Sky," she says to the wide-eyed boy as he morphs and grows. "That is better," she concludes once the transformation is complete. Duggie-Sky stands, and Ella's arms fall from his shoulders. Xlea adds, "Now we can look each other in the eyes."

The boy is two feet taller than before. His features have matured, and his voice deepened, the toddler drawl completely lost.

The company is speechless—all but Duggie-Sky. "Whoa, this is so cool!" He zips across the black rock much faster than before. He disappears, reappears, and laughs heartily. Finally, he slows enough to say, "Thank you, Xlea."

"You are welcome—"

"Enough of this distraction!" The Lord's skin simmers at a low boil. "We have come for a purpose"—his eyes meet those of the company—"and we intend to fulfill that mission. Now, let us pass."

"Why should we?" Tanius steps in front of Xlea.

"Can you not see?" replies the Lord. "Jarr-Wya is dying. Animals morph unnaturally. How long until they turn their hunt to other blood, to those who walk on two legs? Or to the glass city, the Fairy Vineyard, or Baluurwa the Doomful? From your high vantage point, have you not seen the deserts that spew out of the island, consuming the greenery, smothering it alive? Our crops fail to feed us. Everything is dying, fading. Jarr-Wya is poisoned! From the soil to the seas to the sand. The Millia have turned their golden eyes inland. It is only a matter of time before they seek other shores. And the Bangols—their king means to rule Jarr-Wya as Lord of the Star."

Tanius shakes her head. "The Star has no Lord."

"The Star came here to save us," says Xlea. "To save you, too," she adds, addressing the Lord of Olearon.

Nameris speaks up. "Only since the Star's arrival has the land faded and its inhabitants set their anger against each other."

"Perhaps you do not recall," growls Tanius, "that many generations ago, well before the Star crashed into our sea, the Olearons besieged Baluurwa to kill every one of my sisters. For a race that exalts peace, you take much pleasure in pain."

Archie, who has been shifting from foot to foot, finally pipes up. He shuffles into the space between Tanius and the Lord. "Let's all pause here. It sounds like there's a lot of history that neither of you were directly involved in. Why the grudges? I believe we all can agree that peace is what we're after. So why not discuss this calmly?"

"Not one of you will set foot in Baluurwa's tunnels. You will leave this mountain or blood will be shed." Tanius raises her daggers. "The Star is good, and it is here to help us. None of you will lay a hand—or a flame—upon it."

The fiery light in Yuleeo's hands grows to molten balls, and the warrior launches one at the mature Steffanus. The blazing red orb burns through one of Tanius's antlers, and her harsh voice catches in her throat, revealing a shard of weakness. The shard of antler falls with a clatter to the black rock and bounces down, coming to rest at Kameelo's feet. Yuleeo, urged on by the Lord, toys with the second fireball, tossing it in the air and catching it without looking.

"It is true that we believed your race abolished," the Lord says, sneering, "but what can one and a half Steffanus sisters hope to accomplish against eight Olearons?"

Tanius, in a whirl of pink, lemon, and teal plumes, unfurls with a powerful swoosh her great wide wings from behind her back. Her feathers gleam in every hue, with many colors Archie has no name for, and are frosted in silver with splatters of gold. Her wings stretch six feet on either side. Xlea ducks behind one, just as Tanius flicks her wrist so quickly that the company wonder at the gesture. Until, that is, Tessa screams in horror. Archie notices that one silver hand of the Steffanus in the red dress no longer clutches the blade with its hilt entwined in golden vines and leaves.

The dagger has pierced Yuleeo's ruddy forehead. There is no blood at first, only startled skin and slowed breath. Then a drip trickles out of Yuleeo's nose, followed by a stream rushing into his eyes, which remain open as he crumples. The flame at his neck is reduced to a puff of somber smoke.

Archie looks to the Lord, who grimaces, the fire growing behind his black eyes. The Olearons—Islo, Ardenal, Azkar, Kameelo, Nameris, and Junin—step forward for vengeance, while the humans and Luggie, edge back. The Lord sweeps his fingers through the air, igniting his body, and summons a long blade of grass, its green melted to yellow. It whips past him, aiming to coil around Tanius's neck. She cuts it down with one flick of her remaining dagger.

Suddenly, Xlea swoops down on her own brilliant peach- and plum-colored wings. She looks apologetically at Ella and

Duggie-Sky before pulling the dagger out of Yuleeo's skull and zipping into the air once more, out of reach. The Lord creates a ravenous ball of liquid fire between his pulsating hands. Yellow light blinds Archie. Shepherded by Tessa, the humans stumble down the mountain, five paces away from the heat and sparks that erupt from the Lord.

Tanius takes to the sky, her mighty wings whipping the dust and drying Archie's eyes with a belligerent wind. He blinks, wets his lips, and holds Ella close. The Lord twists his body, snapping the seams of his royal suit. Its glass breastplate cracks with the movement, though the grotesqueness of his skin remains concealed. He lurches forward, launching the great fireball, but Tanius tilts her wings and dodges the heat. The fire singes her feathers on one wing.

"You will not succeed," she screams. Turning upward to the shifting pops of lightning, she calls into the moonbeam abyss, "Xlea, it is time!"

As the words leave Tanius's mouth, she is batted down from her elevation by Kameelo, who unexpectedly flew to attack. Winded yet airborne, the Steffanus wrestles the blazing Olearon, flapping and slashing with terrifying ferocity. Her battle cries echo through the dark world. It is not enough.

A tiny voice within the shifting clouds screams, "No!"

Tanius plummets to the black rock of Baluurwa, crumpling at the center of the company. Her charred wings snap free of her burnt, lifeless body. Her red dress is ash grey, her breastplate tarnished, and her eyes, now white, blow away in the storm.

The Lord brushes his gloved palms against the smooth fabric of his royal attire, as if he had killed Tanius himself. "Do we burn the small one from the sky or resume searching for tunnels?" he asks Islo.

Archie is shocked at the Lord's disregard for the bloodshed, for the unbreathing lungs. Grief creeps over all present in a haunting shiver. Yuleeo is not acknowledged for his bravery or his sacrifice. The Lord leaves the Olearon's pale rose body behind him, as he does that of Tanius as well, despite Xlea's reverberating wails, loud despite the storm.

Islo scans the mountain. "The Steffanus child will prove easy to snuff out later, my Lord. We must climb to the shelter of the tunnels."

"It is foolish to believe the tunnels are safe," Azkar grunts, but he lifts his ragged sack, mostly empty, and swings it over his shoulder. He begins to climb.

Kameelo and Nameris bend a knee before Yuleeo and touch him with their hands, bringing his body into their flame so that the three burn but only one is consumed.

The Lord glares back at them. "Did I command your kindness?" Kameelo and Nameris turn, still ablaze, stunned. "No. I did not. There will be a time for ceremony and a time to remember, but not now. Move—find the tunnels!" The brothers leave Yuleeo's body to wilt under the dying flame. "That order is for you as well, Archibald Wellsley. Time to take up your post as my warrior. And you, too, Luggie."

The Lord turns to Baluurwa. The humans collect themselves and timidly follow, with Lady Sophia blubbering out a sad tune between tears as they resume ascent.

A raspy whisper cuts between sharp teeth. "You may have murdered our sisters long ago, but you forgot about our seeds."

This halts the company once more. The Lord grumbles, "Show yourself, child, that we might roast you as we did your elder."

"That's not Xlea," says Tessa to Archie.

"I don't have a good feeling about this," he replies. Nate nods in agreement.

"Me neither, Dad," whispers Ardenal. "Keep our family close. My flame is for us."

Ella touches her father's arm, her pale pink against his deep crimson, and they share a weak smile.

From the settling dust and the dark of the sunless morning emerge three sets of eyes, unnaturally blue and cut by lines of red. Then antlers, tipped with spools of gold. More eyes. The *swack* of air as fifty pairs of wings unfurl. A hundred eyes stare down on the minuscule company, one member less than before.

"We guard the Star," roar the fifty voices in a hellish chorus. "Tonight, we dampen the light of the Olearons!"

The Lord's face switches from determined intent to petrified paralysis, from warmongering to the shame of cowardice. He trips backward. Islo rushes between him and the fire-and-ice eyes, the twisted antlers, and the flowing gowns. Islo ignites, but the Lord reaches through his flame, touching his warrior's shoulder, murmuring close to his ear. The Lord runs past Nate and Ardenal, past Archie, Tessa, Ella, and a scowling Luggie, and down the avalanche of black rock. Islo turns on his heel, dashes behind the Lord, and calls to the company as he passes: "Run! Flee! To the northwest! To the Fairy Vineyard!"

chapter 12

Ella

We're overwhelmingly outnumbered. Thankfully, the Lord isn't stupid enough to attack the Steffanus horde or we'd all be dead. Kameelo has the advantage of flight. Unfortunately, we have only one Kameelo, but hundreds of wings flap behind us.

Apparently, I'm moving too slowly. Grandpa Archie picks me up and runs. He realizes the danger of lingering on Baluurwa. There are too many warrior women and, like us, they're steadfast in their mission. But why protect the Star? I'm baffled that they believe it is good, that it's here to save us.

My skin crawls beneath the heavy stares of the Steffanus warriors from their elevated perches on the miniature floating islands. Ugh, I hate heights. My jaw is clenched tightly; I will not give them the satisfaction of welcoming my green birds to their branches. I wonder, however, if a pair of those eyes above belong to Xlea. However mad I am at what Tanius did to me, my heart still broke at the sound of Xlea's cries, though she is quiet now.

Duggie-Sky is overjoyed with his new stature; I can see it in the way he flees the mountain. He's got a goofy smile on his face as he zooms around, in and out of view like the broken line of a highway. Fine, I admit it—I'm jealous. Duggie-Sky was given a gift—another one—while I'm left mute.

If a Steffanus can work magic like that—growing Duggie-Sky so he's as tall as a ten-year-old—I wonder what else they can do. Great things I bet, like cure cancer. They must have sensed my illness. Why wasn't Xlea kind to me like she was to Duggie-Sky?

Ugh, I hate myself some days. So selfish. *Snap out of it, Ella! Your internal monologue is suffocating.* I'm being carried along on this journey like a queen. When I was captured by the Bangols, a search party came to my rescue. I've been cradled this entire time whenever I can't take another step, my bones aching and my stomach curling with nausea. My family is out here, facing the Steffanus warriors with their leering eyes, the Bangols' power over the earth, and the Olearons' flame, all for me, on some bizarre speculation that we might actually find a cure.

Now that's love.

I despise being a physical burden to others. At least cancer has made me a featherweight—though I doubt it would matter since Grandpa Archie carries me easily. His face is covered in wrinkles like a scrunched-up potato chip bag. At least that's how it was when we set off from Barcelona on Constellations Cruise Line. Now, since Zeno's Tillastrion brought us to Jarr-Wya, his face is a chip bag saved from the trash and smoothed.

Grandpa Archie's hair is the white of freshly whipped icing—except for the new growth. I leave one arm around his neck and reach up with the other. My fingers stroke the baby-bum- soft sprouts where his bald skin was once exposed on his crown and spotted with age.

Why is it growing again? The new hair, from what I can tell in the dark, is chestnut colored like Dad's was before Rolace changed him into an Olearon.

The spiky new hair glistens with perspiration as Grandpa sprints through the twilight-blue trees, the wreckage of the avalanche a short way behind us. Luggie can barely keep up. If Grandpa is tired, he's not letting it slow him down. Is it adrenaline? I've never seen him move this fast—except, however, for the days he snuck into the attic, back home in Seattle, to read the journals Dad left behind when he disappeared two years ago.

No matter how sly Grandpa may be, Mom always finds him out. She too is trailing behind us. She asks me through her mind, in her pestering sort of way, what's changed about Grandpa Archie. She's noticed the difference, too, but kept it to herself. I tell her I don't know, but I suspect it's everything.

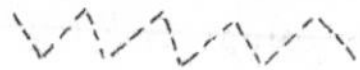

I didn't realize it, but I fell asleep on Grandpa's back. Thankfully, he held my arms and legs tightly. Stupid cancer. It makes me a child needing two naps a day. It's all the walking and the breathlessness of spilling my secrets to Luggie in the cave. The fatigue is a heavy blanket over my head.

How long did I sleep?

I hear Mom and Dad talking about the Fairy Vineyard and pointing ahead. Squinting through the trees, I can see the end of the blue forest and the start of a lush green swath of land. The area is shaded by a massive, twisted trunk with reaching branches of drooping leaves like a weeping willow. Beyond it, I sense the ocean. Its saltiness makes my cheeks tacky, yet its smell is welcome, as if I can close my eyes and be back on the *Atlantic Odyssey,* waking to learn this was all a dream.

Except, I don't want it to be a dream. I'm alive, living more fully than I ever have at school or in the doctors' offices or within the pages of my favorite books. This spark of life burns inside me, like Dad's fire, and I worry I won't be able to keep the flame lit much longer.

Our company huddles as we leave Baluurwa behind us. The ache deepens. Does this mean we leave my hope for a cure behind as well?

A flurry of conversation happens all at once. The Lord listens to ideas about how to outsmart the Steffanus sisters. Islo and Azkar bicker, as usual, always striving to outdo the other. Nameris suggests we take refuge with the sprites for one night only, then return to the glass city to add more warriors to our numbers before "burning alive every last Steffanus." His words, not mine.

The Lord abandons his plotting and replies to Nameris. "What numbers do you imagine we have?" he begins. "With the meager harvest, our flames are starved. Our best warriors are here." He surveys the company.

"We left the glass city with so little when we ventured out . . ." Kameelo mumbles. He toys with the broken shard of Tanius's antler, which he pocketed before fleeing.

"We left them hope," Junin answers boldly. I like Junin. "Hope! What we lack in numbers, we make up for in cunning. We will succeed, but by another way."

I can feel Grandpa Archie suck in a great gulp of air as he resolves to speak. "I have an idea. It's a bit cunning, as Junin suggests."

"Continue, Archibald Wellsley." The Lord frowns.

"We let the Bangols fight the Steffanus sisters for us."

Azkar spits. "Why would they do that? The Bangol king, Tuggeron, is stone-wild, mad, and—" He realizes that Luggie is listening. The gruff Olearon looks over at the young Bangol, son of the king, but Luggie only shrugs.

"You're right, Azkar. My father would never fight for you."

Grandpa Archie clears his throat, and I take this as my opportunity to slip off his back to walk beside Luggie. Braiding my fingers between his, I gaze into Luggie's sad yellow eyes. I squeeze his hand, only once, and hope he understands.

"The Bangols won't know they're fighting for us," Grandpa continues. He's got his hands up, as he does when talking at the television, ordering the Seattle Colts to pass the football. "We trick them!"

The Lord turns his sharp shoulders toward Grandpa without slowing his gait. "Continue."

Grandpa runs over to Kameelo and plucks the Steffanus antler from the Olearon's hands. "Hey!" Kameelo protests.

"We use this." Grandpa holds up the miserable antler. "We plant this in the Bangols' northern fortress, which can't be far from the Fairy Vineyard." Grandpa looks to Nameris, the studious warrior who is never silent about his knowledge of Jarr.

"Less than a half-day's march," Nameris answers. "Faster if we run."

Lady Sophia's face falls.

Grandpa nods, liking his plan more by the minute. "We write a nasty note, pretending to be the Steffanus sisters, announcing to the Bangols that we warrior women plan to invade. We tie the note to the antler and leave it somewhere important—"

"The amphitheater of the stone band shell," Luggie says. "That will get my father's attention."

"Yeah, leave it there," continues Grandpa, not missing a beat, "and mess up a few things on the way out—smash a pot, tip a water jug—all leading a trail south to Baluurwa."

"This could work." A creepy sneer returns to the Lord's usually stoic face.

Grandpa Archie is talking fast now. He's excited. "We provoke the Bangols under the guise of the Steffanus race, and they'll do the fighting for us! We dash into the tunnels when no one's looking—and the Bangols won't suspect us because they don't know we're here."

"A good plan," declares Junin. She takes the antler out of Grandpa's hand. "The Bangols have no knowledge that we possess this." Junin strokes the bony antler, her fingers coming to rest on its golden tip, which spirals out in a fine coil that pricks her finger.

Ella

chapter 13

Ella

The Fairy Vineyard is a dream. Lately, day on Jarr-Wya is close to indiscernible from night, except here. The nights are better. The vineyard is strung with honey-colored lights that warm the cozy corner of the island. Between them are wind-stirred flags of pink, peach, and periwinkle. Sprites fly past in a flutter, a happy hum, and a tickle when they brush against me.

The fearless vines glow a stardust emerald. They spread their radiating leaves in all directions, snaking their shoots along lines of wooden supports, crossing to the neighboring rows and entwining. The vineyard forms lush tunnels of greenery, below which the sprites race to and fro in their daytime chores. Sprite skin is pale sea-foam green but appears darker in places where they nuzzle the foliage.

We are welcomed by Jeo, the queen sprite. She's not afraid, though I'm sure we look—and smell—terrible. I'm always deathly pale, but even the Olearons are the color of red shirts line dried for days in the blazing sun. Azkar and Nameris had taken turns carrying Lady Sophia, and both stretch their aching backs upon arrival. Duggie-Sky, too, is dog-tired. He collapses, snores, and drools on a pile of leaves pruned from the vineyard.

Queen Jeo is elderly. Deep creases accentuate her lively eyes and lips that pucker when she smiles. Jeo has wild white hair braided and twisted into a swan. The bird tips as the jolly sprite takes her leave. She tasks one of her attendants, Quillie, to show us around. Quillie is male, despite his sweet-sounding name.

He's pregnant.

Male sprites grow the children, Quillie tells me, as females are the better horticulturists and prefer to nurture the vineyard until the babies are born. I scrunch my forehead. Grandpa Archie shrugs at the biology and whispers, "We're better off not knowing some things."

The sprites tend the vineyard year-round and harvest its grapes—the ohmi—every fifty sunsets. There are different varieties of ohmi, each with its own color, size, leaf, vine, and magical properties. The sprites tell the ohmi apart by these qualities.

The fat blue ohmi are juicy and give the eater sweet dreams. The firm orange ohmi smell like old socks but remove even the most ornery stains. The purple ohmi, the ones that most resemble what Mom buys at the grocery store at home, are used by the naughty sprites to play pranks on their friends. Yellow ohmi season the stew made from the green, and the black ohmi . . . well, Quillie thinks I am too young to know what those are for.

The sprites aren't like us. They're all related. Every sprite is a part of their great family: all are mother, father, brother, sister, husband, wife, aunt, uncle, grandma, grandpa, friend. They share these roles as they nurture and care for one another.

Queen Jeo gifts the grapes that plant new life in mature males and, after they are consumed, a child begins to bloom within them. These special baby-making grapes—the Life Ohmi—grow in smaller numbers and are hidden within the tunnels of the vineyard. They are white and glow at sundown. The Life Ohmi are protected fiercely, as they are the future of the sprites.

I take diligent notes as Quillie takes us on a tour around the vineyard. The sprites draw pictures on their wooden trellises using a hard drawing tool that reminds me of an oil pastel. It's formed of charcoal from their fires and held together with ohmi juice. The lines it makes are smooth. Quillie sees me struggling with the blue-bark paintbrush and Olearon ink while I stumble through the vineyard. He offers me a piece of pastel.

Whoa! Awesome! I draw faster and more accurately but can also smudge. The pastel works well with the ink, too, which I experiment with when I finally sit down. I need a rest, but my hands are flying across the paper.

A gang of toddler sprites flutter around my head, whispering to each other before laughing and spinning themselves off course. They have broad grins and toothy smiles through their full red lips. Quillie shoos them to bed. I know it's a cliché, but I draw Quillie holding a giant molar. He notices the picture and shakes his head. "We are far too frivolous to do the serious job of collecting teeth," he tells me while rubbing his ballooning girth. Mom looks grossed out, but I think it's sweet.

Quillie—not as mature as he'd like everyone to believe—is twin to his sister Pinne, both born of one Life Ohmi. The pair splash around in my black ink, then dance across my paper with their tiny feet. They make a terrible mess. I love it! This is now one of my favorites. I let the ink dry before folding the paper and tucking it safely inside the pocket of my baby-blue bomber jacket.

The pocket is home to a small puncture wound in the fabric, which I trace with my fingers. It's too small for the paper to escape. I had accidentally cut the hole with Olen's glass dagger. The Olearon had protected me, Mom, and Grandpa Archie when we first arrived on Jarr-Wya. Olen died in the Bangols' attack in the blue forest not long after. That was when I was captured by the stone-heads and thrown into an awakin butterfly balloon fortunately sailed by Luggie and Nanjee.

Those events feel ages ago.

The vineyard's sleepy, silly quality eases my mind into other memories, stories told to me by the glow of my unicorn night-light as I lay curled, precancer, inside my sheets. Childhood stories about my family that were adapted to my age over the years were repeated, expanding in detail and truth.

These stories shift my natural stubbornness into the sweet spot of gratitude. I don't know what I'd do if my parents and Grandpa Archie weren't here with me on Jarr-Wya. My energy is plummeting, the headaches threaten to dice my brain, and the nausea is a constant annoyance. How could I have found my cure alone? No, life isn't meant to be lived in solitude. Whatever Mom overheard the Lord tell Grandpa Archie about family—that it's a weakness—is a lie.

Family is my strength.

Like it is for the sprites.

Like it is for Luggie, heartbroken at the death of his sister.

Oh, Luggie. He's protective. Sweet. Honest. He lives in a world removed from mine, and our communication is unconventional, yet he knows and accepts me. These are alien feelings for me. During my social banishment from hallway gossip, sports teams, and school dances—because I was different, fragile, "contagious"— I learned to be happy with only one good friend: Grandpa Archie.

He wasn't motherly in Mom's way, reminding me to take my medication or put a cool cloth on my head when I was eaten alive by fever. I didn't need coddling. He was a great companion during my forty-eight sick days in grade nine alone. He told me story after story from his life. My favorites are the ones are about his childhood.

Grandpa Archie was raised by a single mom; he never knew his dad. Mom and son were quite the pair, always having adventures, always laughing. Archie and his mom, Great Granny, moved from Arizona to Seattle with their station wagon packed to the roof with books and maps—before GPS—and a mountain of red licorice. They sang along with the radio as their voices slipped out the open windows.

Grandpa Archie told me his mother was a free spirit and prone to embellishment. She was wild in who she loved—reckless even—yet fiercely attached. She told Archie how she met his father, though they never said their I do's. She was twenty and hiking in Africa, independent and determined to see the world. Her canteen had a leak, and she ran out of water.

Young Great Granny was soaked with sweat and delirious from the heat. She saw a mountain bend in half and trees shift horizontally, as if cut along the horizon, though they didn't fall. Through this break in reality, out stepped a man. There was another in his shadow, but that person disappeared. Young Great Granny embraced the tall handsome stranger, whose mind was sharp, even in the swelter of African nowhere. He tracked a water source for her.

They stayed there, living a Garden of Eden existence, for how long Great Granny couldn't gauge. They loved each other immediately, and she knew she had conceived because she felt a tiny flame of life warm her from within. Grandpa Archie always told me that part proudly.

When young Great Granny was eventually found in the badlands, she was alone and asleep, on the verge of a coma. When the search party woke her, she asked for the man. They told her it was a dream, an illusion brought on by dehydration. There was no evidence of another person, and no tracks leading away. She didn't believe them, but after a week in the Nairobi hospital she, too, questioned everything, especially the man and the love they shared.

A month later, when two pink lines appeared on her pregnancy test, she knew that everything she remembered in her heart, despite her mind's raging objections, was true. There had been a man, a love, a sweet season of Eden, and she knew that the gaps in her memory would be filled at the birth of her child. But when Archie was born, fleshy and pink with chestnut-auburn hair and blue eyes—like Great Granny's eyes, and Dad's and mine, too—she had no other clues.

She never told Archie what she expected her child to look like, just that he was nothing like what she'd imagined. "Your father was the love of my life," was all she would say.

Grandpa Archie loves that story, I know he does, and all the others, too, in which he and his mom went treasure hunting and bushwhacking. They hiked the Canadian Rockies and rafted in southern California. That's how he lost her. To the water.

Great Granny saw a glint of red on the river and dove in, without hesitating. She slipped low, beneath the rapids, and the current left her behind, crushed in a pocket of rock, as the raft sailed downstream. Archie screamed till his throat bled and he worried he'd choke. His mother was gone. The light on the water had been the reflection of the autumn sun through a misty morning sky.

When Grandpa reflects on this years later, he resents the rescue officers who concluded that suicide or insanity—possibly both—was the cause of death. He believes his mother saw something so compelling that she risked her life to reach it.

Archie was seventeen then and newly graduated from high school. He was enrolled in college to study African history, something Great Granny had wanted desperately for him, but without her, he couldn't bear it. He slept through orientation, present but absent. He was late for day two and didn't show up on day three.

Archie found a contractor looking for roofers to do a project. The job wasn't far from the apartment he shared with a senior couple after breaking the lease on Great Granny's townhouse. He didn't have a car, so he walked the twenty blocks every morning, uphill both ways (if I remember the story correctly). He learned on the job. Archie jokes that he only staple gunned his hand twice.

He never again went rafting. Or climbing. Or traveling outside Seattle. He roofed and created a man-shaped indentation in his recliner. He married Suzie, who he knew from grade school. He charmed her over the till where she worked, ringing in his meager groceries. He told me he would buy enough for two days' worth of meals, max, so he could go back to the store often to see her. When Suzie criticized his nutritional choices, he knew she was *the one*.

Archie took her out to the edge of the sea and asked her to marry him.

His proposal went something like this: "Suzie, you're the milk that makes me strong, the bread that sustains me, the steak that makes life rich. Will you be my wife?" Grandpa Archie can be so corny! This story made me giggle, especially when I was little and he first moved in with Mom, Dad, and me. I was seven then, and I didn't know the words *tumor* or *cancer*. I did know a little about death—Grandma Suzie's—and the way sadness tastes on the cheek of someone who's been crying. It was also the taste of love.

Grandpa Archie sang his dead wife's name in his sleep. The way he said it—*Suzie*, and on rare occasions, *Suzanne*—made young me wonder if I could ever have a love like that. He spoke her name as if she were still there, his words placed into her mouth like a kiss.

Suzie was beautiful, he told me often. He saw her features

on my face and her character in the person he observed me becoming. She was special in the way she cared for people with such generosity that you'd think there was no end to the kindness in the world, that the more you gave, the more you had to give.

THE plan is in motion. Half our company set off at sundown for the Bangols' northern fortress. They make up three groups. The first is the Lord of Olearon, with Islo as his guard, Luggie as their guide, and Duggie-Sky, who is tasked with using his power of teleportation to place the antler on the band shell's stage. They're heading west and will sneak in from the northern edge of Baluurwa—where the Steffanus warriors would travel if they were plotting a siege.

Luggie seemed overeager to accompany the Lord. He had a strange look in his eyes. His body was tense, and his mind elsewhere. I'm not sure what to make of his behavior. It was like he was readying himself to either pounce or protect. I only hope he doesn't do anything stupid.

The second contingent to depart was Grandpa Archie and the sprite Lillium, plus her pet fly named Gobo. They are the diversion. Grandpa and Lillium will approach the Bangol fortress from the west, cause just enough of a distraction that the Bangols will not detect the Lord's group, and then get out of there.

Finally, Kameelo forms a contingent of one, on a mission to watch from above, ensuring the first two groups aren't discovered. This he must do carefully, so he isn't spotted. The Bangols won't be expecting a flying Olearon, but still, he can't let his uninhibited personality get the best of him.

Of those remaining in the Fairy Vineyard, some opted to stay, waiting for the deed to be done, while others—like me—were not given an option. I wanted to make the decision for myself, to be given the freedom of a choice, even if I would have taken up residence in the Fairy Vineyard anyway. Lady Sophia, too, was not given a say. Also staying behind are Mom and Dad, Captain Nate, Junin, and two of the Olearon brothers, Azkar and Nameris.

Here on this crazy island, when I'd normally find myself falling asleep, I'm awake instead. Luggie's only been gone a few hours, but I miss him. He's my safe place. He treats me like a person, whereas Mom treats me like an illness. When we're together, I don't doubt Luggie's feelings for me. Apart, however, I begin to bite my nails, obsessing over every interaction, replaying and analyzing it all on a torturous loop. Nothing remains of the midnight-blue nail polish I wore when we arrived on Jarr-Wya.

I don't understand why Luggie obeys the Lord. It's not like him. The Olearons callously lump all the Bangols together, vilifying them, but the stone-heads are not uniformly evil—apart from Tuggeron. Luggie is good, which is why I feel uncomfortable with this new plan, though even Mom wouldn't listen to my concerns.

Even Grandpa Archie, too, acts like the Bangols are expendable. He quickly suggested pitting them against the Steffanus race. He must know Bangols are going to die. Those are Luggie's family and friends. They'll be stabbed through the brain by Steffanus daggers, like Yuleeo was, sliced open by golden antlers, and who knows what other fatal gifts the Steffanus warriors will bestow.

Ella

-Blue
-Sweet dreams
-Purple
-tricky
-orange
-Stinky
Black
????
→yellow
+Green
=Stern

Ella

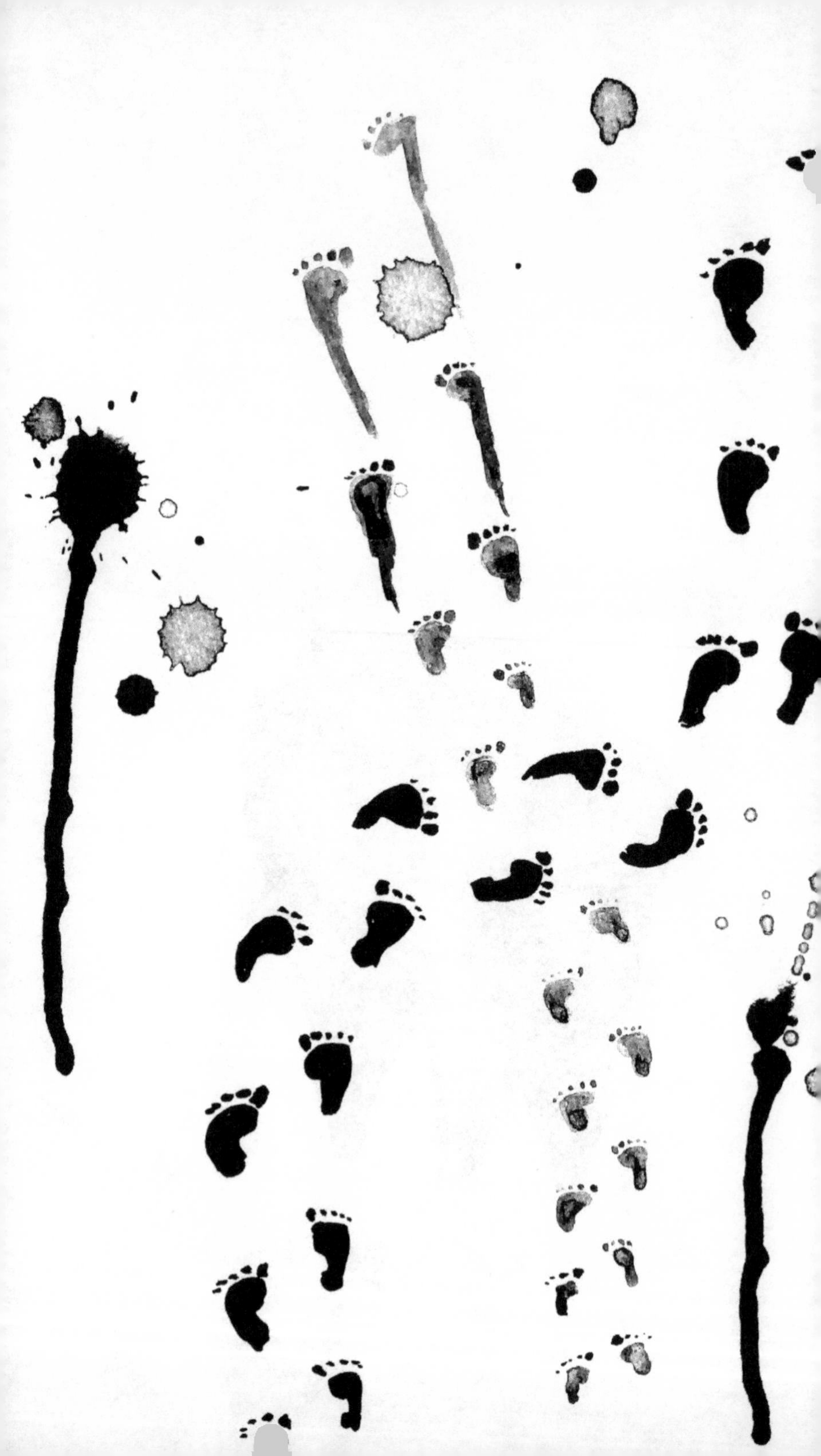

Q+P

chapter 19

Archie

Luggie hangs back as the Lord consults his warrior, Islo. Duggie-Sky listens attentively to them, to the smooth language of the Olearons, which sounds like cursing to Luggie's ears. Their contingent of four arrived at the foot of Baluurwa not long before. The deepening night is cold and carries the cutting smell of frost on the breeze. Luggie shivers. The Olearons refuse to ignite their ruddy bodies for fear of catching the attention of the Bangol night guards. The four crouch on the edge of the black rock, baring their skin as they press up against its warmth.

Luggie feels tense, distracted, consumed with plotting ways to kill the Lord. *I must choose the right moment, but the decision is impossible,* he frets. He concludes that the trepidation hammering in his heart is a warning, not an urging. *Perhaps the Lord still serves a purpose in saving Ella,* he thinks. He puts the matter to rest, for now.

Their contingent has not yet observed the Bangol guard turn to the west. Luggie hopes, for Ella's sake, that Archie is alive. A thundering Haaz creature, cousin to the Bangols, shakes the earth near the western entrance, but the Bangols, including Luggie's father Tuggeron, are not concerned. The Lord insists they delay their advance into the fortress until all bright yellow eyes are on the west.

Of course, the Lord will sacrifice Archie and his sprite companion, Lillium, so we get in and out safely, Luggie thinks irritably. *Just like he will do to me if I am not careful.*

Luggie grinds his teeth. He does not wish to know what the Lord and Islo discuss. *I have heard enough*, he thinks with a grimace. The Lord has only ill will for the Bangols and no shame in cutting them down with his words within earshot of Luggie. The Lord has also never failed to remind him of his role on this journey.

Obedience.

Or the Lord will scorch every Bangol.

Submission.

Or the Lord will murder Ella and everyone she holds dear.

Luggie slips backward into the shelter of a nearby blue-bark tree that has bravely fought its way through the warm rock. When he is sure the Lord and Islo have no interest in him, he slips the stiff leather envelope from his sack and tenderly removes the magical glass from within it. It is a risk, but one he is willing to take. The secret history of the Olearons has beckoned to Luggie every sunset since their departure from the glass city. Delicately, he slides the callused pads of his fingers across the dazzling jeweled surface, and the glass responds in turn.

Storm clouds sweep across the face of the glass, growing from white wisps to angry, foreboding billows that engulf every edge. The clouds melt to black, and white letters appear in Bangol as the Naiu in the glass reveals itself to its reader. As one sentence disappears, another slides in line, the words joining haphazardly, only remaining fleetingly before they are replaced. Luggie reads quickly.

The 22nd Lord, Devi, grew ill after his capture of a Steffanus youngling: ill in body and in mind. Tormented dreams scathed his sanity and planted in him a grotesque fear of the she-race. He shared with his advisors the nocturnal visions he witnessed each night: Baluurwa the Doomful, the great mount of Jarr-Wya, leaking silver-skinned women like blood. The great shadow-giver that towered at the center of the island was pierced through the heart. The silver women, with their eyes of fire and ice, propelled themselves up to the stars on terrible wings, hunger cut across their twisted, angry faces.

Devi's advisors assured him they had set their sights on Baluurwa for forty sunsets, and that the captured one was the sole remaining Steffanus. Devi's father, the 21st Lord, had called forth the flame and passion that pulsed with rage in the Olearons' veins, unleashing himself upon the mount. He burned it to naked rock. Many generations would pass before seed and soil could support new life.

Certain of the truth of his dreams, despite his father's actions, Devi called forth the Olearon warriors. Together, they devised plans to search every tunnel and crevice. These plans never came to be. The captured Steffanus eventually spoke—and not willingly. Her pride was a confirmation to Devi that there were more of the terrifying sisters. The mountain had to be rife with them. Devi and the elder Olearons did glean much from the Steffanus's testimony: the beginnings of the she-race, and the beginnings of all worlds and time and planets with their derivative dimensions devoid of magic. After recording this testimony, Devi took delight in draining the blood of the Steffanus, though it did not give him the peace he desired. On the contrary.

The morning stretch of the sun revealed the end of Devi. His Maiden turned in their bed, within their glass chamber, to find her Lord, her soul partner, ash white, the heat drained from his ruby skin, bleached of all life, as it had been with the Steffanus. Across Devi's chest, cut deeply with a dagger, his papery skin bore these words:

A Lord to destroy.
A Lord to rebuild,
To destroy once more.
Vanity. Foolishness.
The stars be witness.
Peace does not hold hands
With war.
We are coming.

Devi's Maiden, now possessing his spirit and his fear, hurried to appoint their second-born son, Tennam, the 23rd Lord of Olearon. Tennam and his sister Daneelo performed the scorching ceremony on their father's body that dawn and by sundown released a green bird to Baluurwa. Tennam and Daneelo asked the Steffanus for peace, believing it could endure, which it did for two generations.

Tennam passed lordship to his only son, Masillo, the 24th Lord, who bestowed it on his firstborn, Till. It would be the son of Till—Yulan, the 26th Lord—who would unearth unrest once more. The Lords who followed—Jenu the 27th and Teemun the 28th—would become entrenched in a well-worn rut of attack and defense. The Steffanus warriors flew over the glass city, dropping stones that shattered the great hall, the chambers of the Lord and Maiden's attendants, the armory of glass weapons, and finally the Olearon nursery.

The Lords responded with fireballs to the sky and burning grass lassos that bound silver feet and curling golden horns. Olearons aimed, too, for the wings. Steffanus sisters tumbled, landing on jagged fragments of glass that sliced bone from skin and feathers.

In the reign of Teemun, the burning and smashing and piercing and roasting and deeply ingrained hate was a way of life.

By that time, the Steffanus race traveled between Jarr and Earth frequently, growing in foresight—and in anger—with each passage through the threads that pulsed between dimensions. The Steffanus sisters were skilled makers of Tillastrions, some needing no more than a pebble, which they used to call forth their power of Naiu. Others on Jarr-Wya—the Olearons, Bangols, and sprites—would need one from the human world to portal jump to there. The Steffanus race boasted duality of spirit, being birthed at the fusion of human and magical origins.

Steffanus travelers returned with ill omens for the Olearons, which they scratched onto the glass city (always in a state of rebuilding) during the night, so that the dawn would illuminate their dark words. Teemun returned anger for their loathing, fiery boulders for their stones, and words best left unsaid for their dire proclamations. He unearthed his forefather's plans—scrawled by Devi six generations before—and brought his warriors to Baluurwa. No Steffanus child was spared. The mount rained with blazing newborn feathers. Golden antlers were collected, piled, and smelted into the breastplate of Teemun.

Baluurwa was silent. No food preparation fires—evidence that the Steffanus race endured—dotted the mountain in the night. All was Olearon lilac smoke and a windstorm of white. Ash. The red kin emerged, their fire so hot with hatred that their blue jumpsuits, which repelled the lick of fire, burned from their molten skin. They returned to the glass city, naked, proud, and ready for peace.

Teemun bore four children during his reign: two daughters, Mazanoo (called Mazi) and Jeeleano, and two sons. The elder son, Telmakus, joined the Olearon contingent that guarded the Sea of Selfdom on Jarr-Wya's east coast. When Teemun, now more than thirty thousand sunsets old, grew faint of fire, his eldest son was called back from the Olearon ship.

Telmakus was exalted to the glass throne on the eve of Teemun's passing. Having grown up in a time of peace and believing his father that the peace was peacefully won, Telmakus did not concern himself with Baluurwa or the silver-skinned she-race, and only learned of them from fire-yellowed parchment accounts with words ringing as embellishment and myth. He was tenderhearted and sought first his Maiden.

The bloodline of Lords and Maidens is flexible like chain mail. Their spirit has never been linked to a particular race. A Lord may be born in any magical world and inhabit any form. In each world, there is one race to which the spirits of the Lords and Maidens are pulled. In Jarr, they are Olearons. In other lives, they find themselves reawakened in different skin, but always the same race as each other. Never the grey of Bangols. Never the shine of sprites. Never a race of a derivative dimension. And never the silver of Steffanus. The Maidens and Lords are joined to one another, as if by hands held through a fog. One always finds the other.

Telmakus searched the glass city. He waited for the new births in sunny summer's heat, one of two seasons hopscotched between on Jarr-Wya, the other being tepid budding spring. Not even through one-sunset-old eyes could Telmakus find his love. He sought out the sprites, to no answers, and the Bangols, who had left their northern fortress unguarded to trawl the eastern sea. So Telmakus took to Baluurwa. To mourn. To contemplate. To call on the Naiu in him, pleading for his soul partner, as his loneliness was encompassing, confusing, and corrupting.

That was when Telmakus met Laken, the last remaining Steffanus, who hid herself in Baluurwa's heart.

Laken was barely surviving in a tunnel, concealed beneath a broken bough of a slanted tree. She was older than he, by how much he could not tell. Laken's robes were pale blue like the sky. Her face was pinched and puckered by fire's harsh embrace. Her body was rail thin like the Olearons', though she appeared starved, lacking the full breasts, wide hips, and round cheeks of the Steffanus women, whose likeness had been sketched in the Olearon public record. Telmakus nearly confused her with an overgrown sprite, but she was unlike any he had seen in all of Jarr.

Telmakus did not recoil when Laken reached out her silver hand to him; it was scarred and missing three silver nails. She placed it on his heart. He knew she felt his ache, the longing as loud as his unabated cries during the sunset that had just passed to vapor at the kiss of the moon.

They spoke in the common tongue of the land, brought to Jarr-Wya by the Steffanus travelers many thousands of sunsets ago from Jarr's derivative dimension—a language now spoken by all races on the island when not addressing one of their own. Laken held the young Olearon and gave him passage by Tillastrion so he could search for his missing love.

After his return, Telmakus never spoke to the Olearons of what was birthed in him during that journey. He told of meeting pale beings—and his love, his soul companion—and of a land that stretched a distance beyond the cusp of the Sea of Selfdom. He strained to explain the deviation of time from one world to the next—that their rhythms were two parts of the same song. Telmakus was changed, in ways he did not understand—nor did those in his charge.

The Olearons were perplexed that a Maiden would be reborn a world apart from her Lord and that she would be discovered in a derivative. Their questions about their Lord's well-being were repetitive and confrontational, but greater than this was their fear of the Steffanus race.

The elders burned with suspicion. Telmakus referred only to a diviner who lived in the mountain as he struggled to evade the Olearons' dread that perhaps Teemun, his father, had not annihilated the Steffanus race as believed. It was obvious to all that Telmakus felt gratitude for the diviner's kindness. Naivety they blamed, for Telmakus had not known the bloodshed, nor the roasting of the mountain at the hand of his father.

The Olearons rose against their 29th Lord in the name of peace. Telmakus, wishing to display his autonomy from Laken—whom the Olearons assumed was the vaguely described diviner, though they never knew her name—scorched all public records of the Steffanus, vowing to rid the island, and all of Jarr, of the she-race. It was an overcompensation Telmakus would have regretted if it were not for his madness.

In secret, however, he transcribed as much of the record as he could recall, wishing to study it for clues to the blind hatred so easily awakened in his family, his warriors, and all who dwelt within the glass city. The violence in them bled fire from their dreams and caused them to forge of a new arsenal of sharp glass weapons.

Elder Olearons met with warriors in the training paddocks to pass on knowledge and battle techniques. Rumors skipped through the grasses between glass structures and bounced off the smooth, angled surfaces, coating everything with distrust. The words, both truth and lies, crept into Telmakus's brain and began to fester there. He wondered at Laken. Was he too easily fooled by her silver-blue wounds? By her frailty? Was it all a theatrical distraction to keep him from the truth?

Telmakus looked bloated with the weight of his decisions, lacking decisiveness. He consulted his older sisters, Mazi and Jeeleano, who knew the ravages of war when they were young, many sunsets before. Mazi, the eldest, spoke of horrors that became a blade through Telmakus's mind, destroying everything he had come to know through experience—with Laken, in the derivative world, with his love. All of it was called into question.

Jeeleano, a wisp compared to her sister, was soft-spoken and prone to forgiveness in both her beliefs and her manner. She was nursing her newborn then, which Mazi blamed for her sister's sensitivity, but in truth she had always been the gentler of the two. Jeeleano advised her brother that fault is shared, and if it is shared, so, too, is compassion.

Telmakus refused sleep to pore over the secretly recorded testimony of the Steffanus sister told to Devi many generations of sunsets past and of the she-race's escalating threats and prophecies. His hands throbbed with the heat of rage at his growing disorientation, so intense that he felt he did not belong in any world.

Elders banged on his glass door from dawn to dusk, looking to poison Telmakus with their theories and ravenous cravings for dominion, manipulating the vulnerabilities in him that he refused to acknowledge. In many ways, the elders had already succeeded.

Telmakus retreated into the blue forest to the south, needing to relieve himself of the weight he carried via the enchantment of Naiu, a gift from Laken to protect what he and his love had made together. Laken met him there. Her skin shone brightly like the starlight that rained from overhead. She was growing in strength since their voyage through the channel between worlds. She met him so they might again travel to the derivative of Jarr.

Together, Laken and Telmakus delivered the child back to the womb of his love, for her to protect and raise. The Steffanus was leery on this journey. She observed the fear that now encircled Telmakus's eyes, turning their black even darker as he stared at her. His words were few and clipped, secretive. He needed her, as he had before, but this time, their embrace to activate the Tillastrion was joyless, and their parting between Jarr's mighty blue trunks after the earthly delivery had been made was even more distant.

Both Laken and Telmakus turned to look at the other, volumes of words left unspoken, questions left unasked, hearts left hungry for the time they had stolen away for friendship. Yet generations of anger pulsed in their blood and shot outward in one step after the other as they marched off in opposite directions, one toward Baluurwa and the other to the west.

Deflated, Telmakus arrived in the glass city beneath a full moon, which did not lift the shroud of darkness off his shoulders. He was hunched. His anger flared at whoever was nearest. He tolerated the plotting of the elders and the training of the foolish young warriors, blood-hungry and sword ready.

To his surprise, while he had been a world away with Laken, his youngest brother, Dillmus, was primed to become the 30th Lord of Olearon. The transformation was already under way. Never before in the history of the Olearons had the mantle been bestowed while the current Lord still lived. Telmakus felt as if his breath was being sucked from his lungs, his skin severed from its muscle. It was a torture that completed the change in him.

When Telmakus startled a group of warriors returning to the city in the cover of a moonless night, demanding to know where they had been, they told him that Dillmus had ordered them to seek out the diviner in the mountain. They told him they had learned that one lonely Steffanus remained—Laken.

Telmakus decided he must speak with her before events transpired that could not be undone. He was convinced he could draw out of her, because of their wayward friendship, some thread of logic and hope that could bind up all the madness that throbbed in his head.

When Telmakus reached Laken's tunnel, its concealing branch was a black crisp, its leaves completely obliterated. He rushed into the darkness, igniting his skin to reveal the hidden place. There, on the floor of dirt and stone, were five of his most trusted warriors. They had been with the others he had encountered not long before—those who returned to the glass city to inform Dillmus that the deed was done. These warriors before Telmakus were the ones set on performing it. One held a glass blade to Laken's throat. Her wings had been cut from her silver back and lay motionless on the dusty tunnel floor, weeping their spilled blood into the darkness. Laken trembled from antler to naked foot.

The outrage of Telmakus was all-encompassing. The Olearon warriors, now dragging Laken, backed away from their Lord's fire, which reached out to them in their betrayal. They raged in return, sending curling flames toward Telmakus. They spoke to him as one should never address a Lord. The warriors' blades reflected the red of fire, tinged with blue, back into Telmakus's eyes. They released Laken, kicking her forward, and demanded she repeat the prophecy spoken only a moment before Telmakus's arrival. Her eyes were pleading but not harsh. Her voice was but a quiver; no malice was needed as the words themselves were enough.

Laken's Oracle:

"A half-blood Olearon will return to Jarr, and the race of Olearons will cease as they have been known since the first sunrise and their first spark. With this knowledge, the Steffanus sisters will come forth once more to the Olearons, but this time not for help—but for vengeance."

Telmakus plowed past Laken, who crumpled to the ground, shielding herself from the heat that glistened on her scared face. Telmakus's eyes were fixed on his warriors. They did not have a chance to scream.

When Telmakus returned to the glass city, he answered no questions. He shut out the elders. The sun blanketed the pasture, grassy paths, and the glass structures with even, unbiased light. When Telmakus emerged many hours later, his jaw muscles protruded from beneath his sharp cheekbones. His long red fingers were balled. He tore grass from his path and released it, clearing a path for himself through the gossiping crones. The blazing grass traveled before him into the warrior-training paddock, cutting asymmetrical shapes into the earth, where it crumbled into ash.

Elders approached. They asked if Telmakus had seen the Steffanus, if she had cast any ill oracles upon them. He ignored the less ardent elders and shoved down the persistent.

His brother, Dillmus, met his eyes, and in a breath the kin were as close as lovers, but there was no affection left in either. Dillmus demanded to know the whereabouts of the missing warriors. Telmakus did not answer, only glowered back. Dillmus demanded that his older brother release the lordship to him, that there was only one son of Teemun fit to rule the Olearons and wipe out the Steffanus race once and for all. When Telmakus remained silent, Dillmus tripped him with glowing-hot snakes of grass. He called forth nearby objects, setting them on fire in the air, and rained them down on Telmakus's head, only to have the silent ruler obliterate them and smash his brother's attack.

Dillmus, who by now lusted for his half-earned title, proved inept at usurping the rightful Lord. Telmakus embraced Dillmus so tightly that the younger brother lost control of his fire. His flame ripped through the cracks in his flesh and tore through his eyes. The blast emanated through the paddock, collapsing the lungs of many nearby elders. Those who opposed Telmakus shrank away swiftly, while the loyal stood erect and narrowed their eyes.

In the sunsets that followed, many were scorched unceremoniously. Telmakus, his faith lost, set his mind to a singular task. Power. Power and the numbing of his heart. When even these became too great, his fire growing beyond his control, his half-heartbroken, half-petrified spirit shattered him. His loyal warriors collected the pieces of his body—more than one hundred in all—and stored them in a secret compartment beneath the glass throne.

The eldest sister of Telmakus, spiteful Mazi, perished with Dillmus, and thus the lordship of the Olearons was passed to Jeeleano's son. Jeeleano raised him with her kindness, her forgiveness, and most of all, her true love of peace. His name was Dunakkus. I am he, the 30th Lord of Olearon.

chapter 15

Archie

Archie throws himself behind a boulder as another whizzes past him to shatter on a stone-and-earth barricade, narrowly missing his head. Dust and shards of rock cloud Archie's view of the western entrance to the Bangols' fortress. The smooth, grey face of the giant Haaz swings to its left, then to its right. Its body pauses, still and barely breathing, though it clenches its meaty fists where muscles bulge like mountain ranges between its bones.

Lillium, the sprite tasked with helping Archie divert the attention of the Bangols, had warned him that this would happen—that they would meet a Haaz along their way and that the Bangols likely hired their similarly ash-colored cousins to guard their fortress as the stone-heads' suspicion grew. Blooming alongside this suspicion is their lust for the Star and all the lands of Jarr-Wya.

"Over there, Archibald!" Lillium chirps and points to safety as she flutters nearby, hanging in the air an inch out of reach from the Haaz. Her voice, small and high pitched, rings out above the rumble of settling rocks. The Haaz ignores her as it holds its breath, reading Archie's vibrations through the earth. It waits.

The place where the creature's eyelids should part is solid skin, but Archie can see its eyeballs search the inside of its flesh.

When Archie makes up his mind to jump into the crevasses between rocks, where Lillium pointed, the Haaz seems to sense the microscopic shift in his weight and it lunges as well. Archie thrusts himself forward and slides into the narrow opening a second before the Haaz crashes against the rocks. It groans and howls wildly. *Like an undisciplined toddler*, Archie muses where he cowers beyond the fifteen-foot-tall creature's grasp. The Haaz rises and swings its arms about, scratching its knees, which it can easily reach without bending, and punches the stone wall. It howls once more, then disappears into the maze of boulders where it hid when Archie and Lillium arrived.

Archie runs his fingers through his hair, now filling out with deep brown patches where his bald spot once reflected the sunshine. Since arriving on Jarr-Wya, Archie felt invigorated, as if awakening from a deep sleep. His driver's license birthdate may read 1947, but he doesn't feel a day over fifty, as his head of hair and the energy in his pounding veins can attest.

Archie cowers in the stone crevasse, his knees to his chest and his eyes closed, as the trembling of the mound of stone abates. The Haaz is gone—for now. Archie listens. When the wafting dust settles on his khaki pants and the low swoosh of shifting pebbles grows still as they fill the spaces between larger stones, Archie reluctantly opens his eyes. There are no silver-lined shadows cast by the moon. The black is even and velvety and outlined in the bewitching starlight. There is no sound but for the rapid panting of Lillium, who clings to Archie's hair as if grasping the reigns of a horse.

"That was close," she whispers so quietly that Archie can barely hear her fine, singsong voice.

"That was close," he mumbles, contorting his body in the narrow space. He inches closer to the opening and pauses. No grey-as-death hand reaches in for him. No sightless face exhales rank breath into the hideaway. Archie crawls another inch, and then two, until he squints.

The dusty entryway to the Bangols' maze is clear. There the grass—that which fights its way through the sunbaked, cracking mud—is matted and flattened. Bones of fairies, the size of toothpicks, have been collected into spilling piles and wedged between stones in the maze to stab the skin of those who venture between its passageways. The smell of unwashed bodies, caked in sweat and dirt and Naiu, wafts through the breeze.

"I think it's gone, Lillium, but that can't be good," says Archie, sliding on his stomach to gain a better vantage point. "Our job is to distract the Bangols, and therefore the Haaz, while the others sneak through. We need to create a commotion. Draw the beast back."

Archie waits for the sprite to answer, and when she doesn't he turns his head to look over his shoulder. All he can see are the two tiny human-like feet that connect to the sharp angles of her legs. Lillium's femurs jut backward and are thick with strong muscles under her shiny pale green skin. Her thin tibias are covered in protruding bristles that help the sprites catch themselves on leaves, vines, and trees. Lillium notices Archie observe her legs, and she slips her awakin wing dress down to her ankles.

"I thought I was brave, Archibald, but I am not," mutters Lillium. "Maybe I am the silly spriteling the others always call me. I hate that. Silly spriteling. But look at me—it's true. When facing the Haaz, I am small. I have no power."

"Come down here," Archie says, huffing.

The sprite releases his hair and slides down his forehead to jump off the tip of his nose, where a fresh scab rises on his skin. Her foot-length red hair sways rhythmically as she moves. All sprites are born with frizzy ruby hair, and most braid and twist it into the shapes of birds or magical beings. Lillium, on the other hand, lets her curls grow freely in every direction as if she is a tiny Olearon flame. She flutters onto Archie's outstretched palm, where she settles to sit, cross-legged, arms folded, bottom lip jutting out.

"Now, Lillium. Don't talk like that," Archie says. "You are more than your wildest dreams. Believe me."

She sucks in her lip and looks into his eyes. "Tell me more. Please," she replies, suddenly bashful.

"Well, in my life, I've always dreamed of being somebody. Life happened, though, and I got complacent. Comfortable. Scared, to be honest. Terrified. I saw those I love slip away. My mother. My wife, Suzie. Ella. I thought, *Who can be brave in the midst of all this uncertainty? Never knowing how things will turn out?* I wondered if risk would deliver anything but more pain. I was paralyzed. I haven't lived most of my life, Lillium, and that's the truth. But that wasn't my fate. I have this one last chance. Fear isn't your fate, either. You have more courage in your two ounces than I have in all my two hundred pounds.

"When my company stumbled into the Fairy Vineyard, what did you do? Did you curl up and cower in your vine leaves? Did you hide in a nook of a blue tree? Did you fly skyward till the air thinned and no one could reach you? Did you hide behind Queen Jeo?"

"No."

"No. What did you do?"

Lillium shrugs. "Queen Jeo welcomed you, as you say."

"But before that, when our company first set foot in the vineyard, and you spotted us on your watch—what did you do?"

"I pelted you with ohmi."

"And?"

"I bit your nose."

"Right." Archie touches the scab and winces. "And it's quite the bite you have, young lady. My point is, when the moment comes, you'll choose bravery. The strength is in you. I can sense it. Just look." He grins.

The sprite looks down at herself. While Archie spoke, Lillium began to levitate above the coarse skin of his hand. As she rose, her arms and legs spread wide and tense, her jaw clenched, and her red lips spread into a fierce smile.

"Now, if that isn't the face of a warrior, I don't know what is."

Growing self-aware, Lillium shakes her arms and legs and flutters her wings, flipping about in the air. "All right, Archibald. I'll follow your lead. Maybe I *can* do this, but only if you are beside me."

"Deal."

"And please do not tell the other sprites about my moment of weakness. Please! They will tease me to no end. It will be '*silly spriteling this*,' and '*silly spriteling that*.' Oh, I couldn't bear it."

"That's fine by me. Now pop out there, carefully now, and see if the coast really is clear. Maybe you can fly high and spot the others. I do hope the Haaz creatures haven't grown wise to our plan."

"Off I go," Lillium chirps as she whooshes out of the crevasse.

Archie rolls to his back and looks up to the stones above his head. "One wrong move and a thousand pounds will crush me flat. If it brings the eyes of the Bangols here—and Haaz giants—then it'll be worth it. A quick death. A noble death. As long as the others find Ella's cure." Archie closes his eyes to listen once more. The sound of Lillium's wings, a rapid hum, fades as she investigates. "I hope Ella, Arden, and Tessa are safe at the Fairy Vineyard. Nate and Lady Sophia, too, though I'd be fine if Nate was in my position instead. Nate . . ." Archie lets out a throaty growl.

Lillium returns with a flash of red hair and glittering wings, followed by the buzz of her aged pet fly, Gobo. She lands soft as a feather on Archie's chest.

"It's no good. No good at all," she says, breathing heavily, her tiny chest puffing up. "The Haaz we thwarted, along with ten of its friends, felt the vibrations of the others—the Lord of Olearon, Islo, Duggie-Sky, and Luggie—and they headed in their direction. The Haaz pack was running to the southern entrance of the maze, which leads into the Bangol fortress. But I did it, Archibald! I was brave."

"Great, Lillium . . . What did you do?"

"I found the largest stone I could carry and flew over the pack. When I dropped it, the stone shattered. Burst to dust on one smooth head, cutting the giant's skin. At first the group of Haaz stopped where they were, flailing about blindly, their fingers spread and touching the air, feeling the flap of my wings above them. But they could not reach me. The cut one was bleeding badly, the wound spreading. The gash tore open more broadly, and I could see its black skull. The wound split the skin of the giant's forehead in two and continued down the bridge of its nose. All I could do was watch, dumbfounded.

"The other giants put their hands on the cut one. Then the wounded Haaz, he dug his nails beneath both sides of his ripped skin and pulled. Ugh."

Lillium clutches her stomach, wobbles woozily, and faints on Archie's chest. He scoops her up and rolls over, resting his hands on the earth and cradling the sprite.

"Lillium! Please, Lillium, go on!"

The sprite stirs. "The Haaz pulled back its skin from its face," she continues, "which was dripping with red above the rough black bone. That was when I saw it: the creature's eyes. I have only ever known them as shifting mounds of skin, like toy balls rolling beneath a blanket, but they are bone white.

The cleanest white but for a perfect dot of black at their center.

"The Haaz paused to focus its eyes. Eyes that have never before seen anything—not sunshine or moonbeams, stone or sea. Not even its own face looking back at it in those that surrounded it with both curiosity and horror. When the Haaz realized it was okay, it tore away the loose flesh. Then the others around it, their fingers and arms outstretched, still sensing my vibrations, pointed skyward. The Haaz with the crazy eyes looked up and spotted me."

Dust begins to rain onto Archie's hair. A pebble bounces off his shoulder, then another off the crown of his head, and another two off his arms. "What is that rumble, Lillium? Why is the earth beneath me quivering in fear?"

"The Haaz saw me, Archie. Its growl was hungry. Now that it can see, it is faster, too."

"They must be nearly here!"

"By vibration alone they tracked the Lord's contingent to the southern entrance, but they have not left the south unguarded at the order of the sighted Haaz. They pursued me. These creatures love the taste of sprite. That is great, right? Our plan to create a diversion is accomplished! I was so brave, I knew you would be proud! But Archie"—Lillium's voice is pleading—"we must leave. This crevasse will prove only a minor deterrent for the pack."

Archie pulls himself out of the narrow opening, leaping to his feet and racing to the stone entrance of the looming maze. While the Bangols may appear savage, the entranceway is decorated in a sophisticated stone pattern of alternating colors, some the red of baked clay and others marble grey. Just as Archie saw on the apex of the Bangols' arches over the eastern sea, the capstone above his head is skillfully carved in the shape of an island as tall as it is wide.

"Treasures," Archie says under his breath. Treasures was

the name of Zeno's shop in the city of Arrecife on the island of Lanzarote in the Canary Islands. Archie had gone in search of the shop after reading the final clue in Arden's notebooks. There he found Zeno, and so began the domino effect that brought the *Atlantic Odyssey* to Jarr-Wya. Zeno, whom he still considers a friend—albeit a selfish one—stole away at his first opportunity. Archie can only imagine the power-hungry Bangol seeking revenge on King Tuggeron, who killed Zeno's twin brother, Winzun, and their father.

The maze capstone above his head sends a pang of distress through Archie. He worries for Zeno and what has become of him since they parted in the east, but he worries more about the current plan. He begins to wonder what unknown horrors the Bangols have created and what surprises await them. A peach pit of fear forms in Archie's stomach.

"Which way?" Archie's voice is feeble, and with heightened nerves he looks frantically from side to side. Once through the archway, a stone wall greets them dead ahead. "Left or right, Lillium?"

"The Haaz pack run here from the south. At any moment we will see them to the right!"

Archie sprints left. He runs too close to the maze, and the tiny sprite bones protruding from the wall catch the flesh of his arm and leave a flaming scratch. Archie turns a corner to the right and then to the left. Lillium hums nervously at his ear, followed by Gobo. The wild-haired sprite talks quietly to her wings, which she affectionately calls "Wingies."

Every sprite bears a unique constellation of stars on their wings, kisses of Naiu, they say, that sparkle by moonlight. The freckles of light on Lillium's Wingies create the curve of a silhouette in profile. She talks to her wings in her distress, and her yammering muddles in Archie's mind.

His steps propel him farther, faster than he has run in years. The rumbling, bouncing earth from the footfalls of the Haaz creatures increases his pulse, rocketing Archie onward. The growls are deafening and grow like approaching thunder, more terrifying and imminent than the perpetual, erratic wind and lightning in the atmosphere above that never rests. Lillium darts upward till she pops her head into the fresh breeze that whips above the maze walls and its stale, slinking current. She calls down directions, matching Archie's pace.

"Left now, Archibald. No, sorry, your left." The sprite twists and rolls through the air, pointing and counting, squinting and gnawing at her lip. She flies ahead for one long breath, and Archie continues blindly. When a dead end appears ahead, Lillium ducks down below the stone walls to slip into the breast pocket of his shirt. "Right turn here," she chirps impatiently. "Right again. Go human, go!"

"Despite what you may think, I'm motoring to most people's standards. My legs have never felt so young."

Archie can feel Lillium chuckle to herself in his pocket. Gobo suctions his fly feet to Archie's cheek.

"Enough talking and more running," the sprite orders. "Left here. Now straight for a while."

"You sure?" Archie pants lightly.

"Yes. If you had turned at that last left, we would have smacked into a floating orb of tar. Down that turn there is a slippery pit bursting with caged carakwas, their soulless voids filled up with the ghosts of ten nasty Bangols executed recently. I could hear their voices beneath the creatures' clicks. They were feasting on one of them, bickering over who would eat the eyes."

A stone screams through the air and nicks Archie's left ear. "Lillium! The pack! They're catching up. We need to duck out of sight before—"

Archie's sentence is cut off as another stone connects with his left shoulder blade and knocks the words from his mouth and the wind from his lungs. He rolls forward, Lillium spilling from his pocket and Gobo bouncing along the ground. He skids along the gravel path until his back strikes the maze wall. He cries out in pain and clutches his injured shoulder where a sprite bone protrudes from his skin. He pinches the white sliver and yanks it out. Lillium covers her mouth, but Archie can make out her saying, "Oh no," as she slips into the fissure of a monstrous boulder.

The Haaz pack crowds above Archie and blocks the pale light from the indifferent moon. Their lips glisten with thick saliva. The smell of the massive creatures brings up from Archie's stomach the last meal he ate in the Fairy Vineyard.

The bloody Haaz, with its wild white eyes, comes closest. The bulky giant kneels and peers at Archie with loathing bewilderment. "What are you?" it finally croaks.

Archie waves away the creature's moldy breath. "I'm, well, human."

"Not so loud—your vibrations rattle my brain."

Lillium pops her head out of the fissure and retorts, "If you have a brain."

The Haaz flashes his chipped and serrated fangs at her and grunts. His breath blows her back into hiding. The Haaz studies Archie. "It's tiny," it tells the others. "Pale hair, pale skin, pale lips. Not much to look at. Not much to feast on. No obvious gift of Naiu."

"That's where you're wrong," Archie pipes up, improvising. "You may not be able to see my magic, but if I release it, you'll wish to rezip your skin and bury yourself beneath the maze wall."

"Archie?" Lillium says.

He turns back to her and glares.

"Oh . . . yes!" she hollers, finally understanding. "He is so powerful, he can tear you all apart."

"Well," Archie begins, faltering in his resolve, "yeah, and sometimes I don't even know what my magic is until it bursts out —*bam!*"

"He is sweating under his arms. I can feel the vibrations of it oozing from his skin," one Haaz snarls.

The bloody Haaz studies his face, and beads of sweat begin to blossom on Archie's forehead, soon surrendering themselves in weeping drips into his eyes. Archie blinks away their salty burn.

"He is lying!" One of the sightless creatures picks up a large stone and hurtles it toward Archie, who quickly lunges into a roll and out of the way.

The whole maze shudders, and the sighted Haaz swings its long arm and smashes its fist against the blind Haaz that threw the rock. "Do you want this whole place to come down on us?" it says, spitting through broken teeth.

Lillium wobbles out of the fissure, jarred from the impact. Archie whispers to her, "Now what?" The sprite bites her lip. She darts into the air and swiftly away.

"She did not have much faith in your magic, now did she?" The sighted Haaz smiles through its biting words. "Sprites!" it continues. "About all they're good for is smoothing the crinkled edge of hunger." It laughs. The Haaz stares down at Archie as if waiting for him to respond. "Not a talkative race, are you?"

"Pssst." The whisper belongs to Lillium, and there's a faint buzz of a jittery Gobo at her side. Archie tilts his head to listen, keeping his gaze linked to the ravenous eyes that bear down on him. Lillium murmurs between a pass-through in the maze wall. "A flock of black flyers—they will be here shortly. They are coming like a storm. One minute, I promise."

Archie rises, though the Haaz creatures still tower nearly seven feet above his head. "I was taught to speak only when I had something worth saying," he begins. "But when talk fails, I bring forth action like a starless shadow. That is my magic."

The creatures shake their heads at the riddle. "What are your friends in the southern maze up to?" demands the sighted Haaz. "You know they will never make it through." It chuckles wickedly like the clapping of angry waves. "We know the perils on their path, the nasty traps. Now give me something to report to Tuggeron, and I'll make yours a quick death beneath our feet."

"Tuggeron will get his news from me," Archie says, sneering. "Black ones, come forth!"

With this, piercing caws shred the air. The Haaz creatures fall in and out of moonlight as five black bodies appear and circle overhead. The black flyers have mutated further from Archie's last encounter with them. Their twined, serpentine necks hold bird-like heads with piercing beaks. Oily black feathers cover their massive bodies.

"Call them off!" the sighted Haaz demands.

Archie shakes his head slowly, a menacing grimace across his face, disguising his own terror. The Haaz pack shrieks and roars. Their hands are outstretched, their muscles flinching as they sense the weighty vibrations of the enormous black flyers, they and their broad wingspans shrinking the creatures to puny hulks.

"Run now, back to the fortress!" the sighted Haaz orders.

The bulky giants shove and elbow each other as they tramp through the narrow maze. Sprite bones break apart like brittle leaves and fill the air with sweet-smelling white powder.

Archie presses his back to the stone wall and feels his skin punctured in at least four places by the protruding tiny bones. Before the Haaz pack disappears around the maze corner, a black flyer swoops down and hooks its protracted talons through the shoulders of the sighted Haaz. The black flyer lifts the fighting creature off the ground. The raging Haaz cranks its neck back and bites apart the stretched flesh of its left shoulder, then its right; it falls free, landing on the center of a maze wall, which bursts apart under its weight. The Haaz groans vehemently as the wall crumbles beneath him.

The Haaz is weakened yet determined. Bloodied, it exposes its black-boned clavicle, its grey flesh peeling away to reveal an equally gloomy sternum. It stands and lifts a massive boulder from the ground, ready to pitch it at its target. Before the stone is launched, however, the black flyers descend from the jeering storm, swooping in and covering the lone Haaz in a blanket of shiny feathers. The maze unsettles at its dying screams. The beaks turn a haunting shade of crimson, set aglow by the moon. The black flyers toss the large white eyes onto the maze path, which roll in the direction of Archie and Lillium.

"I would say now is the perfect time to run—that way!" Lillium points.

"Yep. Quietly, now!"

Lillium and Gobo slip into Archie's pocket as he loops back to the start of the maze and takes the path to the right, the one that had taken the Haaz pack to the center of the Bangols' fortress. The wails of the dying Haaz grow faint behind them, though new sounds replace the wails. Grinding. Chugging. Screeching, but not of a living thing.

"What's that?" Archie says, unsure of what terror they race toward. There's a *sheeeek* and a *zwiiiing,* like a jigsaw on sheet metal, followed by clicking and clanging and groaning gears. Suddenly, angry sparks erupt ahead, bursting like blooming flowers to greet the multicolored lightning strikes.

In a break between the steadily growing screeches, Lillium

answers, "It's the Bangols. They have dug deep," Lillium says with a sigh. "I do not know what they have built, but it is of a material more resilient than clay."

"Metal?"

"We will soon see for ourselves."

chapter 16

Archie

Archie and Lillium develop a pattern for tracing their course through the winding, perilous maze. Lillium lifts off from Archie's shoulder, embellished with tiny mud footprints, to rocket herself into the murky midnight sky. Once there, she struggles against the manic wind, which whips in every direction. It carries on its bleak current the smell of death, damp and strangling, along with bone dust and the distant caws of the satisfied black flyers.

Lillium traces their route ahead, then dives down steeply, catching her arm on Archie's earlobe. Into his hairy eardrum she repeats, "Left, right, left, left, straight, right, straight, right." In this way, they avoid a magically suspended cage made of rose stems with thorns tipped in deadly green-glowing poison. Down another path, which Archie runs past, they miss colliding with an enchanted stone monster, which stands unmoving as the wall behind it until breathed upon.

Racing along, between her guiding orders, Lillium proudly tells Archie how she made her shining dress. She swooshes the skirt and its silken tips tickle his neck. "My grandest adventure, until now, that is"—her words sing—"was stalking the black flyers, but never too close. It was my job to ensure they passed the perimeter of the Fairy Vineyard and did not return. I would follow their trail of carnage, collecting fallen wings of slaughtered awakins and shed feathers of green birds—you know, the ones your granddaughter spews from her mouth."

"Poor Ella."

"Poor Ella indeed! Although"—Lillium giggles—"I have replaced a few soiled plumes from my gown with newborn feathers from her birds. Ah, are they not lovely, Archibald?"

Archie can hear Lillium spin in a silly dance near his ear. "Don't mention this to Ell. She'll be mortified."

"Pish posh! I am sure, like me, other spritelings would love to bask in her presence as she outfits us in emerald glory!"

"Emerald glory? Oh, Lillium. I do see why they call you 'silly spriteling.'"

Lillium crosses her arms, but says, "Take your next left, then right, then two more lefts."

"I feel like you're spinning me in circles!"

"Maybe so, Archibald, but there are direct routes I reckon you'd rather we avoid." Lillium's voice turns grave. "You think you have seen the worst of Jarr-Wya, but there are greater terrors than the Haaz pack or the mutated black flyers—creatures I wish you to remain ignorant of, at least a little longer."

Archie's feet pound the earth of the Bangol maze, and his joints are silent where they once ground together painfully with the groans of arthritis. Each footfall rattles the stony earth beneath him. Agile as a white sasar, Archie zips around a stack of chewed bones, past an avalanche of rocks where part of a maze wall has given way, and up and down the uneven path. Lillium and Gobo take to the air, surveying for dangers. Only slightly out of breath, Archie turns his chin up. He knows there must be ears against the walls, so he whispers, "I've been running for ages. We must be close."

Before the taste of the words have left his lips, Archie plows headfirst into something unseen. His forehead smacks loudly, and he falls.

It takes a breath for him to slow the rattle of his brain. He is prostrate on the gravely path, winded and befuddled. He blinks away the concussive blackness inside him, even darker than that of the continual night. “Lillium?” he finally manages to say. He scoots to his feet, but he is not in the maze.

Archie stands high on Baluurwa the Doomful.

The rocky edge he finds himself on, alone, is three feet wide atop a steep, sharp cliff. It is nearly nightfall, a pale purple dusk. The sky is full of brilliant gold stars and a moon that looks so close, you could take its hand and leap onto its speckled surface. No lightning fireworks snap and boom. No wind rages wickedly.

Off in the distance, Archie sees great swooning shadows dance through the sky. The black flyers are one headed and soar in spirals in a graceful waltz with pillowy clouds and silver moonbeams. The violet dusk is reflected on the angular panels of the Olearons' glass citadel in the distance. *Like the sky has shattered and fallen to earth*, Archie thinks of the smooth, reflective buildings.

Beyond the glass city, to the northwest of the island, gleams the rowdy Fairy Vineyard. The racing sprites appear as a green glow through their leafy tunnels, their tiny breaths making whole rows of vines quiver.

“Lillium,” Archie whispers again, but he knows she cannot hear him. He is alone. The light of the constellations steal the heat of the day as the sun sets sleepily in the east at Archie's back. *The sun rises in the east and sets in the west*, he thinks, replaying the Boy Scouts lesson from his youth and remembering the first time he noticed the opposite being true on Jarr-Wya. In Jarr, the sun announces itself on the western shore, only to dive into the eastern sea once its light and Naiu are spent.

The sight of the sun's crest around the peak of Baluurwa leaves Archie in awe. It was many days since anyone on Jarr-Wya glimpsed the celestial orb. The Star had sent the island into a turmoil of darkness, robbing the crystaliths in the Olearons' field of the Naiu delivered on sunbeams and channeled into the earth to nourish their crops. The days turned into a maddening, unshifting nightmare. Archie shivers suddenly. He unties the khaki coat from around his waist and hurriedly slips it on, struggling with the zipper as his fingers tremble with cold and fear.

"Hello, Archibald."

"What the—who's there?" Archie jerks fearfully away from the large warm hand that rests silently on his shoulder. As he turns his back to the sky, facing Baluurwa and its sparse trees and knee-high cactus bushes growing through the rocks, his eyes take a moment to adjust.

"Are you . . . Tanius?"

"I am not."

"It was past midnight and storming. Now, it's . . . just a peaceful, quiet sunset." Archie's voice tapers off. The sliver of sun has ripened to crimson, brightening its violet shadow across the melting sky, giving new vibrancy to the gold constellations that sing its farewell. The face of the Steffanus is unfamiliar to Archie when he braves a second look. Her features are distinct from those of Tanius. They are gentler, softer, though her face is ravaged by reddish-blue scars, raised in places, depressed in others, smooth in some areas, rough in others. Archie recognizes the wounds as the caress of Olearon flame.

The Steffanus wears a shredded gown of molten sapphire and chocolate, delicately braided in two thick strands over the slope of her smooth shoulder. Tanius had worn red—bloody, violent red. The antlers of this mysterious Steffanus branch broadly and shine in polished gold. Her eyes, like those who chased the company off Baluurwa toward the Fairy Vineyard, are intensely blue-red and searching. Her lips do not curl in hate but tilt upward with the satisfaction of something earned.

"I am as I always have been, Archibald. Favored by Naiu, birthed of seed and foresight. I did not, however, foresee a visitor this night. The last sunset I beheld you, you were but a fresh-skinned babe with a warm, willing spirit, innocent to life's cruelties. You did not cry at the sight of me, or at the sound of my deep voice, or at meeting my sad, angry eyes. But now, you are changed, and I am left in wonder."

Archie's words are slow and leery. "You know me?"

The Steffanus does not answer.

"Who are you?" Archie shuffles his feet to back away, but there is nowhere to go but down the merciless cliff to the graveyard of broken stones at Baluurwa's foot.

Archie searches his memory for a Steffanus visit in any of the dingy, bohemian homes he and his mother shared before they settled in Seattle. All he can see is his mother's smooth face and rich chocolate hair, and her animated eyes that sparkled when she told him stories. He feels her lips on his cheek; she had kissed him goodnight, every night, no matter whether they slept in a townhouse, a tent, or under the cracked canvas roof of their 1957 Ford Thunderbird.

Archie's mother smelled like spring flowers and spices from the other side of the world. She was a friend to immigrants, both legitimate and undocumented. They painted her hands with henna and filled their bellies with curry. They told Archie that his mother was an old soul, connected to all, as if she had been touched by magic and was no longer bound by the pettiness of all that consumed the mind but mattered so little.

This memory of his mother, so arresting that Archie's skin tingles, fights the image of the face before him. His mother's death is what changed him. It stole his innocence beneath the river's ebb. It robbed him of his adventurous spirit, replacing it with fear and complacency. It changed everything to a life of mindless routine and a recliner so worn that its springs groaned out in welcome each time he plopped himself there, happy to escape through one sitcom or another beside dated floral wallpaper.

"I am Laken," the Steffanus answers, watching for Archie's reaction. She tilts her head to the left, then the right, her blue-red eyes a battle between snow and fire as she digs into his mind with her own, probing for a crack.

Archie resists being known. He is good at this, a trick he learned from Tessa. He had spent sixty years, a lifetime, blocking out all he thought might cause him to feel, sitting so intently still that he could swear he watched life passing him by.

Laken is no match for him. She shakes her head and smiles faintly, though her sculpted face twitches against the gesture. Archie senses Laken's ability differs from Tessa's telepathy; it's more akin to Nameris and his gift of discernment.

"I know the name Laken. Where have I heard it?" replies Archie finally. His eyes broaden with the spark of remembrance. "No, I read it. In the secret history of the Olearons! On the glass square I found—stole—from the Lord's throne. You gave an oracle that terrified the red beings. I thought they had you executed."

"The Olearons write and rewrite history as if they are Naiu themselves. Bah, what do they know? What does anyone know? Our world, Jarr, is in flux, shifting this way, warping in that. Tillastrions take us to places we never intend to visit, time folding and merging and breaking apart."

"Because of the Star?"

"Yes, but that is only part of it, Archibald. Everything is

connected. The life force at the center of it all is Naiu. Its mind is confused. It is everywhere, witnessing so much hate yet perceiving so little love."

"I don't understand."

"Neither do I, in full. In part, yes. I see. There will be a great day of reckoning. Either all of us and everything we know and touch will be destroyed, or we will find new balance, a new peace. As hard as I strain, I cannot tell to which extreme all planets will finally come to rest."

"When are we, Laken? When in time? Is this the future?"

"No, Archibald. This is my past where you are visiting me now. The Star is here, but your ship has still not yet crashed on the southern shore. That event is many sunsets from now."

"I don't understand."

"In your present, I am old and weary, Archibald. I hide within a tunnel of Baluurwa, too weak to protect the Star myself. This I can foresee.

"The lifespan of a Steffanus is often accelerated, thus much shorter than those of humans or even Olearons. We expend the Naiu in us, which removes sunsets from our lives, though they can be returned by generous bounty in the gift of another. Our generations of sisters are the turn of a wheel, not the line of a wrinkle.

"Tanius, of whom you speak, will be of a seed birthed soon, the next generation of Steffanus sisters, who, in your present, must guard Baluurwa and the Star. I will be grateful to no longer fulfill that duty alone."

"Alone?" Archie feels like a child trying to form words as he struggles to piece together the timeline and implications of Laken's story.

"The Olearons burn all they do not understand and those they cannot control. I am the last, scathed but alive in the wake of the wild grief of Telmakus, the 29th Lord of Olearon. I was able to save the seed of our race by giving many years of my own life, gifting of myself so that others may grow. I planted the Steffanus seed here, within Baluurwa, and in as many worlds as I could travel."

Archie shakes his head in disbelief. *Is this all a dream?* he wonders. Then he remembers the warmth of Laken's hand.

"Tell me please, Laken: What did you mean when you said you saw me as a baby? I don't remember." Archie studies her silver skin and unruly tangle of gold-and-brown hair. Her gown's subtly flowing fabrics depict abstracted swells of sea-foam bubbling over broken fragments of silver moon and patterns of churned auburn earth. Studded across her body, like a belt, are a rainbow of plastic buttons, shapes Archie recognizes from dress shirts and jackets, and pins of countries from Earth. France. Africa. Canada. China. Around Laken's neck is a chain fastening a bent shield of tarnished gold over her shoulder and across one breast.

"I knew your father—" Laken answers tenderly.

"My father?" Archie's chest deflates. He suddenly remembers the invisible something he crashed into. "I'm delusional! That explains it. This"—he gestures around himself, to Laken, the blue-bark forest below, the shadowy, sweltering mountain, and heavy sky—"this is all my imagination! I've been knocked out. It's the only thing that makes sense."

"Oh my, Archibald, how you have entangled your mind in forgetfulness! Do you remember nothing of your father's fierce love for you that flows through your veins? Your mother was too fragile for us to visit again; too much time had passed, and her wounds were covered in a beautiful blanket of new life like a field of orchids. We didn't wish to upset everything she had come to know, all she had built up around herself. She would not have accepted that the derivative of Jarr, Earth, was not your true home."

Archie grabs his head and shakes himself. His mind feels as if it will be torn in two. As Laken's words pierce him with bolts of electric revelation, he wonders, and the solid defenses he erected are chiseled away. A crack forms. *What if?* The thought lasts only briefly. Archie chokes out his words, "Tell me. Tell me everything you know."

He follows Laken up a path, illuminated by moonlight, that winds and separates, snaking dangerously both up and down the mountain. She peers over her shoulder to keep watch on Archie as he patters along behind her. Her back is lined with two jagged scars, one on each shoulder blade—where Laken's wings were crudely cut away. Her body is a story Archie wishes to read but also recoils at the sight of. He knows she must have survived brutality he cannot fathom.

Laken rarely looks in the direction she is going, as if the way is deeply etched in her memory, until they reach the edge of a sharp bluff. She slips her wide hand, missing a few silver nails on her long fingers, into Archie's and guides him forward.

Together they step on floating mounds of earth just wide enough for one foot each. The mounds dip slightly under their weight. The land far below, slumbering Jarr-Wya in an earlier age, rests peacefully. The clouds pass through Archie like wandering ghosts as he and Laken take one measured step after another. Small flecks of dirt fall but tumble lazily each time their feet push off. Archie listens, anticipating the sound of the dislodged pieces of earth and stone rattling against the black rock of Baluurwa beneath them, but all is too quiet.

Finally, after what seems like hours of night, they reach a small island floating off one tentacle vine of Baluurwa. "This is my home," Laken says simply, pointing toward a wooden bed carved out of a still-growing tree, softened with layers of leaves. The bed sits low to the ground, and if you rolled over in your sleep, you would tumble over the edge of the tiny floating island. "Sit," Laken says, and Archie obeys.

"Now please, Laken, I need to know. Who is my father? I have so many questions."

Laken perches on a chiseled-rock chair shaped to her long spine. "You know this is the past we are in, Archibald? Much has transpired in the sunsets beyond this one. I cannot tell you what I have not seen in my future, in your past. All I know is what I know. Please, do not be angry."

"That's fine. A part of me still believes this is a concussion."

"I had a strange friendship with Telmakus. Unlike those he ruled, he was not closed-minded and cruel. He was not like the 22nd Lord, Devi, who captured a Steffanus sister generations before me, tricked her into divulging our secrets, then threatening to and nearly killing her.

"Telmakus, the 29th Lord, came up the mountain one night, startling me, inquiring where my sisters were hiding. I told him I was the last, that his kind had burned us to oblivion. Without so much as a sneer or taunting word, he told me he was sorry. He came humbly, begging. He was in search of his love. He knew her from his past life. In her absence his love drove him in reckless desperation.

"I asked the green birds to search all Jarr-Wya for the one Telmakus described as his Maiden from their previous incarnation. They returned the next day, weary and with no answers. In the meantime, Telmakus joined me here, where you are now sitting. We spoke of many things, the human world being one. He found my Tillastrion, given to me by an elder sister before she was scorched. She had left it with me for safekeeping till I was older, wiser, and ready to venture to our derivative dimension, which I did many times after her death. Telmakus asked about the Tillastrion. He said mine was the most beautiful he had ever seen. We decided to search for his love together, thinking that perhaps she had been displaced, for a reason we could not understand.

"We operated the device and found ourselves in a sweltering African desert of the human world. And there she was. Telmakus's desire was so great, it brought us to her shadow.

"The woman was lovely, a part of nature herself, a wild soul, always traveling, as if she, too, was searching. I left the two of them alone in her mirage to spread my wings in flight and soar above your emerald-azure world. I expected your mother would return with us, but Telmakus worried the Olearons awaiting him on Jarr-Wya would be unwelcoming. That is to state it nicely.

"He returned, bringing you with him within his very being, keeping your spark safe, but the Tillastrion did not ferry us smoothly, and Telmakus was confused. He returned to the glass city and was met with fear-mongering and anger at his poorly delivered story.

"Telmakus sent me word by green bird to meet him in the blue forest. He begged me to help him return you to Earth, where you would be safe beyond the Olearons' knowledge, and I accompanied him. He no longer believed his kin would allow you to live. He was heartbroken to leave you and his love on Earth, and return to Jarr-Wya alone once more. Telmakus's mind was shadowed in grief and rage, which, I fear, only grew. The Olearon warriors discovered me in a tunnel and attempted to murder me, but your father intervened. I lost my wings that day but won my life, thanks to him. That was the last time I saw him.

"The Olearons refuse to see the light of Naiu in our sisters. That was not the first time they meant to burn away the memory of us. History tells of other 'last Steffanus' women, but our seed never lies dormant for long. Our love for this world, for all worlds, is undying.

"On my own, I visited you. Your mother believed you were asleep. You awoke when I entered, kicking free of your blankets. You were a babe, not walking or speaking—but seeing you went well. Not one cry left your lips as you smiled at me. You remembered me then. I hoped you always would.

"Your mother was the kiss of love, pure joy, though she was brokenhearted. Her strength of will stitched up the wound Telmakus left behind. She healed herself, though in doing so deceived her own heart, replacing her memory of Telmakus with a smokescreen of logic.

"I knew then," Laken says sadly, "that you would have to find the world of Jarr on your own."

Surrendering to what feels like a dream, to his unconscious mind, Archie accepts Laken's words. "Thank you," he replies.

"Thank you?" The Steffanus is startled. The scars on her face twitch.

"Yes," Archie continues. "If it weren't for you, I might never have been born."

"Ah, I see! The spark of Naiu still lives in you!" Two crystal tears fall from Laken's eyes. She takes Archie's hands—which look small and peach in comparison to hers—and gives him her warmth.

"I read the origin story told by a Steffanus sister to Devi. The secret history of the Olearons said she was deemed worthy of death—was that you, Laken?"

"No, not I, though she told the 22nd Lord the truth. She escaped and informed the sisters of her testimony, warning them of the burning hatred in the west. She did not survive their attack."

"Are you alive, Laken, in my present I mean?" asks Archie.

Laken chuckles, "My foresight leads me to believe so, along with many others. I am the last now, but not in our shared tomorrows, Archibald, as you have witnessed. My sisters' seeds grow in Baluurwa as we speak. I do not have count of the sunsets of my life, but for every one I am gifted, I m grateful for my unexpected friendship with a merciful Olearon."

"Telmakus."

"The corrupted fire-breathers interpreted my oracle for ill, but the words I spoke were meant for Telmakus, as a promise. '*A half-blood Olearon will return to Jarr, and the race of Olearons will cease to be as they have been known since the first sunrise and their first spark.*' This prophecy is about you, Archibald."

"My father was Telmakus." Archie lets the words settle in his mind like softly falling snow. "And I am the half-blood Olearon." He shakes his head. His brow furrows. He struggles to reconcile his image of the Lord that Laken speaks of, kind and loving, with the wicked spirit that sliced through the sanity of his successor in the woods. That version of Telmakus would have killed him by a serpent of fire if Tessa hadn't been quick with the stone. Archie wonders if his father's nobler nature lives on too inside the 30th Lord's body, but as much as he hopes it to be true, he knows no goodness endures in the 29th Lord.

"Arden is in danger," whispers Archie.

"Arden?"

"My son—"

"A son?" Archie nods, and Laken drops his flushed hands and stands on bare silvery feet. "Please, Archibald, who is your son?"

"His name is Arden, or at least that's what we called him on Earth. Here on Jarr-Wya they call him Ardenal. He visited Rolace and was given a gift."

"To be of this world. I know what must have happened. Your blood, the blood of your father, is alive in him. Only one transformation would want so desperately to manifest itself."

"Arden's skin, his eyes . . . they're now red and black."

"Yes," Laken answers, radiating like a shooting star kissed by moonlight. "The half-blood Olearon has come, and so has the one who will save us all from the end."

chapter 17

Ella

The vineyard is alive past midnight with the sprites' lively races. They keep track of: who is the fastest flyer; who can find the prize ohmi the quickest (which Queen Jeo hides in a new place at dusk); who can trace the vineyard from its start, near the Great Tree at the north, to its end by the northwestern sea—blindfolded; who can catch Queen Jeo herself. I'm told the ancient sprite is flown around in an ohmi crate. She once fluttered through the vineyard herself, but now her wings are frail with age.

The sprites are a feather weight when they stand on my palms and shoulders, cheering for tonight's racers. Moonlight kisses their emerald-silver arms, coiled in vines. The tiny creatures wear the very plant they tend and swing on and curl up in each night within velvety leaves. The sprites barely rest—not more than four hours of sleep—before their harried and happy routine begins again at dawn. They're fluttering off now, their races finished, the quickest sprites congratulated and doused in ohmi ale.

My brain is reeling. There's so much to take in that I want to shoo away sleep and explore the vineyard on my own. The half of our company remaining here, though, has other ideas for me. Mom and Dad both coddle me, carrying my bedding and fetching me the dewy water the sprites collect from the Great Tree every morning. Regardless of magical changes and new worlds, my parents have stayed the same: overprotective, concerned, and oozing love.

Others haven't remained as constant.

I've noticed the difference in myself and in certain others since being in Jarr. Grandpa, obviously, who seems to be growing more youthful by the day, but also Lady Sophia, whose change is less obvious.

Lady Sophia's songs, her deep-bellied melodies, once the words of famous lyricists and singers, are now her own creations. She opens her mouth and original words slip out. She is still jolly and self-absorbed—plus obsessed with mothering everyone, which she attributes to lonely, misunderstood cruise director Valarie and her terrible demise—but she's becoming an artist, not only a performer.

Lady Sophia sings a lot about love. Love is a hard topic for me right now, on multiple fronts. First, there's Luggie, my sweet and thoughtful Bangol. It's strange to think I've fallen for a stone-headed creature, especially a member of the race that has caused so many problems for Jarr-Wya, the Olearons, and my family. Luggie is a part of the smaller company that heads to the Bangols' northern fortress. He will lead them to the amphitheater, where they'll plant the Steffanus antler. Why he's falling in line with the Lord of Olearon is beyond me. I'm scared for him.

This worry and so many others make me almost forget my other trouble with love, until the reminder smacks me squarely in the face. Mom and Captain Nate. It's time for bed right now, and ugh! Everyone's getting ready, and the two of them step to the side to talk quietly. Do they think I'm mute *and* blind? I'm not tired, thanks to my rest on Grandpa Archie's back as we fled Baluurwa, plus my skin prickles like cactus bristles at the sight of Mom and Nate. Who can sleep when they feel annoyed? Not this girl!

The way Nate says her name, *Tessa,* all cotton candy sweet yet deep as a bottomless ocean, as if it's coming right from his heart—yuck! It makes me break into a cold sweat, even though the ohmi are warming me from the inside. Nate folds his hand around Mom's when he thinks no one's looking. They talk beneath the canopy of the vineyard. They assume I'm asleep.

The ohmi I ate during the races prove to be not only warming, but rest inducing. I'm sleepy all of a sudden. Or, it could be the cancer. My eyelids grow cantankerous at my mission of staying awake to spy on Mom. As I begin to drift off, while the chattering sprites finish telling each other bedtime stories, I can sense that Mom is still awake. Our bond, the connection between our brains—or is it our hearts?—is like a river we can't dam.

I've begun to hear Mom's dreams. Sometimes I fight them. I scream at them in my head, at Mom directly, telling her to be quiet so I can rest. I don't want to know all the things she thinks about, all her lusty feelings, and her worries—ever the worrier that she is. I'm getting to know her more, which is nice, I guess. She's loved on me hard since my diagnosis, but whether knowingly or not, she's also been painstakingly guarded.

Sometimes her dreams lead me toward her upbringing, but that terrain is protected more fiercely in Mom's subconscious than the Bangols' northern fortress, from what the sprites tell me of their maze. The second my consciousness inches closer to her childhood, Mom wakes up. Snap! That fast. She doesn't want me to go there. I don't get it. What's she trying to hide?

Mom drives me crazy. Why won't she talk to me? Really talk. I know a mother can't be candid with her daughter at all times, like girlfriends, and frankly there's a lot I don't want to know, like what she and Captain Nate do when they sneak farther and farther into the vineyard, beyond my listening ears, beyond the giggles of the naughty sprites who are up past their bedtime. Still, I'd like us to be closer.

When I draw our family—Mom and me, Grandpa Archie, and Dad as an Olearon—when I sketch out our family tree in the slippery ink, Mom's excuses are shallow. There's more she refuses to say. I give up on her being forthright with me. I can tell by the way she gazes at me that I'm ten years old in her mind, childish and naive, but that's the furthest thing from the truth.

I'm fifteen now. If we make it home, I'll be heading into grade ten in the fall. I'm not a child. Cancer will do that to a person; I've grown up faster than anyone should.

I can't recall how many days I've survived out here, which is my failure as an adventurer to keep an accurate record. I should have been etching the sunrises on a tree branch or recording the dates on paper, though I forgot the book Nanjee and Luggie gave me in the cell. The Lord said the Maiden showed him what I drew in that book—in his mind after her death, when they were reunited in one body—but those pages burned with her, or drowned when everything blasted into the sea at her explosion.

What point is there in noting the date now? If we succeed, I'll record my days given to me by the cure. If not, and I die, none of it will matter anyway.

Ella

chapter 18

Tessa

"Is she asleep?"

"I think so," Tessa says as she watches Ella through a break in the leaves.

Nate smiles at her, and she blushes. "Are you turning in, Tessa?" he asks.

"Nah, not yet. You?"

"No." Nate gestures past Ella and the other members of their company, with their sealed-shut eyes, chests that rise and fall heavily, and the throaty rumble of impending snores. Tessa leads the way ahead of Nate. They follow a slender path blanketed in glimmering, dewy leaves, some soft and others frail, which rustle quietly beneath their feet. The sprites are asleep as well, wrapped in their curls of flora. The whole vineyard breathes as one.

Nate and Tessa reach the base of the Great Tree, as the sprites call it, where a garden of exposed roots caresses the edge of the vineyard. The roots ripple upward, peeking out of the earth like whitecaps on a turbulent ocean. The tree's trunk—so broad you could lose yourself running around it—is a peculiar mix of blue bark and the pearl of the white woodland. It shifts and shimmers as Tessa and Nate ascend, climbing its low, tired arms under the cover of night.

Tessa finds it difficult to steal a moment to speak with Nate, what with the inquisitive ears of Quillie and Pinne and the knowing looks of Ella and Lady Sophia. Plus, she is conscious of the Olearons stalking around; they are fiercely protective of Ardenal. The Olearons have taken sides, Tessa feels, and disapprove of Nate and his affection for her, which the man refuses to disguise.

Tessa carries guilt with every choice.

Up in the branches of the Great Tree, Tessa and Nate can hear their whispers clearly, the leaves blocking the whoosh of the disgruntled wind, forming a pocket of sleepy warmth.

"You look lovely," Nate says through a grin as he touches Tessa's hair. Earlier, the sprites wove grapevines around her forehead and through her hair in a living crown. Nate lifts a braided strand, tied at the bottom with a thin, coiling root. He takes the tips of her hair and runs it along her neck and jawbone. Nate scoots closer to where Tessa sits, cupped in a dip of the smooth branch, and brushes a kiss across her cheek.

She lets a rush of balmy air fill her lungs before speaking. "I need to ask you something. And if it happened, then I'm relieved I'm not crazy, but it if didn't . . . I'll be a fool for bringing it up."

"What, Tess?"

"Do you remember the night our company camped by the Creek of Secrets? Before we visited Rolace and his web? Before we reached the Bangols' destroyed fortress and arching bridges in the east, and before the Maiden—" Tessa's voice catches in her throat as she relives the shocking sacrifice and the joy of hearing Ella's voice, knowing her daughter was safe.

"Of course, I remember," Nate answers. "I'm furious with myself for not asking Valarie to move over so I could sleep beside you on the ground. If I had, then I would've felt you stir and prevented you from falling into the creek."

"But if I hadn't, I'd never have learned what Rolace desired—the Banji flowers, which he needed to weave his magical web and form our cocoons, to help me find Ella."

"I'm leery of the magic on this island, Tessa—I've got to be honest. I have been since the beginning. Everything here seems two-faced. Like these Olearons. One moment they're swearing to save your daughter, and the next they backtrack. 'We'll save Ella, but only after we crush the Bangols,'" Nate says, impersonating the stiff red beings and their formal manner of speech.

"I know what you mean. A part of me needs to trust them, but the other part . . . Even this plan. Why send Archie and Lillium to distract the Bangols from the rest of the company?"

"I thought that, too. Archie and a sprite? Really? Out on their own?"

Tessa nods and bites her lower lip. "I wanted to argue with the Lord, but I worried he'd order more of us—like Ella, you, me, even Arden—on this death errand. I bet the Lord sent Archie because of that magical glass. From what you said about the Maiden's reaction when she caught Archie reading it, there's more going on than we know. The way the Lord stared at Archie when we made it back to the glass city, when he told Archie that the two of them needed to talk . . . I could sense it was a big deal. And how the Lord transformed in the forest on the way to Baluurwa. Ugh. Now I feel terrible that we sat back and let Archie go off to die!"

"No, Tessa. You were right not to disagree with the Lord. There's a sinister edge to that guy. We can try to protect Archie, but he's an adult. The only people I've tasked myself with keeping safe are you and Ella. Besides, haven't you noticed Archie's hair? Or his never-ending energy? Something's happening to him. My gut tells me we don't need to worry about him."

"Plus, if the Bangols do capture him, maybe Zeno will be

there. He and Archie have a bond, a complicated bond, but still. I bet that creature would venture to save him, especially from Tuggeron."

Nate nods, then asks, "Was that what you wanted to ask me?"

"No." Tessa feels her cheeks flush and she looks away. "This is hard for me, Nate." She avoids his deep brown eyes, rich like the earth twelve feet below them. She gazes at the island. Jarr-Wya sleeps, like the company and the sprites. Small fires are lit on the side of Baluurwa the Doomful, the Steffanus race unafraid to announce their presence after their reproach of the company. The fires flicker and some are extinguished in a trail of smoke that dances into the night sky, twirling in the wind like wafting ribbons.

The Bangols' northern fortress glows warmly as torches reflect off its clay structures and stones. The Bangols do not sleep this night. The sound of industry, of building, hammering, and drumming continues to rise along with steam and smoke by night, as it had by day. The sprites have only alluded to the Bangols' activities—making weapons, the merry beings supposed.

Digging. Mining. The racket floats above the fortress, raising questions in Tessa's mind.

"Tess?"

She surrenders to the inevitable discussion. "All right, I'm just going to spit it out," Tessa says. "And please don't say anything till I'm finished."

Nate nods.

"When we were by the Creek of Secrets," she continues, "I woke up. Everyone was asleep, even you. I went to the water and drank, then heard someone coming up behind me. I turned, startled, and it was you. At least I thought it was you. We talked. Then you kissed me." Tessa bites her lower lip, remembering the rich taste of Nate's mouth, and his smell—earthy, manly, memorable. "It was like your kiss now, but more of me. My lips. My shoulders. My collarbone." Tessa shuts her eyes as she continues to speak. She hopes Nate will not notice her blushing. "We spent time together. I still remember the feel of your skin, your chest, your hands on me. When I opened my eyes"—Tessa turns on the branch to straddle it as she studies Nate's face—"you were gone. I was alone . . . Did any of that really happen?"

Nate sighs deeply, his strong jaw clenched tightly. "I wish I could tell you it was real, Tess." He balls his hands, opens one, and punches his palm. "You see, it's the magic of this place. How can we know what's real and what's illusion? I tell ya, the sooner we get out of here, the better."

Tessa does not hear anything Nate says after he confirms her suspicion. The kiss hadn't happened. Her shoulders scrunch and she turns away, self-conscious and embarrassed. Nate continues to fume at her side.

Tessa hoped what she experienced at the edge of the Creek of Secrets was real, even if it did make her feel guilty knowing that Ardenal—Arden—rested nearby. That was before he released her from their marriage, giving her the freedom she desired, though she was startled to discover that his words didn't satisfy her either. Once released, Tessa wondered if that was really what she wanted.

Agh, she thinks. *When I first saw Arden in Brown Beans Coffee Shop, with his bright blue eyes and deep chestnut hair, I knew I wanted to kiss him. When I was studying for a nursing final and Arden pulled out his Egyptian history textbooks and passionately rattled on about pharaohs and dynasties, beaming and pushing up his chunky glasses in that charming, dorky way of his, that's when I knew I wanted to marry him. I craved that passion and intelligence in my life. I knew he would be a great father, although I've never really known any father . . .*

Tessa thinks back to the creek. The Olearons call it "the

stealer of secrets." She agrees. It called her *Orphan*. She never breathed her secret to anyone, not even Arden, though he understood in his own way. He was too perceptive to believe her lies. A pang of anger rises in her chest. Tessa wishes she could be brave enough to tell the truth to the people she loves.

She aches to be wanted in the way she felt in Nate's embrace at the creek, for it to have been real—that she was indeed coveted and desired. In the midst of her self pity, her skin begins to tingle, and she becomes aware of being watched.

Tessa peers at Nate from the corners of her eyes.

He is still. His hands are unclenched. His jaw is loose. His gaze is blurred by tears. "What else, Tessa? I can see, I can feel you have more to say."

"No. I'm sorry, Nate. I can't."

She finds herself crying, and Nate reaches out to brush away her tears. As he does, his own cheeks are streaked in damp paths that reflect the bewitching moonlight. Tessa laughs through her sadness and cups Nate's face. She shifts, and they both straddle the branch, knee to knee. Nate rests his hands on her thighs and pauses there before lifting her legs so they cross over his. Their breath hangs in the shrinking distance between them.

"You can trust me, Tessa. Whatever it is, I don't care."

Nate runs his fingers up her arms, and they find their way into the tangles of her hair, beneath the braids and crown of vines. Tessa leans into him, their hearts beating as if drawn together through their ribs and skin and clothing. Nate's lips are warm and smooth. She lets them explore her mouth, and she unbuttons his shirt so his chest is bare. They tap teeth and laugh. Inches away from his face, she reads his eyes and the faint wrinkles he wears from years of smiling. Tessa traces these lines, his cheekbones, and the curve of his strong chin.

Repeating what she said to the vision of Nate at the edge of the Creek of Secrets, Tessa whispers, "I'm scared to want you as much as I do."

"Don't be. I'm not a perfect man, obviously. Just look at Valarie. I'm sorry for my mistakes, and sorry you've become a guarded woman. But I see a tenderness in you, behind your walls. If only you'd let me in, allow me to know you. I'm also terrified. I'm scared by how much I want you, too, Tessa Wellsley."

She flinches at the sound of her last name—of Arden's last name, which she took on the day of their small wedding ceremony. That day, two chairs remained unoccupied at the reception, meant for her parents. Arden never demanded to know what she refused to tell him, and eventually he stopped asking. *Did that mean he didn't care?* In contrast, Nate, his body pressed against hers, neither begs to know nor ignores her pain.

I am guarded. I'm a maze of walls, like those that protect the Bangols' northern fortress. Why do I want to tell this man who I am? An abandoned child who never knew her parents. A lonely girl, so neglected in a foster family overrun with unruly children that she faded into the wallpaper, trapped in silence behind its pattern. An adult determined to appear normal, from a normal family with a normal upbringing. Would it matter if anyone knew? Tessa thinks irritably as she slowly realizes how the seed of fear was planted.

It came from the idea that if people knew where she came from—nowhere—they would start to wonder why: why her parents did not want her; why her foster family ignored her; why she struggled to make friends; why she preferred to be solitary. They would look for her faults, and sure enough, they would find them—one thing or another. Then they would leave. Just like everyone else before them. *Easy to leave.* That phrase planted itself into Tessa's mind at the heartbreak. *Easy to leave.*

As if reading her mind, Nate whispers, "If you let me, Tess, I'll never leave you."

Fresh tears stream through Tessa's gaze, falling quickly, mixing in this new kiss. She slips into Nate's arms and rests her head on his chest. She listens to his heart—one hundred beats she loosely counts. His scent fills her lungs. She feels sleepy suddenly and pulls away.

"I'll tell you . . . everything—but not tonight," she says, yawning.

"We have time," Nate responds. "I'll make sure of it. We'll find our way home, then there'll be a lifetime." He kisses her forehead before they climb down the branches. The curled leaves in the vineyard hum with the sleeping sprites. Down a gentle grassy slope, the company rest in a line between two rows of lush ohmi.

On the path from the tree, Tessa looks back to make sure Nate is still there, that he has not disappeared, as he had by the creek. His grin is playful, and they twist their fingers together tightly, tenderly.

When she returns her gaze to the slumbering company, two blue eyes meet hers. Tessa freezes mid-step.

Ella.

Her fragile head rests on the fine, sprite-woven pillow of vines and green feathers. Ella's body is stiff. Her lips are pursed. Tessa drops Nate's hand, and she rushes to her daughter.

"Ell, you startled me. Did we wake you? Are you all right?" she asks.

Ella remains still and releases a baby bird in response. Not even through their telepathic bond does Ella utter a word. She rolls her frail body over, turning her back to Tessa and Nate.

"Tessa." The deep, tentative voice is Ardenal's. "Can I borrow you for a second?" His black eyes turn to Nate, who nods and steps aside to find his place amongst the row of slumbering bodies.

Ardenal leads Tessa to the crest of the vineyard, which rises on a lazy hill overlooking the sea. He brushes aside a gathering of wayward leaves, and they twirl in the air. Tessa slips down on the dewy grass and shivers, a sudden cold slipping over her.

The moon reflects onto the sea in shattered pieces of light that dance on the turbulent water as the storm rakes the sea. Ardenal graciously released her from their marriage in the white woodland. Tessa wonders what more he has to say. She laces her fingers, nervous that he will notice the confused energy that surges through her—giddy from Nate's kisses, guilty about her own happiness when her daughter is dying and Jarr is poisoned by the Star, and heartsick over her and Arden's lost love.

"Tessa," Ardenal begins.

There is so much Tessa wishes to say to the man looking back at her. His eyes may be black, but they are still Arden's eyes, sheepish and charming. A lump rises in her throat from all the words that want to spill out of her. *I'm sorry . . . I wish . . . if only . . . I love you.*

Ardenal clears his throat. "I do not want this to hurt you, Tess, I really do not, but I need you to think about what I am going to say."

Tessa nods, swallowing down the desires that have not fully formed on her tongue.

"It breaks my heart to see you with Nate. I know I said I release you, but that doesn't mean I do not love you. You will always have my heart."

"Arden—"

"I see the same feelings on Ella's face. She notices your secret smiles and the way you and Nate hang off each other." Ardenal looks away.

Tessa strains to see him, but he slouches, his hunched shoulders guarding his countenance as he stares at the watching moon. He wipes his eyes with the backs of his ruddy hands.

"What I want you to think about . . . What if Ella stays here with me? She is obviously taken with Luggie. I have missed out on so much father-daughter time, and I know that is my fault, but I want to make it up to Ell, however I can."

It takes a few long breaths for Tessa to let Ardenal's idea take shape in her mind. Is this his way of hurting her since she had been so careless in flirting with Nate? She expected that cancer would tear their family apart, not that they would crumble while Ella's heart continues to beat. How could she return to their house, their family home, without Ella and Arden? Would she be strong enough to start a new life with Nate aboard one ship or another? Who would she be?

Tessa defined herself for years as Arden's wife, Archie's daughter-in-law, Ella's mother—then, the mother of a cancer kid, and, finally, a single parent. The idea of reinventing herself brings up old wounds and a haunting loneliness she can never seem to be rid of. Kissing Nate was freeing and fun, but is it enough? Now, she comes alive with him, and a part of her believes his love could heal her.

Still, another love nags at Tessa like something forgotten that teeters on the edge of consciousness. A two-year-long, grudging love that held Tessa hostage in the shell of her life, wondering at everything: her self-worth, her identity, and her doubts about whether anyone would ever want her and choose to stay.

"Think about it. That is all," Ardenal finishes. "I really do want what is best for our family, and that includes your happiness." He leans over and rests his hot red lips on Tessa's cheek. He does not pull away immediately, and she does not want him to. Something else rises in her chest, but this time it is not words but the ache before sobbing. More reckless tears burst from her.

Tessa is uncomfortable with her emotions, accustomed to burying them six feet underground.

Ardenal pulls away, and she catches his hand. Tessa pulls him close, wrapping her arms around his neck, resting against his shoulder. As the warmth of his kiss fades from her cheeks, she weeps out all the pain and regret, the guilt and the words left unspoken, dampening their embrace.

When the hug is over, when the well of tears has run its course, Ardenal pulls away. His black eyes search hers. He cups Tessa's face in his hands, then stands and walks back into the sleeping vineyard.

chapter 19

Ella

There's Mom. She stands on a rock at the top of a frantic waterfall. I crawl along the water's edge, out of the curl of sleep. There's no sprite-woven blanket covering me and no pillow of feathers beneath my head. Am I dreaming? I pinch myself like I've seen people do in the movies, but nothing changes. The rushing water strays into my face and dampens my shirt. My knees buckle and I slip on the wet rocks, but I catch myself and crawl farther. I make it to the edge of the waterfall.

When I look down, there's no end. The fall continues for eternity in a seamless fold of water, air, and distance with no crash of spray at the bottom, if there is a bottom. Whoa, vertigo!

I blink. Is this Jarr-Wya? This place doesn't make sense. Our surroundings look normal but also strange, as if filtered through heat waves, a prism, or Dad's filthy, fingerprinted glasses back home.

I scream to Mom, but she can't hear me through the wailing rapids that carry my voice over the edge.

My voice!

Not the green birds.

Not the screech of brokenness at the hand of greedy cancer.

My voice! I almost forgot what I sound like.

I keep talking—loud and strong and as deep as this waterfall—until my throat cracks and it's all I can do to laugh.

Mom is barefoot and drenched. Her hair is pulled up in a messy bun. She's dressed in jeans and a white tank top, which are clean, something we haven't been in a long time. I'm accustomed to Mom in her cotton dress and pale pink jacket that she chose for Lady Sophia's concert on the *Atlantic Odyssey*. This new outfit is more practical. Where did she get it?

Mom's quivering. She's looking down, too, like me, searching for the waterfall's end. Why is she on that rock? She must know it's slippery and dangerous. Now I feel like the nagging parent!

Mom's toes inch forward.

What's she doing?

She screams.

Then jumps.

"No, Mom!" I rush to the edge and leap after her.

It's hard to breathe. Rocks churn the plummeting water, trapping air bubbles. I reach for them, but they pop at my touch. This time, I stretch gently and catch one between my hands. I pull it to my lips and suck. The bubble shrinks.

I'm descending, but the sensation is closer to floating than falling.

All I see is silvery-white water. Tipping my body, I raise my feet up and angle my head down, as best as I can estimate direction. My arms come together and I squish my fingers into a point. My body slices the water and I descend more quickly. I see a blur of gold and blue beneath me. It's Mom, her hair and her jeans. I continue to drop, then fan my fingers, spread my arms and legs wide, and arch my back. My speed decreases and I whoosh past Mom, just in time to catch her by the wrist. She recognizes me. We hold hands, bellies down, and continue to ride the fall.

Mom's coughing. Tenderly, I pluck an air bubble from the flow and hand it to her. She kisses it, and the bubble dwindles. I catch another and drink the air. We continue this rhythm—I pass her a bubble, she breathes, I catch one for myself, I breathe—while staring at each other. Her green eyes are held fast by mine.

"Where are we, Mom?"

"I don't know, Ella. I was dreaming. Then here you are."

"Are you still dreaming?"

"I think so."

"How did you get onto the rock at the top of the waterfall, in the middle of the river?"

"Choice, Ell. I chose to be there. To be alone. I don't want to be hurt again. I don't want to be left."

"How could anyone leave you if you're alone?"

"Exactly."

"Okay, I guess I'll go with this. Why did you jump?"

"Another choice. I hope there's more for me, Ell. I don't know who I am or where I came from, but maybe there's more than my loneliness, my emptiness."

"At the bottom of the fall is more?"

"I hope so."

Mom punctures her bubble and looks at me desperately. I pass her one meant for me and rest it on her free palm. She sucks in air, and a relieved expression paints her face. Water surrounds us, raining down, with no crescendo visible at the top or bottom. Everything's a silver splash and radiating bands of light, but beyond that, silence.

"If this is a dream, Mom, wake up. I doubt there's another way out."

"I'm not ready."

"Okay. Take as much time as you need." I roll over onto my side, then change my mind. "What, Mom? Not ready for what?"

"I'm scared."

"Why?"

"Because, Ella . . . because I'm an orphan."

I don't know how to respond and so I don't, not right away at least. I can't tell if it's droplets from the falls or tears on her cheeks. I try to get the truth from Mom, who feels more delicate here, in her dreams, than she ever does when awake. "You're an orphan in the dream or in real life?"

"In every life."

"Literally or figuratively?"

"Literally, of course, Ella. How can someone be a figurative orphan?"

"I don't know. Every time we talk you ask for clarity by saying, 'Literally or figuratively?' I'm trying here!"

"Literally. I have no idea who my parents are. At least one was blond, I suppose. One had green eyes like mine. They placed me in an unmonitored pass-through window at the hospital. Left me under the cover of darkness and anonymity, like they were returning an undercooked meal at a fast-food drive-through. That's the story my fourth pair of foster parents told me, but only when I was naughty. They'd say, 'Now we understand why your parents returned you to Seattle Hospital, and don't tempt us to do the same.'"

"I'm sorry, Mom."

"My foster parents took me there, to that same hospital, to get my scoliosis checked after the surgery I had as a baby. I was so young, but I remembered that place. The scars were reminders, too. They were grotesque, raised and red, like the scars on your neck, Ell.

"I remember the fear of entering the hospital again," Mom continues as she swishes her hands through the water. "I screamed and screamed till my foster parents refused to return for the physical therapy treatments. My time in that hospital is my earliest memory, and my foster parents used my fear to keep me quiet. When I was old enough, I left them. I was better off alone."

"Mom, I'm sorry . . ."

"You shouldn't know these things. I'm glad this is just a dream. At least in here I have someone to talk to. Maybe you're the possibility of more I felt at the top."

I smile weakly and scoot closer to Mom. I wrap my arms around her. Even if this is a dream, I want it to be a happy one. I kiss her cheek. "I love you, Mom," I say. She squeezes me tightly.

A rumbling causes us to pull back from each other and turn upright in the water, though it takes a moment for us to find which way is up.

"What was that?"

"How should I know, Ell?"

"Well, this is your dream."

"I have no idea."

Another rumble, and Mom and I collide with the bottom we didn't see coming. It's not a pool of water or hard rocks. Instead, we land on a patch of feathery grass. When we look around, it's clear we're on a tiny island surrounded by calm waves that connect seamlessly to the falling water on every side.

"Hold on!" Mom warns.

"What's happening?"

The land grows larger, rounder, and rises slowly; then, a smaller island pokes out from the water an arm's length away. As we rise, the puny landmass connects to ours. We cling helplessly to the feathery grass. The small island rises fully and turns. It reveals itself to be a creature that points at Mom and me with a short fat beak and studies us with yellow-green eyes.

"Hello," the creature says. I immediately recognize it as a

green bird, a giant one, the same kind that fly out of my mouth since our run-in with Tanius.

"Hello, are you a friend?" Mom asks the green bird.

"Of course, my dear! Are you?"

"Of course," Mom repeats. "I'm Tessa. This is my daughter Ella."

"Mom! Don't tell it my name."

"It's fine, Ell. She's a friend."

"Of course she would say that!"

"My name is Finnah."

"Nice to meet you Finnah." Mom smiles. "Can you take us where we need to go?"

"Where is that, friends?"

"I don't know."

"Oh, I know that place!" Finnah squeals and flaps her wings against the water so they splash waves outward. Finnah adds, "Better hold on. Away we go!"

As the dislocated water flows back with a slap to the center of the rippling expanse, Finnah's body lifts and she bursts upward. Mom and I cling to her feathers. We crawl our way up against the rushing air and splattering water that catches and sprays off Finnah's wing tips. We reach her neck and hook our arms over each of her wings.

"Faster," Mom calls. Her smile is wild, and the bird also appears to be grinning. Finnah rises higher and the light grows brighter and the splashing more haphazard. I bury my face in the green bird's feathers, blinking away the water that pools there from the falls. My muscles scream out, aching from being clenched, but I know if I relax I'll fall back down into the endless falls.

"Faster, faster, Finnah!" Mom sings.

We fly so quickly and so high that we're enveloped in white

light like a shooting star. Mom smiles widely, and I can see all her teeth. She howls with joy. Her messy bun unravels and her long golden mane billows behind her. She curls up to sit on Finnah's wing and lifts her arms, rolling them through the air like I used to when Mom drove me to the hospital, my hand out the window, the breeze pushing it up, then down as I tipped my fingers.

chapter 20

Tessa

Tessa wiggles her toes. They itch and tickle at the same time. She kicks at the sprite-woven blanket she had huddled under in the night, but the vine-like weave, which should be light and springy, is lazy and suffocating. Tessa kicks harder. There is a *sploosh* and her eyes pop open. *Wet.* That one thought breaks through her dream, leaving it forgotten forever in her subconscious, and she swivels where she lies on a bed of leaves. Crawling to a sitting position, Tessa looks around at the sleeping company with terror and incomprehension. Water surrounds them all. It rises four inches from the earth.

Tessa shoves Nate hard, jerking him awake from his rhythmic snoring. His eyes strain at the pink-grey morning; the sun is distinctly absent. He scans the area as if he forgot where he had fallen asleep. He jumps to his feet.

Tessa also leaps out of the water and runs past still-slumbering Olearon warriors to the far edge of the company, where Ella chose to rest, away from her mother. When Tessa's knees splash down beside Ella, the teenager is spattered. She wakes with an inaudible cry and releases three newborn green birds. A look of confusion, then horror and worry, flashes across her face. She turns to find Luggie, then stops. Tessa can read relief in Ella's expression as her sleepy mind remembers that Luggie is elsewhere, though that does not mean he is safe.

The water is warm, so the company did not yet detected its arrival. It continues to creep in from the ocean at the northwestern corner of Jarr-Wya. Nate, Tessa, and Ella rush from one sleeping body to the next, shaking awake Olearons and Lady Sophia. One warrior, who had rested on his stomach, does not rouse when Ella rocks him back and forth. She releases a flock of green birds, which capture the attention of Tessa and Ardenal, who come running to hoist the warrior from the rising flood.

It is Nameris.

Nameris, the studious Olearon who can plot any location on Jarr-Wya as if he is a map himself—the lanky one, who battles using his mind over his brawn—the one who can sense the truth of the spoken word, his gift from Rolace.

Nameris's red face is swollen and creased like a person's fingertips after they have sat too long in the bath. Ardenal shakes him. "Wake up, my friend!" But the warrior's head flops back. His chest does not swell with air. "Help me," Ardenal pleads to Tessa, and she grabs Nameris's feet. The two carry the limp warrior a few feet through the water to where an ohmi crate sits, only its top visible in the swirling current.

Ardenal blows his air and fire into Nameris's mouth, through his pale blue lips. He pounds the warrior's chest, and once more fills Nameris's lungs. The warrior is waterlogged and unresponsive.

Tessa guides Ella away, but her daughter leans out of her embrace. Ella chooses to watch. Tessa bites her lip. As much as she wishes to protect her child from death, Ella is already too familiar with it: Grandma Suzie. The passengers of Constellations Cruise Line. Valarie, the cruise director on the *Atlantic Odyssey*. Their first guard, Olen. The Maiden of Olearon . . .

Lady Sophia mumbles, "Don't look, Ella. It's so sad. So terribly sad." The singer shoos Ella along, toward the sprawling Great Tree. Ella shakes her head, meeting Lady Sophia's blotchy eyes. Ella will not be shooed, and Tessa takes pride in her daughter's resolve.

Are you sure you want to watch? Tessa asks Ella through her mind, a conversation for them alone.

How can I turn away? Ella responds. Her mouth does not open, but she turns to look up at Tessa. *Is that what people will do when I die? Will they look away, hide their eyes from how "terribly sad" I am?*

Oh Ell, Tessa thinks. She pulls Ella closer and keeps her arm around her. *We all want to protect you from this heartbreak.*

Even if I turn away, my heart will still break for Nameris. Ella takes a step closer to the unmoving Olearon, his back propped on the ohmi crate, her father continuing to pound the chest of his fellow warrior. *He deserves that I watch, that I suffer my own pain at his loss. Even when I can't do anything else, I can do this.*

Tessa does not follow, giving Ella space. Instead, she inhales the moment, its tragedy and its beauty, both entangled in the bravery she sees so plainly on her daughter's face.

A deep, rumbling, choking gurgle slips between Nameris's blue lips, then a blast of green-stained water. Lady Sophia shrieks. Ella stumbles back into Tessa's arms. Ardenal wipes his face clean of the expelled liquid and lifts Nameris by the shoulders. The warrior's legs look to Tessa like red elastic bands, too rubbery for him to stand on.

When Nameris focuses his eyes and gains his balance, Azkar relights his younger sibling's flame. The grotesque black scar on the elder brother's face twitches upward as he smiles with relief. Tessa has never seen Azkar smile. It makes her brighten and sigh, exhaling the moment.

As worry morphs to reprieve, the small company become aware of the seawater accelerating its rush into the vineyard. The flowing liquid is dark in the absence of the sun. It covers the feet and ankles of the Olearons and up to the calves of the humans.

Tessa counts the half company, eight in all: Azkar, Nameris, Junin, Ardenal, Lady Sophia, Nate, Ella, and herself. She yells to Junin, "We're all here!"

"We must make for the Great Tree," Kameelo hollers, the sound of the water a roar and crack as the wooden rows of the vineyard bow under the pressure.

"Azkar, take Nameris to the tree," says Junin. "He is weak and cannot help. And the humans, too—Tessa, Ella, and Lady Sophia—but Ardenal and Nate, please stay."

Nate squeezes Tessa's hand quickly before turning to the female Olearon. "What can I do?"

"The sprites. We must wake them!" she replies.

Nate turns to Tessa, who waves him on toward the vineyard. She watches as he sprints behind Junin, his long strides dwarfed in comparison. Ardenal—making sure Ella is in Tessa's care—also races back to the vineyard through swirling water that now dampens Tessa's knees.

Tessa turns to the company. "Hurry," she yells as her feet slosh through the muddy water. She plants her hands on Lady Sophia's bottom and pushes the woman upward, onto a low arm of the Great Tree. Kameelo reaches down from his perch, where he hangs by his legs from a stable branch, to hoist the singer higher. Nameris, still looking the shade of an unripe red apple, is dragged up by Azkar.

Ella scurries from one branch to another, finally resting with her back against the trunk. Her chest rises and falls with the pain Tessa observes etched across her pale face. "All right, Ell?" she asks. Ella keeps her lips pressed firmly shut and nods.

The water rams the tree with force, releasing a handful of leaves with each crash.

The flood is drowning the vineyard, submerging low-hanging vines and leaves. Blue and yellow ohmi float on the water's surface. Junin and Ardenal have the dark liquid up to their thighs, and they leap to make headway. Nate joins them, though he must wade. The three shake the vines and holler, "Wake up! Flood!" Soon many faintly glowing leaves brighten and tremble.

The leaves unfurl like sun-kissed flowers, but there is no sun and no graceful morning. The tiny faces of the sprites are pinched with shock and confusion. Dry sprites flutter furiously like scattered shards of rainbow, making for the Great Tree. They zip to the shoulders of the company or hide behind wind-whipped leaves. From there, their wispy voices call out to their families below. Young sprites wail. Three spritelings hide, whimpering, in the curls of Tessa's hair, clinging to her damp braids.

Other sprites tucked in the foliage of the lower vines discover that their wings are damp and heavy. Some, like Quillie, jump from their leaf, only to find themselves weighed down. Ardenal scoops Quillie from the curve of a wave and places the sprite on his shoulder. Junin and Nate, too, pluck others from the water, where they swoon helplessly, melded to the dark surface.

"Nate!" Tessa yells from her branch, her voice straining to reach him. "Come back to the tree!" He turns at the sound of her voice. His shoulders and head are covered in drenched sprites, their wings rendered useless and the sparkle of their constellations dimmed. They cling to his earlobes and short blond hair. The sprites tuck themselves into the collar of his shirt and make a chain by holding hands around his muscular neck. Nate turns back to the vineyard one last time, taking stock.

He, Junin, and Ardenal are only halfway through the vineyard. Many leaves remain rolled and aglow, hinting of the dreamers they contain. The Olearons and humans holler into the distance, down the rows of vines and playfully painted wooden structures. They plead with the sleeping beings, but many do not wake before the flood surges.

Tessa continues to scream. Her voice is swallowed up by the violent rustle of leaves, the lashing wind, the water's cymbals crashing, and the yells of all—in the Great Tree and on land. They plead with the dreamers in a nightmarish chorus, but they are not loud enough.

Water cuts Nate mid-chest. He struggles to wade through the mess of soupy leaves, floating blue wood, and currents of mud. Tessa notices someone buoyed on the water near him. "There, Nate!" She yells and points. "It's Queen Jeo!" The sprites wail and flutter, animating the Great Tree as their wings stir the leaves and quiver the branches.

Nate cups his water-wrinkled hand around the queen. She murmurs quietly, though nonsensically. "Faster, Nate!" Tessa pleads. She winds her way down the tree as low as possible, dropping from her lookout on a high branch to one that skims the surface of the rising flood. "Faster," she begs.

Nate's eyes hold hers as he wades, though his body is barely visible beneath the sprites cloaking his skin and clothing, holding on with the protruding bristles that line their thin grasshopper-like tibias. Nate's blue eyes are surrounded by white, like the sea around the tree threatening to choke it out. He cradles Queen Jeo in one hand as he is forced to tip his head back, his lips puckered just above the swell of water.

Junin finds Nate's wrist and pulls him forward. Her long legs and high steps make quick strides to the base of the tree. Ardenal arrives behind them. The Olearons, too, shimmer with sprites clinging to their ears and hanging from their lips. Once close enough, Junin and Ardenal coax the sprites from their limbs into the waiting arms of Tessa and Azkar.

Junin dips beneath the water, and at first only bubbles

emerge, until Nate rises swiftly, Junin encircling his waist. She tosses him onto a branch. The sprites who had clung to his hair lose their grip and tumble onto Tessa, pulling at her gold locks, and she yelps in pain. The young sprites flutter nervously, reuniting with the saved and fretting over those entombed in their leaves beneath the flood.

Briefly, Tessa and Nate are blinded to everything beyond each other and the frantic flutter of wings and dull prism of light. They cannot see beyond the vibrant mob. They cannot hear anything but the patter of wings and smacking of lips. Tessa and Nate cling to each other as they balance on the branch. The pale daylight seeps through tangerine, lemon, lavender, and baby-blue wings. The sprites' skin is alive with emerald shimmers, and their hair glows russet beneath steadfast droplets of sea and sky.

The sprites' trembling red lips kiss cheeks and eyelids and tiny water-creased hands and feet. Nate and Tessa pull each other close as the nervous babble of fear, relief, and grief mounts around them in one great trembling cloud. Nate find's Tessa's mouth. Their lips are cold, their teeth chattering, but their hearts beat loudly enough to send warmth from one to the other and back again.

The two entwined humans do not realize when the wings pattering around them have quieted and the intensity of color has faded into the grey morning.

Ella pulls at her mother, and Tessa looks away from Nate. *Oh no, what have I done—and for all to see?* she thinks. Ella is obviously annoyed but also worried.

Queen Jeo—who was passed from Nate to Junin, to Azkar, and back to Junin again—quivers in her cold, damp gown of awakin wings and green feathers. The gown, which had been full and lush, is now spindly and shrunken, like the fur of a drenched cat. When the company first arrived and was welcomed in the Fairy Vineyard, Queen Jeo had appeared plump, a miniature version of Lady Sophia. The two women enjoyed each other's company from the instant they shook hands, the queen's dainty one inside Lady Sophia's broad grip. Now, however, Queen Jeo is frail, spent like an empty change purse.

"What did you say, Your Majesty?" asks Lady Sophia, concern rattling her otherwise smooth voice.

"I can't understand," says Nate.

Quillie, struggling to fly with his damp wings, drops to the queen's side. "Let me listen," he tells the company. He puts his ear to Queen Jeo's trembling lips.

"She's repeating something," Lady Sophia says. "See, she's starting again."

Junin sighs. "Her heartbeat is weak, it is failing . . ."

Quillie leans back. "Queen Jeo wishes all sprites to know that she is proud to have loved each and every one of you. She feels she has witnessed her last sunset and enjoyed her final race through our lovely home. She does not know what home we will have left after the storm of the Star demolishes all we hold dear"—Quillie chokes on his words—"and she wishes to leave us with a gift."

Quillie, with all tenderness and reverence, slips from Queen Jeo's clenched white fingers a tiny sparkling ohmi. He holds it up for all to see before slipping it within the pouch built into his drenched royal attendant uniform.

Quillie's twin sister Pinne flutters beside him. "The Life Ohmi," she whispers, just loud enough for the company to hear.

Queen Jeo wheezes one final time before her head tips back, her neck curving like the swan she wears in her hair. Her eyes drift shut.

Tears blossom on Quillie's emerald lashes. He folds an arm around his twin. Junin straightens her back. When the Olearon speaks, her tone is reverent. "Queen Jeo ventured into the vineyard to retrieve the ohmi that would ensure that you surviving sprites are not the last. Her sacrifice will outlive her through you."

"Our queen is gone." Pinne weeps. "Who will lead us?"

"For now"—Junin cradles the dead queen sprite in one hand and places her second over the small still body, holding Jeo like a pearl in an oyster shell—"follow Quillie, who will care for you with great devotion. Appoint a new queen once the fate of Jarr-Wya has been determined."

The solemn moment is cut short when Lady Sophia shrieks, "Oh, good heavens!" The plump woman clutches a thin branch between her round fingers. She wobbles in her shoes, still impractical even with the heels sliced off. "The flood! Higher, everyone! Higher!"

Tessa strains to see what Lady Sophia has witnessed beyond the drowned vineyard and the northwestern coast. "Wait, where's the coast?" she asks everyone and no one. Ella climbs to Tessa and takes hold of her mother by the elbow. Her eyes are pleading.

What, Ell? I don't understand what's happening. I can't see—

"Leave her, Ella." The voice belongs to Ardenal. "Your mom is a grown-up."

He scowls at Nate and Tessa, who still stand entwined on their branch. The sudden guilt feels as if it will anchor Tessa beneath the sea. The Olearon, frustrated, leaps down to Ella's branch and gathers their daughter's petite body into his strong embrace. Ella fights her father at first, thrashing and stretching to Tessa. In protest, she even opens her mouth—from which two green birds emerge and fly happily away, only to return from the storm to the safety of the Great Tree. After all her effort, Ella's energy wanes.

Still clutching Jeo's body, Junin leaps higher. Azkar and Nameris are close behind her. Nameris drops a hand to Lady

Sophia as he passes, pulling her up as well. Gratitude paints the singer's cheeks strawberry-red.

Ardenal loops Ella's arms around his neck, careful of his flame. He jumps from branch to branch, grabbing tree limbs as he ascends the Great Tree like a broken ladder. He finally slows when their weight bows the branch beneath their feet. Shuffling close to the trunk, he ensures Ella is safe, though her eyes are not on him.

Mom, get up here! What are you waiting for?

I am. We're climbing now, Ell. Not as fast as your dad, but we're moving. What do you see from up there?

The water, it's rising fast!

Really? From here it looks like it's receding. See that branch Nate and I were on a second ago? The bottom of it has cleared the water.

It's getting sucked out to sea. Back into the wave.

Wave?

Yeah, wave, Mom. What did you think Lady Sophia was moaning about? Find a safe spot. Tell Nate to hold you against the tree.

I know you don't like Nate, but really, Ell. Do you have to say his name like that?

Junin's voice interrupts all conversations. "We have mere breaths, everyone. The water will hit us hard. Olearons, bind yourselves to the tree by your belts. Lady Sophia, tie the skirt of your gown to that branch. Sprites, fly high and carry your family too damp to do so on their own. Hold to our company with all your strength. Everyone, do what you must to survive."

Junin ignites her hands and bows her head. Within her fire, Jeo's body turns to brittle ash, which Junin regards respectfully, reverently, before blowing what is left of the fairy queen into the breeze. "We will mourn and remember when the time is right." She places one palm to her heart, leaving a white handprint on her blue warrior jumpsuit.

Junin pounces from branch to branch, catlike, helping the fearful sprites and the stoic Olearons and the trembling humans. Ardenal waves away her assistance. Already he has looped his belt around Ella's body and the shimmering blue trunk. He slips his arms within the belt and around Ella, his body shielding his daughter. He presses his fingertips to the wood and burns small holes where he anchors his hands, bracing for the impact.

Your father has always been your hero, even after he left us.

He left to help find a cure for my cancer.

But did he? Did he help? He was here—for two years—while I was at home, taking care of you every day.

We all make our own choices, Mom.

You're so quick to forgive.

Life's too short not to.

I only wish you'd look at me like you look at your dad, even once. Like I'm the hero.

Whatever, Mom. You could have been the one to wrap your arms around me.

I want to, Ella. All I want to do is protect you.

Really, Mom? And whose hand are you holding, hmm? You're so selfish.

I'm selfish? Really? You want to go there? Right now?

You think I'm selfish? Just because I'm sick? I'm sorry you've given up so much to take care of me. Very heroic, Mom. You should've just let me die.

That hurts, Ella Wellsley.

Ella dips her head beneath Ardenal's arm, straining to peer between the branches, down toward the tumultuous water. Tessa sees the blue eyes gazing down at her apologetically. Tessa smiles, as much as she can with the regret that plunges her heart deeper into despair. Ella smiles weakly in return.

It's okay, Ell, I understand. I'm sorry—for everything . . .

Mom, I—

"Enough," Tessa hears Ardenal say to Ella. "Don't waste

your mental energy with talking. Look!" He gestures, his long arm and finger a red arrow pointing at the impending danger.

Still the Great Tree's foliage blocks Tessa's view. She slips on a branch and Nate catches her by the waist. His hands are tender and guiding. They climb faster, their hands scratching, catching on bark and filling with blue slivers. Nate freezes. "Tessa." He speaks as if the breath has been blasted out of his lungs. He does not need to point. Tessa can now see through the leaves and bodies and Queen Jeo's ashes that hang in the breeze.

The wave.

Beyond the Fairy Vineyard, where the northwestern lip of Jarr-Wya once butted up against the Sea of Selfdom, no coast remains. Rocks that lined the shore have been carried away. Boulders that once rested great distances from the vineyard now peek a sliver above the current, are driven inland, and will soon crush the wooden structures holding the vines in tidy rows.

Tessa chokes on her breath at the sight of the wave. The smooth wall of water inches forward, growing in height. Its azure hue is magnificent in contrast to the pallor of the new day. The pale light only suggests at the creatures that swim in the shadows.

"What are those things?" Tessa manages to say.

Junin answers from the next branch, where her belt is looped around the trunk. She tests her weight to ensure its hold. "They are shellarks. They live in the deep. They don't see the sun unless they are called forth in battle to defend their part of Jarr-Wya. This is my first time beholding them, except in their shattered form as sand on the southern shore, in their wicked incarnation as the Millia sands."

"Are they coming to fight?" Nate asks. "Should we be ready?" He shimmies in Tessa's embrace to retrieve the knife from inside the flap of his boot. He flips open the blade and clenches it between his teeth. He secures his grip on the tree and Tessa once more. She winces.

"If the Star is not our enemy," Junin says, doubtful, "I don't know who is for us or against us. Jarr-Wya is dying. The weather has grown wicked, as you can see. All inhabitants on the island are in danger—from the elements and each other. It is clear: we must be ready for anything."

Junin surveys the company, ensuring every Olearon, human, and sprite is secure and ready. She hollers to her fellow warriors in their language and they nod in reply.

Lady Sophia pipes up, "Will we survive this, Junin?"

"Nothing in life is certain. Only uncertainty."

"That's not very comforting," grumbles Lady Sophia. "May I sing to calm my nerves?"

"Please," Tessa answers instead. Her eyes are closed, her jaw locked.

Through the water, huge shelled creatures can be seen—the shellarks. They carry a circular shell, milky and rose-kissed, that curls innocently like toddlers' hair. Some spiraling shells are tight and compact, while others form loose asymmetrical twists, yet are always firm and menacing. From the mouths of these shells emerge pointed grey heads with emotionless round eyes. Snapping jaws expose jagged fangs that pierce the water and shine through the churning current.

Tessa cannot help but gasp. Also from within the shells sprout strong, stout legs. The creatures' feet fan wide. Between their toes, where sharp talons emerge, grows thick webbing that allows them to slip through the water smoothly, despite their bulbous containers. As the wave brings the shellarks closer, Tessa appreciates the shell details; the brilliant orange with freckles of brown and pearl in twisting patterns. The leader shellark watches the company in the Great Tree as the wave moves steadily closer.

"Warriors, now!" Junin orders.

The Olearons form fireballs between their palms. They hurtle the blazing spheres at the shellarks nearing the edge of the wave. The sea creatures dart backward suspiciously, looking to each other and swimming in jagged patterns.

Lady Sophia pauses her melody to remark, "Not much good that'll do."

"You are right, human," Azkar answers. "This is a show only, a display of our power, our fearlessness, before our flames are squelched and we are forced to fight with glass daggers. Do you have yours at the ready?"

"Yep." Lady Sophia parts her enormous breasts and carefully slides out a piercing blade of glass, its handle wrapped with burnt-ocher leather and sheathed in a similar fold of animal hide. She cradles the dagger in one hand and shouts profanities at the snapping mouths and paddling feet of the shellarks.

"I think the fireballs did the trick," Nate says—but too soon. "They're coming back, hungrier than ever!"

"Yes, the shellarks return, but we hope with trepidation in their pebble-sized brains," Junin answers. "A little fear can determine the winner and loser of battle."

Azkar's deep growl startles everyone. "The shellarks are not alone."

"They departed at our demonstration of strength—not from fear, but for reinforcements." Nameris points, his words trailing off.

Tessa can see something new swimming dangerously around the shellarks.

"Drowned wyverns!" Azkar curses and spits.

"Are they dead?" Nate asks.

"No, simply submerged," whispers Azkar. "But they deliver death, of that I am sure."

Junin's lips part. "No!"

chapter 21

Archie

I don't understand . . . is Arden the one who will save us all?"

"Archie, you crashed into an invisible wall—"

"Laken?"

"Who? No, Archie, it's me, Lillium. I'm so sorry. I didn't see the enchantment coming. It is such an obvious thing, now that I think about it. Hiding a stone wall behind the stardust bark of the blue forest, making it reflect the sky and the walls around it. I bet it trips up more intruders than the pit of carakwas!"

"When am I?" Archie shakes his head as if marbles are rolling around in his skull.

Lillium startles. "Uh, you are now, Archie. Only a few minutes have passed."

"Where's the sunset?" Archie shuffles to his feet. His head throbs, and he cups his forehead where shooting lasers of ice cut through his mind. There is no lingering rose tint in the sky, no brightness of twilight. "I don't get it," Archie says, wincing. "One second I was up there"—he points to Baluurwa and its vine-linked floating hunks of rock—"and now I'm down here . . ."

Lillium purses her lips and makes a puckering sound. "Not sure what to tell you. You were running. *Bam!* Ground. And now. That's it."

"I spoke with a Steffanus—Laken."

"Before you came to the Fairy Vineyard?"

"No! Blast it, Lillium. Just now! Although, it was *then*—many years ago."

"How about for now we agree to discuss this later and continue on? The Haaz giants still track us. They've picked up slingshots, and I do not mean the ones the Bangols hide in their pockets. These shoot boulders. I've been watching them fly over the walls of the maze for my last fifty breaths. I've charted them—where they rise, not where they fall. That's how I can tell the pack approaches. The rising place is getting nearer to us, Archie.

"Plus," Lillium continues, more determinedly, "there is something else we need to worry about."

"Ugh, my head." Archie blinks rapidly as he wrestles with his headache. "What else could there possibly be, Lillium?"

She points. Archie turns his gaze toward the treacherous stone walls around them, then beyond. In the distance, past the western entrance to the Bangols maze and fortress, is a massive wave rivaling Baluurwa in height. It is about to swallow the Great Tree poking above the flooded vineyard.

Archie's hands fall from his head. "Ella," he says. "Arden, Tessa . . ."

"All I can hope is that they woke up soon enough." Lillium's voice is weak. "And that they saved the Life Ohmi."

"The wave is not angled in our direction. It's coming in from the sea straight west. The mountain will take the brunt of it."

"Water will still flood this way, Archie. So, as your sprite guide, I sternly advise you to begin running—*now!*"

Lillium dives into Archie's pocket as he begins to race, zipping around the invisible wall and deeper into the maze. This time, his steps are unsteady. He sprints with outstretched arms and fingers, which slows his pace considerably. He feels pained, fatigued yet crazed, and his brow scrunches in anticipation of another unexpected collision.

"Right, left, straight. Right. Right. Right. Don't argue with me, Archie—I know it doesn't make sense!"

Lillium directs Archie, as she did before, but this time they do not chat or poke fun. He navigates the maze silently but for his padding footfalls, and the grunts of the Haaz beasts that search not far away. Boulders whiz through the sky, followed by thunderous crashes and the rolling and settling of new rubble. Sprite bones claw at Archie's arms as he cuts corners tightly, but he never slows. The disgruntled Haaz pack howl like full-moon wolves.

"So much for the secrecy of our mission," grumbles Archie. "The beasts'll wake everyone on the island!"

Lillium ignores his complaints. She hums to herself and talks quietly to the star-freckled silhouettes on her wings. Archie overhears her. "You really think we'll survive this?" Lillium asks. "I hope so, Wingies! I hope you're right!"

Suddenly, the maze ends.

Archie's feet skid, and he nearly tumbles, and Lillium, too, as she clutches the buttonhole of his pocket. It is a dead end. He runs his hands along the stones. "It doesn't appear to be a diversion. Feels pretty solid to me. Ouch!" He plucks a sprite bone from his palm. "I thought you said go straight."

"I did, and we should have. I do not know how this wall appeared here." Lillium flutters upward, and Archie watches her go, higher and higher till she twinkles like a lonely star above him.

"Lilli, the walls . . . they seem to have grown, or is it just me? They feel taller."

"Definitely taller, Archie. And more of them."

"What do you mean?"

"Well," Lillium begins, "we're closed in."

Archie turns on his heels to look back. There, from where they came, is a menacing maze wall, only an arm's length away. Archie grunts, purses his lips. He approaches the new stones and studies the wall closely, watching it as if it will shift into a different configuration—or be the first to blink. Archie plucks every sprite bone he can find before backing up and ramming into the wall with all his weight.

"Oh no, Archie." Lillium covers her eyes. "Be careful!"

Archie does not tell the young sprite that his shoulder, the same one that was hit with a Haaz thrown stone, feels back to its normal strength. It courses with energy, as if relishing the exertion and longing for more usefulness and destruction. He does not tell Lillium how his blood tingles in his veins—how when he left Earth, his body ached with arthritis and his half halo of ivory hair was shedding steadily, clogging the shower drain, to Tessa's perpetual annoyance. He does not tell Lillium that he feels alive, in an incrementally greater way with each passing day on Jarr-Wya, and that he is secretly pondering the decision whether or not to return home to Earth.

Home. That word has taken on bizarre implications for Archie. He is beginning to forget the smell of his old armchair, the fluorescent sheen from the bathroom light that made his face look pocked, and even his desire for predictability. He never forgets his Suzie, the love of his life, mother of Arden, grandma of Ella. He aches for her, but she is all he misses of his former life.

Archie rams the wall again, and it quivers but does not budge. "How can a two-thousand-pound wall come from nowhere?" he says, fuming. "Nowhere!" He kicks the wall and shoves it with rage. He picks up a loose pebble and pitches it. The pebble ricochets, nearly connecting with Lillium.

She pouts her red lips and folds her arms. As she does so,

she notices the dusty earth beneath Archie's feet. He continues to stomp and huff, unaware. Archie pulls more sprite bones from the walls and snaps them in two.

"What is happening, Archie?"

He follows Lillium's gaze down to where the center of the twenty-five-square-foot expanse quivers, unsettling and funneling itself. As in an hourglass, the dirt and pebbles and sprite bones quietly rush together into one point that dips low. Both human and sprite are without words. Lillium flutters to Archie's pocket. He shuffles backward until his shoulders sting with the cold of one enchanted wall.

The funnel grows wider. The dip tunnels deeper. "Archie, I cannot carry you," Lillium chirps from her hiding spot. "Wherever you go, my Wingies and I go, too." She loops her arm through the buttonhole, shuts her eyes into tight lines, and braces herself. Gobo buzzes and slips in beside Lillium.

"It's been lovely knowing you, Lilli."

Within the vortex of silt and stone, swooshing fills Archie's ears. He cannot hear if Lillium replies. He cups a hand over his pocket, and with the other he reaches. Archie kicks and struggles, searching for a way to break free from the sharp funnel dropping them into the heart of the island. The light of the moon and the dying sun, changing shifts above, is stolen. Even Archie's own voice, his pained grunts, are lost. The funnel continues widening, so there is no up and there is no out.

Then, through the flowing earth and clay and rock, a grey finger appears. Then another. Finally, a whole hand slips through and brushes aside what separated Archie from . . . who? He struggles to see.

The dust and rubble continue to fall, but Archie realizes he is floating, hanging in the air at one fixed spot. The earth fully parts and there, standing before his wafting body, is a short creature.

Stones grow from his head like a crown. His eyes are bloated, banana-boat yellow, and squinting.

Tuggeron!

No. Archie is mistaken. No cheek stones grow from the Bangol's face.

It is Luggie!

"Hello, Archibald," the young Bangol says with a smile. "Here." Luggie pulls Archie, with Lillium safe in his pocket, out of the churning stones and to his feet on stable ground.

"Thank you, Luggie," says Archie. "You saved us—we were going to be crushed to death."

"No, you weren't. This is my home. I have power over it as much as any Bangol, despite my number of sunsets. When I heard the racket of my Haaz cousins, I knew I needed to come save you two. They must be a recent addition to the defenses of my father. I shifted the walls so I could get to you quickly, but you were headed north, a trick of the maze. The only way to stop you from reaching the sea—where there is a steep cliff drop hidden behind an enchanted mirage of unbroken path—was to keep you in the west, then lock you in place. I have never created an earth tunnel before, but it worked. Now here you are."

Archie is speechless. He pats Luggie's back, and the Bangol flushes with pride. Luggie leads him and Lillium to the inner edge of the maze with a view to the epicenter of the Bangol fortress. The fortress consists of a large circular area surrounded on three sides by the stone maze except for the northern edge, which is a peaceful shoreline beyond a rocky cliff, as Luggie said. There, waves lap mischievously in the storm.

To their left is the amphitheater. It is shaped like a band shell, rising and curving over a roughly cut stage. Stairs lead up to one end. A stone throne sits in the middle of the stage, stained with dried blood and caked in crumbling mud and foodstuff. Two passageways like flared nostrils have been cut out of the stone shell behind the throne, allowing the sea breeze to flow into the fortress.

Rock and earth structures are built five stories high with winding stone steps, enchanted by Naiu to float on their own without supports. Archie can see fat Bangols climbing up and down the stairs, each step dipping under their weight. Bangols shuffle here and there. The fortress is alive, as if it were midday. One Bangol hurries alongside a group of rolling boulders, winding a path to a crumbled section of maze across the fortress from Archie and Lillium, under repair.

There is an area of stacked clay baskets still strung to deflated fabric balloons. In pockets around the fortress, wire cages hold weary awakins. The butterflies flutter unhappily in tight mobs. Their purple pairs of wings flap with fatigue and they begin to unfurl their daytime pair, though the light arrives sluggishly.

"The poor awakins," Archie whispers.

Lillium is distracted. "I told you, Archie," she says, her voice the lowest he has ever heard it. Her eyes are locked on the gaping chasm at the center of the fortress, dug deep into the earth. "Metal."

The Bangols have not only discovered metal, Archie realizes, but also its many uses. Below the crust of the island, illuminated by Naiu-enchanted torches burning white flames, rises a mammoth machine. In Archie's estimation, it is comprised of many smaller machines, chugging along together toward a common task. Archie cannot even guess at what that would be.

Gears labor noisily, like squabbling children, while wheels made of brass and inlaid with blue wood interconnect with square cogs and provide steady torque. These keep the whole machine chugging out black smoke and deviant sparks, with more screeches of grinding metal followed by the hollers of dissatisfied Bangols. Sweat drips off the stones growing out of their skulls. Their usual attire—hupper and sasar fur, leather belts, and thick hide breastplates—must only exacerbate the heat they feel radiating out the belly of the machine.

Archie and Luggie slip into a low hollow formed of a crumbling maze wall, just in time for another intruder to appear. "Zeno," Archie whispers under his breath. Luggie looks ready to pounce, but Archie holds him back, placing a warning finger to his lips. Archie, too, wishes to intercept the familiar, scheming Bangol, but Tuggeron, the Bangol king, steps out of one passage hole in the band shell and lounges on the rock throne, surveying the fortress.

Zeno is undeterred. Covertly, he meets the gazes of many of the Bangols stationed around the chasm. They stare at Zeno from the corners of their eyes to avoid drawing attention from the band shell. Archie waits for them to sound an alarm, call the Haaz pack, or worse: send huge boulders crashing down on Zeno, also obliterating him, Lillium, and Luggie where they hide.

The worker Bangols blink their round yellow eyes at Zeno. Some rise from their stations and others resume their tasks, while one contingent reaches for slingshots, stone mallets, and axes. None advance in Zeno's direction, however. To Archie's bewilderment, the Bangols proceed casually to the amphitheater, shuffling along to where Tuggeron awaits them. It is as if their spotting of the rightful heir to the throne, the banished one, is nothing out of the ordinary.

Tuggeron is sprawled on the stone seat, one leg swinging carelessly over an armrest. A part of the stone crumbles, but he doesn't flinch. He grins wickedly down at the assembling Bangols, his warriors and workers.

"How goes it?" Tuggeron asks. "Is the beast ready to transport us to the Star?"

"N-n-not yet." A timid Bangol steps forward. "This is the largest Tillastrion I have ever seen, perhaps that the whole of Jarr has ever beheld. These things take time."

"How much time do you think we have, Borgin? Huh? Chergrin was a much better second-in-command. Too bad he became the carakwas' lunch. Let his death be your lesson: you are only valuable as long as you are useful. Understand?"

"Valuable as long as useful." The timid Bangol nods and backs through the crowd, headed for the open wound in the earth. Borgin is tall for a Bangol, though he hunches in his unkempt garb. His sour odor parts the Bangols along his way, and he disappears into the crater.

Tuggeron laughs from his bulging gut. "I do not sit on the Bangol throne because I am nice. No, no, no. The last king was weak. His heirs were weak, too. Remember Winzun? One of the twins? How he snuck back to Jarr I have no idea, but I took great pleasure in stuffing his pathetic body with stones and filling the bellies of the black flyers with his flesh. That is what happens to those who disobey.

"And the one thing we learned from Winzun—before he returned to the dust and clay of Jarr-Wya—was how to build a *better* Tillastrion." Tuggeron roars the last words. "The Star is calling to me. I can feel its power. Already I am under its spell." He laughs again, which turns into a cough, and he spews green phlegm on the stage. "Bring her out!"

A limping Bangol with aged, yellowing head-stones drags out a lumpy sack. It reminds Archie of a recent drawing where Ella depicted her time as a Bangol captive. She was restrained within a sack like the one that contorts on the stage. Whoever is in the sack now looks to be enjoying the confinement as much as Ella had. The new captive kicks and thrashes, tripping the old Bangol, who responds with a solid punt. The sack is motionless long enough for the Bangol to untie the knot and dump out the body.

Archie's gasps. "Xlea!" he says.

Lillium shakes her head, unknowing.

"She's a Steffanus, just a child," he explains in a whisper. "The only one born so far from the still-growing round of seeds. She may be small, but don't underestimate her. She grew Duggie-Sky two feet taller before our eyes. Ah—she still has her notebook! She's proud of that book. Said she recorded all of her travels between Jarr and Earth."

Lillium bites her lip. "I think she is going on another trip very soon."

Tuggeron roars again, grabbing his spilling gut. "She was so easy to catch," he bellows. "Here I was thinking we had to scoop up one of those swimming humans—the ones with scales—that we spotted beyond the reef! Instead, this little demon came strolling down Baluurwa. In search of more humans, were you?"

The Bangols jeer and throw stones. Xlea is bleeding, a small river of crimson trickling from her temple beneath her youthful antlers, their gold smudged yet radiant.

"Bangols—say hello to our guide to the Star!" Tuggeron booms. The ground rumbles like an earthquake as the assembled Bangols stomp and raise their hands, causing pebbles and boulders to rise from the earth, then crash back upon it.

"I will die before helping you! The Star is our only hope—" Xlea cries, her voice small but commanding. Tuggeron punches the girl across the face and she crumbles.

Archie thinks aloud. "I have a feeling we don't need to plant Tanius's antler on the amphitheater," he says. "I bet the Steffanus warriors are on their way here already."

"Look!" Lillium tilts her head toward the southern maze. "The Lord, his henchman Islo, and Duggie-Sky!"

"They are smart to hide on the periphery like us," Luggie says.

Archie's, Luggie's, and Lillium's attention is called back to the amphitheater by Tuggeron's brash announcements. "This wretched little Steffanus, like her sisters, is made of two worlds. If the Star truly came to rest beneath Jarr-Wya from Ardenal's world, Earth—as the Maiden of Olearon told me on the eastern shore—then the Steffanus is who we need."

Xlea stands feebly, then spits on Tuggeron, who only howls with more laughter.

"Part Earthling, part Jarrwian," explains Tuggeron, "she is an easy world-hopper, drawing on both her identities. For those Bangols unaware: to operate the machine—our great Tillastrion, biggest of any the worlds have ever known—we need one person from one world to build it and someone from another to operate it. That is how these things go."

Tuggeron rubs together the palms of his callused grey hands. "But since we have this helpful little girl"—Tuggeron kicks Xlea to her knees, which scratch on the stone stage and begin to weep blood—"we don't need to obey the usual rules. Like the Steffanus race themselves, possessing both human attributes and Naiu, we can move smoothly between the worlds. And you all know what that means!"

The Bangols roar.

"Right! We travel to the Star, harness it to our will, and own every sunset that will ever be!"

Archie's limbs are weak. He slouches where he squats, feeling altogether overwhelmed and out of his depth. Then Zeno advances. The Bangol does not see Archie, Lillium, or Luggie as he slips by. The hairs on Archie's arms stand at attention.

Zeno, all four feet of him, slinks along in shadow. He scurries up one of the stone pillars that flank the amphitheater, unseen by the king Bangol, and creeps onto the band shell above the crumbling throne. He collects a stone, rubs it between his palms, then chucks it down, connecting squarely with the Tuggeron's head.

Archie covers his mouth. On the journey the first company had taken, Zeno refused to leave Archie's side. On their rest breaks, the Bangol taught Duggie-Sky how to throw a clay ball, without much luck by the boy. "He really does have good aim!" Archie whispers to himself. Luggie scowls.

Tuggeron blinks, though no pain or confusion flash across his sneering face. He bends down and collects the shattered pieces of the blood-tinged rock scattered around his hairy grey toes that peek through his boots. He grinds the rock in his thick grip, then picks up his broken head-stone that a moment before joined with others in a crude earthen crown.

Tuggeron's words are deep, humorless, calculated. "Who did this?"

All bright yellow eyes shoot upward, even those of Tuggeron, who says snidely, "Welcome home, Zeno."

A hush rolls across the stone-wielders, those on the earth and those on the stage, like morning fog, sending a chill down every back. Archie's hands stay cupped over his mouth and Lillium dives again into hiding within his breast pocket.

With a proud, menacing snarl, Zeno grins down at Tuggeron from his perch. Archie knows the expression well, yet now it is fully delivered and drips with loathing. Zeno calls forth a dozen stones that meet his feet as he climbs from the band shell and western pillar onto the stage to face Tuggeron.

"You murdered the true king, my father," Zeno begins. Many Bangols in the audience growl, unaware of the truth. "You imprisoned my brother, Winzun, and me, in a cell on the eastern shore, torturing us with Naiu, which was never intended for such brutality." He takes a step toward Tuggeron. "Then you banished me and Winzun to Jarr's pitiful derivative." Another step. "And when Winzun found his way back here, you slaughtered him, too." Zeno is now within arm's length of the king.

"Guards!" Tuggeron calls, but there is no answer. No feet scuffle across the rocky earth to his aid.

"How," continues Zeno, "would you like me to repay your kindness, Tuggeron?"

The stone king is silent but for the grinding of his teeth. Tuggeron narrows his buttery eyes and scans the faces of the Bangols below the stage. "I am going to lead you to the Star!" he bellows, as if their lust equals his own. Still, no grey-skinned beings advance or even flinch. Archie recognizes faces in the crowd: Bangols Zeno made eye contact with before confronting the king.

Tuggeron roars, grabs his stone mallet, and wields it. Before the weapon can come down on Zeno, a storm that has begun to rage overhead crashes deafeningly. Zeno raises his fingers, calling forth the power of Naiu that makes up every cell in his body —his earth, clay, water, and stone—and rages. Again, a rumbling resounds through Jarr-Wya, bringing with it the unstable scratch of granite against quartz and the crack of separating shale.

The weapon falls, as does Tuggeron, in the downpour of pebbles, carved stones, and one final boulder, which ends the life of the Bangol king. Tiny trickles of putrid blood slip between cracks in the new ten-foot-tall mound of rocks. Zeno is unharmed, only peppered with dust.

Archie turns to Luggie. *No child should watch their parent die,* Archie thinks. *Even if that father is Tuggeron.*

The crouching Bangol wears an expression Archie cannot read. Luggie's lips curl in anger, his sharp teeth bared, and a low snarl emanates from his locked jaw. His eyes, however, betray the well of heartache.

It must be hard to love a father who doesn't love you in return, reflects Archie sadly, *and his death seals off all possibility of reconciliation or even the words, "I'm sorry."*

Archie thinks of the Steffanus Laken and her confession to him on the floating rock of Baluurwa in a different time. He wonders how the 29th Lord of Olearon can manifest himself through the 30th. Archie spent his lifetime knowing neither the love of a father nor his rebuke. He slips down to sit beside Luggie on the ungiving earth and loops his arm around the Bangol's shoulders. Luggie does not pull away as tears plunge from his great, glowing yellow eyes.

chapter 22

Tessa

The shellarks swim lazily, pacing the line between the elevated sea and the trembling island as the tidal wave closes in on the Great Tree and the Fairy Vineyard. Drowned wyverns, the underwater dragons, wind around the shellarks. The wyverns, barely visible except for their ghost-like, glossy, charcoal scales, have strong hind legs and sweeping wing fins. They have no forearms. Webbing connects their toes, the curves of their wings, and even where strong joints bend as they tread the water. The drowned wyverns whip barbed serpent tails. As they turn, their grey scales flash yellow, defining their monstrous forms.

"We call them drowned," says Azkar in a rumbling voice, "but the wyverns are very much alive."

Tessa fumbles to retrieve the weapon she had been given in the glass city before they set off. This is her first time drawing any weapon, let alone a glass one. She had accepted it hesitantly from Ardenal, who told her he would always protect her as he did Ella and hoped she would never have a use for the blade.

Tessa mirrors Nate and many of the others in the company, biting down on her knife. Her tongue barely grazes the glass dagger, and she feels it slice the top layer of her skin. The bitter taste of blood fills her mouth. She wraps herself around the tree as tightly as she can, with Nate holding her close.

The wave cracks through the first branches on the farthest edge of the Great Tree.

Leaves are torn from stems, and branches bow. Many break as they pierce the water and lacerate the smooth wave. All at once, the sea splashes out from where the branches have punctured, opening passages between wet and dry and fatally mixing the two. In the last moment before the wave slaps Tessa's face, she can hear Junin's battle scream, which sends heat through her limbs. It bolsters her belief, however irrational, that the company and the sprites will indeed survive the flood.

The water's affront is brutally intentional, and Tessa feels Nate's nails dig into her as he holds her tightly. She blinks away the soupy water, which temporarily blinds her, to look up to where Ardenal's head butts the water like a battering ram. His hands do not slip from the branch where his fingers have burned deeply into the blue bark. Ella's head is thrust against his chest and bubbles float out from her mouth as she cries, though Tessa hears nothing. It is as if the entire world of Jarr has been muted, muffled beneath the flood. A small flock of green birds drown as soon as they are birthed from Ella's pale lips.

Ella opens her eyes. She and Tessa watch each other as the wave fully submerges them, and they are no longer pushed by its force but pulled in its current. Tessa can feel her tongue again rub up against the glass dagger. More blood trickles down her throat, the metallic taste mixing with the water that floods her nostrils. She swallows it all, feeling bloated and out of breath.

Still, Tessa and Ella watch each other.

Mom, I'm scared.

Me, too, Ell.

Mom! Look out! A shel—

Ella

Tessa turns as Nate releases her, grabs his knife, and jams the blade into one reflective eye. The shellark lets out a rumbling growl that makes the water quiver in radiating ripples. It lifts one leg, retracts its claws, and scratches four long cuts across Nate's upper arm. He chokes on water, pain creasing his swollen face. His features are ethereal in the light of the thwarted sun, which sends weak, haunting beams through the floating debris of leaves, sand, and swirls of mud. Nate's blood leaks into the water and surrounds him and Tessa in a murky cloud of crimson.

Mom, get away! Swim to me!

I can't see where to go—it's so thick. I'm choking.

My mind is going black! Mom . . .

Ella?!

In the same moment that Tessa feels too swollen with water and blood to move, or even continue thinking—her stomach bulging, air gone from her lungs, her body surrendering to the cradle of the wave—she is poked sharply in the ribs. Then she receives a jab to her leg. In her blackening vision she catches sight of a crab scuttling through the water, appearing like an apparition through Nate's curling blood.

The crab turns to her and smiles. *It will be okay, strange one.* It places the thought into Tessa's mind. *I am a blamala crab. Blll-aaa-maaaalll-aaa!* The blamala smiles again.

Its azure shell is enormous, like a small car. It continues to poke Tessa until it has a firm grip on her with two of its legs, covered in its exoskeleton. The blamala's oversized claws begin to move frantically, as if knitting a blanket before its droopy pearl eyes. Tessa studies the creature in her last coherent moments: its quirky smile, its barnacle-covered shell, and the blanket it creates. *But, wait!* she thinks. *It is not a blanket at all, but a bubble!*

The bubble grows between the points of the crab's claws, and, finally, when the creature has judged it large enough, it sets

Tessa and Nate inside. Tessa gasps and inhales deeply, throwing up water and replacing it with air.

With her first breath, she wheezes and sputters. "My daughter, please, she's four branches up, that way." Tessa points. She leans against the bubble, pressing her face to its tacky, sour-smelling film, watching. She is reminded of how she peered through the glass partition at the hospital, viewing Ella's failing radiation treatments. The beam was directed at the soft pink skin on the back of Ella's neck. Tessa was as helpless then—with the fear of the newly discovered cancer, the weariness of the endless exams, with failing hope—as she is now.

The blamala rockets its crab-like body from Tessa's bubble toward Ella and Ardenal, though in its speed it tumbles awkwardly. Turning to Nate, Tessa blows air into his lungs and beats his chest as she had seen Ardenal do to Nameris not long before the wave overtook them. Nate comes to with a jerk and a wince of pain. He reaches for his bleeding arm. Tessa rips a piece of her skirt from her shrinking dress and ties it around the wound.

"I'm supposed to be the one protecting you, not the other way around," says the trembling sea captain with a bashful grin. Tessa laughs and kisses him quickly before she returns to watch the blamala.

When the blue crab nears Ella and Ardenal, its legs outstretched, a shellark appears through the debris. It dives down on the blamala and tears off one azure claw in a merciless bite. Tessa stumbles back in the bubble. Nate steadies her. Suddenly, from behind the shellark, a drowned wyvern approaches. It drops its jaw and releases red breath—not fire as Tessa expects, but boiling water. The wounded blamala points with its remaining pincer, and another crab-like creature swoops in and begins to weave a bubble for Ella and Ardenal. The boiling water encircles the wounded blamala, cooking it. Its shell morphs from blue to electric violet. Its body grows still and it floats to the water's surface, where it floats belly up.

When the second blamala has formed its air bubble, it shoves in the two unresponsive bodies. *Wake up!* Tessa screams in her mind, using her power to pry into her daughter's subconscious. *Ella, you must breathe! Ella? Can you hear me?* Tessa presses her fingers to her temple. Bulging veins throb in angry lines across her forehead.

Mmm. Aaawww. Mmmmm . . . Ella's voice is drawn out, and heavy like soggy bread.

Ella! Oh, thank God! Do CPR on your dad! Hurry!

Ella moves slowly, vomits slimy water, then hustles to help him. To Tessa's relief, Ardenal is revived quickly.

Junin floats motionless in a nearby bubble, rocking within the wave beyond Tessa's reach. Through the murky water, Tessa spots other blamala crabs swimming around the Great Tree, weaving bubbles for the company and the sprites. The blamalas also battle the shellarks, cutting off their heads and legs with their lethal claws before the shellarks can retract them inside their shells.

Tessa jams her hand against the wall of their bubble. It shivers and bounces her arm back with equal force. She takes a deep breath and thrusts both hands forward, fingers fanned out. This time, her hands pass through, but the bubble does not pop. Her reaching arms are inches shy of Junin's limp red body. Tessa pulls back.

"Nate, can you help?" The pale man nods. Together they shift to the far side of the bubble, a mere five steps, and then sprint forward, throwing their weight against the tacky surface. The bubble jerks forward through the water a measly distance. Tessa and Nate keep pushing until Nate needs to sit and apply pressure to his wound, but Tessa continues—until her hands reach through one bubble and into another. She clutches the drenched warrior garb and with all her strength pulls Junin through both bubbles' walls.

The stoic Olearon is unusually quiet, her motherly expression wiped from her face and replaced with green ocean algae. Tessa flips Junin onto her back, repeatedly pumps the Olearon's chest, and blows air down her waterlogged throat. Finally, Junin belches—uncharacteristic of one with her polished demeanor—and water spills out of the corners of her colorless lips.

"Thank you, Tessa Wellsley." Junin's voice is a scratch.

"The giant crabs," Tessa begins, brushing off the gratitude, "they're making bubbles, saving us, and fighting the shellarks, though they're no match for the drowned wyverns."

"The blamala have long been friends to the Olearon. Where's Ella? Ardenal?" asks Junin, sensing Tessa's worry. Tessa points.

"We need to get to them!" Nate says from behind the women. "Now!" He dashes to the far edge of the bubble, preparing to hit the other side. Tessa joins him, beaming. She feels a flutter of gratitude despite the fear coursing through her skin. Ella is not Nate's daughter, yet he has made her safety as important as his own. Tessa tucks the appreciation in the back of her mind, saving it to express later.

"If we run and shove the bubble, we'll get there." Tessa shows Junin. "With our weight combined, we'll move faster."

With thirty pushes the three bounce up against Ella and Ardenal. Nate and Tessa pry their fingers through their bubble, Ella and her father doing the same. They pinch together the edges of both gummy capsules, forming the two into one large peanut-shaped bubble. Ella falls into Tessa's arms. As they embrace, the wetness of their clothing squishes out between mother and daughter and pools at their feet.

Ella takes Tessa's shoulders, fear marking her face. *Mom, another shellark!*

Nate orders, "Everyone, thrust your weapons through. Carefully now. We must wound it before it punctures our ride!"

Ardenal, Tessa, and Junin slash the water with glass weapons, and Nate with the blade from his boot with its hilt carved in nautical symbols matching the black tattoos that ink his arms. Together they shred the face of the nearest shellark. The creature wails with trembling vibrations, causing the five to tumble back onto the sticky bubble. The shellark retracts its head into its shell, and with its meaty legs swims blindly away. It bashes against other shellarks, spinning them off course.

Nate and Tessa spot Lady Sophia, who sits timidly in a round bubble. Her body is hidden under the crinoline of her ball gown, and she nibbles her chipped ruby-painted nails. Then Azkar and Nameris drift into view, also surrounded by a bubble of tacky blamala crab saliva. The company all push their bubbles, which connect to the others, forming one large, lopsided sphere.

"You saved me!" Lady Sophia beams at Tessa, who coordinates the hunt to collect stragglers in their cramped, lonely capsules. *"Muchas gracias mi querido!"* Pink rushes back into the singer's cheeks.

The amalgamated bubble now has enough buoyancy to lift the company swiftly toward the surface. Ardenal, Tessa, Nate, Nameris, Ella, Azkar, Junin, and Lady Sophia reach out of the tacky barrier as they rise. They grab the palm-sized air pockets containing the sprites, pulling their tiny bodies into the sour air of their sticky bubble.

Petite voices surround the company. The sprites cheer and encourage them, flapping water from their wings and stirring the dank air. They also weep for their vineyard and the Great Tree, which floats limply in broken pieces on the surface above them, mixed with the vivid purple blamala crabs drifting on the deathly sea. Under the debris and below the company's rising bubble, the living azure blamalas battle shellarks and dodge drowned wyverns, tangling through a swirl of leafy vines and drunken, wilting ohmi grapes.

"We must direct our bubble," Junin hollers. "See there? The wave has crashed against the side of Baluurwa. The water is retreating now, but not swiftly enough."

"You are right," says Nameris. "If our bubble reaches the surface, it will pop, and we will have to swim a great distance to safety. Surely the shellarks will return when they see us helplessly treading water."

Lady Sophia gulps. "Let's hurry for the mountain!"

Junin nods as she withdraws to the farthest edge of the bubble. The company follows her but for the sprites who waft overhead, keeping out of the way. The company charges the opposite wall of the bubble, turning at the last moment to smash its smooth surface with their backs. The bubble shivers, lurches, and thankfully does not pop. It moves in a jerky fashion through the wave, dragging against the suck of the sea, which pulls its soupy water back from where it came along the northwestern coast. The company continue, undeterred though tiring.

"It's working! We're almost there," Lady Sophia says, beaming. Her plump cheeks conceal her bright eyes.

"Do not stop," Junin chants. "Again!" The company continue bashing the wall of the bubble until they notice they are veering off course. "The wind of the storm, it is . . ."

Nameris continues Junin's thought. ". . . pushing us back out to sea!"

Many in the company drop to their knees, all their energy spent, shivering in damp clothing, their sweat mixing with ocean brine. "We must not give up," Junin pleads. She continues to run and thrust her body against the side of the bubble closest to Baluurwa, but she, too, is weary. Defeat sits in the bubble like another member of the company, languishing in the sadness of their probable fate: being swept out into the vast horizon of watery nothingness and starving; or drowning, their lungs filling with water and ohmi juice and leaves from the Great Tree and tears and blood; or becoming a feast for creatures of the deep.

Tessa closes her eyes. Ella rests her head on her mother's chest. Ardenal covers them with his warm, comforting arms. Then they hear it. Their hearts twist.

A knock.

Awareness crashes over Tessa, and she nearly spills Ella and Ardenal as she shifts to look. There, beyond the blamala's bubble, two shimmering faces float into view. Tessa's first thought: *Death. These are dead bodies drifting to taunt us.* But the eyes that stare at the company are full of life. They blink. Their sea-foam green lips curve in a brief smile.

"Donna and Harry!" Lady Sophia wails. "Oh, I never expected to be so happy to see you two!" She scoots to the edge of bubble closest to the two *Atlantic Odyssey* passengers. Lady Sophia presses her pout against the edge of the bubble, making kissing sounds. "You're going to save us, I can feel it!" She grins.

Junin looks puzzled. "I recall two humans with those names, ones we saved from the Millia's hunger. But humans. These two are . . ."

"One and the same," sings Lady Sophia.

"When our first company ventured east and visited the man-spider Rolace," Tessa begins, relief easing the tension on her face, "he gave some of us gifts of Naiu. Donna and Harry had asked to be bound in Rolace's silky cocoon together. That's how they came to share their power, which made them—"

"Fishy," finishes Nate.

Ella laughs, and a single green bird distorts her mirth when with its two pointed feet it squeezes itself from her mouth. It flutters into the bubble and, confused, bashes its head against the translucent saliva.

"Come here, little one." Junin welcomes the bird to nestle into her smooth, cupped hands.

Lady Sophia points at Baluurwa the Doomful, then makes a pushing gesture. While the company cannot hear Donna and Harry and they presume the couple cannot hear them either, communication continues through hand motions and the shaking or nodding of heads.

"See, Ella," says Tessa, "if we all knew sign language, this would be a whole lot easier."

Ella rolls her eyes.

Tessa works through all the signs she can remember from their family lessons, though that time back home seems like ages ago.

Ella pipes up through her thoughts. *Mom, seriously? You just signed, "Help-play-food-beautiful-finished-day-you-me." That's not a sentence.*

Are you sure?

Ella laughs in her head and Tessa wishes to remember the sound, the long-lost laugh. Maybe her gift from Rolace, Tessa reflects—this telepathy between her and Ella—is the greatest gift of all, as Ardenal had suggested. Here they are, trapped and in danger, in the most fantastical way, and yet Tessa holds her child, as close as she had the day Ella was born, and her daughter's sweet, innocent laugh echoes through her mind.

Maybe this really is the happiness I've been searching for, Tessa muses to herself.

Donna and Harry press their hands against the far edge of the lopsided bubble. They push and strain but only make small headway against the force of the wild wind that hooks and drags the flood away from the mountain. Donna and her glimmer of white hair disappear, her hands leaving impressions on the outer surface of the bubble. Almost immediately, she returns, guiding a lone blamala to the bubble. It is wounded and trailing a crimson line like a ribbon. It raises its mighty blue pincers and snaps them closed. The blamala gently rests its claws against the bubble and begins to swim.

The pace of Donna, Harry, and the blamala is steady, and finally, after Nate has worn a crease in the bubble from pacing, the company and sprites reach the edge of Baluurwa. If Tessa were to stretch, she could touch the warm black rock. Above their heads floats six feet of water.

"Thank you, thank you, thank you," sings Lady Sophia. She presses her hands to the bubble, one aligned with Harry, the other with Donna, and again presses her plump lips to the tacky sheen between them. "SWAK! Sealed with a kiss!" The transformed senior citizens wave before they, and the blamala, fade into the retreating sea.

Tessa waves, overcome with gratitude.

Nate surveys their surroundings. "We're farther north than I anticipated, just above the Bangols' fortress. Maybe we'll intercept the Lord, Islo, Duggie-Sky, and Luggie."

Azkar grunts. "Let us get on with it." He pinches his nose.

"The stench is bothersome to me as well," Nameris concurs, still looking pale and bloated.

Suddenly, the water recedes in one swift inhalation. The bubble and all inside it jerk up and into the air. To the company's surprise, however, the bubble does not pop.

"That was unexpected," Junin mumbles. "I was sure that once the air around us joined the air above water, we would be free."

Tessa touches the edge of their capsule. "We assume it's an air bubble, but we're wrong. It's sticky." Her fingers make a snapping sound when she pulls away.

"Right," Ardenal says. "Tessa is right—it is the tacky saliva of the blamala crabs. Why didn't I think of this before? Now that we are above water, the spittle will solidify. The dampness allowed it to be flexible. We must break through before it hardens fully, trapping us inside." He stabs at the misshapen bubble with his glass dagger, but the weapon snaps at its tip.

"We could have melted it, but the wave put out our flames," laments Nameris, looking to Junin for guidance.

Azkar hulks through the hardening shell. "We must continue to cut at it, smash it. What other options do we have?" he growls.

"We cannot remain here," Junin adds, "balancing on the edge of this cliff." Her words are bold, but her stature is hunched, nervous. She turns her back to the others and begins to saw at the bubble with her glass dagger, which makes a horrible screeching noise against the hardening substance. The sprites cover their ears as they hover near the company's heads. The brave sprites bite at the translucent saliva casing and grind at its joins with the bristles lining their tibias.

"This is useless!" Lady Sophia pouts. "We're going to be trapped in here forever—or at least until the Steffanus sisters find us on their mountain. I bet those she-witches fly down and land on our bubble and taunt us to no end! I should be singing to an audience, not here as a captive to be jeered at!" She folds her thick arms and stomps over to the far edge of the bubble where she plops herself down. With this, those on the opposite end are tossed into the air.

"What have you done now?" Nameris snarls at her. Lady Sophia frowns.

"I think Nameris is right," Tessa mumbles. "You've unsettled us."

Lady Sophia leaps to her feet, a look of terror twisting her round face. "Oh no! I'm sorry! Forgive me!" she wails.

"Everyone," Ardenal hollers, "run toward the mountain side of the bubble—this way!"

It is too late. The awkward sphere wobbles on the sharp edge of Baluurwa, then shifts precariously. The company slide to one corner in a pile on top of each other. The sprites call out conflicting suggestions in their tiny voices, and struggle to lift human and Olearon arms and legs from on top of them to escape the pile.

Oh no, Mom!

We'll be okay, Ella. Brace yourself!

"Hold on, everyone!" Tessa screams as the bubble tips and begins to roll down the northern side of Baluurwa.

chapter 23

Archie
Tessa
Luggie

Zeno turns from Tuggeron's pooling blood to face the Bangols. "Do you see my power?" he roars. "No thick-skulled ruler is my rival. My banishment taught me much. Portal jumping and the powerless inhabitants of our derivative should not be feared. What should be feared, however, is the Star. The Maiden of Olearon lied to Tuggeron. Neither she nor any Olearon can control the Star. Not Ardenal either. It did not come from the land of the humans. Earth reminds me of Jarr in many ways, though it lacks the kiss of magic." Zeno pauses. He laces his grey fingers and cracks them. "We can be that kiss of magic."

A rumble of voices erupts amongst the Bangols below the stage where Zeno stands proudly, making up for his short stature. Some yellow eyes glare; others glow with possibility. Zeno does not rush them.

Finally, he says, "Tuggeron's desire for the Star twisted his mind. I, on the other hand, see clearly. The Star is wicked, poisoning our island. Everyone who believes otherwise has been deceived. Come with me, to the human Earth, where we might start again and obtain whole lands, not mere shores."

Archie's mouth is dry. He cannot catch his breath as it runs away with his strength and is replaced by terrible realizations.

You're a fool, Archibald Wellsley, Archie chides himself. "This was Zeno's plan all along, wasn't it? He meant what he said about helping me get home," Archie says, fuming, "but he didn't mention he'd bring all the Bangols with us."

"Oh my ohmi!" Lillium chirps.

Luggie grimaces and whispers, "The Olearons, even Ardenal—and Tessa, too—have warned you, Archie: Zeno uses you for his will. While I hated my father for the torture, banishments, and death he inflicted, Zeno is the same—only his methods differ."

Across the fortress grounds from Archie, Lillium, and Luggie, the Bangols rally at the amphitheater, talking of the Tillastrion's readiness and other preparations that must be made. Just then, the fringe of the wave subtly slips through the maze and dampens the earth, spilling out from two of the three stone entrances.

All Bangols back away except for one. Borgin, recently ascended from the crater, steps forward. "Zeno, my king," says the timid stone-head, Chergrin's replacement as head guard. "We saw the water approaching in the darkness before dawn. Stay back. We do not know what enchantments from the Star it brings to our northern shore." With a quivering hand, Borgin caresses the water that darkens the earth and slinks into the gorge at the center of the fortress.

The weak sun and glowing torches cast strange shadows on the advancing liquid. It has the sheen and structure of molten mercury. Borgin timidly touches his pale tongue with dampened fingers. "J-just water, King Zeno," he stammers.

The Bangols kick at the water, sneering wearily, and are about to return to their planning when their yellow eyes catch sight of Baluurwa. The black mountain is cut with silver lines of pale light. It stands ominously still and quiet, except for one peculiar apparition: what appears to be a giant water bubble tumbles down Baluurwa's northern slope. Archie can see the other small contingent—the Lord, Islo, and Duggie-Sky—turn around in their hiding place to stare up at the strange sight.

"It is like a tear," Lillium whispers near Archie's ear. "Baluurwa is crying."

The bubble shimmers silver, dream-like. Archie blinks hard, shaking his head as if the sight is a symptom of his concussion. *Not a dream, not a dream*, he repeats in his mind. The bubble is very real. It is oblong, lopsided, and descending quickly. Archie expects it to function normally—to fall, then splash, losing all form. That is not what happens.

TESSA winces in pain. The company in the bubble cry out as they find elbows in their backs and feet in their faces. The blamala's membrane is undamaged by the rocky slope of the mountain and the blue trees that splinter and snap under their crashing weight.

They skid and careen down Baluurwa, bruising and bashing each other as they are mixed. *Like tossed salad*, Tessa thinks. She finds Ardenal's hand and grabs it. He pulls her body close and tucks her head beneath his own, wrapping his arms around her to shield her. Tessa, peering out the corner of her eye, spots Ella clinging to Lady Sophia and Nate as they roll wildly. The other Olearons—Azkar, Junin, and Nameris—have linked their bodies and press themselves to the bubble wall, pushing against each other to maintain a fixed position. Still, the sprites, humans, and Ardenal smash against them.

"We have almost reached the maze entrance," Nameris manages.

"Brace yourselves however you can," Junin says calmly, though she shuts her black eyes. Her smooth red skin crinkles on her brow as a snarl escapes her clenched jaw.

A Haaz at the bottom of the hill, guarding the stone-arched entrance to the maze, stiffens and stretches out its hands, feeling the whoosh of vibrations in the air as the bubble approaches. *What is that creature?* Tessa wonders. The Haaz lunges to the side, too late. The bubble crushes its giant black bones and thick skull in one bounce. Its blood paints a corner of the bubble, which continues to rocket forward over the walls of the maze, leaving it in disarray.

ARCHIE catches sight of the Lord, Islo, and Duggie-Sky, who are forced to abandon their hideout and flee from the maze. The three careen through the stone buildings and across the bare earth, heading toward the east. *Not that way,* Archie thinks. He stands and vigorously waves, capturing his allies' attention. He also steals the gaze of the Bangols, and of Zeno. Yellow eyes radiate in Archie's direction, illuminating the dull morning in an eerie glow.

The small contingent veers west. The Lord and Duggie-Sky are shoved into Archie's arms by Islo, and they all duck as the bubble nears. Maze walls topple like dominos. Boulders soar through clouds of dust. As the bubble nears, Lillium screams as she observes the splatter of blood.

"The other half of our company," Archie says in disbelief.

"And the sprites!" Lillium sings.

"And Ella," Luggie whispers like a prayer.

TESSA clings to Ardenal. His arms give the sense of home amidst the chaos. She breathes him in, and past the smell of salt and sweat lingers his scent. The same scent as her Arden, human Arden; Ella's father, history professor, Seattle resident. Her husband. Then the smell is knocked from her lungs by Azkar's knee as they collide. Tessa is winded.

The bubble travels the great distance quickly, while a swiftly fracturing crack grows across its longest edge. Tessa watches it with dread. As the bubble sails over the last wall of the maze, the crack spreads farther to the left and to the right, eventually joining to form a complete circle.

Hold on, Ell.

You, too, Mom.

The firm capsule smashes down onto the hard earth, cracking open as a nut shell into a million deadly pieces. Sour air pours out like a smoke bomb, along with one hundred frantic green birds. Ella's birds fly frantically in every direction, leaving behind a cloud of emerald feathers and a fading chorus of chirps as they disappear into the storm.

LUGGIE reaches Ella first. *Please let her be okay, please,* he thinks. She is buried under hard, translucent pieces of the shattered bubble. He burrows her out, one shard at a time, until he reaches the last and heaviest. Luggie digs his claws into the smooth, air-dried capsule, but all his efforts fail. He calls to Archie and Ardenal, and together the three heave the fragment from Ella's torso. In doing so, the fleshy palm of Luggie's left hand slices open on a serrated edge and he grits his teeth.

Ignoring the gash, he falls to his knees and collects Ella in his arms. She winces in pain and releases five green birds that Luggie bats out of his face. His searches her body for cuts or broken bones while she gazes longingly at him. Ella lifts a hand to cup his cheek, and that is when they see the cut on her forearm.

"You're bleeding," Luggie says, panting. He clasps his hand over Ella's wound. "Oh no," he wheezes, pulling away suddenly. He looks at his palm, which is dripping steadily where he sliced it on the jagged shard. Ella's arm wears the mixture of their bloods: the violent red of humans and the paler, moss green of Bangols.

Ella, still intently staring into Luggie's bright, frantic eyes, takes the Bangol's cut hand and places it over her gash. She does this purposefully, with smooth motions. The sensation of stirring lifeblood warms the place where their two hearts beat as one.

Many thousands of sunsets later, Luggie will say that this is the moment that changed everything.

"I don't understand," he begins, but then he stops speaking, surrendering himself to understand Ella's meaning—to appreciate her not only as the wounded girl he has come to care for deeply, but as the great love of his life, however bizarre their pairing may be.

Ella cannot speak or even make a sound, however broken. Her gesture, like their own personal sign language, screams Ella's love for Luggie through her fierce gaze.

And so they sit there, content in a flurry of raging chatter and clanging metal. In a swirl of anger and grief, tears and love overwhelm them.

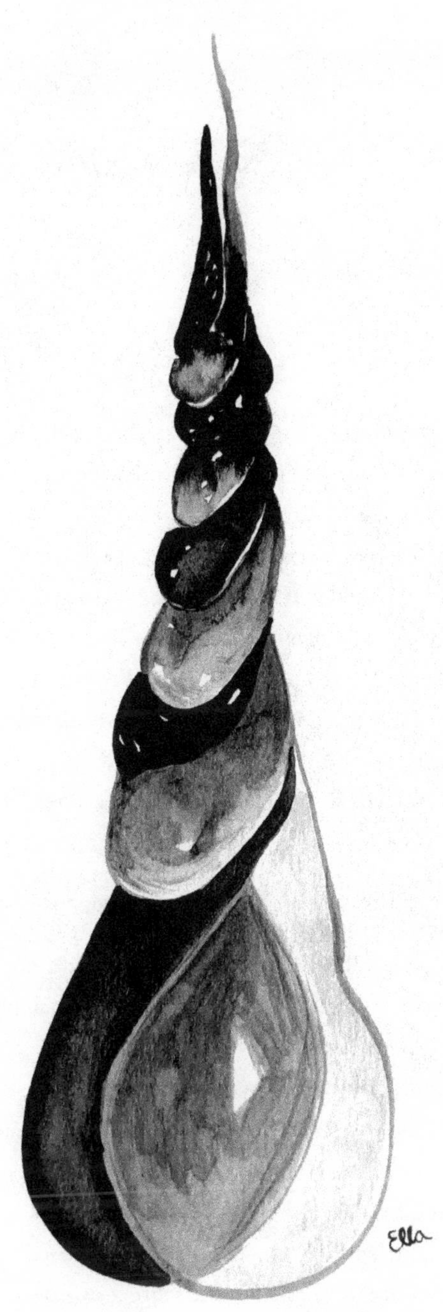
Ella

chapter 29

Ella

I feel different as our blood mixes, though I can't explain how. I'm tired, too, as rain begins lightly, then falls harder. I wish Luggie and I could surrender to the departing stars and the breeze that wishes to sweep us away. Everything's right in this moment as we hold each other on the muddying ground, but also terribly wrong beyond us.

Mom screams. It's piercing, even through the battering rain. I can't tell if the scream is in my head or out loud. Instinctively, I leap from Luggie's arms.

I'm distracted, worried for Mom, and barely notice Grandpa Archie cleaning my wound with his khaki coat. The bleeding has slowed where my skin tingles of Naiu. Dad—his flame relit by the Lord despite the rain—tells me, "This will hurt," and I don't know what he's talking about till he cauterizes my arm. I birth a swarm of green birds with my silent curses. I pull away, both grateful and pissed off.

Tall red bodies block my view. The Olearons from our company look bedraggled, not their usual erect and unwavering selves. The sprites are stained in blood, their greenish skin purple with ripe bruises. The way their hair twists into birds, constellations, and sailboats is no longer beautiful but disheveled and sad. All are drenched with rain and covered in salt and mud, sullying their vibrant clothing. One by one, the Olearons relight themselves with the help of the Lord and Islo. Again, their veins glow molten orange through their skin.

I search for my important people. Grandpa Archie and Luggie are by my side. Duggie-Sky is cradled in Lady Sophia's large bosoms. Then I see Nate joined by Dad. Both are frazzled, worn like the frayed edges of my favorite jeans. I can't hear what they discuss. Their muscles are tense, their backs hunched worriedly. Nate bounces on the balls of his feet, as if ready to bolt at a track meet. Dad stands fixed, unmoving, though the fire at his neck has enveloped his face and thick dreadlocks. His eyes shimmer like black coals from within the blaze. I can see the orange veins throbbing with heat in his hands, as if at any moment a fireball will form on each palm. Dad was rarely mad at home, or at least he hid it better. Seeing him like this scares me.

Where's Mom? There's a sickening acid in my gut, and this time it's not the cancer.

Mom? I call in my head.

No answer.

Shrugging off Luggie's and Grandpa's cautious hands, I inch forward.

"Ella, no!" It's Luggie. I choose to ignore him. He should know by now how stubborn I am, perhaps even more than him, but I'll never admit to that.

I pass by the steaming bodies of Junin and Nameris. There's a figurative line drawn in the sand, though I can almost see one cut into the gravely earth. On one side is our company and the sprites. On the other side, the Bangols. And Mom.

Mom!

Stay back, Ella.

What's going on? What is Zeno doing?

Zeno must sense my question. "Since your commotion

scared away the Steffanus child, the one we needed to operate the Tillastrion," Zeno says kindly, though his words are direct, "we Bangols require human blood." He clutches Mom around the throat as another Bangol ties her up. She thrashes as much as she can, but it's no use.

"Take me instead," Dad says through the lick of fire.

"Funny, Arden. Really," Zeno says, laughing at Dad. Hearing his human name sounds nice to my ears, filling my mind with images of my father with skin that matches mine, blue eyes like ice, and geeky cool glasses. "You did not trust me when you sought me out at my shop on Lanzarote, in the human world," Zeno continues. "You stole my Tillastrion to use for yourself and only made it to Jarr-Wya because of my brother Winzun. Looking at you now—ready to fight for your family. What could possibly make me trust you? Plus, you are not the blood I need."

Grandpa Archie steps forward. "Me, then," he says.

Zeno laughs again. "Archibald! You have taught me the kindness of people, even when they betray you, which I have done to you countless times. You have shown me restraint, which is why I will not kill Tessa Wellsley once we arrive on Earth. You have also extolled to me the wisdom of the kings and rulers of your world, how they earn respect from the ones they lead. So with all these lessons, I cannot take you in Tessa's place. All Bangols here would see the foolishness and weakness of that decision, and the vulnerability it would bring."

Grandpa Archie looks confused.

"I have noticed your strength, Archibald," says Zeno snidely. "It is obvious to anyone who has observed you from your first footfall on the Millia's southern shore until now. I do not know who you really are or where you truly come from, but it is not the human world. And I will not risk my mission on that uncertainty."

"That uncertainty," repeats Borgin fiercely.

"Enough, Cousin!" snaps Zeno.

I'm dumbstruck. What is Zeno talking about? Briefly, all eyes are fixed on Grandpa, who looks like he burns with equal heat as Dad. It's the same look I have when Mom catches me reading my favorite fan fiction horror stories on the internet at midnight. *Busted.* He doesn't speak up, however, and manages to eke out a deep breath. The Lord of Olearon slowly breaks his gaze from Grandpa and turns to Zeno.

The Lord speaks coolly, despite the flame that tickles the back of his neck. "Let us discuss matters calmly, Zeno, and return our shared Jarr-Wya to a place of peace and cooperation."

"Under your rule?" Zeno snaps. "Am I right, Lord?"

With these words, Zeno gestures to the machine behind him that emerges from the earth with blistering speed. The gears begin to move rapidly, with a flashing white light that blinds eyes accustomed to days spent beneath the waning sun. The rain reflects the brightness and glistens like falling silver. The screeches from the Tillastrion transform into a *zinggggg* that spew hungry, stinging sparks. Some come close to me, and I trip backward.

Zeno's hand still clutches Mom. The Bangols behind them, guided by the fumbling Borgin, begin to leap over the cusp of the gorge or summon rocks to catch them as they take faithful steps into the gaping opening. Our company advances, but not quickly. Tentative, leery. I roll to my knees but can't see past the red bodies and the running and splashing of muddy water.

"Goodbye, Archibald," says Zeno.

"Goodbye," echoes Borgin, to Zeno's annoyance.

When I make it to my feet, blood oozes from my scraped knees and granules of dirt cake my eyelids. The machine glows. Lightning forms red daggers through the atmosphere. Everyone runs. Voices bounce off each other. It's all too much, but also too little. The enormous Tillastrion blasts our company back in an explosion of blue. We who remain above the chasm have been flattened; the sky presses down on us, and I can't move. Then the air is sucked out of the fortress like a stolen breath. The sensation of suffocation I remember vividly from being tied in the Bangol sack comes back to me.

I fight to my feet once more, my ears ringing and my eyes playing a cruel game. The Tillastrion is gone. The Bangols are gone. The earth reveals a hollow void beyond my feet; I stand weakly on its crumbling edge.

Mom is gone.

Ella

chapter 29

Archie

Archie curses. Ardenal looks to his father, who is never one for profanity, and rambles hopeless words. Everything aligns in Archie's mind. While his attention was on the company—Ella and the others wounded and trapped beneath hardened fragments of bubble—Zeno and the Bangols realized that the Steffanus Xlea had slipped into hiding. They determined which of the humans would be easiest to subdue—though Archie thinks they greatly underestimated Tessa—and grabbed her when no one was looking.

Borgin, the timid one Archie watched report to Tuggeron on the status of the Tillastrion, snuck down to ready the great machine. Other Bangols grabbed what they needed during the confusion and descended, unnoticed, into the heart of Jarr-Wya. All they required was Tessa.

The Lord stands like a deeply rooted tree. "That is one problem resolved," he says.

"Resolved? Resolved?" Lillium's voice rises with each word.

The Lord glowers at her, though even his most vicious words sound even. "Do you question my judgment? Perhaps I should—"

"She has done nothing wrong!" pipes up Quillie.

Pinne finishes her twin's thought. "We sprites believe even our queen should listen to those she rules and speak kindly in the process."

The Lord, unaccustomed to any kind of reprimand, stirs in a swell of his own fire before Archie steps between the Olearon and the sprites. "We're all friends here," he says.

Lillium's cheeks flush as red as her hair and she flutters away in a huff. The sprites, not prone to confrontation, also disperse. They send pairs throughout the fortress to unlock the wire cages and set free the awakin butterflies, who thank the sprites with kisses before fluttering away.

"It'll be impossible to find her . . ." Nate says. He stands at the precipice of the gorge where once the Bangols' machine bulged out of the earth, reddening the pale clay with rust. It also filled the air with unnatural sounds, which kept the black flyers at bay to the perimeter of the fortress beyond the maze. Now, the morphed two-headed creatures circle overhead, wary of the fortress but close enough to cast grim shadows like the equally ominous storm clouds. Nate watches them and clutches his blade.

Nameris taps his chin, which drips with rain. "The Bangols will be transported to the place Zeno knows best, where he lived while banished."

Lady Sophia covers her mouth, muffling a shocked gasp. Duggie-Sky takes the singer's hand and swings it gently.

"So you can guess?" Azkar growls. He kicks a stone into the cavernous void, past Nate, and the sound ricochets and echoes. "The island from where your ship, the *Atlantic Odyssey*, departed."

"Lanzarote," Nate mumbles. The mention of his ship brightens yet troubles the captain's features. "The Canary Islands . . . When I met Zeno here on Jarr-Wya, on our trek east to save Ella, he grumbled about the shop he operated for years."

"The shop named 'Treasures,'" Archie whispers, remembering. He pictures the splintering wood sign swinging above the door. Its paint was chipped but still clearly depicted an island with a lonely mountain at its center. Archie now knows that island to be Jarr-Wya and the mountain Baluurwa the Doomful, home of the Steffanus sisters.

Inside Treasures, Archie found a shop bursting with dusty parasols, ornately carved furniture likely containing hidden compartments, and incense that smelled oddly familiar. He now recognizes the smell as the spirit of Naiu, which lingered in the dwelling of the displaced Jarrwian. Naiu called to Archie even then. Finally, here in the world of Jarr, he wonders how he lived his life without it.

Treasures boasted brine-rusted necklaces and tarnished green copper tea ware. At the back of the shop stood a pale, illuminated cabinet with a scattering of gold objects—pens and pendants, rings set with opals, tiny figurines of dragons, and a gold-plated skull with diamonds glinting from its eye sockets. That was where Archie first met Zeno.

"The Bangols' powers will be weakened in Jarr's derivative," Nameris points out.

Kameelo swoops down from a sky. "With the Bangols weakened, we will have the advantage and can overtake them," adds the young Olearon, who uses his power to hover a foot above the ground.

Azkar growls, annoyed. "Our flames will be weakened as well, brother. We cannot know the power of our fire until arrival. We need greater numbers or we will be the ones overtaken."

"Wretched Bangols." The Lord's words blossom with hate, and all eyes—last of all the Lord's—turn to Luggie.

Ella slips her hand into the fold of Luggie's arm and intertwines his thick fingers with her own.

"Not you, Luggie. You're different," says Lady Sophia.

"You do not need to comfort him, human," the Lord says evenly. "Luggie recognizes his father's lunacy. Thankfully, Zeno took care of Tuggeron for us. I believe Luggie also sees that the Bangols must come under proper rulership or be annihilated. And the only one fit to rule is here with us right now."

"You," says Duggie-Sky to the Lord, voicing what all assume.

Instead, the Lord turns to gaze at Luggie and wipes a twinge of disgust from his face.

"Oh! Yes!" Lady Sophia sings.

All flick their eyes to look at Luggie, who clenches his jaw without looking up from his broken boots and muddy hupper fur garments.

"My Lord," Luggie finally says, "if they do not comply, I will be honored to be the last of my kind."

Like the rest of the company, Archie finds himself speechless. He tilts his head in bewilderment but knows he cannot ask the obvious question so openly. He will have to inquire later about the Bangol's unexpected submission to the Lord's will. *Perhaps,* Archie wonders, *I can ask the Maiden what's going on. If only she'd appear again.* All gazes but Luggie's flit between each other. No one says another word on the matter.

"And to you all," the Lord says, "you speak as if our course is set for the land of the humans. The Bangols' departure inadvertently removed a rival on Jarr-Wya, one to be confronted at a later time. However, our mission is here: to locate the Star. I am quite confident that once it is found and held in the hands of the Olearons, all will be made right."

Junin stands beside Ella and Luggie, examining their wounds and letting the rain wash out lingering dirt and debris. Ella steps away from her hot hands. Her young face wrinkles in a scowl, her lips locked. She turns to Archie, eyes pleading, and lifts her hands to sign. Ella makes a flat vertical plane with her right hand, while the other is fixed palm up before her. She slices the air, moving the vertical hand in a downward chop on the skyward palm. She signs this, "*Stop*," repeatedly, then rubs her chest in the gesture for "*Please*." Finally, she signs "*Mom*." Her thumb touches her chin, her fingers erect.

"My Lord," Archie begins smoothly, winking at Ella, "there are horrors in my world you'd never believe. The weapons and technology—more powerful than the Bangols' great machine—would be lethal in their possession. If you truly want peace, we must return the Bangols to where they belong. Here. As soon as possible. And save Tessa and all the humans in the process."

Ella smiles and nods at Archie through the pain on her face as Junin tenderly holds her while Ardenal seals her bleeding knees. Junin moves on to Luggie, cauterizing his palm. He stretches the blistering flesh and masks his pain.

The Lord's eyes narrow. "And what if those weapons and technology, as you say, were in the hands of the Olearons?" he asks.

"They do not belong in this world, Lord," answers Ardenal, "and weapons meant for hate belong not in any world. I am a student of human history, and what I have learned is this: peace comes at a cost. When it is bought with blood and violence, those under the new rule do not submit for long."

"You are saying that we must earn peace through peace?" asks Junin.

"True peace, yes. If we can avoid war today, yes. If we can avoid war in the future, again, my answer is the same." Ardenal pushes a finger up the bridge of his nose, lifting his phantom glasses, a nervous habit from when he was human. That gesture reminds Archie of Suzie, Seattle, and the unsuspecting people of the Canary Islands, who by now are reacquainted with the conniving Bangol, Zeno.

Ardenal continues, straightening his posture. The fire at his neck is a low, controlled simmer. "But I agree with you, Lord, on one important point. We must maintain our mission to reach the Star. It is the only way to save Ella and Jarr. If we fail to stop the Star, Earth will be destroyed as well."

Ella's face twists with realization. Archie watches her through the storm. His granddaughter scowls at her father. Archie can see that to Ella, Ardenal's words have sealed Tessa's fate.

Nameris, always one to calculate without emotion, adds, "Since the Bangols needed Tessa to jump portals, they will likely have no use for her upon arriving, what with all the humans readily available. She may not be alive for us to save."

Ella chokes on a green bird. She spits it onto the muddy earth, but it is dead already, trampled under the frantic feet and wings of ten others that fight their way past her pale lips.

Luggie loops his arm around Ella's waist, steadying her. "I do not believe Zeno plans to slaughter the humans he meets on the other side of the portal," he says, and for a moment Ella looks hopeful. "He desires to rule. He will put the humans to work. As for Tessa, because of you, Archibald, Zeno will be reluctant to kill her. She will be safe for now. If we are taking a vote, I am with Ardenal in this decision. Let us save Jarr—and Ella. Then I will pursue Zeno myself."

Ella is frozen in place, glaring, shrinking before Archie's eyes.

"I see wisdom in Luggie's words. No vote is necessary," begins the Lord. "And perhaps, as you so pointedly suggest, Ardenal, the Steffanus warriors will listen to a plea for peace."

"And if not?" asks Ardenal, though his wrinkled brow tells Archie that his son already suspects the Lord's plan.

"Then at least we have her to help in the negotiation," the Lord says, and he yanks from the stone rubble a small bruised and bleeding body.

Xlea, clutching her book, scowls up at the Lord.

chapter 26

Ella

We've taken shelter from this never-ending storm beneath the Bangols' band shell at the amphitheater. Most in the company are scheming. I hate them all. Lady Sophia snore-sings as she sleeps, passed out with a rock for a pillow. Kameelo and Duggie-Sky toy with Tanius's antler, passing it back and forth like a baseball, putting it to use since it will no longer serve to provoke the Bangols. The Bangols aren't here—except for Luggie.

I'm furious with Luggie. I don't care that he's trying to save me. In the process, he's allowing Mom to be held captive, hurt, or even—no, I can't think it. I'm also furious with Dad, for obvious reasons. He's hurt by Mom choosing Nate, so he's turned his back on her. Well, I don't think that's the way to win over the woman you love. Ugh. Everyone's annoying me. I hate their plans. I hate their cocky faces.

I even hate that Kameelo and Duggie-Sky are playing with that antler. It's making sport of an enemy's bone, making light of death. It's not right. I'm sick of everyone, and *argh*, will Luggie just leave me alone already? I glare at him and find a lonely corner of the band shell to curl up in.

Dad warmed me up, dried my clothes moments before, but I bet I could have done it myself with the fire of anger that burns in me. The only one who knows how to talk me down when I'm this mad is Mom—but can our minds connect between portals? Worlds apart?

Mom? Mom, can you hear me? Mom? We need to talk!

I wait. Silence. I scream at her again. Then, I hear her.

You're faint, Ell, and I feel thin. Can't you see me? I can see you there, on the stage. I'm standing, well, hovering here, above the gorge of metal and machines.

You're still here? I can't see anything in the crater. Not you or the Bangols or the Tillastrion.

I jump to my feet as if our company missed something so obvious, but no. The earth is still vacant but for a carelessly broken gear. Nothing hovers in the sky but the hungry black flyers.

I suppose it takes longer to transport such a great number. It's beginning now, Ell. Everything's warped. My arm looks as long as a tree. If I stretch only an inch farther I can stroke your cheek, take your hand in mine.

Something's not right, Mom. We didn't feel this when the Atlantic Odyssey *transported us to Jarr-Wya. That had to be just as many people, and the ship just as large as the Bangols' machine.*

But we weren't the ones who operated that Tillastrion, remember? We were stowaways. It was Archie . . . he must have felt this, as I'm feeling now. Ahhhhhh . . .

What is it, Mom?

The clouds are pressing down on me. The light, it shifts, melting from dusty blue-grey to chalk white and blinding. The magic is morphing into a snaking, slithering violet. The color winds between the folds of my brain. I can't think.

Keep talking to me, Mom.

Jarr-Wya is fading. The grainy smell of the Sea of Selfdom is being sucked from my nose, replaced by the burn of lava, of eyelashes, and of sunshine. I've missed the sun . . . My mind feels cut, Ella. Lacerated into dead and alive, the two sides connected by a singular tract of die-hard synapses. Pulsing. Clouds spin. Claws are on my arms. The Bangols . . .

I'm going to save you, Mom. Tell me everything you see and feel. Our company will follow you, wherever you go. And if not them—I gulp, hearing my error—*then me. You never gave up on me, no matter what cancer threw my way—our way—and that's how much I love you, Mom. I'll go wherever you go.*

No, Ella. No. Your cure is close. Let the others worry about the Steffanus sisters. Sneak into the mountain and find it. I mean this, really: save yourself. My life is a shadow of yours. No child should die before her parent. Please, Ella. Listen to me.

Mom, I can't, I won't. I'm scared, and without you, the fear will eat me alive, cure or no cure. Mom? Are you there?

I'm here. I see the ocean above me, the whole immensity of it. Sea creatures. Blamala crabs. Drowned wyverns, all smug and dragon cruel. The shellarks and other shelled ones swimming so low, diving for the Star, always beyond their reach. I can see the Star, too, but I don't understand it. Its rays of light mix with curls of floating foliage. Waves. A tsunami of color crashing down, down, down, moving closer, shaking my bones. I'm pinned now beneath the sea's floor, buried in the sunken grit of the world.

Which world?

All the worlds.

I'm coming for you, Mom. Nate's with me on this. He won't leave you either. And Dad, well, I know he still loves you, but it's complicated.

Second. Save me second. After you. You first. Save you first.

Mom, I can barely hear you. Your voice, it's broken.

Save yourself, save Jarr-Wya. I'm okay on my own. Ella, I know how to fight for myself. I've done it all my life.

No one should feel alone, Mom, and I think I know a bit more about that than I should . . . Wait! The others are talking. The Lord is grumbling about Dad's plan, which involves delivering Xlea unharmed and making peace with the Steffanus warriors. The Lord thinks we should have wounded them when we had the chance, that the Olearons who remain in the city would have seen the fire and come to help. Then we wouldn't be so badly outnumbered.

I continue. *The Lord wants to return to the mountain and to send a beacon of fire into the sky, calling to the glass city. That way the Olearons can burn in attack from two sides if we're not granted access to the tunnels. The Lord wants to reach the Star now more than ever, while the Bangols are missing in action—to use the Star's power to defeat the Millia before we're transported to Earth to confront the Bangols, though I know what that means. To the Lord, confrontation means battle. It means blood. The Lord is acting strangely, Mom. He's more vicious than he was a second ago. It's like he's a different person.*

Stay away from him, Ella. Do you hear me?

Yeah, Mom, I do. But—

He's not safe. Stay with Dad, Grandpa Archie, and Nate, but still go for the Star.

No.

No? Don't argue with me. I'm the parent here—

And you're also not technically here . . .

Ella? Ella—what's happening there? What're the others saying?

I can't believe it!

What, Ell?

Dad! How can he agree with the Lord? All he cares about is the Star!

No, all he cares about is you, Ella. For your dad, finding the Star means saving you. Oh no!

What, Mom? Are you hurt?

I'm outside of myself. Inside out, upside down. It's either pain or bliss, but the difference between the two is like the thin line of a blade.

Nate will help me, even if Dad won't. Nate has refused the Lord's plan; he says his priority is saving you and our world, our home. He says that Jarr can save itself, that it's his mission to return every last Bangol to their northern shore. Grandpa Archie is pacing. He looks younger, but the frown on his face ages him. He's biting his nails, sinking back into the rubble of the stone band shell. I can tell he's conflicted.

Why won't you listen to me, Ella? You never listen! I tell you to do your homework and you ignore me. I make a schedule for your medications and you forget your pills at home during school. I do everything for you, and now I want you to do something for me: go to the mountain. Stop being difficult with the company, the Olearons, and Luggie, who are all trying to help you, even if it's indirectly. While the others fight, climb into the caves, and find the way down to the Star, kill it, let it go free, do whatever you have to do. Listen to me. This once. Please!

Nate says he needs a Jarrwian to operate the Tillastrion, but all of them have agreed to go after the Star.

Ella, you're not listening! Fine. Give Nate a message for me.

No, Mom—

Ella, tell Nate that I beg him to save you first. Please. I feel so very thin and may not survive this anyway. The Bangols are crushing me. Their bodies are like rock. Their head-stones make the beginnings of a hundred bruises on every part of me. I think we're getting close to the end of this journey. I can hear their language, their moans. They're worried about what's to come on the other side.

Mom, I respect you. I love you. I always heard you when you bossed me around at home. I was always listening, at least with one ear. And I'm sorry for not always doing what you said. I'm afraid this is going to be another one of those times. You're in danger, and yes, you may not make it, but that doesn't mean I'm giving up on you.

I'm being pulled upward, Ell. My body is nearly bent in two. I'll never make it to the other side of this. Everything moves so fast through . . . what is it? Water, or air, or light? And the colors all bleed, the clouds crash, the vibrations shiver through my veins, and I can't speak aloud even if I wanted to. I can make out Zeno, though. His voice is a trumpet, loud and sharp. He says we're almost there. That he can smell Lanzarote and his shop, Treasures, tucked away in the market. Ouch, oh! My back, my head . . .

Mom!

Everything has become so still, and now my head is a spinning top. I'm vomiting blackness. The air here smells . . . familiar . . . the sweetness of grass and brine of the North Atlantic Ocean. Spanish cooking; coriander, red pepper, garlic, sugar cane, and oven-roasted fish covered in salt. We've made it to the Canary Islands! To Lanzarote. To the city of Arrecife, where the Atlantic Odyssey *docked on our cruise. I'm bleeding, Ell. The Bangols are tying me up, carrying me. Not Zeno—he's off ordering the Bangols around. I can overhear them. We're heading to Artesanal Mercado Haria, the artisan market in the town of Haria, to Treasures.*

I can hear people screaming—through your subconscious. What are the Bangols doing?

Their powers are diminished, but they can still control rock. They're bellowing, calling forward the stones of the island. They're crushing people in their way, carving the earth. They're planning to build a fortress of stone. Zeno has approached me. The look on his face is disgusting, greedy, power-hungry. He's boasting. The Bangols are going to construct huge arching bridges—like the ones on the eastern edge of Jarr-Wya—to connect the seven Canary Islands, ruling from here before spreading, hungry to dominate. First Lanzarote. Then Fuerteventura, Gran Canaria, Tenerife, then the three smaller landmasses. All seven Canary Islands will be connected as one. I spit on Zeno. He doesn't like that. He's coming at me. He's got a stone raised in his hand. Oh no!

Mom? Mom?!

Oh shoot, this is not good, not good at all. What do I do? I can't draw fast enough. I'll have to write with the paintbrush, even if Luggie can't read my language. He should have learned when his sister Nanjee pestered him to.

Quiet!! All of You!! Listen to me. I talked to Mom. Zeno's Killing people. He's taking over the Canary Islands. We NEED TO GO NOW!! Stop them or people will DIE! Mom's hurt. Star can wait! Lord- Want to rule Jarr-Wya? Defeat Bangols NOW! Or they'll Kill you in your Sleep. Kill us all. You've got the advantage RIGHT NOW!! Earn our trust. NOW OR NEVER!!!!!!!!!!!

The Lord puts his gloved hand on me, on my right hand, stopping my paintbrush. I forget how to breathe. I wasn't expecting the Lord's touch, and it unnerves me. Mom's warning floods my mind, and I forget how to move. His black eyes are unreadable, bottomless pools at night, dangerous.

"Speak, child," the Lord commands.

What? I'm so confused. Why would he want me to croak out a bird? Oh, owww, argh! His hand is crushing mine, so subtly that I doubt the others can see, and now I can't help but wince and cry out in pain. As I do, one single green bird flaps upward from between my teeth. It has only flapped its wings once before the Lord plucks it from the air.

"Junin, a carrier flask," the Lord orders. She brings him a small metal vial with a blue flip-top from her traveling sack she rescued from the flood. He releases my hand and tears a strip of paper from my stash. He dips my brush into the black ink and writes a message. I glance at it but it's in Olearon. The brush was given to me by the red beings, and it's obvious the Lord knows how to use it. In comparison to my large thick letters, his lines are thin and sure.

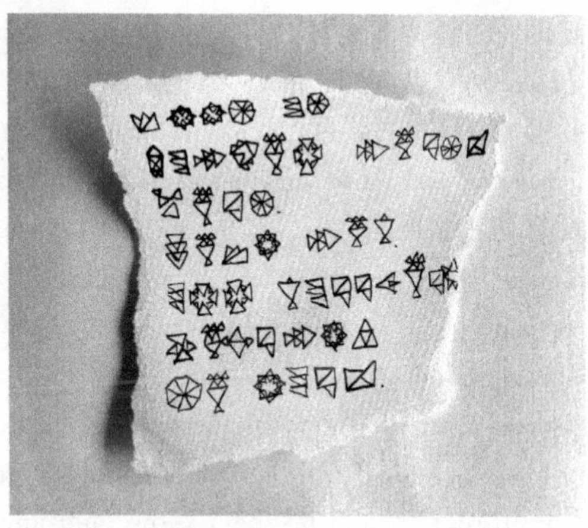

The Lord rolls the paper into a tight cylinder and slips it into the carrier flask, which he straps to a leg of my bird. He secures the lid, then whispers into the green bird's ear. Its human-like eyes bat their long lashes at him, and it chirps and nods. The Lord tosses the bird into the air where it rises hurriedly in a swirl of lacy air to become a green morning star above us.

I scowl at the Lord. My teeth are clenched. I hate him, perhaps more than I've hated anyone—more than the heartless bullies at school, more than my cancer. My illness hurts me, but the Lord has sealed the fate of my world. He's called the Olearons to Baluurwa. There's going to be a war that has nothing to do with saving Mom and the other humans.

My body aches with weakness and nausea, my cancer picking the perfect time to flare up. Otherwise I'd have beaten the Lord, hit him harder than I did Tuggs when I saw him kick Luggie for helping me on the eastern bridge. I need an outlet for my anger, my helplessness. I imagine clawing that ridiculous glass breastplate from the Lord's body, shattering it, and hurting him so badly that he bleeds. I know it's wrong. Dad would pull me off before my fantasy played out anyway. He's not a fighter; it's against his nature, even here. Despite studying history, or maybe because of it, Dad is anti-violence. At least the Dad I knew. That Dad would never go along with the Lord's plan. Maybe it's violence that glows through his orange veins.

The Lord called Grandpa Archie a thief for stealing that magical glass, but it's himself who is the robber. He's stolen my father. He's sentenced Grandpa to servitude, if not certain death. He's abandoned Mom. I hate him.

As much as I want to pound my fists on his chest, cancer is my true lord. Ugh. I need to vomit, but I swallow the acidity back down my throat. I can't let them know—not any of them.

Not Luggie, who will worry and insist on taking an easier road. Not Dad, who will take up Mom's post in coddling me. And especially not the Lord of Olearon, who will feel justified in ignoring my plea to follow the Bangols to Earth to save the humans. I lock my jaw; that's all I can do. I run the remaining ink wetting my paintbrush through my fingers, smoothing the frazzled bristles into combed lines.

"Islo, Nameris, Junin, come," the Lord of Olearon commands. "Preparations are in order. We have one sunset in which to join with these humans"—and the way he says humans infuriates me—"in constructing a Tillastrion."

I can't breathe. Did I hear the Lord correctly? Teach one of us to build a Tillastrion? My mind is reeling. Is the Tillastrion to help save the humans—and Mom? But what about the bird? It doesn't make sense.

Grandpa Archie runs forward, startling me with his swiftness. Confusion scrunches his forehead. As if reading my mind, he chokes out the question rolling around in my head. "The green bird? Pardon me, my Lord, but . . . did you summon the Olearons to battle the Steffanus warriors?"

All that's playing out before me is both too rushed for comprehension and in the same breath too slow, like a video that lags when the audio skips ahead. The vomit rises again, and I cough it down. I dig my fingernails into the simple glass ornamentation on the handle of the blue-bark paintbrush, distracting the cancer with new pain.

The Lord answers Grandpa Archie, "The Maiden in me finds wisdom in the perspective of the child—Ella Wellsley. When my Maiden sacrificed her Jarrwian body, dying to save your lives"—he looms over us humans—"she became my closest confidante. We are as intimate as two souls can be. She counsels me to spare humankind from greater loss, Archibald, advising me to finish what we have begun and to rule peacefully, even if that means Bangol extinction." The Lord turns to Luggie. "As you would agree?"

Luggie nods, his face submissive—though I notice his clenched fists.

I understand why the Maiden would urge the Lord like this; Mom told me she was always kind though unforgiving, faithful yet fierce. She protected Mom and Archie as they wound their way across the island to find me in the east. When Valarie's vengeful spirit transferred into the mob of attacking carakwas, it was the Maiden who paid the ultimate price. She died so that the rest of us could live. That's bravery if you ask me. Slaughtering the Bangols to ensure peace makes sense, coming from her.

What confuses me is Luggie.

Why is he accepting the Lord's plan without argument? These are his friends, his relatives that the Lord talks about so casually. Bangol genocide. The Lord worded it well: extinction. Yes, I want to save the humans, but for their own sake, not as a side effect of hunting down the Bangols. Why is Luggie bending to the Lord's will? When we're alone, I'll ask him somehow, but not now. The way the Lord is staring at him makes my skin crawl.

Grandpa Archie turns to me. "Ell, are you strong enough to portal jump with us?" He takes the hand of my uninjured arm, ignoring its inkiness, and strokes it as he used to do when I was little. I pull away harshly and straighten my back. I won't let any in this company—Grandpa Archie included—see how weak I really am. I nod purposefully, scowling at the notion they'd leave me behind.

"Did your mom find jumping between worlds bearable? Could she handle it?" he asks. I know Grandpa. This is his way of saying that if Mom couldn't take it, neither can I. He continues, "When Zeno and I operated the Tillastrion, being so close to the device, to the Naiu, I felt like I was burning, my brain was bisected, my skin floating apart from the rest of me. I'm sorry if that scares you, Ella. I don't mean to. It was also beautiful, like being up in the clouds, weightless, surrounded by sky, or a part of the ocean—not just in it, but one drop of water among trillions. But I'm worried about you . . . you most of all. I have no idea what you experienced on the cruise ship, if the jump from home to Jarr was as painful for you as it was for me. I worry, Ell. Please don't look at me like that . . ."

I'm scowling, of course, pretending to be strong, though I don't want to injure Grandpa with my forced bravery. So I smile weakly. When Grandpa Archie and Zeno transported our cruise ship to Jarr-Wya, I felt a lesser degree of what Grandpa describes. We all felt something.

We had just returned from touring Timanfaya Biosphere Reserve on the island of Lanzarote. Mom and I were heading to our cabin when I felt a strangeness overcome me. Everyone in the hall was aware of the change of atmosphere inside the ship. It was a feeling of weakness and disorientation, and altogether unlike my cancer spells. Mom chalked it up to turbulence and a bad bout of seasickness as we pulled out of port.

My head seemed disproportionately large compared to my body. The air-conditioning smelled of churned earth and flowers. Wisps of cloud wafted casually down the hall. Mom and I hustled to our cabin, and just in time, because this sweet-smelling, lilac-colored smoke pursued us. I didn't know whether to inhale it deeply—it being so sugary delicious—or to hold my breath. Mom told me to do the latter.

As the lilac smoke toyed with us, as it surrounded our cabin, Mom's words grew slurred. I thought my eyes were tricking me.

Her lips grew swollen, along with her hands and eyelids. Then I felt the fullness of my own lips. Mom and I withdrew to the bed where we waved away the smoke, but it was no use. The color was light and happy, but the smoke made my head feel heavy and covered my eyes with a nearly opaque film. I slept without dreams. I'm not sure how much time passed before Mom woke me up and cleared my eyes. The Maiden of Olearon stared down on us, and then I saw Grandpa Archie lying limp at the foot of the bed. Once awake, he relayed to us that Dad was dead, another of Zeno's lies.

If Dad can survive the trip and live as an Olearon for years, I can do it. If Mom and Grandpa can make the jump between portals—both at the center of the device—then I'll be fine. I hope.

I nod at Grandpa Archie with courage in my clenched jaw. I crack the lid off the ink flask and plunge the brush into it. I draw words for Grandpa, penning each letter as well as I'm able, writing my definitive answer:

Mom said jumping
Portals was a
piece of cake.
She wants us
to come for her
– ALL of us.
Me. You. Dad.
Nate. The Olearons.
ALL of us.
Lanzarote is in
trouble. I feel
STRONG!!

Trust me, Grandpa.
I'll be fine.

chapter 27

Ella

Mom must be sleeping, too, because I'm with her again, in her dream. We still ride the feathered back of Finnah, and the two of them, Mom and the massive green bird, seem to know where they're going. We rise through the sky, which the green birds have a way of spinning into dancing emerald wisps. The breeze is warm and dreamy, and all the edges around us are fuzzy.

"Hey, you," Mom says. She turns back to look at me and smiles, even with her eyes, genuinely unworried.

"Hey yourself," I say, laughing.

Mom's dreams are both the best and the worst place. I love being able to speak and be near her, but to understand her this deeply means seeing and accepting all the pieces I'd rather not know, the things she'd never willingly tell me.

I lean into Mom's back, her long blond hair smooth against my cheek as she turns forward once more. She's as real now as she was bumping up against me as we tumbled down Baluurwa in the blamala crab's spit bubble. I fill my lungs with her smell: spring daisies and cottage nights curled under the quilt Grandma Suzie made for us, our favorite place to hide away from the world. As Mom breathes, both our bodies rise and fall again and again, as Finnah's great rib cage expands between our legs.

"I like you with me," Mom whispers. "When I carried you

within me those nine blissful months, I felt the security of someone as close as my own pulse. After you were born, that love was so tightly wrapped around us. I knew I'd finally found the one who'd stay with me forever."

"But what if I go to school in another state, or another country? What if I live long enough to get married?" My knowledge that neither of these things is possible can't touch me in this dreamland.

"I don't mean in body," Mom answers sleepily. "Being easy to leave isn't about the absence of physical presence. It's the withholding of love, the rejection of desire and affection. Even when we fight—and I'm sorry, Ell, really, for all the ways I do the wrong things, say the wrong things—we share the same blood, the same hair and skin, the same experiences. Even when we run away from each other, we always look back. We always run back. You love me even when I'm a helicopter parent and make life a little miserable for both of us.

"I've always felt like I've grown up right alongside you, Ella," Mom continues. "No one teaches moms and dads how to parent, how to love their kids the right way. What right way? Am I right?" She chuckles. "Especially when it comes to cancer kids. You've taught me what love is. I hope you hear that. You've taught me to love, because even when I make a mess out of everything and fall hard from the pedestal of motherhood, you pick me up. You continue to love me. Which is baffling. Truly baffling to me."

"Mom—"

"It's true. So no matter if we're together or whole worlds apart—like Earth is from Jarr—I know you'll never leave me. I carry you in my heart. Even if I die, Ell—and I may die before I wake from this beautiful place—you're a part of me and I'm a part of you. If cancer takes you—and I say *if* because I am holding onto the hope I once thought so foolish—a part of me will die, too. I don't know if life would be worth living then. Would it, Finnah?" Mom directs her attention to the large blinking eyes, past the three-foot-long eyelashes, of the great green bird.

"Tessa, life is always worth living—however short, however long," answers Finnah. "Some, however, feel that life without goodness, joy, and peace is not worth saving. This is why Jarr is changing, why its inhabitants have grown fierce. When we lose faith in each other, the battle is over."

Mom responds to Finnah as if she's forgotten that my arms are around her waist, that my exhalations flutter the hair at her back. "Ella gave me that faith. Without parents—or any blood family—I began as a lostling. I was lost before I was ever found. The only real family is the one I made with Arden, Ella, and even Archie. But it's all so fragile, tender, losable. As close as I get to happiness, to stability, the situation shows itself to be fragile. Ella's illness. Arden leaving us. Ella's capture by Bangols. I'm sucked back to Earth, alone."

"Being alone is not the worst fate," Finnah answers, ducking beneath a cloud.

"I've clung to Ella so tightly all her life for fear of losing her that I've made fear its own being, and it stalks me."

"If you created it"—Finnah snorts through a golden beak—"you must also have the power to obliterate it."

"I agree with Finnah," I say.

"Oh, Ella, I didn't see you there."

I shake my head at Mom, who yawns and stretches her arms as if only now wakening.

She asks me, "You didn't hear what Finnah and I were discussing, did you?"

"No," I lie.

"Oh good. Well, since you're back there, can you massage a

knot in my back? I feel so tightly wound, Ell—not that I must hold on too tightly, Finnah. Your ride is smooth, I promise."

I scoot back a few inches on Finnah, then rest my hands on Mom's shoulder blades. My arm that broke when we crashed on the Millia's beach has healed to a nagging ache. Here, in this sleepy, distinctly *other* place—where Mom and I can meet worlds apart—my arm feels as good as it did precancer. The gash and burn from our crash into the Bangol fortress is also absent.

Like Mom said, her shoulders are tight and I can feel the knots, firm and round. I push into one, and she cries out. "Too hard?" I mumble. Her hair sways as she nods. I continue to press my fingers and palms against her shoulders, but something isn't right.

I lift the back of Mom's white tank top and nearly tumble, startled, and must grab Finnah's feathers so I don't slip off into the dreamy sky. There, at Mom's scars from her childhood scoliosis operation, grow jagged ridges beneath her skin. From each of her shoulder blades, brown mounds bulge. I wipe my hands on my thighs, as if whatever is seeking to exit her could infect me through my fingertips.

"What is it, Ella?" she asks, turning her chin toward me over one shoulder.

"I-I don't know, Mom." As I say these words, the brown mounds push through the final layer of pink flesh and spill out. Umber-colored vines unfurl from the holes in Mom's skin. They emerge slowly, delicately, thick at first but then thin and yellow-green at their tips. The vines are young and produce stems and buds that bloom into deep dusty-green hearts.

"My back, Ell. It hurts. Please help me."

I can't reply. There are no words to make sense of what's happening. The vines continue to spill out of the two slits on Mom's back. They appear aware. They inch over my legs, and the leaves study my face, caressing my cheeks. They slip behind my head, beneath my hair, to where my cancer biopsy scar lives silently, rippled and red. My eyes grow wide. My scar!

Frantically, I brush the tangled hair from my neck and touch the puckered flesh. It's tender, as it has always been, as if the nerve endings were traumatized in surgery and left to mourn their injury in futile protests. My fingers trace the familiar line, the bumps at either end of the incision, the parallel ridges from the stitches.

I exhale, relieved. My scar hasn't burst open. It remains its own kind of ugly. All the while, Mom's two gashes, one on each shoulder blade, tear wider as the vines leak out like froth on a pot bubbling over. She reaches over her shoulders. Her fingertips are just shy of the gashes. She pushes her elbow and her left hand stretches farther. She caresses the vines, and, to my confusion, seems comforted.

"Oh, I see now," Mom says with a sigh. "My insides are showing on the outside. I've always felt different. Out of place. Nowhere to belong. No one to understand."

"Mom, you're talking crazy. You belong with me. I understand!"

She doesn't hear me. We'd been flying through a peachy sky streaked with wisps of solemn clouds. Since the inception of the dream, a slowly approaching blackness has stolen the scroll of red and margin of blue in the sky, revealing twinkling white flecks that dance around us.

Beside the stars are planets each turning at their own pace. One is a brilliant orange, radiating yellow and revolving quickly. The atmosphere around it is peppered with debris, its content too small to recognize yet large enough that you can appreciate its many forms. This hustling orange world extends a yellow glow, connecting like a stretched sock to a smaller planet. This one is teal with two revolving white rings, situated ninety degrees from each other, spinning in opposite directions. Through this channel of yellow, fragments float lazily from the orange planet to the blue. I can make out small clouds of dust mushrooming off the blue planet as the rubble collides with it.

Finnah chirps, "There are more than a thousand connected realms. There is the mother planet, rich in Naiu, and then its derivative—usually smaller, usually appearing devoid of Naiu, but it is there. The derivative cannot see its mother world, but if it slows down, holds its breath so that time rushes on without it, then Naiu can be felt. Naiu formed the derivative worlds, all worlds, and even unseen it is in everything and in everyone. It is undeniable."

Mom and Finnah cock their heads from side to side, appreciating each planet and its too colorful, too radiant threads binding the mother to its equally vibrant derivative.

"Umbilical cords," Mom whispers. "Everything's connected. One planet sustaining another."

"The bond is not always that peaceful, that respectful," replies Finnah, speaking in hushed awe through her mammoth beak. "Naiu is good, innocent, and naive. It recoils from evil, taking with it its goodness. The evil then has space to grow. Naiu does not recognize that by leaving, it expands the very thing it wishes to rebuke. Not everyone is kind to fellow creatures and the creation they inhabit. In the formation of the worlds, Naiu was spread thin in places, giving rise to unhappiness.

"On Earth, the cruelty between humans is terribly shortsighted. Just as one planet is connected to another, so, too, is everything made of Naiu. When you wound another, you cut out your own heart. Speak words of ill-will, and you slice yourself in two. Touch the land with lust instead of love, and you rape your own identity."

"If we're all connected, Finnah, tell me: Why have I always felt so alone?" Mom is crying. "It's so beautiful. If only all people, all creatures, could see the worlds from here . . ."

Finnah turns to look at Mom. "Is it that you are alone, or that you are running from something?" she asks fondly.

Mom shakes her head, her tears falling to her shirt and watering the vines that have coiled their shafts around us. "What do you mean?"

"If you still yourself, separate yourself from your notion of time, what do you learn? Perhaps you feel alone because you are out of your birth rhythm."

"Because I'm of a different rhythm." Mom's voice contains no self-pity but is crisp and firm and suddenly alive with hope.

"Yes." Finnah nods and glides between the swell of planets. A large purple-freckled sphere dances through the murky abyss. It's surrounded with an iridescent blue sheen, which carries large ships with rippling sails on the cusp of space. The ships drop nets that scoop beneath them, where cheeky fish with spears for noses dart out of the way. One leaps from the blue sheen like blown taffeta and arcs in a perfect rainbow above the hunters. The fish dips beneath the vessel once more and hurries through the flowing atmosphere to the derivative planet, a pale green world with small pockets of blue, like Earth inverted.

"You're right, Finnah," Mom says, snapping me back to the giant bird and the vines and the rushing air and my cancer and my orphan mother. Her voice is full of breath. "I don't know what I've run from all my life, yet I've always sensed it. I've feared it, like a shadow that falls on me from behind. When I turn, whoever was there is always gone. In a way, this presence has created an absence."

Finnah wheezes. I hadn't noticed until now, with Finnah's strained gasp, that Mom's vines have wound themselves more tightly around the three of us. Mom turns to me over her shoulder. Only her neck moves; her arms are coiled at her sides, her legs fixed to Finnah's feathered body. I'm similarly twisted in the firm growth. It's nauseatingly claustrophobic, so I wrench my torso to and fro and pull at the vines, making only small headway. A leaf slaps my hand.

Then I feel it. Something's bulging above my shoulders. There's a pushing, from inside, and the scar on my neck throbs. Then the skin breaks, painfully jagged like torn paper. A trickle of blood runs down the gully of my spine. A newborn vine creeps out of me. It slinks along my skin and inches its way to my right cheek.

Mom's lips are blue. Her eyes are wide as she watches me, the whites glowing in the starlight. They brim with tears, reflecting the twenty nearest planets that dance and spin around us. She blinks, and the reflection drops the planets to her cheeks, where they tumble down to water the vines.

"I'm sorry," Mom says almost inaudibly. Finnah's wings are contorted within the conquest of the hungry vines. The great green bird flaps with strained effort, constricted, and we fall in the shifting expanse of sky and colliding atmospheres. Constellations of one planet butt up against another. All we can do is soar. My lungs bash against my heart, which slams against my throat. My hair, and Mom's, lifts from our shoulders. Still, Mom looks back at me, whispering, "Ella, I'm so sorry."

Ella

Ella

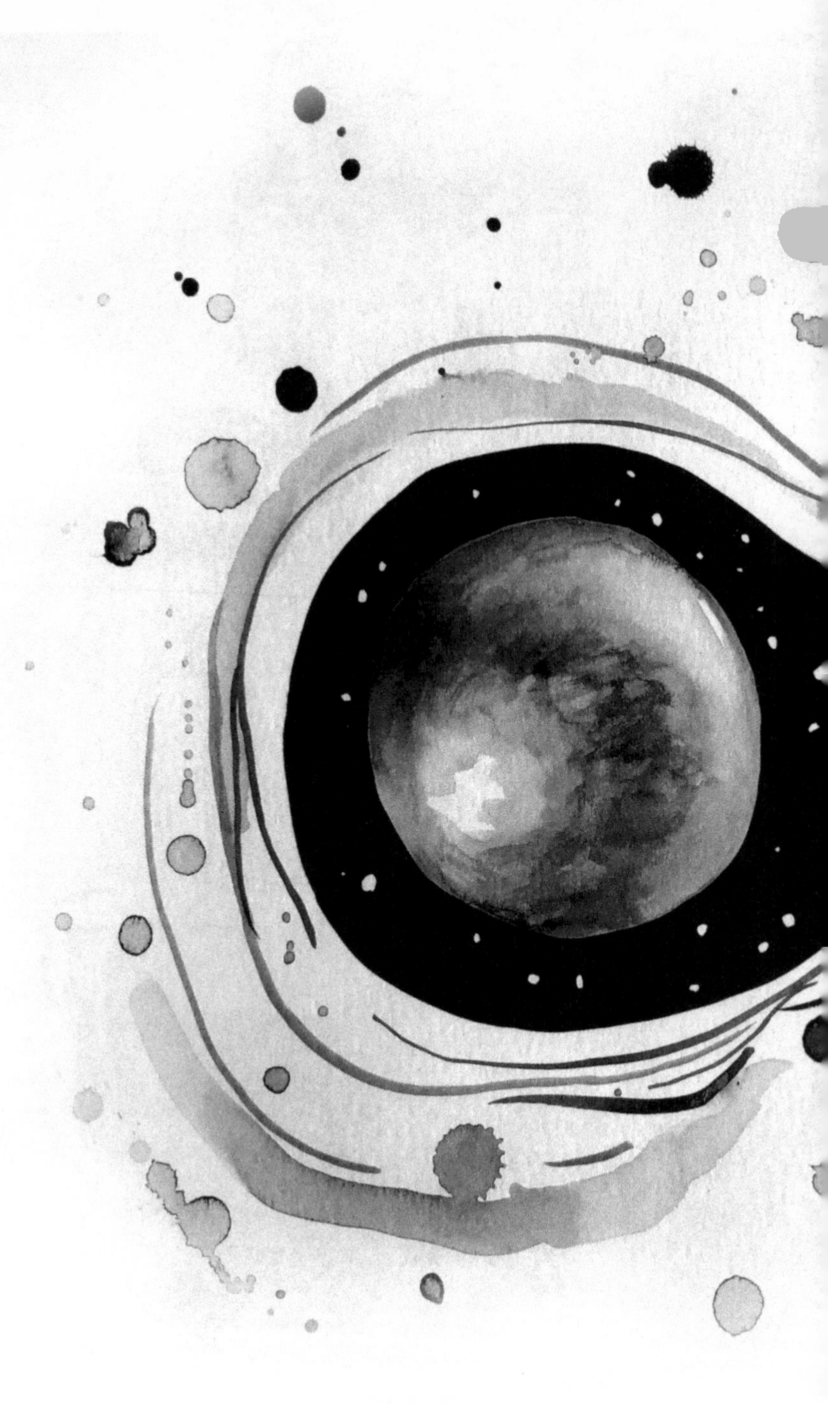

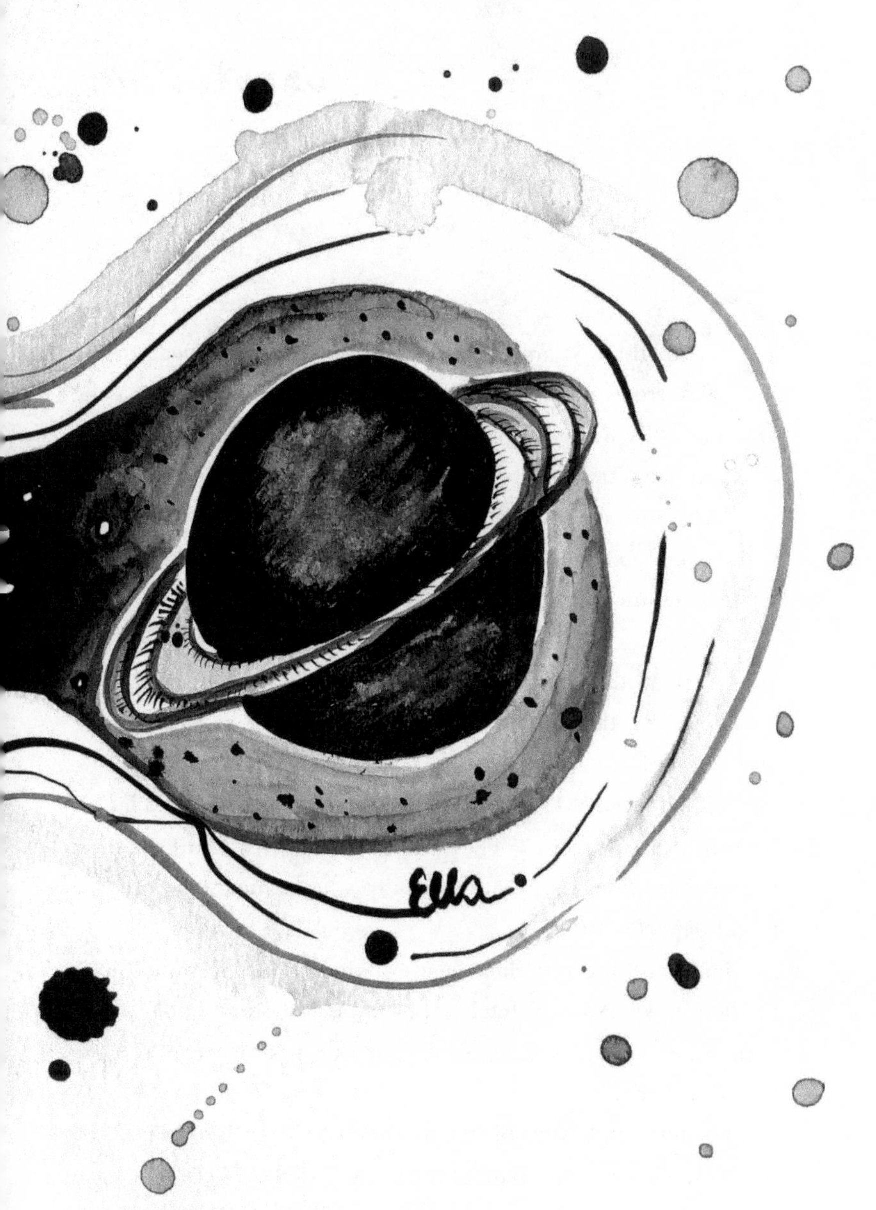
Ella

chapter 28

Archie

Something is amiss," grumbles the Lord of Olearon. He narrows his black eyes as he stares up at Baluurwa the Doomful. "By now, the green bird should have reached the glass city and our warriors a line of red above the maze."

"They are on their way," Azkar replies as he loads his sack with Bangol foodstuffs, a look of disgust across his scarred face.

Islo chimes in, "Right, Azkar. I bet they reach us before nightfall."

Much to the company's surprise, as if Islo had called forth the Olearons, the thin forest beyond the southern maze begins to glow. Archie leaps to his feet at the sight.

"Good, then." The Lord exhales and drops his gloved hands from his narrow waist. "They will arrive shortly. Until then, let us conclude final preparations—only what is necessary—so we might depart swiftly."

Junin and Islo nod their heads of thick dreadlocks and hurry to their tasks. Ardenal fetches Ella a carved stone goblet filled with water, urging her to drink and sit while she can. Luggie hovers at her side.

Nameris and Nate bicker as they construct the Tillastrion on the stage, using the Bangol throne as a table. There they have collected a small group of objects: a flaking ember; a wooden box with a broken hinge meant to hold dried sea plants; an enchanted stone from the maze; a broken shard of the blamala crab bubble.

Archie overhears Nate's objections. "I can't see how this device," he begins, "can possibly transport our company, plus a contingent of Olearons, to Earth."

"What is your issue, human?" retorts Nameris. "Is it our choice of materials, their combination, which is not yet complete, or the size of the device?"

"Size, of course. You saw the Bangols' massive machine."

"From my research of Tillastrions—though I have only studied them, never constructed one myself—it was excessive."

"Okay, fine," Nate grumbles, "but I reckon ours can only move, let's say, eight, but we'll have twenty times that soon."

Nameris shakes his head at the disgruntled sea captain. He sits gently on the arm of the rock throne. "Let me teach you something, human—"

"Nate."

"Nathanial, the Bangols believe size is of utmost importance, hence their recklessness in conquering new territory, even at great cost. This misconception extends to their Tillastrion as well. However, anyone familiar with Naiu knows that it perceives desire, longing. What needs to be great is not the size of the device, but the will to carry it where it needs to go. Think of Archie and the *Atlantic Odyssey*." Nameris waits for his point to resonate.

Archie feels his palms sweat and his shirt dampen with perspiration where he leans against the amphitheater band shell, listening. He vividly recalls his longing to reunite his family, healthy and whole. He and Zeno operated the Tillastrion—which indeed was small, only a box, clay bowl, and glass sphere—in Archie's cabin aboard the *Atlantic Odyssey*. After the swirl of lights, they found themselves still on the ship, and Zeno was distraught. He blamed Archie for not caring enough, when many would argue that Archie cared too much. He inadvertently brought the *Odyssey* and its passengers along with him on his mission to find Arden and Ella's cure.

Nate winces at the memories of his ship plucked from its course across the North Atlantic Ocean, its siege and destruction by the Olearons, and the murders of his passengers by the Millia sands, all because of the size of Archie's desire. Finally, the captain understands.

"So," Nameris says, rising, "how badly do you wish to return to your planet? How much does Ella desire to save her mother?"

Nate is silent but nods thoughtfully.

"We will have no trouble with our little device once it is built." Nameris returns to combining the objects.

Suddenly, Archie feels a hot hand wrap itself around his upper arm. From the way the long fingers bore into him, Archie knows the grip belongs to the Lord of Olearon—but which Lord, he is not certain. *Not the Maiden*, Archie laments, the one Olearon he desperately wishes to speak with.

Archie's heart thuds against his ribcage. He pulls away hastily, high-steps down the stage stairs, and nearly tumbles over a sheet of crudely hammered metal. All around them is the wreckage of foolhardy industrialization, forged greedily from the earth. Discarded gears, bent and beginning to rust, are strewn carelessly amongst the bones of cradle birds and the chewed skins of the Bangols' favorite fruit.

Archie dodges all this and sidesteps the mouth of the cavernous mine. He retreats until his back presses up against a curled piece of clay. The Lord advances on Archie step for step. *Which one is it?* Archie wonders. *The 30th Lord, Dunakkus, or the*

29th? The look in the Lord's eyes is grim, menacing. He towers above Archie, who peers up timidly through his bushy eyebrows. When the Lord does not speak, Archie smiles awkwardly and shrugs, then slips out from between the Olearon and the clay.

"Come back here, Archibald Wellsley," the Lord says coolly. "How am I to trust you when you scurry away like a Bangol?" He corners Archie between a curl of clay and a desolate stone structure. Archie's heels back into a rock, loosening a small avalanche of dirt. "You have nowhere to go. Let us talk candidly, human."

Archie gulps and rests his hands against the wind-cooled stones behind him. His fingers graze the surface until they find sprite bones, and he pulls them loose. He folds the sharp bones into the creases of his palms. *Not much of a weapon*, he thinks, *but just enough if I need to startle him or pick a lock.*

Archie stutters, "My Lord, I'm in your service, as promised . . ."

The Lord's sharp-edged expression trembles momentarily, then his face rounds, he flushes, and his eyes widen.

"Maiden," whispers Archie, blanketed in relief.

"Archibald." The Maiden's voice is hard yet smooth. "We do not have long to talk. The 29th Lord—Telmakus—is growing in strength. While the body of Dunakkus, my love, directs the Olearon warriors, inwardly Telmakus battles us. Unfortunately, I was not prepared for his strength. I grow weary in diminishing Telmakus, to stop him from overshadowing us completely. Therefore, our mission is more urgent than ever."

Nameris was right, Archie reflects. *The 29th Lord is taking over the 30th. But how?*

The Maiden continues swiftly, "Telmakus lusts to wear the mantle of lordship once more, to rule not only Jarr-Wya, but the human world as well. That is why it would appear that the Lord has had a change of heart: from defeating the Star to journeying with the Tillastrion. Telmakus feels a kinship with the humans—I do not know why—and wishes to bring our two worlds together, Jarr and Earth. He is mad! Every Olearon knows this to be true, but as he lives through Dunakkus, none but us two are aware. The Olearons follow, though they do not know the wildness that lives inside this flesh."

"We are not alone, Maiden. Nameris and Tessa know, too—but no one will believe us. You must expose Telmakus," Archie urges.

"It is not that simple, though I wish it were. Done at the wrong moment, I would seal the death for all who witness it."

Archie chokes on his words. "Our company?"

"Yes, Archibald. Telmakus would scorch all evidence, return to the glass city, and continue to rule."

"Maiden, what can I do?"

"Brave human, thank you for your courage. I wish I could protect you and your family. The Olearons, too, are in danger. None are safe. Telmakus has strengthened his mind against me. Be wary. Though I sense you are loath to return to Earth, you must. Keep watch over the Lord. Question his every word and deed. Never rest your attention. The fates of our two worlds depend on it." The Maiden pauses. "And if this is goodbye, Archie," she says, "I do wish you to know—"

Archie shakes his head and argues, "No, Maiden. We will save you and Dunakkus, somehow." He bites his lower lip. "I'll talk with Ardenal—and Azkar and Junin, too—and we'll come up with a plan—"

"Slow your breathing." The Maiden places her large hand over Archie's chest and the warmth calms the jitter of his heart. "I have lived, Archie. I no longer require saving. What I wish you to know is this: it does not matter what world you hail from, nor the amount of time by which you measure your life, nor the ones you have failed, the mistakes you have made. What matters is the ones you have loved. That is the spirit of Naiu. If you wonder which path to take, who to trust, let the love in you be your guide."

The hand on Archie's chest grows hot and uncomfortable, slowly singeing his chest. The Maiden does not withdraw it, even when Archie cries out. The hardness returns to the red face that bears down on him, no longer with compassion but with fury. Archie fiddles with the sprite bones, shifting and rolling them toward his fingers and thumbs. One drops to the ground. A wicked smile spreads over the Lord's face. As Archie is about to stab the fiery hand with the bone, a voice calls out, startling them both.

It is Islo. The stocky Olearon lacks his usual composure. His face is pale red, almost orange, and his voice faded and weary. "The Steffanus warriors," he whispers like a breath of smoke.

"What about them?" the Lord barks, dropping his hand. He turns sharply from Archie to storm gracefully from the interior of the maze.

"Lord," says Islo, "the sisters are here!"

chapter 29

Archie

One hundred Olearons, the young and inexperienced warriors that had remained in the glass city, are herded into the Bangols' desolate northern fortress by an equally large assembly of Steffanus warriors. Black eyes glare at icy reds, and all weapons and flames are at the ready. The Olearons band together at the center of the commotion and form a monstrous fire, surrounded on every side by fierce women in scorched yet vibrant gowns, their antlers dripping gold.

"Command your warriors to squelch their flames," one tall, full-bodied Steffanus demands. "We wish to speak with your Lord."

The Lord of Olearon steps from behind a stone structure to stroll across the fortress grounds, past the gaping crater. He reaches the southern maze and faces the new arrivals, saying, "Let us begin with manners. Who addresses me?"

"I am Callisto, and I have questions for you—"

"Callisto," Ardenal interrupts. "That is the name we humans gave to the second largest moon of Jupiter, one of the four that orbit it."

"Yes, mother world Jupiter and one of its derivatives, Callisto," replies the Steffanus. "And who are you that speaks out of turn?"

"I am Ardenal, or Arden on Earth, where I was born."

There is hushed chatter amongst the Steffanus sisters, but Callisto only narrows her eyes.

"Now you know my name. Tell me the meaning of yours," Ardenal demands.

The fierce red of Callisto's eyes softens. "I found Callisto an inspiring planet and changed my name in its honor. Callisto's terrain is craterous, which some find unsightly. To me, from a distance, that moon appears like its own galaxy, containing a host of stars in constellations yet unmapped by my sisters and me. It is believed to be a world long dead, lifeless, and desolate. I do not believe that to be true. Rumors in the human world say the icy planet holds a living sea at its core. One day, I hope to visit it."

Archie watches as his son slips into his role as a scholar. Ardenal pushes up the glasses he no longer wears as he begins to speak. "I first came upon the moon Callisto in my historical studies. In Greek mythology, Callisto was the stunning daughter of King Lycaon. Callisto took up a virgin's vow as a follower of Artemis. Unfortunately for her, she was seduced by the great god Zeus—also known as Jupiter—in disguise. Callisto became pregnant and her bad luck continued.

"Artemis believed Callisto's pregnancy and the son she bore to be the woman's betrayal. She was barred from the company of Artemis, to whom she was loyal, and after the birth of her child she was turned into a bear by Hera, wife of Zeus. Then, as if she had not been through enough, Callisto's offspring nearly killed her on a hunting mission.

"I cannot recall which god had mercy on her—though in all irony I suspect it was Zeus, who began the whole fateful chain of events in the first place. Callisto was plucked from the Earth and placed amongst the stars as a new constellation: The Great Bear, or Ursa Major. She became mother of the Arcadians through the son she bore by Zeus."

The face of the Steffanus flushes red. “You tell me what I already know, Ardenal—Arden,” says Callisto in a deep voice. “What purpose do you have with this history lesson?”

“Well”—Ardenal clears his throat—“as someone who knows the mythology, I wonder . . . In reality, Zeus was the deceiver, Callisto the deceived. So Steffanus who chose the name Callisto: Are you and your sisters fooled by the Star? Do you seek to mislead us as well? Perhaps you do not know the lies you believe as truth—lies like the ones revered by the Millia and Bangols, which seem like logic but are a betrayal of all races on Jarr-Wya, if not all of Jarr.”

“You do know your history, Ardenal, though I suspect I know more about you than you do about yourself,” says Callisto with a sneer.

The Lord, who had watched stoically until now, rages. “What knowledge could you possibly possess?”

“Our sister, Laken, has told us much.”

Archie lunges forward at the name. “Laken,” he says, wheezing. “Is she here?”

“No, human. She is not. Nor back on Baluurwa, at least not in body. Laken was murdered, despite her old and weary form, when these Olearons passed near the foot of the mountain not half a sunset past.”

Archie covers his mouth with his hands, muffling his shock and sorrow. He can see Laken’s scarred though gentle face. He remembers her voice and the shapes her lips made when she spoke, revealing the truth that still leaves Archie reeling.

“They pursued us first, my Lord,” says a red-skinned warrior. “We defended ourselves while hurrying to you.”

“War disguised as peace!” says Callisto with scorn. Her wildly flowing gown is blue, silver, and earth brown, as Laken’s had been. Callisto’s face bears no similarity to the wise, kind Steffanus who sat and talked with Archie on her crumb of earth high above the blue forest. "Before she died," continues Callisto, "Laken spoke of beings from the human world. Ones who would save us all. She told us to look for the one named Archibald Wellsley, and that he would help us regain peace in all worlds."

"Archie?" says Lillium near one of his ears. "Is this true?"

"However, the wind carried a disturbing story up to our ears. A story about this very man, who plotted a war between the Bangols and Steffanus sisters, all to gain advantage over the Star," Callisto finishes.

"It's true," Archie mumbles, "but that was before I went back in time and spoke with Laken."

"Dad, are you delirious? What are you talking about?" asks Ardenal, all confidence flushed from his ruddy face.

"I did hit my head, but that's besides the point. I don't know how it happened, but it did, Arden. I believe it as much as I believe in the ground we stand on. I spoke with Laken, but it wasn't now; she was young and alone. Oww—"

The Lord rests his gloved hands on Archie's shoulders, squeezing tightly. "There is much for us to discuss, Archibald, in private, before you divulge too much that may be used against us. What use is there in wasting breath on a dead Steffanus? No, we must focus on the living and how to keep them so." Releasing Archie, the Lord steps forward until he is face-to-face with Callisto. "I agree with my loyal warrior, Ardenal. Why would the Steffanus sisters wish to protect the Star, which has poisoned our world since its arrival, driven mad the Bangols, and formed the Millia sands?"

"Dim your warriors' flames, and I will tell you what I know," answers Callisto.

The Lord looks to Ardenal, without words, for his estimation of the trustworthiness of the Steffanus. Ardenal nods briefly. The

Lord turns to his warriors, the ones equipped with provisions from the glass city and weary from their travels. He raises his hands and lowers them gently. All crimson skin is extinguished, and flames return to the napes of the warriors' necks. They push out of the circle of Steffanus sisters and join the company.

"Gestures of peace. Thank you. Now I will begin," Callisto says, more kindly than before. "My sisters and I were birthed from the fusion of the creature Naiu and a human girl, right there"—she points at the towering mountain of warm black rock—"on Baluurwa. Because of this, we experience Naiu's emotions through our collective beings. We feel the heartbreak of Naiu, of its laments in response to what it has made—the hatred amongst the love, the evil amongst the good.

"Over five hundred thousand sunsets ago, when Naiu created all the worlds and their derivative dimensions, it unknowingly expended its power. Along with it, Naiu gave its magic, love, creativity, joy, and light. Those were its true gifts which, it believes, have become a corrupted. Naiu created time and life from nothing, but over many sunrises and sunsets, that spark of curiosity has morphed into what Naiu is not: greed, lust, distrust, dishonesty, fear—and greatest of all, hatred.

"Naiu, alive in its creations, mourns what it has made, wishing to undo it. It withdraws those disparate parts of itself back to where it throbs and pulses the loudest in any universe: here, in Jarr, on the island of Jarr-Wya.

"Our island is where Naiu crashed in exhaustion after creation. Its impact formed the mountain at my back, though it was not always called 'Doomful.' I believe that was a name given by the Olearons many sunsets ago."

The Lord's face is enveloped in flame. "The Lords before me bestowed that name out of respect for the Olearon blood shed on its stone and as a promise to those who spilled it."

Callisto inhales sharply. "As the Naiu in me withers, I wish to pierce you through the eyes, slicing away your smug stare with my daggers."

All Olearon flames crackle and simmer.

Callisto continues, "But being aware of why I feel so prone to hate has lessened its grip over me.

"Naiu wishes to die, to cease, and in doing so, remove its enchantment, its life force, from the worlds it has formed." Callisto pauses. "In Naiu's heartbreak, it desires to abandon these worlds, leaving them to consume themselves with malice and greed, to eventually wither away, to crash out of their orbits and destroy the unique system of time Naiu fashioned for each one.

"Naiu longs for the greater expanse to return to peace, silence, blackness, to meditation and hum and possibility, without the corruption of impetus.

"During this removal of magic, which has already begun, whole orbits of the worlds and derivative dimensions will be thrown beyond themselves, bursting, fracturing, crashing together. Races of the most exquisite beings you could ever imagine will be destroyed forever. Stars and moons will crumble into the dust of dreams. The moon Callisto may one day soon cease to be.

"What once was, will be no more. Laughter will die along with sorrow. Lovemaking will perish with disease. All that was once beautiful will be lost."

Ella chokes on a sob, releasing a scattering of green birds that fly gloriously from her lips, chirping merrily in contrast to her gloom. Archie shuffles through the crowd to Ella's side, where she leans on Luggie. He helps support his granddaughter, sensing her weakness despite her will. She looks up at him with imploring eyes as he and Luggie bear her weight. Archie rests his lips on her forehead, kissing a vow of protection upon her.

Archie collects tears from Ella's cheeks. "We'll figure this out, Ell," he manages to whisper. "Somehow . . ." He is left with the weight of his promise and Callisto's words, feeling as if the enormity of all life balances unsteadily upon his shoulders. *How can we possibly figure this out?* he wonders.

"But hope is not lost," continues Callisto, as if knowing Archie's fear. "While my sisters grow hypnotized to the longing of Naiu—as Callisto was to Zeus—they have not, nor have I, given over to despair. We fight the withdrawal of Naiu within and around, choosing goodness."

"This is much to receive," says the Lord, skepticism cut into his face in the subtlest creases. "Nameris, you are the wise historian of Jarr amongst the Olearons, as Ardenal is amongst the humans. What is your estimation?"

Nameris scratches his ruddy chin. "We have believed all manner of speculation about the poisoning of Jarr-Wya, first that the Bangols were to blame. But as this human helped us to understand"—Nameris points to Ella—"that idea was incorrect."

"We Bangols are of the land, its soil, rock, and clay," adds Luggie. "It is a part of us, in our blood. We would do anything to protect it."

Nameris nods respectfully to Luggie and continues. "The other theory is that the Star is the culprit, leeching into our lands an evil that weakens our crops and corrupts our minds. To be honest, Lord, I have never considered Naiu, or I should say, the lack of Naiu to blame. We have only known Naiu to imbue our crystaliths with power that floods our fields, nurturing our crops. We have only ever known it to give, not to take."

"This sounds to me like the foolish deception Ardenal proposed," Azkar says with contempt. "The Star has deceived the Steffanus race, as they seek to do to us."

"It is not a deception, my friend, if I might call you that," says Callisto, gesturing to Azkar and requesting his name.

He answers her with a grunt.

"Azkar," she repeats. "As I have said, we Steffanus sisters are battling the same war within us I see mirrored on your divided face." She approaches the hulking Olearon, who wears a scowl that scrunches the black scar twisting from his left eye to his collarbone.

As Callisto nears, Azkar bristles, but then she touches him. Her long silver fingers trace the scar so tenderly that Azkar shivers and moisture simmers on his eyelids.

Archie watches the bizarre embrace as the deep scar smooths and brightens. The black flesh glows to a pale orange. Though it cannot return to the fullness of red, it is far less gruesome.

Azkar raises his hands to his face and neck. "No one has touched me here," he says, marveling quietly, "since I returned to the glass city, wounded, and the healer cauterized my wound, which was so badly separated that it could not be properly rejoined."

"This is the power of love, when we fight for it, against all odds, against the convenience of apathy and the evil of hate that seeks to divide us," answers Callisto.

Ardenal lays an apologetic hand on Azkar's shoulder. "I did not know your pain, my friend," he begins, his words for Azkar alone. Then to all gathered he says, "Without love, what are we fighting to save?"

"Ardenal is right," Callisto says. "We Steffanus sisters have hope based on fact. We have traveled to Earth, searching and learning. We have ventured even farther—drawing on the Naiu in us to operate Tillastrions of our own making—to places from which many Steffanus sisters have failed to return. The ones who survived those unimaginable places brought back knowledge. They discovered a way.

"Naiu was not the only one that spread its wings through

the expanse before it formed consciousness on marbles of earth and sent them spinning. There was another, perhaps many others, though the one we found was the playmate of Naiu. She was called Finnah but has gone by many names since."

Ella bristles at Archie's side, while she listens intently.

"Like Naiu," Callisto continues, "Finnah once flew with wings; she had no need for legs or feet or toes as there was nowhere to land. Together, Naiu and Finnah batted their feathers through the velvety expanse of peaceful black nothingness, curving around each other like strands of a braid. Their flight was the first dance.

"Finnah observed Naiu spinning time and giving of itself in reckless creativity. Finnah warned Naiu that time was not a toy and that creation was a responsibility, but Naiu turned its eyes away, lost in delight and with no foresight of what might come.

"When Naiu crashed onto Jarr-Wya, forming Baluurwa, it perished in perceivable form except in the shadow of all it has made, and most tangibly in my sisters. Finnah was in mourning. Without her companion, the vastness seemed icy and unfriendly, but for the worlds and derivative dimensions that looked—unknowingly—to Finnah for guidance and protection.

"Finnah was tender and wise. She knew what she must do. She shut her eyes tightly, inhaled the expanse, and burst apart into flecks of light that scattered broadly. Finnah has swollen into suns and frozen into moons for each orbit, seeking to give order to the worlds, and their sunsets, sunrises, and the pacing of time, disciplining the seconds like an infant—though they often rebel, running away or falling behind. What we call stars on Jarr and on Earth is Finnah watching over us. Many human years ago, we sisters discovered Finnah, her primary consciousness, living as a sun in a faraway world, her fingers spread out across the galaxy.

"We told Finnah of the change of heart in Naiu and the

beginnings of its withdrawal from the universe, which was barely perceptible then, even to us. Naiu believed goodness was dead in the worlds, thus true death should follow.

"Through all the sunsets since the creation of the mother and derivative worlds, Finnah has observed. She has watched from afar, noticing the restraint of a child to spare the wounded spider, though she could easily crush its fragile legs beneath her foot. Finnah has seen the passion of lovers, thoughtful gestures, sacrifice, the magic of skin's touch, the heart's swell of love.

"Finnah has seen the creativity that is the birthright of all Naiu has formed—creativity untarnished, released in purity and joy, in art and music and invention and movement and song. You have seen the striking glass formations of the Olearons. You have partaken in the ingenuity of Rolace, who weaves enlightenment into a web so all whose will is strong and heart is brave may blossom into the fullness of their being. Even in the Bangols, Finnah witnesses the magic of creativity through their stone-made inventions and architecture.

"Finnah believes that what Naiu created is good, despite the pain, the hard lessons, and the early evolutions of these worlds as they seek order out of disorder and fail in the process. Yet failure is not forever. It opens each race to new dimensions of the Naiu in them—the good in them."

Archie emboldens himself to ask, "What will happen once Naiu is gone?"

"If Naiu continues to recoil from all worlds," Callisto answers, "our magic, our potential for life and love, will be stolen away. It will be the first death, an invisible death. We will remain like a body but without a spirit. In some places, in the far reaches, the life force of Naiu has already disappeared. These places need saving, but not yet. We sisters see this, and so, too, does Finnah. Their time for salvation will come.

"The first to be saved is Naiu itself. It must be convinced that the worlds are worth redemption. That must take place here, on Jarr-Wya, where Naiu collects itself."

Azkar clears his throat. "And how might that be done, Callisto?" His voice trembles with gratitude.

"When we Steffanus sisters found Finnah in the corner of the galaxy where her heart dwelt, we implored her for help. Finnah suspected what was happening even then; she sensed that Naiu was growing stronger in the core but abandoning its creations on the periphery.

"Finnah regretfully said goodbye to its closest world, leaving it in chaos once more. She soared between the orbits, around the spheres of blue and emerald and ocher and magenta, where races were left to fend for themselves without their stars. Finnah pulled back her fingers as she traveled toward Jarr, gathering her strength.

"At first Finnah planned to crash into Jarr-Wya to snuff out Naiu, her friend through all the ages. She hoped that what love remained in the world would remain where it was so that some worlds could live on. In the last second, however, as she streaked through Jarr's sky, Finnah changed her mind. She conceived of a trickier course, but one that could save all."

"Let me get this straight," Nate says, scratching his blond crew cut. "Finnah is . . ."

"The Star," Archie finishes.

Ella shivers from her feet to the tangle of her hair, but keeps her mouth shut tight.

"You see," adds Callisto, "it is not the Star that is poisoning our land. The Star, Finnah, is here to convince Naiu. It is the withdrawal of Naiu—growing greater with each passing sunset—that leeches life from Jarr-Wya, our home. In its absence, the Olearons, Bangols, sprites, and even we sisters grow conflicted at the true meaning of peace, believing it can be won through bloodshed. And as for the ill-formed Millia—"

A sneering voice cuts through Callisto's like a serrated blade. "I wondered," the gravelly voice begins, "when you'd turn your story to us, to us."

Archie forgot how Senior Karish repeats himself in the pompous puff of his words. That is the only thing he failed to remember. He turns his head and sees the golden form of Senior Karish, the mouthpiece of the Millia sands, mimicking the form of a mammoth sasar. Archie recalls what Olen, the now-dead Olearon warrior, told Tessa, Ella, and him about the Millia. Olen said they were once the shells of the sea creatures who desired the Star and dove deep, though they could never reach it. Their bitterness at their unfulfilled mission bled their wickedness into their shells. At the creatures' deaths, these shells broke apart into millions of grains of golden sand on the southern shore. It was sand so corrupt that it formed a village, made of itself, and continued in fruitless toil after its only love: the Star.

Archie witnessed the cruelty of Senior Karish and the hive mind shared by the enchanted sand. It transformed itself into a beast, biting into a female passenger of the *Atlantic Odyssey*. It stabbed sand-formed claws through the belly of an Olearon. A sandstorm shattered part of the Olearons' glass ship. Worst of all the memories is the nightmare that stalks Archie whenever he closes his eyes: the Millia's demand for blood and the way they blew through the humans, shredding them only to suck every drop of their blood from the crimson-stained beach.

Archie pushes Ella and Luggie behind him as the golden sasar descends upon the company.

chapter 30

Archie

"You foolish Olearons and equally dim winged women. Foolish. Dim," snarls the beastly form of Senior Karish. His long golden tongue licks his sandy face. "You talk as if this island is worth saving. Ha! You talk, and talk, as if one of your races could ever be worthy to rule Jarr-Wya."

The Lord of Olearon wears a robe of fire. "If not our races, then who?" he asks coolly, betraying his composure with his flames.

"Is it not obvious?" Senior Karish howls with laughter.

Jarr-Wya begins to rumble. Huge footfalls are felt on all sides, except the north, where erratic waves slap the shore with the broken discipline of the storm. Out from the eastern, southern, and western maze entrances bound a dozen Haaz headed for the heart of the fortress. The blind giants move their meaty legs with vigor, the fastest Archie has seen them run.

"What are they afraid of?" Lillium asks. She slips low in Archie's pocket, where she chatters to her Wingies.

"I don't know—" Archie begins, then stops. Peeking just above the tops of the maze walls, he can make out waves of glittering gold, tearing through every turn and finally spilling out of each of the three entrances. The sand curves in a wave, bouncing off the muddy earth to rise up once more.

The Haaz pack leap into the cavernous earth, where the Bangols' Tillastrion once churned, and cower in the mud. Sand trickles over the edge of the gorge in golden falls that taunt the sightless beasts.

"You see, you see," begins Senior Karish once more, interrupting the whimpers of the sprites. "This blasted storm has done wonders for us. No longer are we contained to our southern shore. No longer do we remain at sea level, which changes by the day . . . have you noticed? This crazed wind has blown us across Jarr-Wya and up Baluurwa, and even here, where we are more than delighted to stumble upon this gathering."

Nameris bites his bottom lip. "This is terrible news," he whispers.

Azkar clenches his fits, his bold knuckles cracking with loud pops. He sets his body aglow and stalks up to the sandy creature. "Return to the south, or we will return you ourselves."

Again, Senior Karish howls, spewing silt in Azkar's face. "I cannot imagine how! Are you going to collect us one grain at a time? Best of luck to you, best of luck . . . You will need it in this tornado!"

The golden sasar stands on its back legs, towering two feet above Azkar's dreadlocks. The Olearon warrior is unmoving, blackening the ground with a charred halo around his feet. Senior Karish moves his front paws toward Azkar, who does not back down, and at the last moment before they collide in flame, he retracts his deadly claws.

The claws enter Azkar's fire, sparking and solidifying. Senior Karish rests back on all fours. He inspects the change to his claws, which cool to melted glass. "That's better, much better," he says. "These will do the job."

Archie stutters, "Wh-what job?"

"Well," begins Senior Karish as the Bangols' fortress continues to fill with sand, as if there is no end to it. "We will kill you all—we have been craving human blood since that derelict ship crashed on our beach—and then sink the island."

Luggie says, "Sink Jarr-Wya?"

Ella calms him with a touch, though the Bangol's teeth remain bared.

"Why would you do that?" Junin growls, her lit body simmering in the rain. She moves to stand shoulder-to-shoulder with Azkar. Islo and Ardenal do the same. Together their flames overpower the downpour and glow orange and blue in one unbroken wall of heat.

"It will take a little time," Senior Karish says, "but we can drown the island in sand and in water. Since the arrival of the Star, new pockets of desert have appeared; I presume you have noticed. There is the one to the east, which grows by the sunset, and another that chokes out much of the blue forest in the south.

"And for the water, well, have you forgotten where we originated? We Millia began as the shells of mighty shellarks and other deep-dwelling creatures you have only imagined in nightmares, in wicked nightmares. We Millia remain friends to ocean dwellers. Even as I speak, the shellarks and drowned wyverns maneuver seaweed ropes woven a human's height across, connecting them to the crust of the island. Already they pull downward, anchoring Jarr-Wya deeper and deeper."

"You will crush the Star! Not collect it as a treasure. You will bury it alive!" says Callisto. Silver tears fall from her silver cheeks.

Senior Karish ignores Callisto and continues. "Have the Steffanus sisters not told you, Lord of Olearon? Within Baluurwa, they have tunneled to the island's deepest crusts. These wicked women might have drowned you all already, were it not for their enchantments. Even now, there are weary sisters at each of these lower caverns, standing guard over the magic that holds back the sea."

"Everything we do," shrieks Callisto, "is to guard and protect the Star and Naiu and Jarr-Wya. Even if it means the death of our sisters. But you! All you lust for is your imaginary treasure."

"Oh so dramatic! So dramatic, Steffanus!" Senior Karish mocks. "Do not worry about the Star, or Naiu, or the island. You have other more pressing matters to concern yourself with."

The Lord and Callisto exchange a glance before their eyes turn back to the writhing sand. Senior Karish is joined by other golden sasars that flare retracted claws and piercing fangs. The company, Olearons, sprites, and Steffanus sisters back away slowly toward the Bangols' amphitheater.

"It is only a matter of time, a matter of time. Our plan is already under way. We Millia have been patient long enough, long enough. We will ride Jarr-Wya through the sea to the Star."

The Haaz pack, once only whimpering, begin to bellow until their voices are choked out, along with their lives.

chapter 31

Ella

Everything happens at the speed of red lightning.

Luggie pulls me up into his arms. Grandpa leads us through the Bangols' fortress, always only a step ahead of the Millia. Our company flees the evil sand, which has morphed from sasars to a giant octopus with too many arms for me to count as I peer over Luggie's shoulder and am jostled about. The Steffanus warriors weave among us, along with the Olearons from the glass city. All the red bodies look alike, which makes it hard for me to spot Dad.

There he is! I know the way his black hair falls past his shoulders and the shape of his back.

Dad's a touch shorter than the other Olearon men, about the same height as the women. It's like he hasn't fully grown into his new skin. I get it. I'm always the shortest one because my body spends all its time fighting cancer, neglecting my need for height.

Dad is running backward, his face turned away from me. He's staring squarely into the hundred gold eyes that cover the sandy face of the octopus. Fireballs glow like burning roses on his palms and grow into black holes of heat and malice. He throws them at the eyes, melting glass tunnels through them. He calls the tall grasses from the distant blue forest, and they sail to him, aglow with orange light. Dad directs these flying slivers of flame with his fingers, tangling them around the Millia's tentacles, binding them briefly.

The Steffanus warriors fight as they run, jabbing daggers into sand and breaking apart the form of the monster, only to have a tentacle crash to the earth in tiny pieces bearing no resemblance to what it once was. Then the sand reforms somewhere else. The sisters unfold their wide wings—lovely pinks and teals and sunshine yellows with splatters of silver—and beat the air till they stand on the staggered roofs of the Bangol fortress. They are eye-to-eye with the sand creature. From the building tops, they catapult loose boulders, which crash through the octopus but do nothing to slow it down.

Luggie shifts me to Grandpa's arms. Grandpa Archie sprints—unnaturally fast—past Luggie, and I scream for him, a silent scream, releasing fifty green birds that are shredded to pieces by the mammoth gold beast. The sand spills streams of blood. My poor green birds. As much as I hate them, they are a part of me.

Even as we reach the band shell's stage, I reach back for Luggie, but Grandpa won't let me go. My eyes feel clouded with liquid fear that streaks my cheeks and dampens my bomber jacket, which Grandpa gave me back on Earth. Our company—and the sprites, Olearon warriors, and Steffanus sisters—gathers here. Nameris and Nate tinker with the Tillastrion, which still looks to me like an odd collection of garbage.

I'm blubbering now. We can't leave Luggie behind! I grip Grandpa Archie's shirt and shake. I point from Luggie to Nate and Nameris, again and again, but either he doesn't want to acknowledge that we're leaving Luggie behind or he's thinking up a plan. I hope it's the latter.

Luggie stands fixed in the fortress. His arms are spread at his sides, his fingers whitening with tension. In the corner of the band shell, where Grandpa shields me from the attack—amplified by the storm crackling through the sky—I can see flashes of Luggie's grey face. His cheeks flush and crack open, dripping his strange-colored blood. Only adult Bangols have cheek-stones. Through his torn skin, sharp edges of newborn rock emerge. I'm watching Luggie grow up before my eyes.

Luggie summons the Naiu in him, wielding his Bangol power over the earth. He crumples four-story-tall structures. They topple in a landslide of boulders that explode through the gold octopus and sprays sand into the murky morning like the petals of an immense yellow chrysanthemum.

That's when Grandpa Archie leaves me. He leaps from the stage and dashes to Luggie. I can hardly believe his courage—and his strength. He swings Luggie onto his back and races through the rubble and charred earth cratered with fireballs that billow lilac smoke.

Lilac smoke . . . I remember it from the *Atlantic Odyssey*. When the Olearons first boarded our cruise ship, the magic purple gas was how they subdued us, incapacitated us.

The voice of Senior Karish rumbles. "You think you can lock us behind your wall of purple?"

A woozy tentacle parts the lilac curtain, the enchanted smoke taking effect. The Millia's speed begins to lag, though Senior Karish continues to threaten and curse, slurring his wicked words. Translucent slugs slip across the hundred eyes of the octopus, but the massive creature moves onward, unblinded, seeing with every grain. Tentacles flail, looting the dense smoke for bodies big or small, though finding none.

Painfully, I push myself up from the stage and shuffle through the buzzing sprites and icy winged sisters to Nate and Nameris. Their hands are busy and Nameris mumbles about "desire" and the "right combination of things," but it's all futile.

Their frustration is my salvation. I cling to the sleeve of Nate's shirt and pull like an impatient toddler yanking on my occupied parent. I don't care. Plus, Nate isn't my father. Finally, I capture his attention and point to the Millia monster, to the place where Grandpa and Luggie disappeared in the silky folds of lilac clouds.

"We can't wait," is all Nate says.

So I pull and claw at him. I bash his arms away from the collection of objects, scattering them across the rubble of the rock throne. He gets angry, not at me, I know, but at the situation—at his and Nameris's failure to operate the Tillastrion; at his inability to save Mom; at the sense of being lost that surely bites at him in this weird world beyond his control.

Nate shakes me loose, and I fall. My hands scrape across the stone stage and tiny buds of blood sprout and blossom. I watch the smoke. It's all I can do. I pull on the long chain I wear around my neck with Grandma Suzie's locket, which I clutch for comfort. The Bangol key—the one I found in the secret pocket of the book Luggie gave me to draw in—dangles limply against the back of my hand.

Tiny fingers, greenish and warm, try to comfort me, but I can't even gaze up at the sprites. Xlea appears and startles me. What will she take from me this time? I inch backward on the stage, leaving a pattern of my blood behind on the stones. Xlea folds my hands in hers. They feel like static, yet soothe my wounds. When I break my gaze from the smoky lilac wall and wobbling golden octopus, the blood on my palms is gone and my skin glows pinker than I remember it.

That's when I realize my error.

The chain, locket, and key are visible for all to see. Instinctually, I cup my tingling hands around them. No one appears to have noticed, and thankfully all eyes look beyond the band shell.

"There they are!" Dad hollers and jumps down from the stage.

With his free hand, Luggie waves the lilac enchantment away from Grandpa's face, but still, both of their sets of lips are swollen like ripe tomatoes. Their eyes, even Luggie's large yellows, are blinded by the smoke's opaque film and nearly crusted shut with sand. Dad reaches them, and I'm hit with a wave of relief. Then, to my horror, I realize that the three of them—Luggie, Grandpa, and Dad—might be left behind if Nate and Nameris are successful with the Tillastrion.

My arms quiver as I push myself up from the stage and fall headlong toward the throne. Not close enough. My head is a sloshing mess of cancerous fatigue, deafening me to all sound but Lillium's high-pitched chirp near my left ear. She's ordering the sprites to lift me. Digging their spindly barbed legs into my bomber jacket, they haul me forward, inch by inch. The toes of my shoes drag, drawing two parallel lines in the rock dust.

The face and hundred eyes of the golden octopus emerge through the smoke as it pursues the three left on the ground. Dad pulls along Grandpa, who nearly buckles under Luggie's weight. Grandpa stumbles and falls, and Dad fights to rouse him and Luggie.

"Sisters!" The voice is Callisto's. She takes to the air, flanked by two other Steffanus sisters, each descending upon my favorite people, encircling them in an embrace. Lifting off from the wrecked surface of Jarr-Wya, they fly feverishly for the band shell.

A sandy tentacle pierces the group, separating them. Callisto and Luggie spin off course. Dad and Grandpa arrive, carried by the other Steffanus sisters, and collapse into a heap. Dad rushes to the edge of the stage, but Callisto and Luggie are still three arms' lengths away. Still, he reaches for them.

"This will work!" It's Nameris.

"Now or never!" Nate answers.

I can't let them operate the Tillastrion before Luggie is saved from the Millia. Callisto, too. My mind wills my throbbing arms and legs to cooperate with the sprites, who are tiring quickly. I aim my feet, one after the other, and throw myself on top of the Bangol king's throne. I clutch the locket in my sweaty grip, praying for strength.

Time moves at half speed—so slowly that I wonder if I am released from the prison of the long and short hands of the clock to achieve all that is needed in these fateful moments.

Dad's hand is just shy of Luggie's . . .

Dad is held from falling from the stage by Junin and Lady Sophia, who are linked to Azkar and Duggie-Sky, who hold hands with the Lord and Islo and Kameelo, who cling to the Steffanus sisters and other Olearon warriors, and Pinne and Quillie, who hold fast to Nate and Nameris, their tiny hands dug deep in the men's hair.

Dad's fingers curl around Luggie's!

Nothing happens.

Nate curses.

The Tillastrion remains a pile of garbage.

Stupid garbage!

The golden octopus approaches.

I open my hands to look at Grandma Suzie's locket one last time before we all die. The Bangol key slips down the slack chain. It touches the pile of garbage.

The second it touches the Tillastrion, everything changes.

There is light. There is pain. There is bliss.

The sandy voice of Senior Karish wilts and vanishes.

We're moving between worlds, just like Mom described. I'm torn in two, my body dissected organ by organ. My mind can't hold on to the unsettling image of myself.

As we pass through bands of color, like blurring scenery seen from a car window, I notice a shape repeating every blink or two. A keyhole. Many keyholes. Why hadn't Mom mentioned this? Unless they only appear to a person with a key. My key. Or, I should say, the Bangols' magic key that made the pile of garbage come to life.

I'm so weary I can barely move, and still my body seems to be floating all around me. Somehow I manage to get the ornate metal key into a hole. The bands of red, blue, and green open in a perfect circle as if on hinges, and I peer inside at a white world with patches of azure surrounded by a vividly yellow sky. At first I hear nothing, then an eardrum-cracking blast. The planet cracks in two, spilling from its core hungry lava that drips out through the surrounding atmosphere. When it connects with the great black beyond, it forms hard marbles of gloom.

I pull my head back through the door and slam it shut. The bands of light continue seamlessly past me once more. Again, I spy another keyhole, and I can't help but give in to curiosity.

Past this doorway, I find myself peering into an overgrown forest much like the white woodland of Jarr-Wya. Broad emerald foliage shadows the forest in warm, diffused light. There is a rustling sound above my head, and I inch beyond the door to gaze up. What I see would have terrified me if it wasn't for my connection with Mom. In our many conversations since her power was unlocked by Rolace, we talked about the giant spider with the head of an old man. Rolace was alone in the world of Jarr, but here, through this mysterious passageway, I see his family. There are easily forty of these spiders hanging and swinging from the leafy canopy. Their round bodies are hairy, with twelve skinny legs jutting out at all angles. The bodies carry the heads of white-bearded men who remind me of Grandpa Archie before he came to Jarr-Wya.

The men-spiders are chattering loudly as they stroke silvery beards that droop low from their wagging chins. They look to be sharing steaming drinks while grabbing at pieces of a dying creature tangled in their web. Suddenly, my face touches something silky—smooth, yet also tacky like glue. I hadn't realized that I'd taken a full step into this faraway world, until now. The men-spiders also notice.

All their eyes are on me—human eyes at first until their faces morph, stretch, contort, pinch, and finally disappear into a fully arthropod form. I shudder and tear at the web adhering to my cheek, but it stays in place. In one fluid motion, knowing cancer is no match for my fear-fueled adrenaline, I turn and leap back through the doorway, which thankfully was held open by the toe of my shoe.

The bands of colors streak once more as I'm back in the flow of the Tillastrion. My heart is beating hard and I'm sweating. I set my attention on Mom. Picture her face. Remember the feel of her skin against mine. Replay her voice over and over.

I don't dare place the key inside any of the other waiting keyholes that whoosh by. The spiders' web is still on my face. It was real, not just a mirage of portal jumping. I slide the chain with Grandma Suzie's locket and the key back inside my shirt.

I understand now why the key has tingled against my skin since I first looped it onto my chain. Luggie and his sister Nanjee had no idea what I was up to. They had steered the clay basket, held in the air by the wing power of a cluster of awakins. The butterflies, never sleeping, had carried us over the blue and white forests to the eastern shore. There, far above the ground, was when I discovered the key. The tingling felt like love, right from the beginning. Now, I recognize that love as life instead. *Life*. The heartbeat that keeps us all here.

If we can trust what Callisto told us, then that life force that

I feel is Naiu. Soon it will depart from all worlds. I think of the poor white planet dripping lava, sad and heartbroken.

I've never visited that white world or the men-spiders' forest, yet I was just there, and it was as real as any of the color around me. I'm piecing it all together. While a Tillastrion can take you and your traveling companions where at least one of you has been before or where you're from, the key unlocks *all* worlds. Immediately, I realize the immense potential of the object resting against my skin.

This reaction makes me aware of my body in the portal—my weakness, the insurmountable fatigue, the inescapable side effects of cancer—even between worlds.

At my back, where the Olearons' sack is slung loosely, I feel a dampening pool. The cap on the ink vial must have cracked opened in the kerfuffle. There's nothing I can do but let it fill the inside of my bag with black, which is also what's happening to my mind. Everything fades from grey to soupy onyx as I slip under the cloak of sleep, but not the restful kind; the cruelty of illness has stolen away my resolve.

My eyes are vaults closed tightly. All I know now are smells: burning; the saltiness of my favorite potato chips; water—the sensation when water enters your nose and gets caught in your throat and you can smell and taste it at the same time; sunshine on skin, warm, sweaty, and sweetly perfumed. Then, it's flavor: spice; the burn of hot chili peppers on pizza.

Pizza. That is my last thought, and it lingers with me until smell is replaced by sight. Pure white light envelops me and clears away all corners of conscious thought.

Ella

BEWARE
Ella

chapter 32

Tessa

Tessa nibbles her lower lip. She is alone with her own voice in her head. She had pulled at Ella's consciousness as long as she could as she tumbled through dimensions with the Bangols. They held the connection even after Zeno began redecorating the island of Lanzarote. Then the link was severed.

Tessa realizes that without Ella's efforts, holding onto each other's minds worlds apart is nearly impossible. Tessa suspects Ella is asleep or perhaps unconscious. She won't consider a third option. When she calls out to her daughter, there is no answer, only her echo. Tessa moves on to nibble her already-bleeding nails, and the nagging pain at her fingers snap her out of self-deflating talk and the loneliness that bites at her.

She leaps to her feet from the cool tiles, nearly frozen by the air-conditioning that blasts from a hidden vent. The place where she is held captive is modestly furnished with a simple floral loveseat and water-stained wooden coffee table. Tessa flicks on and off the sole light switch, watching with befuddled awe as the linen-shaded lamp in the corner comes alive, then fades, then comes alive once more. They lived for weeks, she guesses, on Jarr, with no electricity or heat apart from what the Olearons and the sun provided. By the end, the sun dwindled and so did its warmth, leaving only the moon to hint at the burning star's endurance.

The room has a whitewashed interior, like most exteriors on Lanzarote, except for one wall, painted such a blinding neon green that it amplifies the migraine jackhammering the front of Tessa's brain. She can feel a goose egg at her hairline where Zeno struck her with a rock. Tessa is no longer bound by ropes or chains, so she can wander the space freely, though she is not free.

All doors to the room where Tessa paces are either locked or barricaded shut from the other side. Wooden steps lead to an elevated door on the green wall: a study. That was where Zeno plotted with Borgin—calling for maps of Lanzarote and the other Canary Islands—before venturing out with a troop of Bangols to begin construction. Tessa listened through the door, but the Bangols spoke in their own language—harsh, clipped, and gargled sounds. She strained her power to enter the minds of the stone-heads. Her telepathy was only marginally successful. What she did discover, however, was that her gift also translated the Bangols' plotting into a language she could understand. Or was it the other way around? Was she suddenly able to comprehend Bangol?

Tessa cringes at Zeno's plan. He will construct a fortress on Lanzarote, a place of refuge and protection, that will withstand weather and intruders. Then they will link the islands with arching stone bridges. This is easy for Tessa to picture. She witnessed the Bangols' skill with stone firsthand on Jarr-Wya's eastern beach.

Tessa has no doubt the Bangols will succeed—if they are not stopped. She knows she must act, but fears it is not a job for one. True, Tessa is accustomed to being alone, but this challenge feels hopeless. She does not wish for Ella and the others to transport themselves to Lanzarote, but instead press on to find the Star. At the same time, she frets that their eventual arrival on Earth will be too late.

The first stone bridge will span north from Lanzarote to the island called La Graciosa, a craterous volcanic landmass with little in the way of civilization. La Graciosa is not considered one of the main Canary Islands, being so close to Lanzarote and with a minuscule number of inhabitants. It would have been a perfect island to build a fortress on, but Zeno insisted the Bangols need humans to work, grow food, and soldier for them in the likely chance of attack by sea. Lanzarote provides such humans. Also, Zeno's familiarity with the island affords him certain advantages. For the first time, Tessa realizes that he had been planning this new fortress all the years of his banishment.

Once La Graciosa is overcome, which Zeno wagers will be the easiest of all takeovers, the Bangols plan to expand their stone bridges south, across the sea from Lanzarote to the heavily populated island of Fuerteventura, from where they will build the longest bridge in Bangol history to the circular mountainous island called Gran Canaria. Then they will spread to the last of the larger islands, bird-shaped Tenerife. Once Tenerife is overcome, Zeno believes the smaller isles—La Gomera, La Palma, and El Hierro—will easily fall under his rule.

The arching ceiling above Tessa is held in place by aged wooden supports given new life with a coat of shellac. The wood surrounding the windowsill has been painted white to match the walls and ceiling. Tessa winds a crank, opening the window and allowing floral air to waft in. Its smell is laced with salt and construction dust.

Beyond her window is a narrow road lined with whitewashed buildings. Tessa does not know what day it is or even the time, only that the artisan market, Artesanal Mercado Haria, with its green tents, is closed. No shops are manned or assembled. Instead, terrified people yell to each other and rush through the streets, loading vehicles and bicycles with belongings and food and hurrying away to one of the coasts to board boats off the island. One lonely tented structure remains along the street, with its roof of white and mustard yellow stripes that flaps in the sweltering breeze.

The sight of small compact cars—a red Nissan, a blue Mini Cooper, a grey Hyundai Elantra—zipping through the streets unnerves Tessa. The contrast of the Bangols' balloons to the puttering vehicles is a sharp one. Tessa's old life—her job as an emergency room nurse, their family's dated Seattle bungalow, Ella's plethora of doctors, and Tessa's smattering of casual friends—still feel removed from who she now finds herself to be, even though she is home. Earth.

Most buildings in Haria are a story tall, but the one holding Tessa is two. She contemplates jumping, but the asphalt-and-stone sidewalk is unforgiving. Below her sole window are enchanted rocks spanning many feet in all directions. Chosen for their sharpness, the stones balance magically, their piercing ends pointing up, destroying any hope Tessa might have of dropping from the window and surviving. *Plus*, she reasons, struggling to see good in her ill situation, *I may be safer in here*. Her eyes are on the activity of the Bangols in the distance, and she shudders as yet another piercing human scream reinvigorates her migraine. Already the Bangols are wrangling humans to their will.

Beyond the white buildings with green and blue doors, past archways of thorny bougainvillea bursting with lush pink flowers and rows of forty-foot-tall palm trees, are dirt roads with shoulder-high rock walls. *No wonder Zeno felt like this was a familiar place to hole up in during his banishment,* muses Tessa. The walls and roads lead up stout hills on all sides of Haria. The small town is a half-hour drive by yellow cab from Arrecife on the coast, where the *Atlantic Odyssey* had been captained by Nathanial Billows. Nate. Tessa's heart pangs with confused notes.

Up on the low mountains, Tessa can make out hupper fur garments and sweating grey skin. Clearly, the magic that surges through the Bangols' ancient veins has diminished, though it is not fully abated, in the human world. On Jarr, the Bangols herded rocks like obedient children, whereas on Lanzarote, the stone-heads are forced to exert greater effort. Rocks crash and crack against each other. Tessa can hear the high wail of a Bangol whose foot has been crushed under a boulder. She can also make out Zeno, who stands astride a mound of upturned earth, barking orders at those bustling below.

The whole island is abuzz with activity. A second contingent of Bangols rounds up humans, testing their ability for manual labor. Those who refuse are persuaded by the sharp edge of stone. From the corners of her eyes, Tessa watches a group of children fill backpacks with candy bars looted from a local confectionary, then cower behind a white wall as a pair of Bangols troll by.

Tessa recalls the day excursion she and Ella took to Timanfaya National Park, a half-hour drive west of Arrecife. Their rickety bus wove around volcanic craters that pocked the island like the face of the moon. Archie opted not to join Tessa and Ella, which Tessa now knows was his plan all along, despite feigning disinterest. The sole reason he emptied his bank account to take his daughter-in-law and granddaughter on Constellations Cruise Line was to find Zeno and, through him, Arden.

Tessa and Ella learned that Timanfaya was one of Spain's national parks, covering nearly a quarter of Lanzarote and butting up against the North Atlantic Ocean on the western coast. Their guide told them that the name translates to "Fire Mountains," and with this memory, worry overcomes her.

What if Ella doesn't obey me, which is likely, Tessa thinks, *and she comes here with the Olearons? The people of this island may call its volcanoes Fire Mountains for another reason. Who knows what the Lord of Olearon will do. Burn down the island? Burn the entire Earth? Ugh . . . No. Ella will listen. She'll go on with the 30th Lord, Archie, and Ardenal to find the Star. They'll locate her cure and right everything that's gone wrong in that world, then do the same here. I'm worrying for nothing.*

A thundering crack shakes Haria as Zeno and fifty Bangols remove a chunk of mountain. It hovers ominously above the earth before they place it as a stronghold for the new fortress. The crust of Lanzarote breaks through civilization with clouds of orange dust, the upturned ground peppered with uprooted shrubs. Everything is dry, brittle, and crumbling. In the distance, the ocean batters the island with ferocious waves, though it cannot match the one that swept through the Fairy Vineyard.

Along with worry, fatigue also tugs at Tessa. She recognizes the difference in time from Jarr to Earth. It is not the jet lag of changing time zones but of seconds that pace themselves in one place and race forward in another. Tessa cannot remember the last time she slept—peacefully, that is. Her dreams had become turbulent zones of unrest since she plunged into the frigid water of the Creek of Secrets, following the bubbling voice of Rolace and the evil that dwelt in the enchanted current.

Fatigue cloaks her. Tessa drops onto the couch. Her vision blurs and her eyes close.

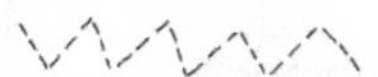

TESSA is weightless, extracted from gravity, a thing of the air. Her hair tangles into a windswept golden braid. Her vines sit nicely in her hands—unlike in her nightmare, where they choked the life out of her and her companion, Finnah. She strokes their smooth green leaves. Now, Tessa and Finnah soar through a cold shiver of air and emerge above the cloud cover. The blue here encompasses them. Tessa hopes they can remain quiet, but Finnah enjoys the company.

"Hello, sweet human," the massive green bird chirps happily.

"Hi, Finnah." Tessa yawns. "Where are we?"

"In a pocket of peace before the things to come. I want you to be rested—you will need it."

"Will I? I'm all alone again. Would anyone even notice if I didn't wake up?"

"Oh yes! You would be greatly missed by many, some of whom you have yet to meet."

"That's sounds nice, Finnah," Tessa says sleepily.

"Everything is coming together according to plan, Tessa, and you must trust me. Always trust me. Everything will appear grim and hopeless before the end, but still you must trust me."

"As long as Ella lives."

"*That* I cannot promise, Tessa."

"As long as Ella lives, Finnah."

Now the green bird does fly on in silence. Tessa's eyes flutter, and she falls asleep inside the dream.

chapter 33

Archie

Archie spits sand from his caked lips and feels the grains crunch between his teeth. He wipes his tongue on his shirt till his mouth is dry. His eyes are covered in a glossy substance, like looking through Vaseline. He rubs them clear of the slinking, crawling creature born from the Olearons' lilac smoke.

Archie is knee-deep in sand. He remembers the quicksand on the eastern side of Jarr-Wya where they trekked to find Ella a day after arriving on the island. Tessa carried a bouquet of Banji flowers for Rolace—its potent hallucinogenic quality becoming quickly apparent. The quantity she carried was great, and so, too, her delirium. She conjured a ship made of blood and fire; a tornado of sand and vines; the Millia . . . The visceral memory crawls over Archie's skin, and he kicks himself out of the sand and nearly leaps onto a grey- and red-brick path. When he surveys his surroundings, he spots the rest of the company—and the contingent of Steffanus sisters, Olearon warriors, and sprites—also digging themselves out. Ella is not moving, and he rushes to her. Luggie is frantic.

Archie places his fingers on Ella's throat. She has a pulse; it is weak but steady. He brings her to the edge of the beach, to the sidewalk, and rests her frail body on a wooden bench. "She's sleeping," he tells Luggie, who rubs the slimy slugs from his eyes and shakes sand from his hupper furs like a wet dog. Luggie sits beside Ella. His sharp nails delicately untangle the knots in her blond hair, and he blows sand from her eyelashes.

Archie studies their location. They are on a beach in Arrecife. Facing the sea is a deserted skateboard park to his right and the Gran Hotel Arrecife to his left, which Archie pointed out to Tessa as the spot where he would acquire a coffee and newspaper when he opted out of the tour to Timanfaya National Park. He never made it to the Gran Hotel but knows that beyond it lies Marina Lanzarote.

The road behind them, Avenue Fred Olsen, is a mess of locals and tourists fighting over vehicles, bunches of bananas, and convenience store loot. Cars with locked doors weave around the unpredictable pedestrians and speed away. One motorbike is tackled by a crazed elderly woman who knocks the rider off his seat and mounts it, leaving the man in her dust.

"We escaped the Millia!" shouts Duggie-Sky. He and Kameelo laugh and chase each other across the beach, where, like the others, they shake themselves free of the grit and mud of Jarr-Wya that traveled through the portal caked to their grimy clothes and the bottom of their feet.

The Lord stands erect as Islo brushes clean his mirrored breastplate and golden robes. Frustrated with the formal garb, the Lord unhooks the trailing fabric from his pointed shoulderpieces. "Archibald, you have been to this island, which is so terribly unfamiliar to me," he begins, grimacing at the vehicles and bleeding humans. Sirens blare in the periphery. Two cars collide, sending their side mirrors bouncing along the street. "Where do you presume we travel to from here?"

Archie has never heard the Lord sound so leery and uncertain. "Well"—Archie scratches his stubbly chin—"Our best bet of acquiring any form of transportation not already in use is the marina. When the *Atlantic Odyssey* docked there, the place was a mess of buses—a real traffic jam."

"I agree with Archie," says Nate. "And judging by the state of Arrecife, we better get a move on."

Nameris approaches the park bench. "Ella must first speak with her mother," he says, "to know the exact location of the Bangols."

Ardenal lays a gentle hand on his daughter's shoulder, rousing her slowly.

Lady Sophia points a plump finger inland. "I can see the Bangols from here," she says. "See, on that mountain, and that one, and that one."

"Zeno," says the Lord, his voice a deep rumble. "We must find Zeno."

Ella wakes sluggishly and Ardenal explains their need. Ella swings her thin legs off the bench and rests her elbows on her knees and her chin in her hands. She places her fingertips along her brow and stares at the brick sidewalk. Archie knows the gesture; his granddaughter is fighting nausea. Luggie pulls what is left of Ella's ink and unsoiled paper from her sack and passes her the paintbrush.

She looks up at Archie. He can sense she has already communicated with Tessa. "Go on, Ell. Whatever directions you can manage will be a great help," he says.

TREASURES
ZENO
MOM
Ella

BANGOLS
Ella

Once the drawing is done, the Lord says, "Please, Archibald, Nathanial Billows; lead us." He brushes his hand in front of him, gesturing to the humans to take up the first line. "We must locate the Bangols and restore order. I feel ill in this place lacking in Naiu."

"Do you need assistance?" asks Junin. The Lord nods faintly. Junin and Islo flank him as they follow Archie and Nate. The company and other Jarrwians trace the sidewalk of the avenue. Upon reaching the Gran Hotel and its tower of blue glass, Archie suggests a quick meal inside for strength, as he notices the sluggish pace of Lady Sophia and even Azkar, who walk lethargically side by side.

They enter through glass doors beneath angled tan and grey pillars and are greeted inside by a greenhouse-style lobby with marble tiles, polished wooden balconies, and palm trees. There is a distinct absence of hotel staff, only trembling, nervous tourists who pull half-zipped suitcases in and out of the building. At the sight of the Olearons, Steffanus sisters, sprites, and Luggie, a frenzy erupts. Children point and stare with bulging eyes while their parents drag them by the arms or throw them over their shoulders and run in the opposite direction. The lobby and attached restaurant clear out in minutes, leaving a buffet of local dishes—*papas arrugadas*, *miel de palma*, *conejo al salmorejo*—warming beneath heat lamps in broad metal dishes. The Jarrwians, Luggie, and humans eat their fill, while also sampling the island-grown wine.

"These walls remind me of home," says Kameelo. The Olearon touches a tall pane of glass. When it does not shimmer and shift in its transparency, he adds, "Strange."

The company and Jarrwians venture farther along the coast, heading north on Avenue de la Mancomunidad past its abandoned restaurants. They travel the street beside an eight-story apartment building with windows facing the sea. They navigate past one whitewashed building after another with street-side restaurants barricaded with overturned tables and wicker chairs. The coast and North Atlantic Ocean are to their right. They walk more quickly after the meal and arrive at Marina Lanzarote in half an hour, Archie guesses, as the sun is beginning its graceful dip in the sky and melts into the water.

The marina's modern eateries and shops boasting wares of copper, leather, pottery, and wood are separated from the sea by elevated black walkways. All seafaring vessels have been commissioned or hijacked, so the marina is a bare skeleton drifting on the water. Land vehicles, too, are occupied, crashed, or gone from their parking spots—except for one.

A dilapidated, rusting school bus hums near the tourism information office. Inside the office, Archie sees frantic travelers arguing with a bald man in uniform. A tourism officer. Archie cannot read the man's lips beneath his full black mustache, but frustration bulges in thick veins on his forehead. He finally pushes past the tourists and out the glass door, jumps into the sea, and swims away.

The company load themselves onto the bus, leaving the Steffanus sisters and sprites to fly and the large contingent of Olearon warriors to trek behind. As Archie shifts the creaking beast into gear, a pot-bellied man wearing the bus company logo on his breast pocket appears in the open doorway, hollering profanities. He is quickly silenced, however, by the Lord's glare. The man's loot from the nearby shop slips from his hands and he flees in the same direction as the tourism officer.

The vehicle lunges forward and blasts black smoke from its exhaust pipe. "You're sure you can drive this, Dad?" Ardenal's red jaw is locked as tightly as his hands clutch the metal storage rack above the seats.

"I'm fine. Getting the hang of it, see?" Archie grunts as he turns the enormous steering wheel. "Er, well, the bus needed a new paint job anywho."

The Lord is murmuring to his warriors a few rows back from the driver's seat. Archie overhears, "Ignite your flame," and "Burn them all," and "Zeno must die."

"Excuse me, Lord," says Archie. "I know the Bangols have caused us heaps of trouble, but perhaps I can reason with Zeno. I know him better than most here—"

"You trust that bond?" Junin asks.

"Well, yes, actually," answers Archie. "It's not a perfect friendship, but a bond nonetheless. Why not proceed with diplomacy first, Lord?"

"Archibald's suggestion is good," says Nameris. "If you wish to maintain your firm hand, let the human"—Archie sees the Olearon gesture toward him in the dangling rearview mirror—"speak first to the Bangol king. If it goes poorly, then we may approach with our flames."

"The Bangols will interpret this as weakness from the Olearons," the Lord says with a grimace.

Archie shakes his head. He navigates the road based on Ella's map and what he recalls from the cab ride he took to find Zeno before they were transported to Jarr-Wya. "Nah," Archie says, brushing off the Lord's concern, "they won't even see you right away—just stay put in the bus."

The Lord, not accustomed to being on the receiving end of orders, leans back in his olive-green plastic seat.

"I'm going with you, Dad," says Ardenal.

Archie raises a thumbs-up, causing the unyielding steering wheel to jerk out of his grip. He steadies the beast and takes another turn toward Haria. "It's settled." Archie steers too wildly around another corner and knocks over a decorative wall, creating a small avalanche of stones.

Out the windows of the bus the company watches the destruction wielded by the Bangols pass them by. White buildings bear the scars of collisions with boulders, and trees are flattened, their leaves nibbled by the hungry, gray-skinned race. Frightened people peek out from behind rubble and work to board up their homes and shops with chairs, cabinets, cardboard, crates, and books. Groups of Bangols dig into the earth, both with magic and handmade tools. Mounds of rock are piled high every few blocks. The Bangols use clay and mud stuck to white walls along their path to form crude arrows and give directions in their language's graphic symbols. The company duck from view at the sight of the Bangols, and Archie shields his face with a hand to avoid being spotted.

Ella

Luggie translates. "That clay message means: Main fortress this way."

"Thank you, Luggie," says the Lord evenly.

"So Dad, what are you going to say to Zeno?" Ardenal asks. "How are you going to convince him to leave?"

Archie wipes his perspiring forehead with his arm. "I thought I'd make it up on the spot. It's more authentic that way." The truth is, Archie is unsure what he can offer to entice Zeno back to Jarr. He runs scenarios through his head but is called out of his ruminating and back to the bumpy road as Ella pulls on his sleeve.

"She wants to find her mother," explains Luggie. "Tessa is a captive in a different building—not Treasures—and Ella thinks she knows the way. She does not want you to worry, Archie, or you, Ardenal. I am going to stay with her. We will find Tessa and then stay put, if it is safe there. Here is a copy of the map to Tessa's location. Careful, the ink is still wet."

Archie parks the bus beside a fallen building reduced to rubble and tree branches. The building provides an unexpected alcove, hiding not only the bus but also the remainder of the company and Jarrwians who assemble there.

"Islo, begin preparing our warriors," orders the Lord. "We must learn the limitations of our flames before the Bangols do."

Islo nods and turns to the Olearons. "Steffanus sisters, we leave old grievances behind in our world. Here, we battle together. Sharpen your daggers!"

"And what about us?" pipes up Quillie.

"We sprites are capable of fighting," adds his twin, Pinne.

The Lord regards the sprites, the sixty who survived the flood in the Fairy Vineyard, the crashing roll of the blamala's spit bubble, and the Tillastrion's journey to Earth. "Fly amongst the buildings, listening," he finally orders. "Do not venture too far or let yourselves be seen. Travel in twos and threes. Report back here—the intelligence you gather will help us chart our attack."

"If attack is needed," adds Junin.

"I have faith in you, Dad—you will find a way to end this peacefully," says Ardenal.

chapter 39

Ella

I hug Grandpa Archie like it's the last time, just in case. Luggie and I set off on our own trajectory, and, thankfully, he gives me the dignity of walking on my own, at least while we're in sight of the others. I feel every step as if my legs are firing pins and needles.

In my peripheral vision, I keep an eye on Grandpa and Dad as they head toward the plaza of Haria, lined in attached white buildings with green doors. It's the place, they've told me, where there's usually a bustle of outspoken street vendors offering things hand-carved, hand-painted, hand-picked, and hand-stewed, bringing the color and spice of Mercado Artesanal to life. There the trees are given square sections of the tiled road to grow up tall, their leaves forming a tight canopy that banishes the light, like the spindly trees in the white woodland of Jarr-Wya. I wish I could have seen the artisan market under different circumstances.

Grandpa and Dad become a part of the shadows. They search for the low flat roof of Treasures—Zeno's shop—squished between two larger storefronts, its cracked white wall and entrance tucked beneath a splintered hanging wood sign. It's the place Mom tells me Zeno plans to use as the entrance to his fortress, flattening everything else. He must be at work because loud crashes shake the dry earth, and clouds of clay dust form plumes above the plaza. Buildings collapse. I suppose I'll never see the market after all.

"Ella, you should know," Luggie begins, "I will not shed Bangol blood unless it belongs to Zeno. Then I would happily tear the stones from his brain."

I nod my understanding but hope he'll choose to protect me above everyone else, as selfish as that may be. I try not to wonder what Luggie will do when we cross paths with other Bangols. Will he fight his friends and family to save me? I slip my fingers between his where they feel safe, warm, and at home, at least for now.

We dodge a group of bloody humans, mostly beefy men, who roll boulders like barrels. We duck behind a mound of rubble as a pair of Bangols stomp by. "I know them," says Luggie. "They are a few hundred sunsets older than me. We grew up playing together and learning to direct the awakins in the training balloons. These Bangols follow Zeno's orders now, but under a new king, they'll be different. Ella, believe me."

I respect Luggie's compassion. It will make him a good ruler, unlike his father, Tuggeron. Still, why the Lord of Olearon supports Luggie and wishes him to be the next Bangol king, I don't know. There's a motive there I haven't put together. It makes me suspicious of the Lord, of Luggie, of everyone. What are people keeping from me? What side deals have they struck? I can't ask. How can I draw these delicate questions?

The artisan market is up Plaza León, an angled street to the left from where Luggie and I walk along Calle de la Cilla. We pass a gutted supermarket where there's a welcome mat of splattered food. The wooden doors to a cafeteria have been wedged free and are nowhere to be seen. Maybe Zeno has a use for them elsewhere. A children's playground looks like a junkyard for rejected abstract metal art. The twisted slide is beautiful in its own way.

I wonder how long Mom and the Bangols were here before

the rest of us arrived to have already caused so much damage. Dad told me that time moves differently between a mother world and its derivative. That's the only way I can explain the Bangols' progress.

We begin up a slight incline, not even a hill, and it's too much for me. Luggie—like the clichéd knight in shining armor—lifts me from my plodding feet and carries me. The cancer in me knows we've returned home, and I feel it stewing. A headache blooms between my eyebrows and I press hard on the spot, in the failed hope for a fraction of relief. The road continues upward, appearing to lead us into the fading sky. I'd been so happy to arrive home to see the sun, but dusk has settled in. At least it's a rosy one.

I'm almost asleep, lulled like a newborn in Luggie's arms, but then I see it: an outdoor lamp, the kind for a street with no room for a post in the ground. The lantern style is traditional with frosted glass and brass fittings. It's held upright by a metal arm that juts out like someone playing tag and is affixed to the front of a continuous white wall. It is one marker Mom told me to look for.

There, across from the lantern—which flicks on, almost like a beacon, as the dark descends—I spot what seems like one of the only two-story buildings in the area. It has a faded green door, in front of which balance fifty or more stone spearheads. They're aimed up, deadly arrows pointing me toward Mom.

I'm nodding like a bobblehead, something I've gotten used to since being unable to speak. I jump down and wobble. Luggie banishes the enchanted stones with one sweep of his hand. I reach the door first and find it locked—big surprise. Luggie calls back one of the stones and hides it between his palms. I've never seen him control rocks this way, and I think his skill startles him as well. His fingers mold the rock as if it were clay. He forms a key-shaped pick and slips it into the lock. A moment of fiddling and the door swings open.

A deafening blast occurs down the road, behind us, back at the plaza of Haria. *Dad! Grandpa!* My worry is converted to adrenaline. Somehow, I sprint up the decaying stairs to the door at the top guarded by an enchanted puzzle of soccer ball-size rocks. I press my back to the side wall and Luggie sends the stones past me and crashing down the stairs.

I'm in Mom's arms. There's crusted blood on her forehead, turning a lock of blond hair a muted pink. She says all the words I'm thinking: "You found me," and "I'm so glad you're safe," and "I love you."

More crashes of earth and scraping of lava rock follow.

"Have you seen?" Mom asks Luggie. "How far along is the fortress?"

"It is hard to estimate." Luggie looks around the simple room, then spots what he's searching for—a ladder leaning in the corner, then a trapdoor to the roof. The three of us climb up—even me, since I want to see—past the angled wooden beams and through the trapdoor.

The roof is flat and brittle. Mom squeezes my hand so tightly it hurts. We all cough, even Luggie who is made of clay and earth, and shield our eyes from filling up with dirt. Mom peers toward the plaza of Haria, where Zeno's shop is being outfitted as the entry to the new Bangol fortress. Luggie, in contrast, is gazing north toward the low ranges of volcanic mountains and their porous craters. "They will head there next," he says. "What a magnificent field of rock."

I want to tell him, "Now's not the time to admire the landscape, Luggie!" but I'm distracted. My eyes are pulled much farther south than the plaza of Haria. The building where we stand, at a higher elevation than sea level, affords us a lookout over the rest of the island. I distinctly recall the size of Arrecife's beach where the *Atlantic Odyssey* docked while we visited Lanzarote. The sweep of sand was broad before, but nothing like this. The lip of yellow now forms a huge stretch of shore along the coast.

More sand.

A thick, long beach.

A black hole of dread opens in my stomach, sucking in every hope I had for a peaceful negotiation with the Bangols and for a quick journey by Tillastrion back to Jarr. Everything has become a million times worse.

I point, but Mom and Luggie don't see. I make a fuss, but they're still blind to it. My mind is a landslide of turmoil and Mom can't hear my troubled thoughts. Her head is too noisy with panic, too distracted with plans to stop the Bangols, to save me.

Yanking a piece of paper from my sack, I quickly communicate my message. Mom reads it and drops to her knees. She says the word to Luggie, who can't read our language. Mom covers her mouth but through her fingers I can hear her say with a gasp, "No!"

MILLIA

chapter 39

Archie

Ardenal releases a lone grapefruit-sized fireball, which captures every Bangol's attention as it sizzles through the air before colliding with the base of the gentle mountain to the north. Two guards abandon their watch of the green door leading into Treasures in Haria's artisanal market. Archie and Ardenal slip inside the shop and bar the entryway with a flip of a lock.

"I wondered when you two would arrive."

"Zeno," Archie begins, panting, then speaks too quickly for his tongue to keep up. "You must stop this. People are hurt—they're dying out there. You've destroyed whole communities, homes . . ."

"And what of my home? My community? My family?" Zeno waits for a reply, and when Archie stands mutely, the Bangol continues. "You see, you have no answer for that. Tuggeron brutally murdered my father, the true king, and my twin brother. Tuggeron tortured me, using the power of Naiu against me. He sent me to live here—away from every Bangol I have ever known, to be treated like a freak instead of a king."

Ardenal hangs back in the wisps of incense and the shadow of a ceiling-high wooden cabinet, allowing Archie to approach the rear of the store. "Zeno, you've had it rough—I don't take that away from you," Archie says, kindlier now, his mouth catching up with his mind. "But Tuggeron is gone and you have this one chance to rule the Bangols justly, as I know you can. Remember our talks on the way east? A king who is loved is one who leads with wisdom and restraint, not with careless violence."

"Jarr-Wya is dying, Archibald. A good king saves his subjects, which is what I have done. I have given them a chance to thrive. The Lord of Olearon is obsessed with the Star, and that will be his downfall."

Zeno sits on a stool behind a glowing glass counter. When Archie first met the Bangol here, Zeno had hidden his face beneath a camo-patterned wide-brimmed hat. It wasn't until Archie neared and the creature looked up from the oxidizing jewelry behind the counter that he noticed Zeno's radiant yellow eyes. Archie stumbled back then, petrified at the sight of someone inhuman, someone birthed of nightmare. Now, however, Zeno is clothed in hupper fur across his chest; his arms are bare, as is his head of sharp stones that encircle his skull like a crown. He no longer hunches where he sits but stretches his neck tall, which straightens his whole posture as if he is strung together on a pulled string. And this time, Archie approaches the cracked glass display as a friend.

"Oh, do not look at me like that," Zeno says with a sneer. "You cannot convince me to go back."

"This isn't your world, Zeno—I don't care how long you've lived here," Archie retorts. "Your world is Jarr. Mother worlds must nurture their derivatives, not overtake them. You must feel the weakness in your hands, your blood, your mind since returning. You must feel this absence of magic, of Naiu, more than any of us. Now that I've smelled the air on Jarr-Wya, I know the scent in this shop is a reminder of the fullness of Naiu. The smell reminds me of the island, but not this island—not even close."

"Arriving in Jarr after my banishment was amazing. The Naiu in me came alive. I could tell because of my power in our fight." Zeno inclines his head past Archie to where Ardenal hangs back in shadow. "I was as strong as I ever was."

Archie nods. "That's right, Zeno. You're meant to live close to that source, a source of life and goodness that everyone—and I mean everyone—will lose, along with our lives, if we don't work together to save it."

Zeno holds a ball of rusty-orange clay in his stout grey hands. He rolls it like cookie dough into a smooth ball, then squashes it flat. "Back on Jarr-Wya, I could levitate this piece of clay while I slept. Here, it took forty mature Bangols, full cheek-stones and all, to break off that piece of mountain. I am sure you have seen it—the foundation of the eastern wall of our new fortress." Zeno balances the clay ball on the fine tip of one sharp fingernail. He drops his hand and the ball stays in place, hovering before his eyes.

"It is a pity," continues Zeno, "to lose the strength so innate to the Bangol nature. However"—the ball falls into his waiting palm—"can you not feel it, Arden? That we grow stronger by the minute?"

Ardenal contemplates the Bangol's claim, then slowly nods. "I did not notice until now, but . . . yes," he stammers. He tests his abilities, igniting and extinguishing himself in a flash. The wooden floor is scorched black. The puny fireball he conjured just moments before seems feeble, powerless in comparison. "But how can this be?"

"I do not know," says Zeno slyly, "and I do not care." His eyes narrow, and the meager foundation of Treasures rumbles, dislodging small rocks and cement debris. Zeno collects a rock into his hand and tosses it to Archie, who fumbles it. The pebbles continue to roll out from the building's walls and foundation, along the stained, splintering floor. They behave like lines of ants crawling up Ardenal's and Archie's legs. The father and son kick and brush away the stones, but they hop over their hands and encircle their necks, choking them slowly.

"Now, Arden, Archibald . . . we have far too much history between us for me to kill you both without even the smallest sliver of regret. Instead, I will show the mercy you taught me, Archibald, which is so honorable in a king. Return to Jarr-Wya and tell the others, tell the Lord of Olearon, that we Bangols give them our land there, that we will not be needing it any longer—"

Zeno's speech is cut off when a group of Bangols send a boulder through the locked door of Treasures. Green fragments of wood fly through the shop. Sawdust settles on the carved cabinet and glass display case and onto the brown ash of spent incense. The stones around Archie's and Ardenal's necks fall to the ground with a clatter. Borgin enters through the blast hole, his voice chiming above the ringing in their ears. "My King, forgive our intrusion. The door was locked."

Zeno flushes with anger. "What is so urgent, Cousin?" Under his breath he mumbles, "I was fond of that door."

Borgin pushes forward two humans, followed by a third captive, all with rough sacks pulled over their heads and shoulders. Archie recognizes the prisoners' clothing immediately and runs to them. Ardenal makes it there first.

"Tessa, Ella!" Ardenal exclaims, smiling. He yanks the sacks off the women's heads and singes the fraying ropes around their wrists. He kisses Tessa and Ella, leaving behind warm red lip prints on their cheeks that linger before fading.

Archie pulls the sack off the third captive, and immediately Luggie's face is contorted in fury as he locks eyes with Zeno.

"Ah, Tuggeron's heir . . . now this *is* more interesting," says Zeno.

Borgin says, "I thought you would want to kill this one yourself."

A wide, wicked smile spreads across Zeno's face. "For once, Cousin, you have done something right!" With a flick of his wrist, he commands the marching pebbles that choked Archie and Ardenal, directing them through the dank shop to encircle Luggie.

"Wait," Luggie says, wheezing. "I am not the enemy on your doorstep. Neither is the Olearon army, or the Steffanus sisters, who are also here, only a block away."

"A block away? It might as well be a world away. They will never arrive here in time to save you."

"The Millia," Tessa cries. "Zeno, the Millia are here!"

The pebbles drop one by one from Luggie's neck, and he speaks. "We saw them first as a broad golden beach, many ships' widths from the shore. As we watched, pillars of sand rose into the sky, nearly touching the clouds. They crashed down onto helpless buildings, people, animals. Even now, the Millia slink inland. When they arrive here, your fortress will not protect you. We will all be dead."

"That's not all . . ." says Tessa with a whimper. She looks to Archie and Ardenal for strength.

Ardenal holds Ella in his muscled arms and gives her his warmth. Tessa steps forward. Archie can see his daughter-in-law burying her fear, pushing it down beneath a deep sigh before continuing. Her eyes flick open, and they no longer tear with worry but blaze with bravery.

"Jarr-Wya is here, too," she says flatly. "The Millia weren't lying when they confronted us at the Bangol fortress, your old fortress, after you slipped away with the Tillastrion. They said the storm spread their grains of sand across the island. The flood brought their shores farther inland. They attacked us"—

Tessa's pale green eyes meet those of every Bangol in the room —"and when our company operated a new Tillastrion, well, we must have worn enough flecks of sand that were touching other flecks of sand and—"

"You brought the Millia and Jarr-Wya here?!" roars Zeno.

"*You* brought them here!" repeats Borgin.

"Silence, Cousin!"

"No wonder our powers are restored," muses Ardenal, a sober edge to his voice.

Zeno grinds his teeth and the sound sends chills up Archie's back. The Bangol king storms past Tessa, past Borgin, and past the other guards pointing stone mallets and rock-cut spears at Archie, Ardenal, Ella, and Luggie. Zeno disappears through the hole in his shop with the crowd in Treasures filtering out behind him.

Zeno digs his piercing nails into the bark of a nearby tree, one of only a dozen left unbroken, and scales it. He then leaps from its branches to the roof of Treasures. He calls forth stones from the rubble and climbs up them one step at a time till he stands on the roof of a still standing two-story building. He peers south.

"We are fools! All of us," Zeno calls down. His voice is resigned, and Archie detects a hint of sorrow behind his words. "How long have the Millia sprouted up in deserts across Jarr-Wya without our suspicion?" Borgin begins to suggest an answer, but Zeno cuts him off. "And now they will be the death of us all. There will be no happy ending."

Luggie calls forth smooth stones from a flattened building nearby and walks up them from the square-tiled pedestrian plaza to the crumbling roof. He stands shoulder to shoulder with Zeno. Luggie points a grey finger to the sea beyond the golden beach.

"We do not need to play the fool any longer," Luggie growls. "We can right the wrong we have neglected for too many sunsets."

"Call every Bangol," Zeno orders Borgin. "Bring them down from the mountains, craters, surrounding towns. We need every stone wielder. Every Jarrwian." Zeno looks at Luggie and down at Ardenal, Archie, and Tessa. "Olearon. Steffanus. Sprite. And human, too. We must face the Millia and Senior Karish. Now is the time to fight!"

chapter 36

Tessa

Adrenaline courses through Tessa, as if she, too, is strengthened by the presence of Jarr-Wya. The creatures of Jarr clamber through the streets—the Olearons, Steffanus warriors, sprites, and Bangols—descending in elevation as they march and fly toward Arrecife.

When Lady Sophia catches her first glimpse of Jarr-Wya, she nearly faints. *"O, Dios mío,"* she wails. "The eighth island! Just like you told us, Captain Nate! Before we boarded the *Atlantic Odyssey*. You said some sailors and locals believe the Canary Islands are the mountaintops of sunken Atlantis. Or, that a mythical thief captured the sun and buried it inside one of the islands. Or, what I now see before my eyes!" Lady Sophia fans her face with a plump hand. Lillium flutters over with a leaf and fans it to cool the flushed singer.

"The eighth island," Nate says gruffly. "But this isn't that myth, Lady Sophia."

The opera singer objects. "You told the passengers that only the setting sun will reveal the location of the eighth island, and the sun is almost spent—"

"Folklore. Children's stories to keep the young from venturing out in boats by night." Nate storms forward at a pace Lady Sophia is unable to match. He hulks past Azkar and Nameris, who exchange a look. Warriors silently bolster each other for battle. Kameelo flies low overhead, watching the shifting sand and reporting to the Lord.

Nate finds Tessa in the mob and takes her hand. His touch sends a shiver across her skin. Conflicting emotions flash through her: the comfort of protection, fear of the unknown, trepidation for the future, and, even in its most frail stage of blooming, *love*. Nate watches Tessa's face with a wrinkled brow. He squeezes her palm against his own and waits for her to mimic the gesture. Tessa does, though it is weaker than she intends, and she forces a smile, which Nate appears to accept.

Ardenal jogs to Tessa and Nate, and says, "In my research, I encountered the legend of San Borondon. He and his troupe of Irish monks set sail across the Atlantic Ocean. An old poem told of an island discovered by the monks. They came ashore, only to have the landmass begin to move. They realized they had landed upon the back of a giant sea creature."

"Another children's story," grumbles Nate.

"I am not supposing that any of the myths are true," Ardenal answers.

Junin, stalking along nearby, continues his thought. "But they can lead us to wonder: is this the first time Jarr-Wya has visited the human world?" The question is left to hang in the air.

The hodgepodge army reaches the coast, near a tiny square town called Los Ancones, with low lava-black cliffs supplying a direct view south. What they see causes Pinne and Quillie to cling to each other and Lillium to dive inside Archie's breast pocket. Ella tears her eyes from the sight to bury her face in Luggie's hupper furs. Tessa drops Nate's hand and covers her lips with trembling fingers. She feels a warm hand on her shoulder and turns to see Ardenal.

The Steffanus sisters sharpen one dagger on the second they carry with a *shing* sound that frays Tessa's nerves. The Olearons stand tall, unwavering, and all but Ardenal are aglow from head to foot in the seductive curl of flame. The Bangols dig their feet into the earth, strengthening their will to win.

From the coast of Lanzarote, Baluurwa the Doomful can be seen, along with the smaller islands, with their vines and rocks, that float airborne around its midsection. The glass city of the Olearons reflects the fading Earthen sun, which is a mere sliver of orange on the horizon. The dilapidated arching bridges of the Bangols are silhouettes on the opposite side of the island. Between the two extremes, the southern shore is naked earth in the absence of the Millia's gold village.

The sea between Jarr-Wya, the fateful eighth island, and the coastal town of Arrecife is turbulent, but not from wind or storm. Massive spiraling shells emerge from the surface. Tessa knows the shark-like rows of teeth and strong, treading legs that emerge below. The shellarks carry sandy figures on their backs. The Millia have assumed human form. Drowned wyverns leap from the sea with their webbed wings, spewing boiling water and leaving a trail of floating electric-violet blamala crabs belly up behind them.

One golden figure reaches the beach, forgoing its ride to stand at the center of the rising columns before becoming a column himself. A despicable voice snarls out as loud as thunder—Senior Karish. The sand continues its relocation from Jarr-Wya to Lanzarote, then up the northern coast, rushing, amalgamating, and dispersing repeatedly—until it arrives at the feet of the waiting Jarrwian.

"Your idea, your idea, Zeno, was a good one," says Senior Karish, hissing his words. The sand settles with a patter like rain. "We listened, always listening. But why should the Bangols have all the fun, all the fun?"

Zeno steps out from the grunting Bangols and past the

Olearons that part for him like splintering trees in a wildfire. "This is my island, Karish. My world. Conquered and built upon. You are too late."

"Oh no, I do not believe so—right on time we are, right on time. You dimwits underestimate we Millia. Our expansion across Jarr-Wya was calculated. Our new pockets of desert allowed us to wipe out the Banji flowers, which gave Rolace—rest his hairy legs—and the Steffanus sisters, and even you Bangols, added strength."

Tessa notices Archie's eyes grow wide. He fumbles in the pockets of his trousers, digging for something. She watches him shift to the periphery, where he retrieves a pale and brittle leaf that crumbles to reveal a folded sock. He retucks the stained sock and whatever it conceals back into his drooping pocket. He leaves his hand there, too casually. Duggie-Sky also has his eyes on Archie. Tessa can tell the boy knows what the old man's hiding.

"As our deserts grew, so did our dominion over Jarr-Wya," continues Senior Karish. "Truly we are now the rightful Lord of that island, rightful Lord. And thanks to you all, we are not limited to Jarr-Wya alone. This place looks lovely." The sandy wave gestures without hands to Lanzarote. "And the land is not all we want," adds Senior Karish, menace beneath his belittling tone.

"What else?" demands Zeno.

"We Millia crave the Star more than anything. We overheard the winged women in our desert nearest Baluurwa the Doomful. They were speaking of their tunnels through the mountain, which reach down to the Star. We also overheard that there is one in your company intimately connected to what we desire. That this human's life or death—her death—is a key to releasing the full power of the Star in all worlds."

"No!" screams Tessa. Her heart feels as if it will explode through her chest. Her breath is stolen from her lips. She pushes through bodies, oblivious to who they are, and pulls Ella to herself. Ella's face is the white of new snow and her hands are icy, despite the blanket of nearly suffocating humidity hanging over them.

"We should have left her hidden in Haria," Luggie whispers to Tessa.

"I have heard enough!" bellows Ardenal. He heaves a fireball twice the size of himself that slices through the muggy air with consuming flames. The ball bursts through the Millia's wave, turning a gaping section into inanimate glass that shatters on the lava rock below.

"You underestimate us," the Lord says firmly, his lips parting his flames. "Our powers are restored through the presence of Jarr-Wya. We unite in its defense until our last fire, flight, and stone."

Senior Karish cackles, "So be it, so be it."

chapter 37

Ella

The moon is shining on us once more. I've grown used to seeing its pale face beaming down on my equally waxy-looking cheeks. The sky here is clearer than it has been for days on Jarr-Wya, where the storm shielded the moon with leaf-spinning wind and lightning bolts of a thousand magnificent colors.

This is the calm breath before battle.

Dad is the first to charge, all brave and strong. His body is a beacon so bright, I can't look at him too long or my vision fills with spots as if I've been staring at the sun. He's joined by Junin and Azkar, then Islo and Nameris, and more Olearon warriors, who link together to form a bonfire so massive that the Millia are forced to lurch back or be melted to glass.

The Millia are driven south, and briefly I think this will be easy—but I'm dead wrong. Senior Karish is cunning and relentless. The wave transforms back into a hundred tornado-like columns that funnel sand sky-high above the tallest flames. The tops of these columns form black flyers of pure sand with massive gold wings that sprinkle sand into flame. The Olearons are forced to separate and flee or be pierced by the melted granules that have now turned to raining slivers of lethal crystal.

The Steffanus warriors meet the gold flyers in flight and force their daggers into the twin necks and snapping beaks. The women's eyes freeze and burn, their shredded gowns twisting through the breeze. They are both glorious and terrifying at once. Part of me wishes to be up there, to feel as light. Mostly, though, I want to help but I don't know how.

"Sing," Luggie says, and it takes me a second to realize he's talking to me, not Lady Sophia. I shake my head, but he implores, "Let out everything you want to say, Ella, and tell your birds what you want them to do."

Finally, I understand. I step away from Luggie and Grandpa Archie and Mom, not wanting to hurt them. My chapped lips part and I scream out all the anger I've buried inside my silent world, all the things I've been incapable of saying. A flock of green birds—which I both loathe and love—erupts from deep in my gut. Their feathers floss my teeth and carry the force of my breath, hot and horrifying, into the blackening sky. A green wind that curves and snaps like garden snakes trails behind them. My eyes are on the gold flyers and the Steffanus warriors, who tumble through the sky by the Olearons' firelight.

My green birds pierce through the sandy fowl, separating their grains in rocketing bursts. Steffanus wings beat and break the writhing, struggling-to-fly Millia, who rupture into smaller birds that wrangle my green flock, impaling their hearts. Steffanus daggers dice the petite golden birds which, along with the decimated gold flyers, crash to the lava rock below in glittering mounds. These piles rest still for the duration of a heartbeat and could easily be mistaken for the start of children's sand castles built on lazy beach days.

The stillness is consumed by blood-chilling howls as the sandy mounds reconstruct into famished sasars. The deadly massive wolf-like creatures prowl in packs. They're a head taller than my nearly five feet and their shoulders are twice as wide as my hips. Mom and Luggie brace me, holding me up, and I release more green birds, which fly alongside the Steffanus sisters in the war for the sky.

The gold sasars lunge for an Olearon arm or a human leg or a stony head. A tall ruddy warrior buckles under the weight of one golden creature. Then a Bangol falls, too.

"You will tire, will tire fast," Senior Karish growls through a sasar's sharp fangs. "But we will not. It is only a matter of time till this island, whatever it's called, is submerged in a fallen rainbow of Jarrwian blood."

"With blood flows life, real life, not its sandy impersonation," says the Lord of Olearon, who has a devilish look in his black eyes. He scowls in a way I've never seen; it's distinct from his usual stoic stance. He quivers, and his burnt red lips retract. "You are the fool, Karish. You! What effect did you suppose the island of Jarr-Wya would have on its creatures once brought to the derivative world?"

Senior Karish doesn't respond right away. In sasar form he digs at the earth, sharpening his claws, and turns in circles as if chasing his tail.

"I can see," continues the Lord in a vicious snarl, "that you are coming to appreciate your predicament. You have brought to this battle the very island that equips your enemy to prevail against you. Naiu, radiating through Jarr-Wya and alive in us who breathe, is stronger than any evil enchantment trapped in the rubble of shell."

The Lord lets his words sink in, like Mom does when she's intent on making her point. He laughs, deep and wicked, and orders those at his sides, "Drive the Millia to the beach! Drive them across the sea to Jarr-Wya!"

Boulders rush past us; I recognize them as pieces of Haria that had been used to construct the Bangol fortress. A sacrifice on the part of Zeno, I recognize, and hope that Grandpa Archie is right about him after all.

The stone-heads roar and run as fast as their short grey legs will carry them, wielding rock mallets and fatal slingshots. Other Bangols approach empty-handed. They fan their fingers to detach the unforgiving lava rock and project it forward. A cluster of Bangols unite their Naiu, forming a towering three-story-tall stone monster that throws punches at the sand. The lifeless rock formation attacks so fast that a section of sand is unable to take on new forms between hits.

Many Olearons create projectile weapons of fireballs and burning coils of grass and shrubbery. Dad, Junin, Azkar, Islo, Nameris, and the Lord assemble groups of Olearons that once more link into mobile bonfires that pursue and drive the Millia toward the coast, cornering the sandy shapes on a broad sweep of beach.

Glass covers the earth, and I'm careful where I step. Grandpa Archie swings me gently onto his back, giving Luggie leave to join the fight alongside the Bangols. Luggie passes me his sack before running off.

Luggie, stubborn and brave—my heart twitches in my chest. I want him to stay with me—through the growl and stab of sand, the Steffanus warriors' shrieks, and the trembling of excavated earth—but I sense he desires to test the limits of his maturing powers. The skin on his cheeks, around the newly budded stones, is still tender and flushed. I watch Luggie go until I'm forced to look away.

Mom is pulling Grandpa Archie and me inland, away from the screams of the wounded and the dying. We find ourselves in a vineyard of white grapes planted in black volcanic-ash soil in individual shallow hollows. On the Lanzarote tour Mom and I had taken during the port break, we learned that the vines on the island are pruned based on a lunar cycle. I tear my eyes from the battle at my back to where the moon I grew up watching hangs innocently in the twinkling night sky.

We hide inside one of the hollows, surrounded by a knee-high semicircular stone wall called a zucos, a word I learned on the tour. Zucos protect the grape vines from the ruthless sea winds that easily uproot unguarded plants. We're in a field of zucos.

In these heartbreaking moments, as our friends and their families risk their lives to protect those they love and their home, I realize I'm with two of the people who have given up so much for me and for our family. For the past two years, it's been me, Mom, and Grandpa Archie—for family dinners, attending my doctor's appointments, cleaning the house, and the hundred other normal things that make up daily life, so different from what I now know in this mixed-up place.

We peer over the zucos and watch a wave of sand splash down hard on a group of Olearons. I pray with everything in me that Dad isn't in that group. The Bangols direct the earth to fold and collide with a pack of Millia sasars, which bursts apart. The Steffanus warriors continue to battle the gold flyers and the smaller golden birds that break off from cut chunks of sand. I release new flocks of green birds that race to the battle. The sprites mount my green birds' backs. Lillium organizes the sprites into groups, each determined in their goal. She leads the fowl into the heart of the sandstorm, her red hair twisting through the breeze like Olearon flame.

Pinne and Quillie aren't with Lillium. They've taken shelter in a nearby zucos. I can make out their sparkling wings in the distance, inland, well beyond the reach of the perilous battle. Their mission is clear: they must protect the Life Ohmi, the grape that ensures the existence of future generations of sprites.

My throat hurts, and my mouth is dry and caked in feathers. Mom urges me to sit. I can't do anything but obey. A bunch of white grapes makes a squishing sound beneath my weight. A headache threatens to split my skull. *Cancer, why now?* I think. Mom overhears me.

How are you feeling?

Fine! Gee, don't worry about me, Mom. We've got more important things to focus on right now.

As my harsh thought snaps out at her, Grandpa Archie flattens us onto the vine. A boulder wielded by the Bangols has burst apart at the hand of the Millia. A piece of rock flies through the sky and crashes a foot beyond our zucos.

"Ell, you okay?" Grandpa Archie asks, panicked.

I nod. Then I look at Mom. Her head is bleeding. A steady gush streams from a cut near the goose egg from Zeno's blow. The shard of rock did its damage. More of her blond waves are stained crimson.

Grandpa applies pressure to the gash, but Mom doesn't respond. Nor does she stir at my pleading hands that clutch hers. "She's knocked out cold. Ell, stay here with your mom. I'm going to get Arden."

I shake my head, "*No*," and drop Mom's hands and sign the word. Then "*Stop*"—a downward chop with my right hand that connects to the flat palm of my left. I rub my chest, signing, "*Please*." My whole body trembles. Mom can't die. Mom can't die. Mom can't die. Grandpa can't leave me here alone!

"Ella, deep breath," Grandpa says. "I feel it in my bones: I'm not going to die here, on Earth. Which means we're going to get back to Jarr—*alive*—I'll make sure of it. Olearon blood flows through my veins. Which means it also flows through yours, Ella Wellsley. I'll explain it all soon, but for now, please hear me: you're stronger than you look, stronger than you feel. Now is the time. Muster your courage and draw on the Naiu that lives within you."

Ella

Ella

chapter 38

Ella

Grandpa Archie leaves me in the white grape vineyard, tucked in a zucos, stunned, alone with Mom, whose bleeding has slowed, and also alone to stew on the bizarre reality that I'm only part human. This news has me squeamish, uncomfortable, as if I haven't ever really known myself. If I don't do something with my hands, the shaking will overtake me and I'll enter into a full-on panic attack.

I dig into my bag for paper and my paintbrush, but it's Luggie's bag I grab by accident. In it is the royal-blue tunic from the Olearons, unused, and something else—a leather envelope and inside—oh! This must be the glass square Grandpa Archie stole from the Lord's citadel. How did Luggie get this? Hmm.

There's no one here to get me in trouble, so of course I pull out the piece of glass. Its surface is bordered in glimmering rubies, emeralds, and diamonds. I brush dust from its surface, which is frigid and tingly to the touch with the electric prick of static. Whoa! Billowing clouds appear and flow across the square, melting into black. White words emerge through the darkness in a language I know by sight to be Bangol, thanks to Luggie and Nanjee, who taught me what they could while our awakin-flown balloon carried us above the blue and white woodlands.

I can't read Bangol, but the glass, as if sensing it is no longer Luggie who holds it, bleeds the letters away and new words appear. These I understand.

What I found beneath my glass throne, the pieces of him, have fully adhered to my skin. Ashamed, I hide the new flesh below the royal Olearon robes, the sleeves and pant legs rolled down. I am regretful of my decision to trust him. At first this transformation granted me unmatched strength, but also, I have discovered, unyielding fear.

My uncle Telmakus, the 29th Lord of Olearon, experienced such terror and rage that he was driven to madness. These now plague my mind as well. Telmakus was broken in spirit, having lost his love from another world, and been betrayed by his warriors. He allowed anger to multiply in him, to consume him, tearing out the good in his heart and replacing it with evil.

This secret history has taught me much, but knowledge is not always accompanied by wisdom.

I have been a fool.

Believing I was greater than Telmakus, I wore his ravaged life on top of my own, wielding his power but also growing in his delusions. Wisdom would have insisted I burn the pieces of him, destroy the wicked enchantment that preserved his being inside that drawer. But now I am becoming him, slowly, and I cannot stop it. Telmakus takes over my mind at his will. He speaks through me, fights through me, plots conflict and destruction, contrary to my desire for peace.

My Maiden has suspected for many sunsets the ill fate I have set in motion for us all. Within the shell of me, since her death, the three of us struggle like twisting ropes, and I weep for my soul's companion. I did this to her, to us, and I fear there is no way to undo it, except for death.

If my body dies before Telmakus assumes full control, then all will be saved from a terrible fate. If not, he will rule through me, and I will be prisoner along with my Maiden. Telmakus must be stopped.

My mind is going crazy. With this all-consuming headache, I can't process what I've read. Do Dad and Grandpa Archie know that the Lord is out to get us? Is his possession by the evil Lord complete? Which Lord is fighting right now, Dunakkus or Telmakus?

A new thought creeps in and hurts more than the migraine. Why did Luggie not share the Olearons' history with me? Why would he keep it a secret? My cheeks flush with fury. What is love if not honest? Maybe he doesn't care as much as I thought.

Then I remember the fancy metal key around my neck. It tingles against my skin, even now, beckoning to me. It was hidden in a covert pocket in one of King Tuggeron's books, inside the decorative leather and metal cover that bound pages meant to be filled with the king's exploits. I didn't tell Luggie or his sister; I wasn't convinced I could trust them back then or even after our bond grew deeper. Still, I kept my secret, as guilty as Luggie is with this glass history.

The fight is loud—crashing rock, howls and wails, the crackle of fire—and smells like death—burnt bodies and blood. If I had anything more than green birds in me, I'd be sick. Too many questions ram my brain. Too much is at stake all around me. Pushing my hands (covered in Mom's blood) against my temple, I apply pressure.

My life doesn't make sense, and it's not fair. I need a minute to myself, for pity, before I take to heart Grandpa Archie's words —about finding my inner courage, or whatever—and choose to be strong.

I think about Mom and Dad and the mess they're in. Our family is together but broken. I decide to tell Luggie about the key. Since the adults aren't fixing things, that leaves it to me.

The throbbing in my head careens down my neck where the cancer poisons me from the inside out. It makes me woozy. All I know for certain is that everything is getting worse—much worse.

Needing an immediate outlet, I begin to draw. In a continuous stream of consciousness, I paint until I'm surrounded by curling vines covered with inky-wet pages and a river of tears.

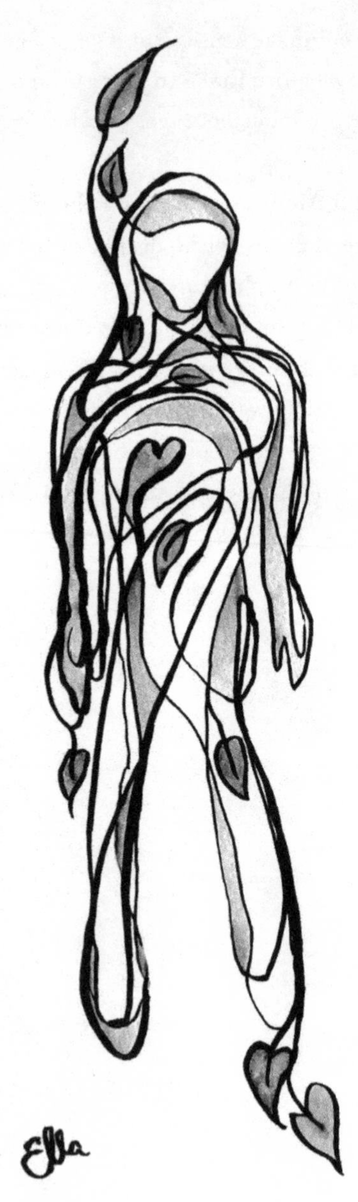
Ella

Ella

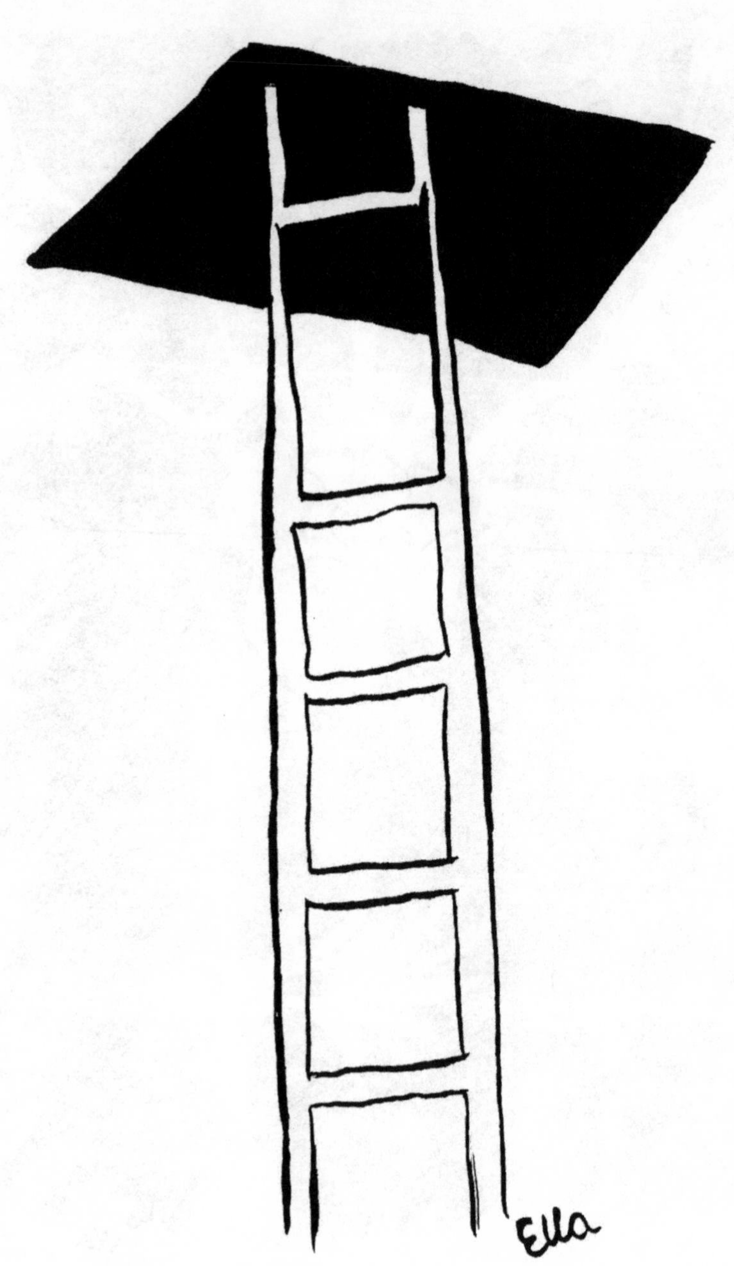
Ella

Grandma Suzie,
I miss you...
I love you...
Give me strength.
Love Ella

chapter 39

Tessa

"How is it we can communicate at a level beneath my consciousness, Finnah? I can only speak with Ella telepathically when awake and eavesdrop on the Bangols with all my effort, but here—wherever here is—I easily find you."

"Oh, Tessa." Finnah laughs, and it is bells and wind chimes and echoes and raindrops. "You are unconscious right now; that is true. You will learn to harness your power, in time. Do not fret."

"Will I survive?"

"If I answer that, will it not spoil the fun?"

"You have a strange idea of fun . . ."

"When you are awake, Tessa, your inner voice tells you what is true and what is false, which is not always accurate. It does this to protect you, though I do not believe you are a woman who needs protecting. You see, I am incomprehensible to that voice, and so our conversation is rejected before it has begun."

"How do I quiet myself so I can hear you? When I'm awake, I mean."

"Surrender. Welcome belief and disbelief as sisters, without judgment. You are not of that world, Tessa, but, indeed, there is magic on Earth; it is the derivative of Jarr, but not lesser than it. Its magic is different, hidden more deeply, harder to find, yet just as powerful. Fortunately, something even greater dwells inside of you.

"Embrace that which you are, that which you have always been," Finnah continues to chirp happily. "It is not faith to say that you claim your power. It is faith when you choose bravery in the face of terrible odds and cling to hope."

"Who are you really?"

"You already know, Tessa. Look inside yourself and you will see."

chapter 40

Archie

Archie's legs move like a shooting star. He covers ground quickly, smoothly, and leaps over debris and bodies alike, never slowing. On all sides of him, Jarrwians fight the Millia. Olearons combine efforts with Bangols, surrounding the stone monsters in fire so that with each thunderous punch, sand is melted and the Millia are beaten back. The Steffanus warriors and sprites also unite, attacking from the air, from above and below, from in front and behind, trapping and thwarting many great golden flyers.

Archie monitors the battle as he weaves his way through it. The smell of smoke, carrying burnt flesh, lodges in his nose. Ardenal stands at the center of the sandstorm, a dome of fire encircling his crisp patch of earth. Golden grit pummels him from every side as he melts it to glass rain. Sweat stains his royal-blue warrior's jumpsuit, damp despite his blazing heat as he strains against the Millia.

In Archie's peripheral vision, he notices Zeno and the Lord propel forward a massive boulder burning with the heat of the absent sun. It bounces twice before rolling toward the heart of the sandy storm in Ardenal's direction. Archie follows it. As the molten boulder advances through the Millia, it melts a cylindrical glass passageway through the sand. The soles of Archie's shoes reek of burnt rubber as he follows the boulder but finds himself protected within the smooth tunnel.

From inside, Archie observes the blackened earth, burned of

its shrubbery and vines, littered in grey and red bodies and scorched wings. There are human remains as well, though he cannot tell the bodies apart through the sheen of the glass.

The boulder passes Ardenal, and Archie skids to a slippery stop. He smashes his way through the glass and to the edge of Ardenal's fiery dome. "Arden!" he hollers as loudly as he is able, choking on smoke as the heat coats his throat. "Arden!"

Ardenal cannot turn; all his effort is spent in deflecting the attack. Archie takes a gravelly breath and dashes through the fire. He envelops his son in an embrace so tight that it creates a heat all its own.

"Dad!" Ardenal says, maintaining the shield. Wrinkles of confusion ripple his otherwise creaseless face. "How did you make it through my fire?"

Archie only says, "I need your help." He fills in his son on Tessa's condition. Ardenal shifts the burning shield to the opening in the tunnel, then extinguishes it. They slip inside the rounded glass passageway and sprint through the battle toward the zucos field.

The screams, crashes of stone, splashes of gold, and sizzling of fire become quiet in Archie's and Ardenal's ears, replaced by the thudding of their feet on glass. Ardenal touches Archie's arm, slowing him. They peer through the shimmering tunnel once surrounded by pelting waves of sand.

"Where'd they go?" Archie mumbles.

"The Millia," Ardenal answers, "are leaving."

He shatters the glass to their left, and they emerge into air devoid of silt and sand. The vibration of the silence is deafening, trembling through their ears. Junin and a bedraggled Lady Sophia appear beside them.

Lady Sophia smiles through her sooty face and says, "Oh, wonderful! I'm so relieved to see you two up and about!"

"Are you wounded, Ardenal? Archibald?" asks Junin. She offers them a glass vial of the silvery wryst drink to restore their strength.

Lady Sophia adds, "Or vulai bread?" She gestures to her sack. "From my stash. I knew it would come in handy."

Archie spots the Lord and Zeno approaching the coastline where Jarr-Wya floats in the distance, a black blotch on the horizon. They are at the cliffs' edge, some hundred feet away. Senior Karish twists in a writhing column, slowly shrinking into human form.

"Can you ladies take this"—Archie gestures to the wryst and vulai—"to Ella and Tessa? They're just past those first semicircular stone walls. Tessa is injured—she was unconscious when I left her. Ella's . . . well, fading . . ."

"We're off to help!" Lady Sophia says brightly, hoisting her dress where the stitching ripped and now brushes through the volcanic ash that covers one-third of Lanzarote. She and Junin head for the vineyard.

WHEN Archie and Ardenal reach the coast, the sour voice of Senior Karish hisses through the air. "More trouble than it's worth!" he says with a sneer. "More trouble! We will return once the Star is ours, the Star is ours. If I were you all, I would be far away by then. Perhaps in a new world entirely." Senior Karish cackles—a twisted, wicked laugh through wide sandy lips. From his breastplate of unbroken shells, still containing their aquatic life form, he detaches a conch shell and blows.

His golden shape begins to crumble, first his head and then his shoulders and torso, until he is a mound of sand. The shells containing crabs and other creatures scurry away. The Millia, taking with them every fleck of ash, grain of sand, and tiny shard of lava rock from the eastern coast of Lanzarote, funnel into the air in a black-gold tornado. A rumble of disgruntled voices emerges from the sparkling vortex. Archie cannot make out their words, but the bloodthirsty tone is unmistakable.

The sandstorm levitates toward Jarr-Wya. In the distance, across the Atlantic, Archie can see a hint of yellow. The tornado spins above the angry ocean, casting muted shadows on the water where the shellarks in their twisted exteriors can be seen ferrying sandy figures. Other monstrous shelled creatures emerge from the moonlit sea like great whales and then are gone. Drowned wyverns stir the water and leave a trail of half-eaten blamala crabs in their wake.

"We must return our island to where it belongs, in Jarr." Callisto is the first to speak.

"All the boats are gone," says Nate, his eyes on the marina.

"It will take far too long for us Steffanus sisters to fly there," Callisto says, pacing, "and till midday tomorrow for the sprites, if they make it at all."

Lillium shifts from one grasshopper-like foot to the other, whispering to her Wingies.

"What about a Tillastrion?" Azkar suggests.

Nameris shakes his head. "No, that will not work. A Tillastrion may transport us between worlds, but not from one place to another within the same world."

"What are our priorities here?" a voice says behind them.

Archie startles at the sight of Tessa as she approaches.

Ardenal runs to her and hugs her in an embrace that lifts her from her feet. He kisses her wounded forehead, where blood still glistens, though it no longer flows. His warm lips seal the cut. His hands cup Tessa's face briefly before he grows aware of the eyes gawking at them, including Nate's. Ardenal turns to Ella and lifts her weak body, returning to the gathering.

"Our priorities, as I see them," continues Tessa, "are, number one, find the Star, then return Jarr-Wya to Jarr."

Archie knows that when Tessa says "find the Star," what she means is locate Ella's cure.

"No," Callisto says. "Jarr-Wya must be returned first. Our battle with the Millia is far from over, and we cannot risk them remaining on Earth where this firm sea wind can scatter them to the farthest reaches. No."

"I have an idea." The timid, boyish voice is Duggie-Sky's. "I know it looks far but, well, I can get to Jarr-Wya with my gift from Rolace."

"That's too far for you to teleport, little fella," says Archie, stumbling over his words as he takes in Duggie-Sky's new stature. "What if you don't make it and end up treading water in the North Atlantic?"

"I've done that distance before, Grandpa Archie." Duggie-Sky smiles with gleaming white teeth. "Maybe not quite that far, but close."

Xlea steps past Callisto. Her face and arms are bruised from her imprisonment by Tuggeron, her wings blackened from the battle on Lanzarote. She still clutches her notebook, which, Archie notices, has a leather strap hand sewn to its binding. Xlea wears the notebook slung over her neck and around one shoulder. "I will help Duggie-Sky," she says.

Zeno snorts and the Lord shakes his head. "This is not an errand for children," the Lord says.

"I possess more bravery in my wing tips than you do in all your fire," Xlea retorts hotly. Callisto hushes her with a firm hand on her back. Xlea takes a deep breath before continuing. "Please forgive me, Lord of Olearon—but let me explain how my size can be an advantage to our mission."

The Lord turns to Azkar, Islo, and Nameris, who nod. "How can you be of help?" the Lord says evenly.

"Well," begins Xlea, "Duggie-Sky can teleport me with him to Jarr-Wya. The added weight may make him fall short of the island, as you suggest, Archie, but just how short I am not sure. Whatever the shortfall, I can carry him the rest of the way."

"You need to find the core of the Millia's storm, which has not yet traveled half the distance in its return to Jarr-Wya. It made it there in a matter of breaths, so we have none to spare," says Callisto. "The sandstorm is connected to our island, its golden teeth still firmly sunken into Jarr-Wya. If Duggie-Sky gets you close, then, Xlea, our best course is that you operate a Tillastrion midair, while surrounded by the Millia. This mission is perilous—you must be wise and careful. Xlea and Duggie-Sky, you two will transport yourselves, the Millia sands, and Jarr-Wya back to the world of Jarr."

"Then the rest of us will use a Tillastrion to transport ourselves to Jarr-Wya once we see the eighth island disappear," says Lady Sophia eagerly.

"And find the Star and Ella's cure," Tessa adds.

Archie nods. Ardenal and Ella as well.

"Lord?" Xlea inquires.

"Yes," says the Lord, standing tall and with steady eyes. "Jarr-Wya must be returned. We will await your success, then follow you."

Callisto retrieves a small device from the fabric of her piecemeal gown and places it tenderly in Xlea's hands. Archie can see the delicate objects that make up this Tillastrion. There is a small brass box, and on its top is fastened a fired-clay Banji blossom. Xlea opens the box. Inside is a tiny blue feather, a black pebble from Baluurwa, a tarnished pocket watch, and a pink plastic button.

Archie remembers what he read in the secret history of the Olearons as the first company ventured east. The Steffanus sisters, being Naiu-born and part human, can operate a Tillastrion by drawing on both aspects of themselves. Most Tillastrions, however, as Archie learned from Zeno, must be created by someone in the world wished to be reached and operated by someone from the world presently occupied. A Steffanus is one and the same.

"Set your intentions on home, my dear," Callisto says. She slides her silver hand from Xlea's back to her tumbling sugar and cinnamon-colored hair, stroking it kindly. "Your desire will save us. Now go!"

Xlea and Duggie-Sky find the edge of Lanzarote with their toes. Xlea wraps her arms around Duggie-Sky's neck. Turning back one last time, Duggie-Sky smirks happily over his shoulder at Archie before saying, "See you in Jarr, Grandpa!" The human boy and young Steffanus girl disappear in a blink.

"Prepare yourselves to be transported," the Lord commands. "But not you." He is looking at Zeno with a bizarre expression Archie cannot read. The Lord's shoulders quiver ever so slightly.

"What do you mean, not me?" growls Zeno.

"Of course, not you," says the Lord, a nasty curve to the corners of his ruddy lips. "Only Bangols loyal to the rightful heir, Luggie, and loyal to me, may return."

"Loyal to you?" Zeno says. "Why would any Bangol be loyal to an Olearon?"

"Life will be different upon our return to Jarr-Wya. I will oversee all races, ensuring peace by the power of the Star."

Callisto bristles. "The Star is for us to protect and aid, not to manipulate to our will."

"If that is your belief," begins the Lord slyly, "perhaps the Steffanus sisters must remain here as well."

"You have no power over us, in this world or any world," roars Callisto. Her eyes take on more red than blue, and her wings part with a *thwack*.

"He's not who he seems. The Maiden told me, and I believe her. He is the 29th Lord of Olearon," announces Archie.

chapter 41

Archie

He's the 30th Lord, Dad," Ardenal corrects.

Archie shakes his head. "No, Arden. The 29th."

Tessa pleads, "Archie, be careful!"

"It is true." A soft, kind voice creeps out of the Lord's mouth, but it is not the Lord's. "It is me, the Maiden of Olearon, partner to the 30th Lord. When I died, I joined my love inside this shell but soon discovered, as I had feared that we were not alone. *Argh!* No!" The Maiden in the Lord's body clutches her throat. "My end . . . has come . . . Archie, you must . . . stop him!"

Archie knows these words spoken by the Maiden are her last. As the body of the 30th Lord straightens itself, smoothing its royal robes, the wicked sneer returns to his mouth.

"My Maiden rudely spoke out of turn," says the Lord in a mocking way. "But she will not be doing that again.

"Luggie join me—remember our agreement," growls the Lord. "All Bangols loyal to King Luggie, to me, step forward and join us. The rest—Olearon warriors, ready!—shall be scorched into the black rock of this earth."

Luggie steps to align himself beside the Lord. "Ella, I am sorry. I promised to obey the Lord if he did not hurt you and your family. I didn't know it would resort to this."

The Lord laughs, but the sound sets the hair on Archie's arms and neck on end. "It does not matter what you think, Luggie, only that your actions have proven you faithful. You have spared the Wellsley's. Now let us continue with those not so fortunate—"

"Olearons, don't move!" The command sounds weak from Archie's lips, and he clears his throat. "This isn't the Lord you promised to serve. Before you stands the 29th Lord of Olearon, Telmakus, who went mad with rage and killed his brother, Dillmus, and was corrupted by the evil desire for blood over peace. He grew so powerful and power-hungry that he burst into a thousand pieces, which were stored in a magic compartment beneath the glass throne, where I found the secret history of the Olearons."

"You propose to know me," says the Lord, cackling. "But I know you as well. A pathetic, powerless human!"

Luggie speaks up. "I found the secret history glass in the sea when the Maiden took the life of the incarnation of the human cruise director, in the hive mind of the carakwas. I am sorry I didn't tell you, Ella. I regret it with all my being. Through the enchanted glass, I read about what the 29th Lord wanted the Olearons to forget, and what the 30th Lord sought to destroy. But it wasn't the 30th Lord at all. Telmakus has taken over the mind of Dunakkus, along with that of his Maiden, who bravely resisted."

The Lord slowly removes his gloves, revealing sickly orange skin beneath. His fingers are a patchwork of red and ill tangerine, with pale yellow lines dividing chunks of skin like stitches. "Well done, all. You have discovered the truth. I applaud you. It only required four hundred sunsets. Yet, what you have failed to recognize is that it does not matter. I am alive, the rightful 29th Lord of Olearon. The 30th Lord should never have been, nor his Maiden. And they are no more." He rips the Maiden's patch of vivid colors from his shoulder and grinds it into the earth beneath his boot.

"No!" Lady Sophia covers her trembling lips.

"It is done, you weak human. All of you—it is done. They are dead. My power is fed by them and all that is around me. My flesh is alive once more, thanks to an elder's spell and Dunakkus's foolishness in adorning himself in its treachery. I grow in strength with every the sunset. And now that I may speak freely, Ardenal, I have a matter to address with you."

"Lord?" Ardenal stutters suspiciously. He places Ella on her feet, and she rests her head against Tessa's chest. He steps forward.

"Arden, don't," Archie says, but the Lord advances on Ardenal.

"There is an oracle that bothers me, which I must address here and now before we return to Jarr," says the Lord with a snarl. He takes another casual step toward Ardenal. "And it has to do with you." With an outstretched arm, he grabs Ardenal's throat. The Lord's grotesque flesh is reeking.

"Arden!" screams Tessa.

Telmakus glares. "The Steffanus, Laken, once my friend, proclaimed this: 'A half-blood Olearon will return to Jarr and the race of Olearons will cease as they have been known since the first sunrise and their first spark.'

"So, you can see, Ardenal, why I must disallow you to accompany us to Jarr. When I learned through the Maiden and Dunakkus of your transformation from human to Olearon, I knew what must be done. I will protect the purity of the Olearon race with the heat of a thousand suns."

"Put him down." Archie says pointedly, his rage seeping out from his level tone.

"And when I kill you, Ardenal, the power Rolace gave to you, his Naiu, will be mine. My reign will be restored, and peace, as I wish it to be, will govern Jarr-Wya."

"You can never rule hearts with hate." Ardenal chokes on the words through the Lord's unyielding grip.

"Save your breath, Arden," Archie says in a low voice.

"Archie! Your eyes!" screams Tessa. She recoils with Ella, backing up behind Azkar and Junin.

Archie feels the pulse of Naiu pump through his heart, drumming in his ears. He looks down at his hands. The age spots and wrinkles are gone, and through his veins flows red heat in branching lines beneath his skin. Archie cannot see himself, but he knows what Tessa witnessed, what all now see plainly. His eyes are a solid onyx hue, a bottomless black from corner to corner—Olearon eyes.

Archie smelled something familiar in the scent of Zeno's incense in Treasures—back when he was a hunched, nearly bald old man, when he snuck off during the cruise, lying to Tessa, following the notes scribbled in Arden's notebooks, when he first sought out the yellow-eyed, grey-skinned creature with stones growing from his head.

The smell of that incense hinted at what he would slowly begin to understand—abstractly at first—after arriving on Jarr-Wya: The feeling of home. The strength he had long forgotten from his youth roofing in the hot Seattle sun. The part of himself, and of his mother, that had come so close to magic, that when he lost them both, he misplaced who he was—who he is.

Ardenal's face pales to a sickly orange as the wicked Lord's grip tightens.

"I said, put him down!" Archie yells, stepping forward. "It's not Arden you want, Telmakus. It's me."

"What are you yammering on about, Archibald?" The Lord

breaks his gaze with Ardenal and meets Archie's eyes. The mangled hand releases Ardenal to fall to the volcanic crust of Lanzarote. Luggie rushes to Ella's side, braiding his fingers between hers, and allowing Tessa to race to Ardenal. She drags him to safety, the Olearon who was once human, once her husband, once the love of her life. Tessa places her lips against Ardenal's and gives him her breath, forcing his chest to rise and fall. Archie notices the change when her lips turn from life-giving to loving.

Archie takes a step closer to the Lord. "I spoke with Laken before she died, and she told me who you once were, Telmakus. You were a peace-loving Olearon, a lovesick Lord searching for your Maiden. And you did find her. Here, on Earth."

"So what?" says the Lord with scorn. "None of that matters. It is all past. What I am concerned with is the future."

Archie calms the fire in him, or more accurately, he thinks, channels it. "The past teaches us who we must be and gives us a choice about who we wish to become tomorrow."

The Lord snarls. "I have no time for platitudes!"

Archie continues, undeterred. "I didn't know my father, but Laken revealed to me the truth of my past. You, Telmakus, once loved a woman, a human. That woman was my mother."

"N-no," stammers the Lord.

"My mother was heat stricken and dehydrated from hiking, so your red skin didn't disturb her in her delirium. You carried for her the child you conceived together—me—till she was well enough to do it herself. But she never saw you again. Laken checked in on me, but by that time, you were changed. I believe my mother knew, deep in her heart, who you were. She saw the red glint of the sun on a river and dove in. She died trying to find you."

"My son . . . is alive . . ." The words of Telmakus are bittersweet, tinged with resentment at the loss of his former self and his potential, and new hatred for the man standing before him with pale skin and Olearon eyes.

Archie feels strength throb through his limbs. His mind is sharp and his reflexes heightened. In one split second, he can sense the cool of Callisto's warning hand on his back, the tiny flecks of salt on the breeze, and the dormant lava beneath Lanzarote. All the hundreds of eyes of the Jarrwians and humans, who watch with bated breath, are focused on Archie and the Lord, and so it is only Archie who notices when Jarr-Wya—the eighth Canary Island—fades from the horizon.

"I am the half-blood Olearon," Archie says. Lady Sophia faints.

"There can only be one Lord of Olearon," says Telmakus, sneering. He ignites his hands into flaming embers and charges Archie.

With the thrill of adrenaline and the power of Naiu, Archie moves swiftly, accelerating into double time. With one arm, he reaches back to grip the sheathed dagger of Callisto, who stands beside him. With his other, he retrieves the Banji from his trouser pocket, shaking the enchanted flowers free of the sock that hid them.

Archie feels his veins burst open with fire, which burns through him, yet he is unburned. He lunges toward the Lord. Their two flames—one burning sickly orange and the other a vibrant newborn red—collide in a deadly embrace. Before the Lord can choke his life out of him, burning him alive as Telmakus had done to his brother Dillmus, Archie smears the Banji across the seething red face.

The Banji flowers take effect immediately. Though weakened from the days spent wilting in Archie's pocket, they still possess enough hallucinogenic properties to disorient the Lord.

Briefly. Archie finds his mark and digs Callisto's dagger deep into the Lord's heart.

Slowly the red flame envelops and extinguishes the orange, and both fade to deep azure, a blue so hot that Jarrwians and humans alike—even Olearons—must back away. So bright is the light that all must turn and shield their eyes. These moments, unlike before, are long, half-speed, and measured—a time outside of the ticking clock of Earth or the sunsets of Jarr.

When Archie emerges from the blaze, he is alone. The scene dims to moonlight. The Steffanus dagger and a mound of ash is all that remains of the 30th Lord's body and the enchanted pieces of the 29th Lord. Telmakus, at last, is at rest. Archie pulls the fire back inside his veins, where his skin is unbroken, unblemished with a hint of rose, yet still pale.

The first voice to shatter the near-reverent silence is Callisto's. "What do you stand for, Archibald, half-blood Olearon? Do you seek power, like your father"—all eyes linger on the pile of ash and the metal dagger, on the cracked glass breastplate on the lava rock island—"or peace, like your family? Who do you choose to be tomorrow?"

"Peace loving," answers Archie. "Always peace."

Azkar and Islo, rivals in all but this, approach Archie with the same expression. They each bend one knee and bow low before Archie.

"Our 31st Lord of Olearon," says Azkar.

"Our 31st Lord," repeats Islo.

Junin approaches and also bows. She is followed by Ardenal, Kameelo, and Nameris, then by all Olearon warriors.

chapter 42

Ella

The silvery wryst drink that Junin poured down my throat has finally spread warmth and energy through me, if not a drunken giddiness. Grandpa Archie, Dad, Mom, and Luggie are alive! I'm beyond relieved.

All the events with the evil Lord happened fast. I was confused when I read the secret history of the Olearons, which I now see is only part of a convoluted story spanning many decades and worlds. All the pieces have slid into place: Grandpa Archie—how he changed, inside and out—his mother's bizarre love, and her tragic, mysterious death. It explains why Dad, inside Rolace's web, was transformed by the power of Naiu into a red-skinned being who can fight with fire. Of course, he became an Olearon! Olearon blood flows through his veins, as it does through mine. Dad's transformation was dramatic for me and Mom, especially Mom, but in fact is the most natural change in the world.

Dad and Grandpa Archie are wrapped in a tight embrace, just beyond the mound of ash that was two Lords and a Maiden. The briny wind sweeps in from the North Atlantic Ocean and picks up the white flecks of burnt skin and bone and carries them over Lanzarote and out to sea beyond the other side of the island.

Grandpa cups Dad's face in his hands. Their foreheads—one pale, the other red—touch in a smear of dirt and sweat. "I am so sorry you lost your father," Dad says.

"He made his choice," is all Grandpa Archie replies.

They whisper so quietly now that I can't hear them. Their black eyes, however, sizzle with happy tears I recognize from home.

The melodious sound of Lady Sophia, who has risen from the charred earth where she fainted, is carried on the curling breeze. She sings in Spanish, and I imagine I can understand. The melody is a drumming heartbeat: resilient, reflective, and enduring. The frazzled locals of Lanzarote and stunned tourists who huddle watching at our periphery hear Lady Sophia's voice, and fear is washed from their horror-stricken faces. She lulls them like a mother; her aria places peace in their hearts, the confidence that the worst has passed and it's safe to return to the places from where they came.

I, too, am soothed, and I squeeze Luggie's hand. He turns to me and apologizes, again. It's easy for me to smile, forgiving him completely. In a gesture of trust, and of love, I place the key to all the worlds in his grey hands. I close his fingers around it. Soon I'll explain, once we've returned to Jarr-Wya.

Jarr-Wya! I nearly forgot! My eyes whip past the carnage of Lanzarote, which looks like burnt toast, and search for the magical island. Is my mind playing games with me? Have Duggie-Sky and Xlea been successful?

It's gone! Jarr-Wya has been wiped clean from the razor-sharp horizon, like a black ink drip on my pad of paper that is painted over with white. I forget myself and call out to Mom, Dad, and Grandpa Archie. A cluster of green birds are birthed from my lips. They flutter around me for a moment, hiding in my hair and stroking my cheek with their newborn wings.

I point, and everyone sees. Callisto's blue-red eyes burn and her skin shimmers in the moonlight.

"We must go, now!" she urges. "There are not enough Steffanus sisters left guarding the Star in the belly of Baluurwa. If the Millia find their way through the tunnels—"

"Ella's cure!" Mom says aloud, but in her head adds: *Don't worry, Ell. I'll find it. We'll find it.*

"And the cure for Jarr. Olearons, prepare yourself," commands Grandpa Archie. The red warriors cauterize wounds and secure their sacks over their shoulders, lining up. "Zeno, we need the Bangols in this fight. Please join with us in saving Jarr, Earth, all the worlds."

Zeno studies Grandpa Archie's black eyes. "Tell me the truth, Archibald. Did you know the truth of who you are when we met in Treasures?"

"No, Zeno, I had no indication then of what I now can't deny."

"And who do you support as Bangol king?" Zeno is sneering, yet his eyes betray his hope.

"Zeno"—it's Luggie who speaks—"I do not wish to be king, only that the Bangols live our sunsets in amity in our world, and not at the expense of any other."

Zeno considers Luggie's conditions. For the length of one rumbling sigh, the stone-head regards Lanzarote with sentiment, as if saying goodbye to a dear friend.

"Leave this place to rebuild itself," Grandpa says. "They've endured volcanic eruptions and thrived in this black ash soil; they'll survive this devastation. Be the king I know you are, Zeno. We need your help."

"Of course I'm coming with you," says Lady Sophia. It's both a question and a statement.

Grandpa Archie, once annoyed by the plump singer, now grins and nods. "We'd have it no other way," he answers.

Lady Sophia appears relieved.

Dad points and directs the last lingering humans toward

Arrecife. They cower from him, but not from Lady Sophia, who shoos them along a dusty road. The singer brushes herself clean and joins the Olearons, who tower over her; she looks right at home among them with her round cheeks narrowing her eager eyes as she beams, ready to jump portals.

I watch sadness flash across Dad's features. He realizes, as do I, that he no longer belongs in this world. How can he ever rejoin our family? Things can never be as they were at home in Seattle, even with my cure.

"Jarr-Wya is dying, Archibald," says Zeno huffily. "You ask me to return to a world where my kin might never flourish, or even endure as these humans surely will."

The tall hunched Bangol, Borgin, shuffles up and whispers in his cousin's ear. Zeno huffs in response and scratches his boots against the earth. He reaches deep beneath his hupper fur and retrieves a wooden box with a brass latch. Zeno places the Tillastrion in Grandpa Archie's hands.

"My dim-witted cousin has informed me that the Bangols had hoped I would lead differently from Tuggeron, who was bloodthirsty and hungry for new power and lands." Zeno compresses his lips and takes another deep breath. "I do wish to rule justly, as you have taught me, Archibald. Perhaps you will allow us Bangols to build our bridges out over the western waters, to learn what lies beyond the Sea of Selfdom, where none have gone and returned."

"I think that can be arranged," Grandpa says, chuckling. He clicks open the brass latch and strokes the shifting glass orb and simple clay bowl contained inside the wooden box. "But first we must unify—Olearon, Bangol, Steffanus, sprite, and human."

"The Millia cannot be destroyed," adds Callisto, "until the Star fulfills its purpose."

"Then we know what we must do," Grandpa says with the hint of a grin.

Ella

chapter 43

Tessa

Nate slips his hand inside Tessa's. His strength surrounds her, and her heart swells. She looks up at him. Nate's shirt is ripped and stained with black ash and blood.

"I see the way you look at him," Nate begins. "Have you chosen him?" He looks at Ardenal, who crouches to Ella's height, smiling and preparing her and Luggie for the portal jump to Jarr-Wya.

Tessa searches Nate's wide brown eyes. They are easy to read. Kindness. Protection. Love.

She turns her gaze again to Ardenal. He leaves Ella and Luggie to assist an elderly Spanish man onto the shoulders of two local youths, who carry the senior inland toward a partially destroyed town. He checks in with his friends and fellow warriors—Azkar, Nameris, Kameelo, Junin, and Islo—then turns toward her.

Tessa is startled by Ardenal, as he is by her. There is an unseen heat exchanged in their stares, a longing beyond words and worlds, and a hope, just a sliver of a hope, that refuses to die.

Ardenal's black eyes slip to Tessa's hand, folded within Nate's. His chin falls, and he turns away from them to join his father at the edge of Lanzarote, where the sprites flutter excitedly.

"I haven't decided." Tessa is surprised by her words, spoken from lips wet with tears and trembling with fear.

"Then I'll follow you back to Jarr-Wya," answers Nate. He squeezes her hand. "I'll fight for the island, for Ella, for you, until you make your choice."

chapter 44

Ella

Steffanus sisters, closer," Callisto orders. The sprites, directed by Lillium, land on the winged women's shoulders and tangled manes, bracing themselves with their legs bristled for the turbulent journey ahead. Lillium calls shrilly, and Pinne and Quillie fly out of the zucos field. The twin sprites still cradle the Life Ohmi. Lillium's pet fly Gobo hides in the tangle of her copper-red hair. Jarrwians and humans embrace in one massive huddle, and Luggie slips me into his arms.

Grandpa Archie and Dad rest their hands on the Tillastrion. Dad spins the clay bowl and it doesn't stop. Grandpa Archie lifts the glass orb, a giant marble containing rushing clouds in an emerald sky. He drops it into the box and latches it. Their black eyes slip closed as a silver wind begins to slip out from the seams of the Tillastrion. My heart leaps—for a hundred reasons, for all that's to come—as the landscape around us blurs and melts into a sea of blue.

Ella

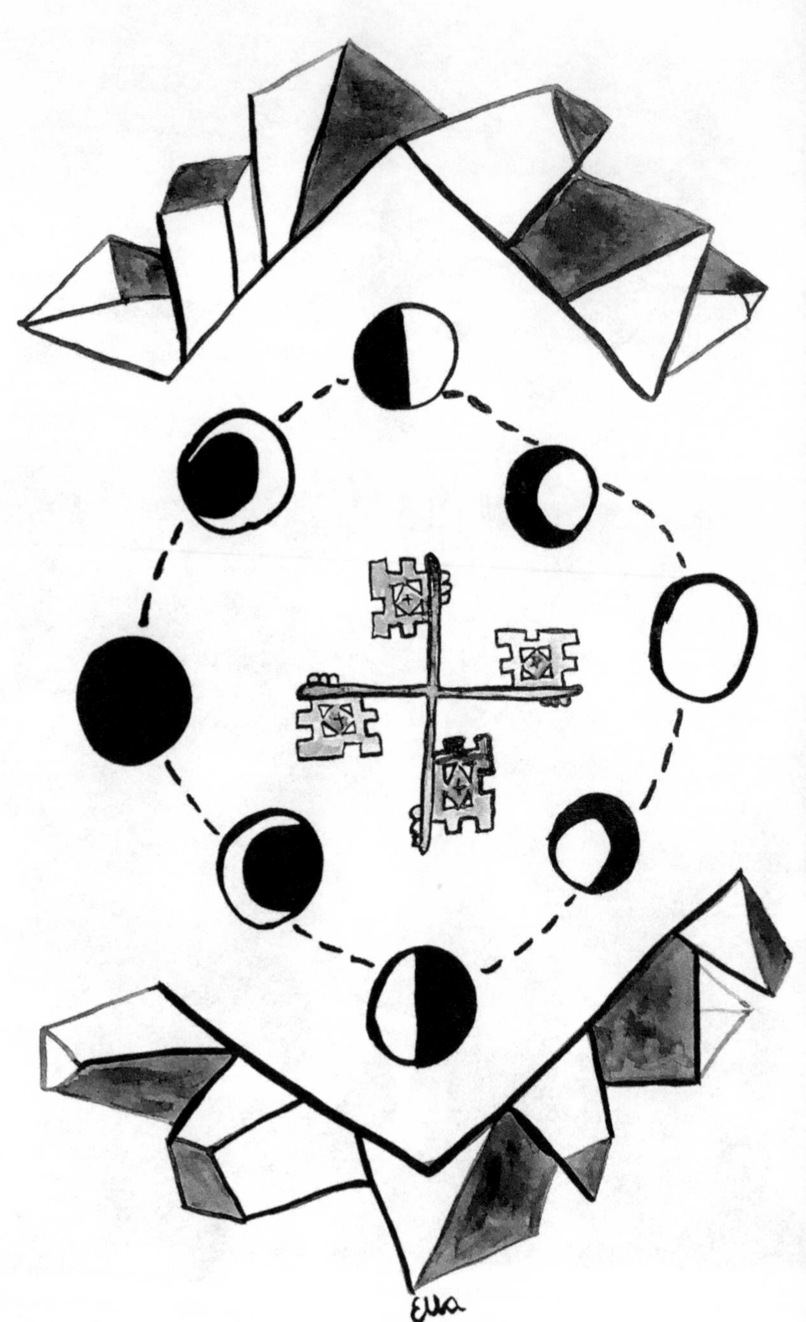
Ella

Ella

epilogue

The Star smiles beneath the sea, shadowed by the crippled island of Jarr-Wya. *All the happenings beneath the moon are unfolding according to my plan,* it thinks merrily, *and finally we have the attention of Naiu.*

glossary

of Characters, Creatures, Plants, and Places

ARCHIBALD "ARCHIE" WELLSLEY

A white-haired senior citizen—born in 1947—and a retired roofer from Seattle, Washington. He is father of Arden, called Ardenal on Jarr-Wya; father-in-law of Tessa; grandfather of Ella; and widower of his late wife, Suzie. He moved in with Arden and his family after Suzie's death, when Ella was seven years old. Archie has noticed changes in his body since arriving on the magical island. He also faces repercussions from stealing the secret history of the Olearons from the glass throne of the Lord, though it was not the only object he pocketed. He carries a small bouquet of the Banji flowers wrapped in a sock and leaf inside a trouser pocket.

ARDENAL (PRONOUNCED: ARE-DEN-ALL)

As a human, Arden Wellsley was a professor of Ancient Egyptian dynasties at Seattle University. He was the adult son of Archie, husband of Tessa, and father of Ella. He had dark brown hair, blue eyes, and chunky glasses. He disappeared when Ella was twelve years old, using a Tillastrion to portal jump to the island of Jarr-Wya. There, he was changed into an Olearon inside the web of the man-spider, Rolace. Reunited with his family in the mother world of Jarr, Arden—now called Ardenal—continues his search for Ella's cure and a way to make peace with his broken marriage.

ARRECIFE (PRONOUNCED: ARH-AY-SEE-FAY)

A real-life port city on the island of Lanzarote in the Spanish Canary Islands, in the North Atlantic Ocean. The city faces the African continent and the country of Morocco.

ATLANTIC ODYSSEY

The name of the cruise ship that carried the Wellsley family and sailed through the Canary Islands in the North Atlantic. The ship was run by Constellations Cruise Line and was captained by Nathanial "Nate" Billows.

AWAKINS (PRONOUNCED: A-WHAY-KINS)

Large magical butterflies with two sets of wings: by night, they are airborne with a purple pair, and by day, with a yellow-orange pair. They never land for fear of the hallucinogenic Banji and other predators. The Bangols capture the awakins for use in their air transportation balloons.

AZKAR (PRONOUNCED: AZ-CAR)

An Olearon warrior and the eldest brother of Nameris and Kameelo, and deceased siblings Olen (OH-len) and Eek (EE-k). Incredibly strong and often gruff, Azkar is known for his scowl, his bravery, and the jagged black scar stretching from below his left eye to his collarbone.

BALUURWA THE DOOMFUL (PRONOUNCED: BAL-OO-R-WHA)

A mountain that rises sharply at the center of Jarr-Wya, created when Naiu crashed onto the island. The Steffanus race, who call Baluurwa home, have carved tunnels into it. Baluurwa has many small fragments of land jutting out from its sides that connect to the mountain by rock chutes, vines, or that simply float on their own.

BANGOL (PRONOUNCED: BANG-GUL)

A race originating from the rock, clay, and earth of Jarr-Wya. They possess power from Naiu, the magic in the world of Jarr, to manipulate earthen materials at their will. They have large, glowing yellow eyes, grey skin, and stones growing out of their cheekbones and bald heads.

BANJI (PRONOUNCED: BAN-GEE)

A magical flower that contains large quantities of Naiu. It has the power to distort perceptions and is often used as a weapon. In the presence of the Star, the growth of the flowers wanes.

BLACK FLYERS

Large coal-colored birds whose appearance has morphed since the arrival of the Star. The most notable changes are their growing wingspan, the talons that curl from their wing tips, and the splitting of their necks into two; each has two terrifying beaked heads.

BLAMALA (PRONOUNCED: BLAA-MAL-AA)

Enormous crab-like creatures with blue exoskeletons that live in the oceans surrounding Jarr-Wya. They are slow swimmers due to their oversized claws, so to battle their aquatic foes they use their skill at blowing saliva bubbles. Their spittle contains unique properties that allow it to be strong yet flexible while wet, and to solidify into a hard form when exposed to air. If a drowned wyvern cooks a blamala with its boiling breath, the blamala's shell turns an electric violet and it floats on the surface of the sea belly up.

BORGIN (PRONOUNCED: BOAR-GIN)

Zeno's soft-spoken cousin and primary henchman. Borgin is tall for a Bangol, with hunched shoulders and uneven eyes. He immediately repeats Zeno's orders to the Bangols, much to his superior's annoyance. Borgin aspires to be an exemplary second-in-command, though he cannot take care of himself; his clothing is untidy and he smells sour.

CALLISTO

A fierce Steffanus sister with a vast knowledge of the origins of the worlds. She is the lead she-warrior and intent on protecting the Star, whom she believes has come to help Jarr-Wya.

CANARY ISLANDS

Real-life Spanish islands of volcanic origin, which are connected in a chain called an archipelago. The islands are located off the coast of Africa in the North Atlantic Ocean. The seven main landmasses are Lanzarote, Fuerteventura, Gran Canaria, Tenerife, La Palma, La Gomera, and El Hierro.

CARAKWA (PRONOUNCED: KA-RACK-WA)

A clicking, screeching creature the size of a small dog. It has the body of a lizard and the hard shell and head of a beetle. It has fly-like compound eyes, half-moon claws, and sharp, lacerating forelegs. It has no soul and thus is easily possessed by evil spirits, which was the case with Valarie—cruise director of Constellations Cruise Line—at her death.

CHERGRIN (PRONOUNCED: CHAIR-GRIN)

A Bangol who was a faithful warrior and leader of defense to King Tuggeron. He died in Valarie's carakwa attack, abandoned by Tuggeron. His replacement is Borgin.

CONSTELLATIONS CRUISE LINE

The name of the business that offers passengers voyages through the Canary Islands on the *Atlantic Odyssey* cruise liner.

CRADLE BIRDS

Fowl that live on Jarr-Wya, which flock in migration around the island. They are named for their curved, U-shaped backs, where they carry their eggs.

CRYSTALITHS (PRONOUNCED: KRIS-TALL-LITHS)

Light-transferring prism-shaped crystal columns that channel the sunshine, converting it to Naiu. The columns aid in dispersing the magic through the soil to nourish the crops that grow in the Olearons' fields.

DONNA

A cruise passenger from the *Atlantic Odyssey*, once a human before receiving the gift of Naiu within the web of the man-spider, Rolace. Now Donna is part amphibian with gills on her neck and shimmering, scaly skin. She is a senior citizen, though her transformation has smoothed the lines on her face and given her body renewed strength. She and her husband, Harry, who possesses the same gift as his wife, parted ways from their fellow humans and cruise passengers for a life lived beneath the surface of the sea. The company has not seen Donna and Harry since the carakwa battle on the eastern beach.

DROWNED WYVERN (PRONOUNCED: WHY-VERN)

Water dragons that are very much alive, named because they live in the sea. Webbed feet grow from their strong hind legs. They have no forearms, instead swimming with broad wings that allow them to be quick and make sudden turns. Their tails are barbed, and their yellow-hued bodies are smooth with serpent scales. They breathe out boiling water to wound their enemies.

DUGGIE-SKY

A four-year-old African American passenger on the *Atlantic Odyssey.* He is a good-spirited boy with a love of aviation and superhero-themed clothing. His name refers to the Douglas A-3 Skywarrior airplane, designed by Ed Heinemann and introduced in the 1950s. Duggie-Sky traveled on the cruise with his father, who died at the hand of the Millia. No one knows Duggie-Sky's real name.

DUNAKKUS (PRONOUNCED: DONE-AK-US), 30TH LORD OF OLEARON

Dunakkus, his birth name, is the current leader of the Olearons. Dunakkus stands a foot taller than other Olearon males and wears a thick dreadlock decorated in jewels. He aims to rule with peace but is unafraid of war and sacrifice to achieve that goal. He has united with his soul partner, the Maiden of Olearon, who died defeating the carakwa manifestation of Valarie, the *Atlantic Odyssey* cruise director. Now the Lord and Maiden inhabit one body—that of the 30th Lord—where she passes her knowledge on to him. His two main warrior guards are Yuleeo and Islo.

ELLA WELLSLEY

The blond, blue-eyed fourteen-year-old daughter of Arden and Tessa Wellsley, and granddaughter of Archie. She is a considerate, creative young woman with a quick wit and a humorous approach to life. When she was ten, doctors discovered a cancerous tumor at the base of her brain and wrapped around the top of her spinal cord. She lost her ability to speak six months before boarding the *Atlantic Odyssey*. On Jarr-Wya, Ella has befriended and begun a romantic relationship with a young Bangol named Luggie. She has also given up sign language in favor of communicating through ink drawings. Her illness grows worse by the day and her family searches for her cure on the magical island.

ELLAG CURRANTS (PRONOUNCED: EEE-LAG)

A food of the Olearons made into a sweet liquid that is poured onto the bland vulai bread to make it more appetizing. Ellag currants are purple and sweet like honey.

FAIRY VINEYARD

A vineyard located on the northwestern corner of Jarr-Wya. It is tended by the sprites, who draw on the vines' wooden supports and sleep curled in their leaves. At the edge of the Fairy Vineyard grows a massive tree, called the Great Tree, which is a hybrid of the blue and white woodlands. The vineyard grows ohmi grapes in many varieties, each with their own color and magical property.

FINNAH (PRONOUNCED: FIN-AH)

A magical being that Tessa and Ella meet inside of Tessa's dreams. There, Finnah takes on the form of a giant green bird and carries the women on her back. Finnah's presence is mysterious as she often indirect in her answers, and, while Tessa is trusting, Ella is suspicious of the large magical being.

GOBO (PRONOUNCED: GOW-BOW)

Pet fly and friend to the sprite Lillium. The small silver insect is immensely protective of Lillium and growls, with a high-pitched hum, at those who come near her. Gobo flies circles around Lillium, often tangling her hair, but he also engages in reconnaissance missions for her, scouting a place before she arrives. Gobo is an old fly. In Jarr, flies are black and turn silver as they age. Gobo was abandoned by his young horde, like a black cloud they were, and so Lillium plucked him out of a lonely puddle and made a home for him at the Fairy Vineyard.

GREEN BIRDS

Small, gentle birds that inhabit Jarr-Wya and are friends to the awakin butterflies. They have human-like eyes, long eyelashes, and spin emerald wind behind them when they fly.

HAAZ (PRONOUNCED: HH-AA-ZZ)

A giant, dim-witted cousin of the Bangols. The Haaz creatures are grey-skinned and stand a towering fifteen feet tall with shoulders like sun-bleached boulders. They have smooth skin over their eyes, rendering them blind. Their noses are no more than a slight ridge, punctured twice. Their skulls are small, thick, and black beneath their skin. Since they cannot see, they rely on perceiving their enemies' vibrations through the ground and air.

HARRY

A human passenger of the *Atlantic Odyssey* who was wrapped in the magical web of Rolace and gifted, along with his wife, Donna, the ability to live beneath the sea. Harry can breathe underwater and swim quickly, aided by webbing between his fingers and toes. He looks mostly the same as he had as a white-haired human, though now his features are less wrinkled and his youthful energy renewed. Harry and Donna said goodbye to their company of humans and Olearons, choosing to live in the sea around Jarr-Wya instead of walking on land.

HUPPER (PRONOUNCED: HUP-PURR)

A rabbit-like creature with a corkscrew tail and foot-long, shaggy ears that stand erect. They hop from tree to tree, held by an unseen magnetic force, and, like chameleons, take on the color of what they touch. Hupper whiskers form a perch for fireflies that coexist with them, until the hupper is hungry and thus has an easy snack.

ISLO (PRONOUNCED: EYES-LOW)

An Olearon warrior and one of the close advisors to the 30th Lord. He is quiet and controlled, analytical but slow to speak. When he does advise, his voice is a low rumble and his words few. Yet because of his cunning, he has earned the respect and honor of the Lord. Islo is tall, like all Olearon warriors, though his build is not willowy. Instead, his arms are firm and muscled, his neck thick, and his hands like boulders. He was a childhood schoolyard adversary of Azkar, and the two still harbor unspoken resentment, all the while serving the same Olearon rulers.

JARR (PRONOUNCED: JA-RR)

A world formed by and filled with magic known as Naiu and connected to the derivative dimension of Earth. On Jarr, days are measured in sunsets.

JARR-WYA (PRONOUNCED: JA-RR-WHY-AH)

A magical island in the world of Jarr. The island has long been ruled by three dominant races: the Olearons, Bangols, and sea creatures that were turned into the Millia sands after the arrival of the Star. None of the island's inhabitants, known as Jarrwians, know what lies beyond it in their world. In the past five thousand sunsets, the magic on Jarr-Wya has changed, with all creatures feeling the effect.

JEO (PRONOUNCED: GEE-OH)

Jeo is the current queen of the sprites. She has white hair that is twisted and braided into a swan that sways on her head. She is old and tired but friendly, jolly, and kind. A queen sprite is chosen from amongst all sprites upon the current queen's death.

JUNIN (PRONOUNCED: JOO-NIN)

A female Olearon, mother, and warrior in the contingent tasked with protecting the surface of the sea at Jarr-Wya's southern shore, next to the Millia's beach. She is brave and thoughtful, and the Lord turns to her for assistance with new missions.

KAMEELO (PRONOUNCED: CAM-EE-LOW)

A youthful Olearon warrior and brother of Azkar and Nameris, and deceased siblings Olen (OH-len) and Eek (EE-k). He is known for his eagerness and free spirit. Within Rolace's web, Kameelo was gifted the ability to fly. This power he uses playfully but also in reconnaissance missions and battles for the Lord.

LADY SOPHIA

A portly Spanish opera singer and the entertainer on Constellations Cruise Line. She is a loud talker, flamboyant, and self-centered, though not unkind. Despite being out of shape, Lady Sophia relishes the adventure on Jarr-Wya while also complaining about it. She is motherly to those in the company, singing them to sleep and distributing hugs.

LAKEN (PRONOUNCED: LA-KEN)

The last of the she-race called the Steffanus—for a time until the new seeds blossomed. Laken has rich auburn hair, blue-red eyes, silvery skin, and horns wrapped in gold growing out of her skull. She once flew on large wings until they were cut from her back. She is prophetic, though her visions do not always unfold as expected.

LANZAROTE (PRONOUNCED: LAN-ZA-ROW-TAY)

A real-life landmass, one of the seven Canary Islands located off the western coast of Africa in the North Atlantic Ocean. Two popular tourist destinations on the island are Timanfaya National Park and the artisanal market of Haria. The capital city is Arrecife on the coast, with its hub of Marina Lanzarote.

LIFE OHMI (PRONOUNCED: OH-ME)

The special ohmi grapes grown by the sprites who continue

their race. Queen Jeo gifts the male sprites Life Ohmi, which they consume and grow a child within them. They are small, white, and glow at sundown. To protect the Life Ohmi, the sprites hide them in the tunnels of the Fairy Vineyard.

LILLIUM (PRONOUNCED: LILLY-UMH)

A sprite from the Fairy Vineyard, Archie's sidekick. She has an ancient silver pet fly named Gobo. Lillium is proud of the design of her gown, created using the most awakin wings of any sprite's but Queen Jeo's. Her grandest adventures, before meeting Archie, were stalking the black flyers and their trail of carnage across Jarr-Wya to collect awakin wings. She is proud and stubborn but also timid and shy. The pattern of Naiu on her wings is shaped into silhouettes, one on each side. Lillium calls her wings *Wingies* and talks to them when she is afraid. Lillium, like all sprites, has untamed reddish-orange hair, though she refuses to braid it. Instead it flies free, like a curling frame around her round, pink cheeks.

LORD AND MAIDEN OF OLEARON

Titles given to the male and female rulers of the Olearons. The Lord and Maiden must find each other in every age, as their souls are always connected. As with all Olearons, when one dies, the other inhabits the living one's body until his or her demise. The Maiden stands approximately eight feet tall and the Lord approximately ten feet tall, a full foot above his male warriors.

LUGGIE (PRONOUNCED: LUG-EE)

A 5,800-sunset-old Bangol (roughly sixteen human years), son of the current king, Tuggeron, and brother of Nanjee. He is next in line to rule after Tuggeron and is tasked with learning to lead the Bangols, including inflicting punishment and flying their transport balloons. Luggie and Nanjee befriended Ella when she was their father's prisoner. The siblings gave Ella food and a book with ink so she could draw. Nanjee was wounded when their balloon crash-landed, and she died at the attack of the carakwa horde led by Valarie; this was also when Luggie found the secret history of the Olearons in the eastern sea. Luggie strives to do what is right, often going against the warring rulers of Jarr-Wya.

MILLIA (PRONOUNCED: MILL-EE-AH)

A race on Jarr-Wya formed of crushed seashells, their name meaning "soul of the shell." The sea creatures desire the Star beneath the island, but they cannot reach it. Thus, the shells crash on the shore and break into millions of pieces that make up the Millia sands on the southern beach. The sand contains all the bitter unfulfillment of its past masters. They can change to any shape but remain the one solid material.

NAIU (PRONOUNCED: NY-UU)

The magic in the world of Jarr and on the island of Jarr-Wya. According to the secret history of the Olearons, as told by a Steffanus, Naiu was a flying being and created all worlds and all time, which extended its power to each of its creations. Naiu crashed onto Jarr-Wya and, before it died, fused with a human child, creating a new race called the Steffanus. Since the arrival of the Star, Naiu is waning in Jarr.

NAMERIS (PRONOUNCED: NA-MER-IS)

An Olearon warrior and brother of Azkar and Kameelo, and deceased siblings Olen (OH-len) and Eek (EE-k). Nameris discovered his power—the ability to tell if someone speaks the truth—after visiting the man-spider Rolace with Arden, who at the same time transformed into Ardenal. Nameris is often grumpy and skeptical, yet he possesses great wisdom about Jarr-Wya: its terrain and size, its weather patterns, history, and races.

NANJEE (PRONOUNCED: NAN-GEE)

Older sister of Luggie and a Bangol princess. Nanjee was favored by her father, King Tuggeron, and was skilled at penmanship and therefore tasked with recording the Bangol history—Tuggeron's part of it—in ornate books. It was one of these books that Nanjee and Luggie gave to Ella. Nanjee was wounded and later killed, and is deeply missed by Luggie.

NATHANIAL "NATE" BILLOWS

A brown-eyed, blond-haired, tattooed sailor who captained the ship named the *Atlantic Odyssey*. Theatrical in his gestures, he loves to tell stories. He is young, brave, and flirtatious. He is not afraid to make known his feelings for Tessa and has vowed to protect her and her daughter, Ella.

OHMI (PRONOUNCED: OH-ME)

The magical grapes grown by the sprites, each variety with its own unique color, shape, leaves, smell, and magical power. There are ohmi to aid sleep, to be used in jokes, to enhance night vision, and for other useful purposes. The Life Ohmi is the most prized and protected as it is the seed of new life and represents the future of the sprites.

OLEARON (PRONOUNCED: OH-LEE-AIR-ON)

A race of creatures on Jarr-Wya with red skin, full black eyes, and dark Mohawks with adorned dreadlocks. They can release fire from the backs of their necks and envelop their whole bodies in flame. Their warriors wear royal-blue jumpsuits and, in addition to their fire, wield weapons made of glass. They are ruled by the Lord and Maiden of Olearon. Olearons live in western Jarr-Wya in the glass city.

PINNE (PRONOUNCED: PIN-EE)

A middle-aged sprite with eight daughters and seven sons. She is giggly and fun loving. Her twin brother is Quillie, and unlike most sprites, their wings are identical in their Naiu patterns. Sprites do not typically have more than one baby at a time, though their gestation period is a mere sixty-seven sunsets. Pinne has shaped her reddish-orange hair into the shape of a flower.

QUILLIE (PRONOUNCED: QUIL-EE)

A handsome middle-aged sprite, twin brother of Pinne and male attendant of Queen Jeo, from whom Quillie learns all the news of sprite royalty. Quillie is pregnant with a child, as it is the male sprites who carry their children until birth; the women are the better gardeners and refuse to give up their passion for the vineyard.

ROLACE (PRONOUNCED: ROW-LIS)

A huge spider with twelve hairy legs and the head of an elderly man. He uses the enchantment of Naiu, found in the Banji flowers, to spin a cocoon around an individual to expose his or her unique powers, but only if the will is strong and the heart is brave.

SASAR (PRONOUNCED: SA-ZA-RR)

A white wolf-like creature the size of a bear. Since the arrival of the Star, sasars no longer have a sense of smell and must use sound and touch to hunt their prey, primarily the huppers and the cradle birds.

SEA OF SELFDOM

The mysterious ocean off the west coast of Jarr-Wya, near the Olearons' glass city. Those who venture far on its waters never return.

THE SECRET HISTORY OF THE OLEARONS

A square of Naiu-infused glass that responds to touch, revealing writing in one's own language. Archie discovered it in a hidden compartment of the Lord of Olearon's glass throne. The historical record documents the 30th Lord's private search to understand why many of the public records, especially those of the 29th Lord, have been destroyed. Archie was discovered with the secret history by the Maiden of Olearon before her death. She confiscated it, threatening to scorch him, and the glass was lost to the sea—or so everyone believed. Luggie found the secret history and keeps its knowledge to himself.

SENIOR KARISH (PRONOUNCED: KA-RISH)

The leader of the Millia sands and spokesman on behalf of the evil race. He wears a crown and breastplate made of shells that are still inhabited by their sea creatures. Selfish and consumed with desire for the Star, Senior Karish strikes deals that bend in his favor.

SHELLARK (PRONOUNCED: SHELL-ARK)

A creature of Jarr-Wya's sea, a shellark has the smooth grey skin of a large swimming mammal but carries a tall twisted shell on its back. Shellarks may curl themselves into these shells and sit dormant at the bottom of the sea, only to unfurl in their hunting seasons. During these times, their kills stain the water with blood as the shellarks gnaw their prey with rows of dagger-sharp teeth. They have no allegiances, though the Millia wish to employ the shellarks' strong bite in their favor. Their shells, at their death, are transformed into the Millia sands.

SPRITE

A petite flying being about four inches tall. Sprites live in the Fairy Vineyard on Jarr-Wya where they harvest ohmi grapes. They have the hind legs of grasshoppers, allowing them to jump far, though with delicate padded feet. Their femurs jut backward, thick with strong muscles under their shiny skin, and their thin tibias are covered in bristles that help the sprites catch themselves on leaves, vines, and trees. Their legs are hidden under clothing made of creased leaves, flower petals, and the shed wings of murdered awakin butterflies. They have one palm-sized wing growing out of each shoulder blade. Each wing is nearly transparent and sparkles with Naiu as if sprinkled with stars that make up tiny constellations, each configuration unique. The wings of the sprites glow in the night and they tell each other apart by these glittering patterns. Their skin is a pale sea-foam green, their eyes are chestnut and sprinkled with blue like rain on bark, and their wild, thick, and tangled rusty-colored hair is braided into ornate and regal headpieces of winding shapes. Sprites do not choose one partner. They are all family, living and working together, sharing roles.

STAR

Five thousand sunsets past, the Star flew through the sky, heading for Jarr-Wya, which it chose to spare. Instead it crashed into the ocean, coming to rest beneath the island. The Star incensed the Bangols. The shellarks' love of it turned them evil, forming the Millia sands. Much plant life and many creatures have been altered by it; the island has not been the same ever since. Everyone is searching for the Star, but each for their own distinct purposes.

STEFFANUS (PRONOUNCED: STEFF-AN-US)

A she-race created by the fusion of a human girl and a magical being, Naiu, at its death. They have large wings that extend out from their backs, antlers from their heads, and skin that shines silver. Their weapons are long daggers with gold coiling handles. They collect gold and silver—particularly buttons, brooches, and beads—and have a fascination with traveling to Earth, which they do by building their own Tillastrions. They can operate Tillastrions on their own, drawing on both their human and Jarrwian identities.

TANIUS (PRONOUNCED: TAN-EYE-US)

A Steffanus sister who wears flowing red garments and has squinty, judgmental eyes. She has transported herself between

Jarr and Earth many times, and with each portal jump, she grows in foresight and doom. She is suspicious, looming, and razor sharp. There is not even the smallest trace of humor in her, and she is guarded and protective of those she loves and of her home.

TELMAKUS (PRONOUNCED: TELL-MAK-US), 29TH LORD OF OLEARON

As a young Olearon, before becoming the 29th Lord, Telmakus was brave, determined, and foolhardy after love. He was later corrupted by the demands of his reign and his thirst for power. He killed his brother, Dillmus (Pronounced: dill-MUS), and lost control of his fire and the glass throne. His death is shrouded in mystery.

TESSA WELLSLEY

A Seattle nurse with long blond hair, green eyes, and a feminine style. Wife of Arden, mother of Ella, and daughter-in-law of Archie. She is the sole breadwinner and caregiver for her family since Arden's disappearance two years before. She is stubborn and passionate, with a quick tongue and an unbreakable motherly love, though she often gives off an air of suspicion. Tessa is an orphan, raised in a dysfunctional foster family, though these are secrets she has told no one. She had scoliosis as a child—a crooked back—and underwent surgery and has scars from it. Within the web of man-spider Rolace, Tessa gained the power of telepathy, though it is a skill yet to be honed. It has allowed mental conversation between Tessa and Ella, which has proven helpful on their quest but also a channel for arguments between mother and daughter.

TILLASTRION (PRONOUNCED: TILL-ASS-TREE-ON)

A portal jumper between one magic-filled world to its connecting, derivative dimension. Two beings are required for the device to function: one to build it and the other to operate it. The one who builds it must be from the world the pair wishes to reach; the one who operates it must be from the world they wish to depart.

TREASURES

Zeno's shop in Mercado Artesanal Plaza Haria, on the island of Lanzarote. There the banished Bangol sells antique jewelry, baubles, lamps, and furniture. It is a small building with a zigzagging crack and is squished between two larger storefronts.

TUGGERON "TUGGS" (PRONOUNCED: TUG-ER-ON)

The murderous current king of the Bangols, and father of Luggie and Nanjee. He is a fat, selfish Bangol who wields a stone mallet and desires dominion over Jarr-Wya—and beyond. He lusts for immortality and, most of all, for the Star. He wears a sleeveless outfit of brown and grey fabrics, decorated with animal hides.

VALARIE

The spunky brunette cruise director of the Constellations Cruise Line's ship the *Atlantic Odyssey*. She was the scorned lover of Captain Nathanial "Nate" Billows. After a challenging youth, she became jaded and spiteful. After her death within Rolace's web, her wicked spirit was hosted in millions of carakwas that linked together to form one massive monster. Valarie attacked the Bangol bridges over the eastern sea, desiring to kill Ella and Tessa most of all, as she believed the blond passenger had stolen Nate from her. The hive mind carakwa monster was defeated by the Maiden's blast.

VULAI BREAD (PRONOUNCED: VUU-LAY)

A loaf of square-shaped bread made from the Olearons' harvest. It is grainy, pale yellow like corn bread, and dry.

WINZUN (PRONOUNCED: WIN-ZUHN)

Twin brother of Zeno and blood co-heir to the Bangol kingship. The twins were banished to Earth by Tuggeron, but Winzun found a way back when Arden Wellsley came looking for the magical island. Unfortunately for Winzun, he was murdered by Tuggeron upon his return to Jarr-Wya.

WRYST (PRONOUNCED: RR-WHY-ST)

The silvery drink of the Olearons, given to strengthen the weak or weary, and consumed at times of celebration. It can produce a drunken effect in the young.

XLEA (PRONOUNCED: EX-LEAH)

A young Steffanus, too trusting and awestruck. She was birthed from the last group of blossoms and is a fearsome 3,761 sunsets old, which is approximately ten human years. Xlea is perceptive, fearless, and friendly. She and Duggie-Sky are instant friends. Her wings are the color of a pale newborn rainbow, and her robes flow in yellows and greens. In a side pouch she carries a worn paper journal bursting with drawings, writing, scraps, mementos, and dried flowers from her travels to Earth.

YULEEO (PRONOUNCED: YOU-LEE-OH)

A trusted henchmen-warrior to the 30th Lord of Olearon. He is diligent in following orders and unafraid to confront an enemy.

ZENO (PRONOUNCED: ZEE-NO)

A Bangol and rightful co-heir to the throne. He and his twin brother, Winzun, were banished to Earth by Tuggeron, a wicked Bangol who killed the twins' father to become king himself. Winzun helped Arden—Ardenal—travel to Jarr-Wya. When Archie discovered Zeno, who was operating a trinket shop called Treasures in Lanzarote on Earth, Zeno was ready to say and do whatever it took to return home. Zeno is often conflicted between doing what he wants and what is right, and is curious to learn from Archie how kings in the human world earn the love of their people. One of Zeno's closest confidants is his clumsy cousin, Borgin.

The Olearon Alphabet

A		N	
B		O	
C		P	
D		Q	
E		R	
F		S	
G		T	
H		U	
I		V	
J		W	
K		X	
L		Y	
M		Z	

The Bangol Alphabet

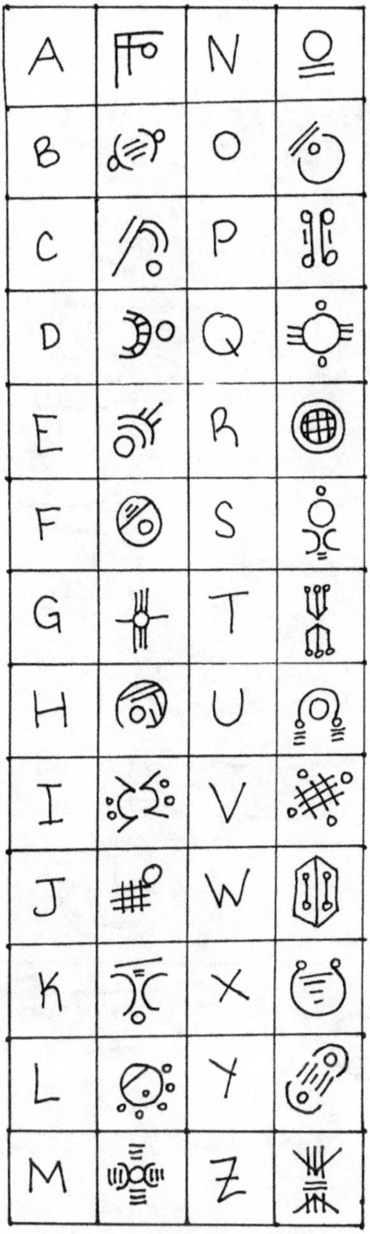

A		N	
B		O	
C		P	
D		Q	
E		R	
F		S	
G		T	
H		U	
I		V	
J		W	
K		X	
L		Y	
M		Z	

Family Tree of the Lords of Olearon

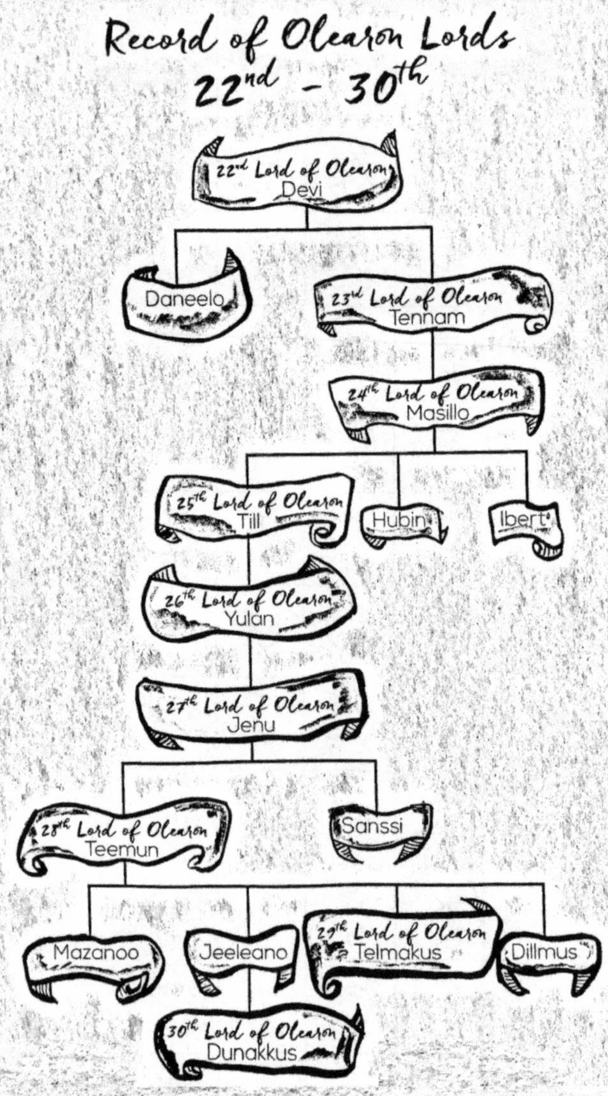
Record of Olearon Lords
22nd - 30th
22nd Lord of Olearon
Devi
Daneelo
23rd Lord of Olearon
Tennam
24th Lord of Olearon
Masillo
25th Lord of Olearon
Till
Hubin
Ibert
26th Lord of Olearon
Yulan
27th Lord of Olearon
Jenu
28th Lord of Olearon
Teemun
Sanssi
Mazanoo
Jeeleano
29th Lord of Olearon
Telmakus
Dillmus
30th Lord of Olearon
Dunakkus

Decoder Challenge

Decipher the language and the words. Email the decoded message to secret@8thislandtrilogy.com to receive a secret clue to an important revelation for book three in The 8th Island Trilogy.

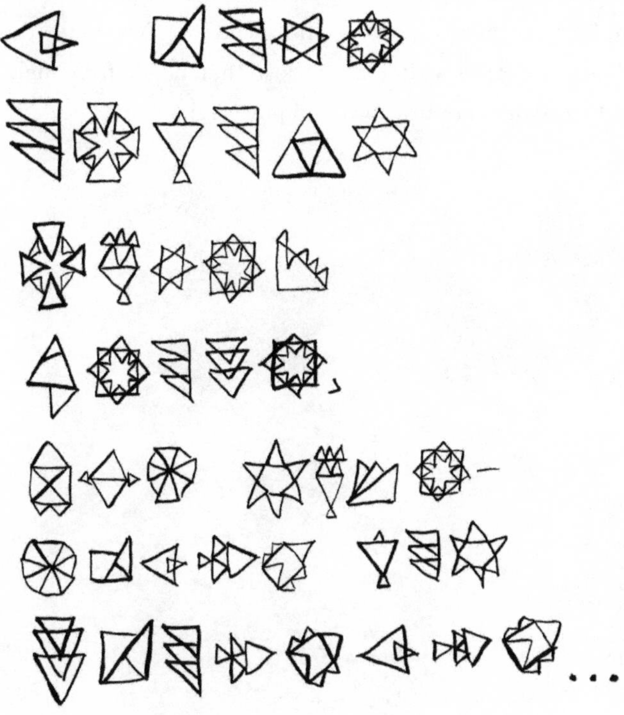

Acknowledgments

Thank you to my family and my publishing team. Thank you to street team and book trailer crew. Finally, to my readers. Thank you for your emails, reviews, and social love. You make the often solitary life of a writer and artist that much friendlier. Keep reading. Words are precious and powerful.

A Note from the Author

Dear Reader,

Thank you for portal jumping with me to Jarr-Wya! If you enjoyed the journey we have taken together, please send a note to info@alexismariechute.com, as I would love to hear from you. For free downloads of Ella's drawings, wallpapers for your phone and computer, discount codes, secret chapters, character profiles, book tour info, and more, please visit:

www.AlexisMarieChute.com
and subscribe to the e-newsletter at
www.AlexisMarieChute.com/contact
Thank you!
Alexis Marie Chute

About the Author

Alexis Marie Chute is an award-winning author, artist, filmmaker, curator, and inspirational speaker. Her memoir, *Expecting Sunshine: A Journey of Grief, Healing, and Pregnancy After Loss*, was a Kirkus Best Book of 2017 and has received many other literary awards. *Expecting Sunshine* is also a highly acclaimed feature documentary film produced and directed by the author. The film screened around the world in 2018. She is also the author of the epic fantasy adventure series called The 8th Island Trilogy. *Above the Star*, Book 1, was released in 2018, and *Below the Moon*, Book 2, in 2019. *Inside the Sun*, Book 3, will hit bookstore shelves in 2020. Alexis Marie holds a Bachelors of Fine Arts in Art and Design and a Masters of Fine Arts in Creative Writing. She is an internationally exhibited painter and photographer, curator of the InFocus Photography Exhibition, and a widely published writer of fiction, nonfiction, and poetry. Alexis Marie is passionate about creative living and coined the term, "The Healthy Grief Movement." She is a highly sought-after keynote speaker and teacher across all her artistic and healing disciplines. In her spare time, she loves traveling, reading, canoeing, paddleboarding, sharing thoughtful conversations with friends—old and new—and spending time with her family. Alexis Marie lives in snowy Edmonton, Alberta, Canada, with her husband Aaron and their three living children.

Connect with Alexis Marie Chute

WEB: AlexisMarieChute.com

EMAIL: info@alexismariechute.com

E-NEWS SUBSCRIBE: AlexisMarieChute.com/contact

INSTAGRAM: @alexismariechute

TWITTER: @_Alexis_Marie

YOUTUBE: youtube.com/alexismariechute

FACEBOOK: facebook.com/AlexisMarieProductionsInc

PINTEREST: pinterest.com/alexismarieart/

When sharing on social, please use these hashtags:

#alexismariechute, #abovethestar, #belowthemoon, #8thislandtrilogy

Help Spread the Word

Please join with readers around the world in spreading the word about *Above the Star*, *Below the Moon*, and The 8th Island Trilogy!

HERE ARE 10 IDEAS:

1. Write a review of the book on Amazon and Goodreads.
2. Recommend the book through word of mouth to your friends and family.
3. Share the book on your social media accounts—and post a photo of you and your copy on Instagram and Twitter to be in the running for a special prize. Social Sharing Hashtags: #abovethestar #belowthemoon #8thislandtrilogy #alexismariechute
4. Read the book at your book club (email the author: info@alexismariechute.com, for the club study guide, using the words "BTM Study Guide" in the subject line).
5. Order the book from your local bookstore and request it at your local library.
6. Purchase a copy for the waiting room of your doctor or dentist, or leave a copy for strangers to pass along on the train.
7. Invite Alexis Marie Chute to speak at your organization or community event, or to teach an art or writing class.

8. Write about the book on your blog or talk about it on your podcast or YouTube channel.

9. Invite people to the book launch events—and if there isn't an event near you, join with the author in planning one.

10. Subscribe to the e-newsletter at www.AlexisMarieChute.com/contact for more ideas and ways to connect.

BONUS: Email the author at info@alexismariechute.com to share how the story has impacted you.

Thank you!

With gratitude,
Alexis Marie Chute

Other Books by Alexis Marie Chute

Coming Soon…

Inside the Sun

Book 3 in The 8th Island Trilogy

(SparkPress, 2020)

www.AlexisMarieChute.com/8thislandtrilogy

Above the Star

Book 1 in The 8th Island Trilogy

(SparkPress, 2018)

www.AboveTheStar.com

Expecting Sunshine:
A Journey of Grief, Healing and Pregnancy After Loss
(She Writes Press, 2017)
www.ExpectingSunshine.com

Expecting Sunshine:
A Journey of Grief, Healing and Pregnancy After Loss
Second Edition
(She Writes Press, 2019)
www.ExpectingSunshine.com

Also Available from Alexis Marie Chute

Expecting Sunshine Documentary Film

www.AlexisMarieChute.com/expecting-sunshine-documentary

SELECTED TITLES FROM SPARKPRESS

SparkPress is an independent boutique publisher delivering high-quality, entertaining, and engaging content that enhances readers' lives, with a special focus on female-driven work. www.gosparkpress.com

Above the Star: The 8th Island Trilogy, Book 1, Alexis Chute. $16.95, 978-1-943006-56-4. *Above the Star* is an epic fantasy adventure experienced through the eyes of three unlikely heroes transported to a new world: senior citizen Archie; his daughter-in-law, Tessa; and his fourteen-year-old granddaughter, Ella. In this otherworldly realm, all interests are at war, all love is unrequited, and everyone is left to unravel the truth of who they really are.

But Not Forever:A Novel, Jan Von Schleh. $16.95, 978-1-943006-58-8.When identical fifteen-year-old girls are mysteriously switched in time, they discover the love that's been missing in their lives. Torn, both want to go home, but neither wants to give up what they now have.

The Alienation of Courtney Hoffman: A Novel, Brady Stefani. $17, 978-1-940716-34-3. When 15-year-old Courtney Hoffman starts getting visits from aliens at night, she's sure she's going crazy—but when she meets a mysterious older girl who has alien stories of her own, she embarks on a journey that takes her into her own family's deepest, darkest secrets.

Wendy Darling: Volume 1, Stars, Colleen Oakes. $17, 978-1-94071-6-96-4. Loved by two men—a steady and handsome bookseller's son from London, and Peter Pan, a dashing and dangerous charmer—Wendy realizes that Neverland, like her heart, is a wild place, teeming with dark secrets and dangerous obsessions.

The Revealed:A Novel, Jessica Hickam. $15, 978-1-94071-600-8. Lily Atwood lives in what used to be Washington, D.C. Her father is one of the most powerful men in the world, having been a vital part of rebuilding and reuniting humanity after the war that killed over five billion people. Now he's running to be one of its leaders.

About SparkPress

SparkPress is an independent, hybrid imprint focused on merging the best of the traditional publishing model with new and innovative strategies. We deliver high-quality, entertaining, and engaging content that enhances readers' lives. We are proud to bring to market a list of *New York Times* best-selling, award-winning, and debut authors who represent a wide array of genres, as well as our established, industry-wide reputation for creative, results-driven success in working with authors. SparkPress, a BookSparks imprint, is a division of SparkPoint Studio LLC.

Learn more at GoSparkPress.com